P9-DFY-968

We All Fall Down

We All Fall Down
Goldratt's Theory of Constraints
for Healthcare Systems

By Julie Wright and Russ King

The North River Press Publishing Corporation

Additional copies of this book can be obtained from your local
bookstore or the publisher:

The North River Press Publishing Corporation
P.O. Box 567
Great Barrington, MA 01230
(800) 486-2665 or (413) 528-0034

www.northriverpress.com

Copyright © 2006 Julie Wright and Russ King

All rights reserved. No part of this book may be reproduced or utilized
in any form or by any means, electronic or mechanical, including photo-
copying, recording, or any information storage and retrieval system, without
permission in writing from the publisher.

"We All Fall Down" is a work of fiction, any resemblance between the char-
acters herein and real persons living or dead is purely coincidental.

Manufactured in the United States of America

ISBN: 0-88427-181-1

To John, Monica, Russ, Oded, Carol, W.G. and the team at Frendoc - without them this book would not exist.

Chapter 1

Three little words! Just three words were capable of igniting the wrath of Fran the Fearsome. It was strange, I didn't regret saying them. I don't even remember allowing my mouth to let them out into the open. Sure, they were buzzing round my head like a flatulent bumblebee, but they should have been for my ears only.

Perhaps I had better explain. It was Monday, a day despised by nine-to-fivers around the world and dreaded by the Health Service. The family doctors get it first, the wave of patients dragging themselves in after a weekend of sickness. This delay in seeking medical attention results in many of them being so poorly that the overrun doctors have to admit them to hospital. The result? Their Monday morning rush becomes our afternoon rush, turning our daily *crisis* meeting into a *catastrophe* meeting.

We were all crammed into the Trust HQ Board room. It's a long narrow room with a ridiculously thick pile carpet that lurks silently, waiting to trip anyone accustomed to the smooth, polished floors of the corridor. The walls are decorated with expensive portraits of long dead Head Surgeons who view every meeting with justifiable distaste.

A long gleaming, solid wood table dominated the room. Chairs were packed around it and still more were crammed against the walls, but there were still some people standing. Me? I had grabbed my favourite spot, opposite the door with my back to the wall. The perfect spot for a manager who may be trusted to dole out bad news to dangerously ill people, but not to wear suitable clothes to work.

If you glanced in the room, it would have been easy to miss me, Mrs. Average with shoulder length mousy hair, just a mischievous glance away from being plain. I was trying to blend into the background despite the distraction of my horrific uniform of a navy blue synthetic skirt with a matching polka dot blouse. Yeuch! Here in my back-against-the-wall location I can watch the reactions of the others as they wait to hear just how bad it's going to get today.

Opposite me Fran the Fearsome, my boss, the Associate General Manager of Surgery was fulfilling her role as Duty Executive of the Day by starting the meeting. She looked effortlessly chic as she smoothed her elegantly tailored designer jacket and expertly flicked back her long, blonde hair as she started to speak. Not a synthetic polka dot in sight, but then she was senior management.

'Welcome everyone, despite the fact that we have just entered the month of July, we are still suffering from *Winter Pressures*,' Fran announced and paused. There were groans all round, just like every week I can remember. We spent all winter telling ourselves that the bed crisis would ease in the summer, only to find we have just as many patients now as in the cold months of winter. So what's new? I started to drift off as she waffled on about rocks and hard places, hitting the ground running and rising to meet the challenge. At last, she invited reports from the other members of the meeting and a tired and harassed looking male nurse from the Emergency Department kicked off proceedings.

'I'm afraid that unless five beds are found within the next hour we will have to report five, 24 hour trolley waits to the Department of Health, with another four, 12 hour waiters due before the end of the morning.'

There was a pause as everyone absorbed the depressing news before the ED man continued. 'As it's Monday we're not expecting the flow of admissions to slow down. In fact the usual Monday afternoon rush has been getting worse in recent weeks, not better as had been predicted.'

Next up was Joan, the Head of Nursing. Now here's someone who should be forced to wear a uniform. The poor woman has a severe problem with colour co-ordination and she was currently making a bold statement with an orange blouse and lilac suit. I think she's worked so many early shifts that she dresses in the dark. 'We have regular staff shortages on two thirds of the wards', she announced sternly, 'so please, please, be patient with the agency staff we have employed to fill the gaps.'

The Ambulance Liaison rep was just as critical as he reminded us that they 'cannot and will not' tolerate their ambulances being used as holding bays for patients that cannot be offloaded due to a lack of trolleys in ED. He stressed how this repeated behaviour is seriously impeding the services' ability to respond to 999 calls and threatened to take serious action if the management of the hospital cannot rectify the situation.

The reps from Trauma and Physio did a fine double act by listing *all* of their current patients along with their possible discharge dates. This was a totally unnecessary level of detail for this meeting; all we really needed to know was the number of patients they intended to discharge today. However, no one tried to stop them, as they seemed to be using this forum to justify their lack of discharges.

Eventually, it was my turn as Manager of the Admissions Department to spill my bad news and I started by gently correcting my ED colleagues. 'As you already know we have five, 24 hour trolley waits in ED with, I think you will find, another *six,* twelve hour waits to be reported before mid-day.' The ED Reps muttered to each other, but I ploughed on regardless. 'We have thirty routine surgical cases due in today, over two thirds of which are cancer or suspected cancer cases.'

I nodded to the Maxillio Facial Surgery Team, or Max Fax to those in the know. 'One of the cancer cases is a Max Fax patient, whom we cannot cancel.' I was rewarded with a weak smile from the Max Fax team. 'We have nine routine medical patients due in. Three of these have been rolled from last week because of the lack of beds,' I continued. 'We have four outstanding requests for transfers from other hospitals, two to trauma,' I continued the nodding ritual with the trauma team, 'who have surgeons standing by to operate as soon as we can clear the necessary beds. The other two are waiting for medical beds, both terminal cases that need to be moved to this area to be near their families. 'Day surgery was opened over the weekend and we've already used all 10 beds in there. The teams on day surgery are furious as this goes back on last weeks promise not to use their beds. They are pushing my staff to move the patients off their unit before anyone else is allocated a bed.'

This comment provoked angry muttering from the ED, Ambulance Liaison and the Max Fax and Trauma teams so I was quick to continue. 'We have one critical care bed empty out of a total hospital bed-stock of 500 and the wards have only declared three definite, and eight potential discharges for the day. Leaving aside the possible discharges we need 61 beds to get the hospital back to normality, if it can be called that, and that doesn't account for any further requests for beds from ED.'

I sat down taking in the extra air of despondency my presentation had created. However, a *bed temperature* of minus 61 is certainly not the worst it's been and no one commented on my report. Fran nodded at me and turned her attention towards the other representatives in the room. As expected they couldn't produce any spare beds and the catastrophe meeting appeared to be drawing to a close without incident. However, I had an inkling that something bad was going to happen. Fran looked different, much too happy and my heart started bumping it's way down my spine the moment she asked the Heads of Departments to stay on for a few minutes.

The number of people in the room quickly reduced to a third of the original number and the remaining ten of us waited for Fran to continue. 'I appreciate that the Monday meeting is not the customary place to announce such a major new project, but we concluded that the bed crisis was so acute that we could not afford to hang fire until the next scheduled monthly meeting,' Fran announced. 'I anticipate that my announcement today

4

will encourage us to push the envelope and conclusively kick these problems firmly into touch. From next weekend, we will have a new team managing the hospital's beds. They will be called the Clinical Bed Management Team and they will be made up of Senior Nursing Staff.'

Bzzzzzzzz! Those three little words were already forming in my harassed little brain. Joan as Head of Nursing glowed in her lilac bloody suit and quickly scanned the room for a reaction. She didn't get what she expected as everyone was staring at me, waiting for my reaction. I looked down at the table, unable to meet their gaze, my head buzzing furiously.

'We all know the recent inspection by the Department of Health reported that we are working at a dangerously high capacity,' Fran continued. 'A major incident would leave us in dire straits. Their report demonstrated that we would struggle to get patients in and out of the hospital and it is for this reason that the Board has decided to appoint a new team to tackle the problem.' Bzzzzzzzzz!

'Does anyone have any comments?'

Everyone in the room was looking at me, taking in my scowling face. The words were buzzing relentlessly inside my head and somehow I heard myself take a deep breath and quietly say. 'I don't understand.'

As uncomfortable silences go it wasn't the worst I've never heard. It was shorter than the time I called Mum from the States to tell her I'd just become engaged to Max. That lasted at least six seconds and was followed by a thud as Mum's backside landed on a chair. This one lasted about half the time, but there were no congratulations for me after it. The other reps looked embarrassed and Fran, well she looked as fearsome as I have ever seen her. Finally, she broke the silence. 'Details of the project will be emailed to you before the close of play today. Thank you for your time and Beth, please, will you stay for a while?'

I had to calm myself down, I pulled out a half written shopping list and started to jot down random items. Carrots, potatoes...I could hear the other people leaving, there were a few muttered words of congratulations to Joan. Onions, toothpaste, pizza...

I could hear Fran tidying her folder. Frozen peas, toilet cleaner, razor blades... It was just her and me. I looked up slowly to meet her steely gaze. We stared in silence for a few seconds, there was no way I was going to break it. I was boiling inside, the carrots and frozen peas hadn't helped. All I could think of were the razor blades. Eventually Fran decided to speak.

'Beth, Beth, Beth.' I tried to ignore the sickening maternal tone to her voice.

'You must have known something had to be done. You must see this is the best solution for everyone.'

She was obviously expecting a response from me, but I was on fire with a rage that I was determined to keep locked in. After another chasm of a pause, Fran continued, her voice sharper than a fresh hypodermic needle.

'This just will not be tolerated. Your position hasn't changed, you will be expected to step up to the mark and run with this project. The Board are depending on you. I have told them you will, but with your current attitude I am beginning to doubt your ability to be a team player.'

I sensed that my silence was really getting under Fran's skin. I kept simmering quietly and restricted myself to looking at her with contempt.

'You have worked for me for five years and I can honestly say that your attitude has shown a marked deterioration during that time. You are developing a reputation for being uncooperative, at times downright obstructive.' Another pause, but I wasn't going to say a word.

'You must realise that this attitude will land you in trouble very soon. You know you will never get promoted if you keep this up! What do you have to say for yourself?'

I decided it was time to leave, I quietly picked up my file, checked my bleep that had silently gone off eight times during the meeting and walked towards the door.

Finally, I turned to Fran. 'I shouldn't have said, "*I* don't understand",' I said before pausing to wonder if I should really continue. A smirk crept across the Fearsome One's face so I drove the insult home. 'What I should have said was, *You* don't understand.' I turned sharply and strutted out of the room, leaving a stunned and very angry Fran.

Chapter 2

The lift I felt after getting one over on the Fearsome One quickly diminished as the implications of her new plan zipped along the synapses of my brain. I clomped down the corridors en route to my office feeling more claustrophobic with each step.

Like most hospitals, Hartfield Infirmary is a rabbit warren of old and new buildings, plastered with direction signs and divided by busy roads. I decided to take the over-ground route and choke on a few fumes, rather than sharing the underground tunnels with the steady stream of migrating patients.

My bleep went off as I reached the almost fresh air, but I had already listed the number. My mind was whirring as I waited for the pedestrian crossing lights to change in my favour and I jumped when someone touched my shoulder.

'Minus 61 eh? Is that a record?'

I turned to see the warm features of Professor John Summers, one of the Surgical Consultants. He is a fascinating man, a slightly crumpled, younger version of Sean Connery with extra bushy eyebrows. Many of the nurses claim he is the most eligible bachelor in the hospital, but I've been away from the single scene for far too long to have an opinion.

He's one of those academics with the ability to have an intelligent conversation about any subject under the sun. In fact, the sun is one of his obsessions; being a South African, he misses it constantly.

'Sorry Prof. I was miles away,' I replied with a smile. 'No, 75 is our all time record, but that was during a winter flu epidemic and this is summer. I really don't know how much worse it can get.'

'Ach!' he exclaimed. 'I know you'll do the best you can Beth, but I'm getting really pissed off with the whole situation.'

The Prof, as most people like to call him, really does have the most intense frown I've ever seen. It's as if his whole face folds up of his own accord leaving just his bushy eyebrows poking out the top. It appears with impressive speed and vanishes just as quickly.

'It makes me so damn angry when I can't operate on patients just because we don't have a God damned bed,' he continued before checking himself. A small crowd of people had joined us at the crossing and we have to be so careful what we discuss in public as we've already taken a beating from the press.

'By the way Beth, you didn't ask me how I knew what the bed count was,' The Prof continued, the twinkle returning to his eye, 'I heard it from someone in the car park as I was getting out of my car. Would you believe it? That's some set of jungle drums the Trust has. I have never known a Department of Health directive that actually communicates properly. I'm intrigued, who set the system up?'

I smiled; my bed number report was certainly becoming famous. 'I set it up a few weeks ago and within 15 minutes of issuing the first report I was getting calls from all over the hospital.'

'So you put it on the Intranet?'

'That's the strange thing, I don't. When I arrive at 7:15, I gather the figures and tell my bed board staff. When they start phoning the ward at 7:45 they tell the Ward Clerks today's *lucky number* and it just flows from there'.

'Ach! That's amazing!' The Prof exclaimed as the lights finally changed and we set off across the road. 'I've never known information to travel so fast. Just shows this old institution can communicate when it needs to. I've even heard the operating theatre porters discuss it before the sports results. Tell me, what made you do it?'

'Simple really,' I replied. 'I was sick of the surrounding hospitals closing their Emergency Departments when the going got tough. As you know, our policy is *open all hours* despite the chronic bed shortages. So I began to wonder what trigger they used to decide when they would close to blue lights. All I got was, "It's really bad" or "It's the worst it's ever been", but no cold hard facts.

'So one day I did my totting up exercise and when Edgeworth General phoned to say they were closing their Emergency Department, I told them we needed 55 beds that day before we could even start housing any new emergencies. Their Admissions manager was dumfounded. Within half an hour she called back to say they were just 15 beds down and would not be diverting their blue light calls to us. Now all of the hospitals in the area use this measurement.'

The Prof laughed and his eyes twinkled mischievously, 'So, it's true then, good news may travel fast, but bad news travels faster! Keep up the good work Beth and by the way...'

'Yes I know Prof,' I interrupted kindly. 'You've got three breast cancers and a thryroidectomy to come in today. I really will do my best, but I can't promise.'

Both our bleeps went off at the same time and we laughed and parted at the main entrance. As I turned to go The Prof told me to have a nice day, but there was no chance of that. From such a disastrous start, there was only one way forward, a downward spiral 'till the bitter end. Roll on 5:30. I glanced at my watch; it hadn't struck 10:00 yet.

There was certainly no respite for me as the moment I reached my department Eddy jumped to his large, flappy feet and followed me so closely that he nearly tripped me up.

'Eddy, can you give me five minutes?' I asked drawing on depleted reserves of patience. 'At least let me get in the door.'

Eddy is a first class pratt who spends as much time and energy trying to undermine my authority as he does locating empty beds. Perhaps that's a little harsh, he does care about his work, but unfortunately for me, he is obsessed about being promoted to my job. He's worked in the Health Service since leaving school and at 32 years of age has worked in Admissions for 10 of his 16 years service.

If he were a dog he would have been described as a mongrel. He is tall, lanky and clumsy, his fetching, synthetic, blue trousers finishing a good few centimetres from his over-large feet. However, he is always immaculately turned out; his red hair is cut every two weeks and kept rigid with generous amounts of gel, while his polished shoes shine brighter than operating lights. His personality shows similar contradictions. He swings from his usual mode of angry competitiveness to his amiable, helpful alter ego at will, usually when he wants something.

Eddy was an innocent; he applied for my job but, as I discovered later, was only granted an interview 'for the experience of facing an interview panel' not to actually prove himself good enough for the job. That was five years ago and he constantly tries to put me down, especially in front of senior members of staff.

Having shaken off Eddy for the time being I dived into my *bubble*, a small glass walled office that acts as my transparent refuge. There are no external windows in the whole department so we are blessed with bright artificial lights that are supposed to recreate daylight. Unfortunately, it just makes the staff look more in need of a bed than the patients.

I dropped my file on top of the existing pile I keep on my *guest chair*. This is not a case of being messy; I cover the chair to discourage people from staying too long. My bubble is so small that if visitors cannot sit down they have to stand in the open doorway. This allows me to listen to the general hubbub and if a visitor becomes too annoying I can turn any conversation between my staff into an excuse to push past my visitor and end the meeting.

But today was different. I didn't invite Evil Eddy to stand in the door and report; in fact I closed the door so he couldn't. Then I started the process of catching up on my messages. I fired up my computer and listened to the two messages on my voice mail. I needed to respond to them, but I wanted to check my email first. The details of Fearsome Fran's plan were probably already lurking in hyperspace.

I dialled the first number from my bleep list while my PC was whirring through its start up. It was Day Surgery and although the receptionist had no idea who bleeped me, she found the time to scold Admissions for using their beds over the weekend. I cut her short and reminded her that her ward reports were late. I wasn't listening to any more accusations that morning.

My email account was open by the end of this call, but despite 20 new messages there was no sign of the details of Fran's new project. I spent the next 10 minutes working through my bleep numbers and ended up with a list of the patients that *cannot be cancelled.* These are provided by various secretaries and junior doctors who have been given the task of pleading the cases of the sick and dying patients scheduled to be admitted today.

These calls always make me foam at the mouth. The junior doctors try to baffle me with medical jargon, while the secretaries try to pull rank with words like "absolutely" and "definitely" cropping up in alternate sentences. The Prof's dragon of a secretary, Marge, even threatened to *report* me if I did not allocate a bed to one of The Prof's patients. Who was she going to report me to? Me?

I used the same response on each call, 'We will do our best, but we cannot produce beds out of thin air.' I used to get jokes about bunk beds and hammocks, but this tailed off a few years ago. They are still used by the newer members of staff who were yet to be ground down by the futility of the process, but thankfully I haven't heard them for a while.

When I was ready, I opened the door and called out to Eddy to bring in the day lists. He bounded over like an overzealous puppy and before I could object he swept the files off the visitor's chair, dumped them on the floor, and started ranting. He was in his Eddy the Eagle mode. You know? After the foolhardy British ski jumper, who despite his lack of skill or technique, leapt off the ski jump, and kept going till he crashed at the bottom. Here was Eddy, all suited up and ready to fly off into a world of biased plans and personal grudges.

'I've already told Joan how excited we are about the new Clinical Bed Management Team and that we'll do everything possible to support them. I suppose this means you'll be moving on now they will be managing us?'

You slimy toad!

'No matter, they can't do without us on the front line, so *our* jobs will be safe and Joan has already told me that I'll be okay.'

You disgusting little weasel!

One of these days I'll actually say these comments out loud to Evil Eddy, but for now I was content to restrict them to my head. I've caused enough trouble today by voicing my opinions.

'Of course I haven't said anything to the rest of the staff yet,' he continued enthusiastically, 'but they did overhear my conversation with Joan, so they know something's in the wind. When does the new system start? I've heard it will be this week, can you confirm this?' Eventually Eddy drew breath long enough for me to interrupt him.

'Eddy nothing is definite yet,' I said with commendable restraint and I was pleased to see the light dim in his eyes. As quickly as the prospect of assuming the Admissions crown had arrived I was snatching it right back.

'But...'

'No buts Eddy. At the moment the plan has only been announced. The details have yet to be hammered out and no-one knows what will happen.' I felt bad lying to Eddy, but I couldn't afford another one of his mutinies. Last year I was hauled into the personnel office to discuss my time keeping. Eddy had kept

13

a diary of my movements and, as I was not the ever-present manager Eddy thought *he* would be, he assumed my time out of the office was spent skiving and, even worse, shopping.

His records were meticulous and perfectly matched my diary. Every absence from the office corresponded with meetings throughout the Trust. After clearing the air with the head of personnel on my time keeping, we went on to discuss Eddy's motivation for such a nasty plan. Concluding that my instinct to keep my schedule to myself was the right thing to do, I still keep my diary to myself and exercise my right not to report my movements to my juniors. This is essential, as Eddy's habit of gossiping had armed my staff with enough objections to proposed changes in working practices to sink a battle ship.

'Now, before I went to the meeting we were 61 beds down, how's it looking now?' I continued.

'Umm, we have another 10 discharges planned, but Day Surgery are pushing to take these beds and I don't blame them.'

'How do they know about them Eddy?'

'Umm...'

'You didn't? How many times have I told you not to give out specific information on beds until we know the whole picture? It just causes panic. How could you?'

'Mr. Smith asked me and he's a consultant, I wasn't about to lie to him no matter what you say. He's over *you* so when he asked I told him.'

Dirty little cockroach!

'You know that by 11:00 we will have more discharges!' I exclaimed. 'I suppose Mr Smith's already hassling the ward managers to take his patients, unless of course you managed to resist the urge to tell him which wards the beds are coming up on... Oh! You didn't...Eddy! How many times do I have to tell you? We run an information service here and we have to be very careful what information we give to what people.'

'I suppose you will be pleased to tell Mr. Ahmed that his 17-year-old trauma patient with two broken legs can't be re-admitted because you let Day Surgery decant a drug addict into the Trauma cubicle? And what about The Prof's cancer patients? Are you prepared to tell their husbands that although we know their wives are riddled with breast cancer, we cannot operate on them because some sweet old ladies need their beds for some TLC?'

'Eddy, the plan was to hold these patients in Day Surgery and aim Mr. Smith's activities towards their admitting consultants to get them discharged directly from Day Surgery. We let the ED use the beds on the strict understanding that they only put *treat and street* patients in them. Short stay, obs, IV antibiotics. If we start moving them out we won't get today's electives in. I hope you realise what you've done Eddy...?'

By now Eddy was fiddling with his pen, his head hung in shame. When I finally paused he looked up and any feelings of sympathy I was reluctantly developing for him disappeared. His face was contorted with hatred. 'Well if you were here as you should've been, this wouldn't have happened!' He spat out.

'How many times Eddy? I give you instructions for a reason. If you followed them you wouldn't make these stupid mistakes. You're not going to lay this at my door, but yet again I'll have to sort out your mess. Get back to the bed board and do what you're paid to do. No more, no less, do you hear me?' Eddy stormed off, muttering something under his breath.

'I heard that! Get to work. I'll be out in a while,' I called out after him. Luckily I didn't hear what he said, but I try to keep the greasy snake on his toes. I returned to my email, voice mail and bleep numbers. Nothing could be done with the bed situation for another half an hour so I resolved to deal with the other fires. Another day out of control, so what's new?

Chapter 3

It was 1:30 by the time I managed to escape the confines of my bubble. I usually cram down food on the run, but I've recently set myself a new rule. If my stress levels rise over 10 on my personal barometer I burst out of my bubble before I'm rushed into the ED with chest pains. Thankfully, the rule works, but I always feel guilty about taking a 30-minute break. It's 30 minutes that could be spent trying to find a bed for one of those breast cancer ladies.

I reassured myself that if I didn't take some time out I would go doo-lally. I needed some thinking time, to drag the day back into perspective before re-engaging in battle. Unfortunately, my peace was shattered by my bleep going off the moment I sat down at the canteen table. Just as I strained to read the number without removing it from the waistband of my slacks, I heard a familiar voice with a South African accent.

'Mind if I join you?'

'Of course, please do,' I replied and started to form an apology as The Prof arranged his lunch on the table, placing his tray on the empty seat next to him. He was looking more crumpled than usual today; his casual consultant's attire of slacks and designer polo shirt didn't appear to have met an iron between the washing machine and being worn. His housekeeper must be on holiday.

'Shame on you Beth,' he said with a mischievous glance at my lunch. I looked down at the unappetising offering of a limp sandwich, a bowl of salad and a yoghurt.

'You obviously have no sense of adventure,' he continued. 'Now I think I have bought moussaka, but I have to admit that it closely resembles the spaghetti bolognaise I had yesterday.'

I laughed as John forked a large chunk of the mystery mince dish into his mouth. 'Maybe it's part of a drive to promote healthy eating in the workforce,' I suggested. 'Just ensure that everything apart from the salad is inedible.'

'Ach, I wouldn't call this inedible,' John mumbled around his food. 'Tasteless certainly, but it's probably edible.' There was a pause as we both ploughed into our food. A pause that started to grow slightly too big for it's boots.

'I'm so sorry we couldn't get all your ladies in today, Prof.,' I said. 'We'll try to get them in early tomorrow in time for theatre but...'

'Good God Beth! I didn't sit here to make you feel guilty.' The Prof interrupted with a smile. 'I know you will do everything you can. I really wanted to continue with this morning's discussion. You spoke more sense in those few minutes than I have heard all year in this Goddamn place. I am just here for some sensible conversation.'

'Sensible! You must be joking?' I laughed. 'I feel I'm talking another language to everyone else. I just can't seem to make myself understood. If you understand me, you must be as nuts as I am!'

'Don't talk yourself down.' The Prof's eyebrows started to beetle together. 'I thought I'd finally found a Brit who was over that particular ailment, now you are beginning to disappoint me.'

'What do you mean, "ailment"?'

'I've been working here for ten years since leaving the sun of Africa,' The Prof continued. 'I thought landing the professorship was my lottery win—the opportunity to work at one of the foremost teaching hospitals in the UK with the added bonus of strong University working ties. It was my dream job. I planned to stay here for about fifteen years then return to Jo'burgh with a raft of knowledge to pass on, but nothing's going to plan.

'For months now I've been trying to figure out what is happening, but I can't get a handle on it and today I thought, ach no, I know I saw a little ray of hope. You are the first Brit I have spoken to who managed to state a problem in plain English.' 'So what's this ailment you're talking about? You've got me worried.'

'Poor choice of words,' he laughed. 'No Beth, I don't think you are ill, or lacking anything for that matter. I was simply trying to say that you're the first colleague who has explained to me what a problem was and how you went about solving it, without claiming you're a bloody genius, or using the results to angle for promotion!'

'You mean the bed count?'

'Yep I mean the bed count. How do you do it?'

'Well I explained this morning about Edgeworth and...'

'No, I don't mean that. You explained that very clearly. That is what I mean. How do you manage to identify a problem so clearly and just put it right? These things usually take months of debate and audits and you did it in hours. How?'

I picked at my half-eaten sandwich as I tried to work out the answer. John looked at me with intense irritation as he tentatively chewed his food. 'That chip was still frozen! Brown on the outside and frozen in the middle, they are trying to kill us!'

I laughed. 'I'm sorry John, I wish there was a cunning plan, but the truth is that I just did it.'

'Don't you dare apologise, I suppose it was too much to hope that I was finally on the trail of Holy Grail, but if you ever figure it out will you let me into the secret?'

'Sure,' I grinned at him. 'Talking of sacred icons, what on earth is up with your secretary? Forgive me if I'm speaking out of turn, but Marge is becoming a right royal pain in the butt. She's even taken to threatening my staff with disciplinary action if we don't find beds for your patients. You know we do our best and we really don't need another battle to fight.'

'Good God, she's off on one again is she?' The Prof replied, his eyes twinkling mischievously. 'You know she thinks I'm not good enough to be a professor don't you? Oh, yes. She is convinced that her mission in life is to turn me into a gentleman. That's a bloody laugh. You should hear her when I announce that I'm going surfing for a weekend. She even suggested that I should take up more refined pastimes such as golf or shooting. Ach, just what I bloody need, a half-day hike, or an afternoon spent killing things when I spend all week on my feet trying to save lives! She really is on her own Goddamned planet!

'My only consolation is that if she is giving your team a hard time I'm off the hook for a while. I'm really sorry Beth. I'll have another word with her. Now. I must dash, but remember if you figure out where your magic powers come from, let me in on the secret, okay?'

As I said goodbye I flipped open my notepad and thought about what The Prof had just said. I scribbled down two headings: Fran and Prof. Under Fran I wrote, 'Will never get promotion,' and under Prof 'Not using an answer to angle for promotion.' I reworded the two statements 'Not given a promotion', and 'Not trying to get promotion'. Something was missing, but what? I scribbled down 'Do I want promotion?' but there was no answer in my head. I sat there with my pen poised, but I couldn't decide whether to write yes or no. I recalled my earlier clash with the Fearsome One and was surprised how quickly my anger had faded once I returned to the office. Was I just too busy to stay mad, or was I really not bothered about my career stalling? Oh bugger! Where was the magic when I needed it?

Eddy's chair was empty when I returned and I automatically started thinking the worst. Luckily, Sally was there. Sal is Eddy's counterpart on the Bed Board and she's everything that Eddy should be; stable, hardworking and quick to take instructions. In fact she is one of the few people who actually looks good in our uniforms.

I could make sarcastic comments about her perfect figure, but I know it's not just down to her genes. Her raw material isn't quite perfect, she may have cute dimples when she smiles, but she was gifted with a nose several sizes too large for her. However, Sal is a gym bunny; she gets a buzz from exercise and often tries to persuade me that a session after work is perfect for relieving stress. She's probably right, but the gym and I are as compatible as drinking and driving.

'Hi Sal, where's Eddy?' I asked.

'Hey Beth, he's gone to move some notes,' Sally replied.

'Again! I must have told him a thousand times that moving notes is not his job; we have the couriers to do that. Did he take a bleep?' 'Nope, but he said he won't be long, I think he's gone to see Mr. Smith to apologise for this morning's cock-up.'

I managed a wry smile. Apologising my arse, he was sticking the knife in and twisting it as much as he could. I didn't tell him about taking my break so Eddy probably assumed I'd nicked off to Day Surgery to give them a piece of my mind and make him look stupid. He'd made up an excuse to get in there before I did and was probably badmouthing me to the staff on the Unit. If he got lucky he would bump into Mr. Smith and spread his hatred even further. Oh, happy days!

'Not to worry Sal. How are things now?'

'Ticking over, we've cancelled fifteen of the surgical routines, all over the phone, thank Buddha, but the two outstanding breast ladies are starving themselves from midnight. We might be able to get 'em in tomorrow, but I don't rate their chances.'

I nodded sadly and sitting in Eddy's seat at the bed board I carefully wrote down the names of the two cancer patients in my notebook.

'So, how's the ED looking?'

'We've identified beds for all of yesterday's patients, but the last of them won't hit the ward 'til tonight. Beth, do these count as twenty-four hour trolley waits? I never know which way the bods are measuring these times, it changes every frigging week.'

'I really don't know Sal, so your guess is as good as mine. Just fax the details over to the general office as usual. It's not our problem if the powers that be decide to cut off the trolley wait time when a bed has been identified, rather than when the poor patient actually gets in it.'

I decided to be brave and look at the new requests and pulled the ED register towards me. The register is an A3 book with a sheet for each day of the month. There were enough lines on each page to log 40 bed requests from the ED each day. Recently we were fortunate if we only used the front of the page for any given 24-hour period, it was now a regular occurrence to log requests on the back of the page. Today's page was already three-quarters full. I picked up the phone and dialled the number for the Major End of the Emergency Department.

'Hi, can I speak to the nurse in charge?' I asked before recognising the voice at the other end. 'Hi, Chris, I thought you were on an early?'

'Hiya, Beth, I was, but guess what?'

'Short staffed eh? You have my sympathy. This is becoming a regular Monday afternoon occurrence isn't it?'

'Tell me about it! The Monday morning shift has become less popular than the Black Death. Now, how can I help?'

'Just wanted an indication of your expected list. I know it's early, but for some strange reason I want to know how bad it's going to get.'

'Hang on to your seat, we've got twelve on it already, and the SHO[1] is currently taking a call with another holding.'

'How did I know today was going to go from worse to bad?' I moaned. 'Thanks Chris, I'll send the girls up to start interviewing if you don't mind. At least this way we can get the patient's notes for you before the medics get to see them. This seems to help a bit, but it won't create any more beds.

'By the way have you managed to convince any consultants to join the Monday afternoon party as we discussed at the last meeting?'

'You must be joking Beth. You and I know that if we could get senior doc's to see the patients in the Emergency Dept on Mondays we would have fewer admissions. The young doc's are really foundering and being so cautious it drives me nuts.

---

[1] Senior House Officer - despite the title this is a junior hosptial doctor role

'I'm just a nurse with more experience in my little finger than some of these kids, so who am I to complain? You know how it is, the brass either have teaching sessions or clinics on a Monday and they are set in concrete. Sorry, Beth, have to dash, sounds like a serious RTA coming over the radio.'

I put down the phone with a grimace. 'Sally, phone the Trauma Wards and see if you can identify any more possible discharges for this evening. It sounds like we may have casualties from a road traffic accident coming in. Promise to only put trauma cases in their beds if you have to. I know they hide beds for fear of being lumbered with a long-term medical case; a promise might lubricate things a bit.

'Also, when the girls get back, ask them to go to the ED to interview as many patients as possible and to request their notes before the Medical Records staff go home for the day.'

'No worries Beth.'

The doors flung open and Evil Eddy rejoined us at last.

'Ah, Eddy; just doing your job for you. Where the hell were you? No don't bother, I know. Just don't let me hear that you are moving notes again, all right? Sal will fill you in.'

I quickly returned to my bubble before Eddy had a chance to respond and I finally saw the email I had been dreading, 'Clinical Bed Management Team—the way forward.' God, how ` pretentious! I printed it off and walked out to collect it from the printer in the main office before Eddy got his greasy paws on it. I needn't have worried; Eddy was on the phone to Chris in the ED.

'Hi Chris,' he chimed, 'can you give me the hospital numbers of the expected patients?' I couldn't believe it. I strode over to Eddy.

'Pass me the phone please Eddy,' I ordered. He looked stunned but he thrust the receiver towards me. I grabbed it.

'Sorry, Chris, ignore that last request. Bye.' I put the receiver down with a bang and turned to the Evil One.

'Eddy don't you understand plain English? Didn't Sal tell you to tell the girls to go up and get the information on the patients?'

'But they aren't back yet,' Eddie protested. 'I was just trying to get the information.'

'Eddy, the reason I asked you to send the girls up to the department to get the information was to help relieve the pressure up there. You phoning them is just adding to it. Remember, we are the clerical staff, they are the medics. We are here to support them, not the other way around!'

'But you said we have to get the notes before Med Recs closes in half an hour,' Eddy whined.

'In that case Sally, you go up and get all the hospital registration numbers you can, then request the notes. Eddy, when the girls get back tell them to go and interview and remember to tell them that the notes are in hand, I don't want a double request going to Med Recs or them zooming off on a wild goose chase. Understand?'

'But, we don't know if they will all be admitted!' Eddy bleated. 'We don't do it this way. We wait until they request a bed, then interview, then get the notes. It's always been like this!'

'Well Eddy things change and it's about time you got used to it. Just make sure the girls do not tell the patients they are going to be admitted. They can say they are just checking that the records are correct. Can I trust you to do that one small thing? And before you start criticising another of my decisions I'll tell you why we are doing it this way today.

'The medical rotation took place two weeks ago. The junior doc's are out on their own for the first time in the ED, it's Monday afternoon and they don't know their stethoscopes from their tongue depressors and we all know what that means. They are overcautious and will admit anyone with a pulse.

'To try and remedy this situation I want them to have all the available notes to refer to. Hopefully, they will provide some of the answers the patients would normally be admitted to find. So maybe, just maybe, they will not feel it necessary to admit quite so many patients. Got it?'

'Shall I write a new procedure for this?' said Eddy sarcastically.

'No Eddy just do it today and I will monitor it. If we need to change a policy I will tell you first alright?'

'Yes,' Eddy mumbled.

I returned to my bubble picking up the pages from the printer on the way. As I closed the door, the two couriers, or my girls as I call them returned to the office. I smiled as Eddy made a great show of giving them their new instructions before shooing them out of the office. I took a bottle of water out of my desk drawer, opened it, and took a big swig before I read the dreaded email.

Clinical Bed Management Team - the way forward
Presented by Joan Norman - Director of Nursing

In an effort to overcome the bed shortages at Hartford Infirmary the following plan will be implemented from Saturday 6th July.

The Clinical Bed managers will visit each ward at the start of the early shift to ascertain how many beds would be available that day.

They will then meet in the Admissions office to review the expected list for the day and will allocate beds on the basis of clinical need.

They carry bleeps 3001 and 3002 and should be contacted for any issues relating to bed allocation.

A second ward round will take place after lunch and any beds identified on this round will be allocated to ED patients.

Any questions should be directed to the Senior Clinical Bed Manager - Tessa Pringle

Short and sweet, but loaded with problems. What the hell did Joan think she was doing? Tessa of all people - the scourge of the nursing staff. She had been ward manager of three different wards this year already and each time she prompted an outright rebellion among her staff. Now she would be terrorising every ward in the hospital.

Hmmm, I paused to consider this tactic. It was true the ward managers tried to hide beds until they knew they would be allocated patients in need of their own particular skills. Getting the ward staff to admit they had empty beds was a real battle that I've been engaged in for years, so perhaps sending Tessa the Terrible to each ward twice a day might cure them of this practice. But what about the rest of the plan?

How long would it take them to do the rounds and get to admissions? My staff need to know about any empty beds or beds being vacated early in the day, especially when they have patients waiting at home, starved and ready for surgery. Most patients need to know a bed would be available by at least 08:00 in order to get through the rush hour traffic to be here by 10:00 in time for surgery.

My mind was whirring, but it didn't know which direction to turn to first. There was so much wrong with the plan and so many questions that couldn't be answered. Why? Why? Why! It won't make any more beds, or more accurately will not result in the admittance of any more patients. Yet the piece of paper in my hand clearly stated that 'in an effort to overcome bed shortages' this would happen. How?

I sat back and thought about my lunch with The Prof and laughed out loud, 'I know I seem to speak another language, but this sure as hell isn't English as I know it. It doesn't make any bloody sense at all.'

Chapter 4

I was the first to arrive the next morning, this is usually the case, and it's just the way I like it. It's my favourite time of the working day, the department is empty, and I can get my thoughts in order to face the chaos prowling around the next corner. Normally I hit the department at around 7:15 but today I managed to get into work earlier than usual as my husband Max was away on business Without his company at the break-fast table I prefered to use the time to get a jump start on the day.

I always wake up earlier when he is away and, to be honest, I've been enjoying a little bit of space from him. He has become obsessed with the notion that I should resign and find a less stressful job. He will probably go on another rant when he finds out about yesterday's nightmare so I have a few days grace to try and patch up the frontline here before he returns.

I slipped my makeup bag out of my briefcase, grabbed a form from the box on the wall in my office, settled in Eddy's seat at the bed board, and selected the necessary items from my makeup bag. I often put on my face as I survey the board. It may not be a logical pattern of behaviour, but it works for me. We all need time to think and performing the mundane task of making myself presentable each morning does not stop my brain whirring around. It may even help it.

The bed board is 12 feet wide and about two and a half feet deep. It's made up of moulded plastic strips - the kind that fac-tory time cards are kept in - only these cards are smaller, about 3 inches by 2 inches. Running across the board are 30 columns of slots, each one representing a ward and at the top of each column is a hand written label with the ward number written on it in thick black felt pen. As a system it was very basic, but it worked. If only the whole health system could be as simple!

I was engrossed in the tasks of applying eye shadow and scrutinising the board when there was a knock on the door. I knew it wasn't one of the staff, they all have the code, so I opened the door to find Prof. John Summers looking very uncomfortable. He was obviously perturbed at catching me at one of the more personal aspects of my morning routine.

'Ah, morning Beth, I'm sorry, I didn't mean to disturb you.' There was no need for me to apply any blusher; I was as embarrassed as he was. It's one thing for Sal, or even Eddy, to walk in while I'm applying the war paint; it's quite another when it's a professor.

'Not at all Prof,' I replied, trying to make light of the situation. 'I'm afraid I do things in a bit of a random order in the mornings. What can I help you with?'

'Well,' John started, he was still looking uneasy, 'it's just me being nosy I'm afraid. Why don't I explain while you finish the other eye?'

I realised with a start that I had put colour on one eye and not on the other. No wonder he looked uncomfortable! I quickly grabbed the brush and daubed my unpainted eye.

'I was contemplating your delightful bed temperature system last night and I was trying to formulate a similar system to make more use of our beds. I'm afraid I failed completely; I couldn't even work out the best way of monitoring the bed situation in the first place. I just ended up surrounded by bits of paper and sticky notes.'

I laughed. While The Prof didn't live up to the stereotype image of an absent-minded academic, I could easily picture him scowling at the mess around him.

'You'll like this then, welcome to the bed board.' I declared and ushered him closer so he could get a clearer view.

'Ach!' He exclaimed, his quick eyes darting over the board. 'Lots of different colours, I appreciate that, helps the old grey matter digest it all.'

I laughed again; it was good to know that two minds don't have to be great to think alike.

'These columns each represent a ward,' I explained 'and the different coloured cards in the slots provide all the information we need. A pink card represents a female patient and a blue card represents a male.'

'Right, I've got that, I also see you have written basic notes about the patient on the cards.'

'Yes, that's just admin information, the patient's name, the admitting consultant's initials, admission date, and the ward they had been admitted to.'

'Excellent, but you also have blue plastic cards, what do they represent?'

'The blue plastic cards show how the wards are laid out. For example, a blue plastic card followed by four pink cards then another blue plastic card shows a female four-bedded bay so only a female patient can be put into the bed. Likewise there are wards with ten bedded areas and dotted throughout the hospital are the single bedded bays or rooms we use for patients that need isolation or privacy.'

'Ah yes, the ones we all fight over,' The Prof remarked with a wry smile.

'Correct,' I confirmed.

'So what denotes an empty bed?'

'We use red plastic cards to show empty beds.'

'I can't see any of them.'

'Correct again, I'm afraid. I haven't seen a red plastic for months, since at least, well last Christmas when the hospital tried to discharge as many patients as possible. Unfortunately, they didn't stay empty for long as we were swamped by a flu epidemic the day after Christmas.'

'Ach, I remember that one,' The Prof mused, 'I was one of the many who was struck down by the damned thing. So why is the board split into two sides?'

'Ah, one side is surgery and the other side is medical. Although the hospital has approximately 500 beds the wards numbers don't run across the board sequentially. The left of the board represents the surgical wards while the medical wards are on the right hand side.

'We normally have two people working the board and they always used to squabble over who worked the surgical side. Surgery is always harder to manage, as the turnover of patients is much faster in this discipline. They used to complain that the medical side was 'as interesting as watching paint dry.' Now no-one wants to work surgery as they also have the job of phoning patients to tell them their surgery had been cancelled due to lack of beds.'

'Yes, I see,' The Prof replied thoughtfully. 'Is the surgery always cancelled because of lack of beds?'

'You should know Prof, but I would say that only one in every 500 cancelled operations were due to other reasons, like a sick surgeon or lack of theatre space.'

The Prof rubbed his chin, his eyes darting around the board. 'You really are on the front line here aren't you? We should be thankful that you have such a robust and simple system to monitor all the bad news.' He glanced at his watch, 'Oh damn it! I have to be elsewhere. Thank you for showing me this Beth, it has been absolutely fascinating. And keep up the good work.'

'Don't worry Prof, I will, and I'm just about to try and find a space for your two breast ladies.'

'I had better leave you to it then, thank you and stay well!'

The Prof disappeared as quickly as he arrived; it was good to hear a senior person acknowledging that Admissions are on the front line. Telling a patient they are being cancelled is the most heart-wrenching task we have to do.

When beds started to become an issue, some of the staff would be in tears after telling anxious patients, and even worse anxious spouses and offspring, 'Yes, we know your wife/ husband or mother/father is very sick, but we are really sorry, there is nothing we can do, we just don't have the beds'. It was a distressing task that left the messenger emotionally exhausted by mid-day.

Over the months, we have developed various coping mechanisms. We tried many different ways to deliver the news, but in the end found the only way to perform the task with sincerity was to tell the truth. 'Mrs. Smith, this is XYZ from the Admissions Office of the Hartford Infirmary. I am sorry to have to tell you that we're not going to be able to admit you today for your surgery, because all 500 of our beds are full and there are not enough patients that are well enough to be discharged for us to be able to admit you.'

Sometimes we would point out that if the current patients were not being discharged early then neither would they when it was their turn to be admitted. The patients who actually accepted this response took comfort with the thought they were at the head of the queue so they will be next in line. How little they understood.

This method of passing on bad news worked well in the majority of cases. Although it was the truth at the time it was delivered, there was one important factor that was not mentioned unless the staff were really pushed and fighting to rationalise the decision making process: the effect the Emergency Department has on the hospitals' intake.

A growing number of patients who were waiting their *turn* at home were deteriorating and with depressing regularity these patients ended up being admitted via the ED as referrals from their own family doctors. These were the uncomplaining British General Public who tended to be elderly and when questioned on how long their condition had been worsening invariably replied, 'I don't like to make a fuss.'

These were always tough to deal with because by the time they were finally admitted, often after an excruciatingly long wait in the ED on a narrow trolley, usually without pillows, they frequently had more symptoms than were presented at their original consultation. This extended their treatment time, as they were generally medical patients whose treatment meant devising, applying and checking new medication routines.

I diverted the tracks on this depressing train of thought and returned my attention to the bed board and my make up bag. I noticed that five patients had stayed overnight in Day Surgery. At least I had managed to stop Mr. Smith from taking all the beds that became available yesterday. Further scrutiny of the bed board showed that at least a third of the surgical beds housed medical patients. No wonder they have to cancel so many surgical procedures! In the past a short-stay surgical bed could have three occupants in any given week, now we were lucky if a single medical patient in a surgical bed would be well enough to be discharged after three weeks. That's a 9:1 ratio! How long can this hospital sustain that? I had the uncomfortable feeling that it would not be long before the whole system experienced a slow and painful meltdown.

Most women can put on their face whilst doing other tasks; I have developed the ability to slap on the war paint around the phone headset. This useful skill allowed me to phone all of the major departments and complete the Temperature Chart for the morning, before closing my make up bag. Just 55 beds down today, an improvement on yesterday, but I was acutely aware of the two breast cancer ladies. I knew they would be waiting by their phones, overnight bags at the ready, having starved themselves of food and water since midnight the night before. I felt sick at the thought of them waiting for the call to come in for surgery later that day.

I called the Short Stay Surgical ward. It was 7:45 so the early shift of nursing staff should have finished their handover meeting by now.

'Hi, it's Beth in Admissions. Who's the nurse in charge today? Can I speak to her?'

'Good morning Beth, is it cold today?'

I recognised the voice instantly.

'Morning Niamh, just minus 55, a tad warmer than yester-day.'

'Warmer? Jeezus! That would be considered arctic weather anywhere else. So what can we do for you?'

'Niamh, I've got two breast ladies rolled from yesterday who are due for surgery today. Prof knows about them and I've promised to move heaven and earth to get them in. Can you help?'

'Well, we are here to please, have you got any suggestions?'

'Glad you asked. I know you have two young ladies on the ward with self-inflicted abscesses—you know, our regulars who like to dabble in illicit substances? Well, I know the surgeons saw them yesterday and they decided that conservative treat-ment would be appropriate. Any chance someone could put some pressure on the drug rehab team to take them off of our hands before 11:00?'

'That's a hell of a tall order Beth. That team are a walking ad for Prozac so they are. They take an age to move their people on.'

'But, Niamh, if you could get the Registrar to consent to discharge during the morning ward round they could be put in the day room. The rehab team would have to take them then.'

'The day room! Jeezus! That's right next to the drug store and you know the problems we had last month when one of our delightful drug abusing patients tried to walk off with half our stock.'

'I know but I'm begging here Niamh. These ladies deserve more than this and quite frankly unless we put a bomb under our rehab colleagues they will miss surgery this week and next week's slots are already allocated. It will be two weeks before they get another shot at this. I couldn't wait two weeks could you?'

'I'm with you there Beth, but I can't make any promises. I really will try my best, so I will. Ah, wait just a minute. You know the rotation has just taken place? Well what if I tell our new wonder boy of a Registrar that this is our Ward policy? He won't know any different. I'll probably get a black mark on my otherwise perfect copybook, but what the hell? I'll try and con him into it. Leave it with me. I'll call as soon as I have some news. Ah, here comes my man now. Hello my fine little registrar! Have I got some interesting cases for you this morning...'

The phone line went dead. What a trooper! I was so pleased Niamh was on duty this morning. Any other senior nurse would have given me a hard time but Niamh and me go back a long way. Her copybook looked like a leopard with chicken pox, but she always got the job done. She was smart and used her mixture of charm, flattery, and wonderful sense of humour to head disciplinary actions off at the pass. No matter how bad things got, Niamh floated through the sea of flotsam and came out in one piece.

She recently let me in on the secret—figure out the most deserving patients and fight like hell for them. The patient and the consultants were always pleased so any flack she got from her peers and superiors were always overridden by the *top of the food chain*. As I said, she's a smart lady.

Eddy and Sally arrived just as I was pinning the bed temperature chart to the wall.

'Good morning Eddy, Sally,' I chirped. I was determined to be enthusiastic about the day. 'Are the girls in yet? I think we'll continue with the system we set up yesterday. Interview, get the notes, then admit when a bed comes up. The charge nurse on night duty said the junior doc's were able to treat and discharge two patients last night because they had the notes. A little victory, eh?'

Eddy sat in the seat I had just vacated and put on the headset. 'Warm seat and warm ears. What have you been doing Beth?'

'I've been trying to sort out some beds for your two breast ladies,' I replied. 'Niamh will get back to you as soon as she has some news, but in the meantime would you phone the ladies to assure them they've not been forgotten and we'll get back to them with some news as soon as we have it? Thanks Eddy.'

Eddy breathed out an audible sigh of relief. 'Sure. I hardly slept last night. I couldn't stop thinking about them. I thought a job should get easier the longer you did it.'

Eddy's voice trailed off as he began to dial the home number of the first patient and I retreated to my bubble. It was nice to see Eddy in one of his agreeable moods and I knew how hard those calls are to make. He certainly didn't need his boss breathing down his neck. I switched on my computer and checked my diary as it powered up. No meetings! Brilliant! I had a strong feeling that today was going to be better, but I instantly stopped the thought, no point in tempting fate.

Chapter 5

I have never been fascinated by spreadsheets, but the task of reducing spending in my departmental budget was taxing so much of my brain that I didn't hear Eddy knocking on my office door. He almost thumped the door the second time to get my attention.

'Come in,' I said without taking my eyes from the screen. When I looked round I was surprised to see a broad grin splitting Eddy's normally sour face.

'I've got two beds for the breast ladies!' He announced proudly. 'It's going to be tight but the teams are on standby and I should get them here in time for surgery. Just thought I'd let you know.'

Ah, so *he* managed to find the extra beds did he? I let the weasel continue his story.

'Thanks Eddy. How did *you* manage it?'

'Short Stay Surgery have managed to get two ladies discharged,' Eddie chirped. 'They're in the day room, the staff there aren't too happy but I made it work.'

I smiled as I thought of Niamh's antics. There was no point in bursting Eddy's bubble. It would only end in another nit-picking row. The breast ladies were the only important factor.

'Well done! How're the beds looking?'

'Oh, about 6 foot long with white sheets and full of patients,' Eddy was determined to milk *his* success for as long as possible.

'Yes, very funny. How many do we need?'

'It's getting better. One of the trauma wards phoned down to declare some early discharges; the ward sister said something about a reward for yesterday. Don't know what she meant. Anyway, I've cleared the orthopaedic patients from the ED, which just leaves us with four up there to find beds for.

'Umm, it's Tuesday today so some of the medical teams are doing early rounds, so we hope to have a few more empties to play with before 11.00.'

My, *this is too good to be true,* antennae were working overtime with this news. 'What about the surgical electives?'

'Ah, well. Same old, same old. By getting the two breast ladies in we're going to have to cancel more than we hoped, but I got them in and the Prof. will be pleased. I'm sure the Max Fax team won't mind us cancelling their two, their cancer case got in yesterday and the two scheduled for today were fairly minor non-cancerous operations. The only real sticking point is the Whipples op that is due in, Joan is duty exec for today so I'll throw that decision at her, if I need to.'

Eddy's eyes seemed to narrow slightly as he paused and looked carefully at me before continuing. 'Are you out of the office today at all?'

'No Eddy, you've got the pleasure of my company all day.' His face plummeted as fast as a Sumo wrestler jumping off an aeroplane. I knew his game. He wanted a private chat with Joan about the new project. Tough. I watched him skulk out of the office and started musing over the upcoming daily crisis meeting.

These meetings have grown over recent months. In fact there was a time we didn't have any bed meetings and the Admissions teams were just left to get on with it. That was before we were inspected by two very nice people from the Department of Health. They observed our day's work from start to finish and concluded that the team were not wasting any of our most precious resource, beds; in fact we were over utilising them.

The final report that went to the board announced that the hospital was running at 98 percent capacity. I'll never know how they reached that figure, as the maximum time a declared bed had been empty on the inspection day was less than 15 minutes. Still, who knows where they pluck these figures from?

In short, the report concluded that 'whilst the hospital was maximising it's bed stock' it was 'operating at dangerously high occupancy levels' and that if it 'could address the problem of getting patients in and out' it should 'be able to increase the flow of patients through the system.'

This sounded very similar to what I've been saying all along. Get 'em in. Get 'em treated and get 'em out! Nothing has changed since that report and the 11:00 Tuesday to Friday bed crisis meetings that were held from then on achieved nothing other than taking a number of senior staff away from their posts for half an hour.

The Board reacted to this failure by putting their *best brains* on the case and introduced the *Duty Exec of the Day*. Working on a rota, the most senior of the management team were duty bound to chair these meetings and collect as much information as possible. From this they were expected to gather enough insight and wisdom to broker deals between the relevant medical teams.

Unfortunately, these *relevant* teams were not represented at these meetings. It seems to me that *they* were the *best brains* as they had predicted the futility of the meetings before they even started. The surgeons and medics had been happy to rely on the Admissions staff to page them if there was a conflict over patients and beds and they would sort it out between them. However, when the bed situation worsened, they threw the decision making back at the managers, citing their Hippocratic Oath as their get-out clause from having to make life and death decisions. This left the managers, who were not bound by the oath to make the decisions on their behalf.

Some awful decisions were made and the Duty Execs now found themselves trying to broker deals between the increasingly belligerent teams. Perhaps the best indication of the difficulty of this job was the number of times the Duty Execs call in sick on their duty days. When this happens the role is delegated to junior Associate General Managers, who for the first few meetings jump on the opportunity to prove their worth. After all, they were smart, well educated, and have written numerous essays on National Health Service management. However, despite their best efforts, no one had broken the code. No one had managed to figure out how to keep pace with demand.

Eventually, the Board had decided that as Mondays were statistically the worst days they warranted the Monday morning briefing or Catastrophe Meeting, as I called them. For the rest of the week we continue with the crisis meetings in the Admissions Department.

I was brought back to the present by my PC chiming for the 11:00 meeting in its irritating know-all way and I opened my office door just as Joan walked in to the department.

I don't have an axe to grind with Joan. She's a nice person; not to mention a very experienced nurse with a history of putting the patients first in any disagreement. I may not agree with the plan, but I had no right to take it out on Joan. So I ignored the frightening impact of the bright scarlet suit she had chosen to dazzle us with today and made a point of being friendly.

'Hi Joan, how are you?'

'Hello Beth,' she replied in her lovely soft West Country accent as she treated me to a tired half-smile. 'I'm fine, I'm always fine, there's never time to be ill in this place.'

Joan was never one to over-indulge in smiling. Her front teeth looked as if they had gone out for a night on the town and jammed themselves back in wherever they could find room. As a result she tended to hide them behind her lips as much as possible. It is a shame because Joan was born to care for people and beneath her tough exterior was a smiley person, desperate to get out.

I returned her smile and suddenly felt confident that I could get her on my side over the coming weeks. As we made our way towards the bed board I placed my hand on Joan's scarlet elbow and whispered in her ear.

'I'm going to give the staff the details of the new project after lunch, when it will be quieter, so I would appreciate not mentioning it now.'

Joan looked serious for a second before she relaxed and nodded. 'Right you are Beth, but I hope they will be ready in time.'

'They will,' I assured her.

A quick look at the board showed much more movement than this time yesterday, but there were still no empty beds. I picked up the two elective lists, one for surgery and one for medicine and asked Sal to hold the fort until the meeting was over.

I could feel Eddy's eyes burning into me as we walked towards the coffee room at the back of the office. No doubt he wanted to present the day's figures for the department because of the success of admission of the breast ladies. Should I let him have the glory? I wasn't sure.

There were about a dozen people waiting for us in the coffee room so the seven chairs were already taken. I stood alongside Eddy in front of the staff lockers and smiled inwardly at the sight of Eddy watching the elective lists like a hawk. I reasoned that this afternoon's meeting to discuss the new project would give his ego a thorough bruising so I handed him the lists as the meeting was called to order.

After the meeting Eddy was like a cat with two tails, happily taking the congratulations from the staff and the backslapping from the representative of the Breast Care Team. In fact he was more like a dog with two tails, wriggling around the floor in ecstasy as these influential people scratched his tummy.

Being Eddy he chose to ignore the scowls of the representatives from the Emergency Department and Day Surgery who were still fighting to clear their backlogs. However, I could hear Eddy on the phone from my bubble after the meeting, cancelling some of the minor surgical patient's admissions. I was delighted that he actually sounded professional and caring for once rather than his usual impression of a depressed donkey. He was definitely on a roll today.

I could also hear Joan talking to the Surgical Consultant of the patient who was due to be admitted for the palliative Whipples operation.

'Of course I am aware that the patient has cancer,' she snapped. 'After all I've been a theatre nurse for more years than I care to remember. But, if we cancel this particular operation I can use the same bed for three other cancer cases whose prognosis is much better than the Whipples case.'

I couldn't hear exactly what the surgeon said, but he spoke at length and when he finished Joan turned to Eddy and told him to put the Whipples case into the only bed becoming available on the GI ward. As Joan turned away she caught my gaze through the glass and I noticed she had tears in her eyes. My heart melted and I sprung up to ask if she had time for a coffee.

'Thank you,' she replied, as she rapidly blinked back her tears. We returned to the now empty coffee room and I busied myself making the drinks.

Joan sighed heavily as she got her emotions under control. 'Oh Beth, it gets tougher every day. At least the patients had names when I was nursing. We only dealt with people who were in hospital and receiving treatment. Identifying them by their condition was something I vowed I would never do, but here I am sounding like a surgeon. Beth, when is it going to get better?'

'I know what you mean,' I replied with sympathy. 'We try our best to be compassionate, but at the end of the day I try to tell myself that what we are doing is operating a large factory with very different types of raw material going in the front end. Each patient's needs are different from the rest. Trying to rationalise what we do seems impossible and I've been racking my brains for years, but now it's becoming critical and I'm not sure how much *I* can take, let alone the patients.'

I was horrified to see that my attempts to show Joan we're not personally responsible for each and every patient had failed. Joan was now sobbing.

'Beth, when I moved into management I was going to revolutionise this hospital, make it something the local people would really appreciate. Now I just feel useless.' She pulled a tissue out of her pocket, blew her nose and composed herself. 'You know what the toughest thing is? Making decisions. I know what to do when treating a patient, but I just don't know how to make these kinds of decisions.'

Tingalingaling! An alarm bell that was much louder and more irritating than the one on my PC started to ring in my head. I had heard this so many times but it never really registered before. I slowly formed a question

'Joan, how much training did you have for this job?'

'I have a degree in nursing and I'm doing a Masters in Healthcare Management,' Joan replied briskly. 'Why do you ask?'

'I was just wondering if your training included decision-making.'

'We cover many subjects both managerial and clinical but not how to deal with this. This is too different to be part of our course work, too particular to this hospital.'

'Is it really though? Surely almost every hospital in the country must have similar problems. Are there no guidelines? Nothing you can refer to?'

Joan looked pensive, 'Perhaps there is something. This new project was modelled on another hospital's successful project so it should help, and the New Clinical Bed Managers are full of ideas. I'll have to do some digging, but there must be some more help out there somewhere. I just hope that together we can come up with the goods.' She glanced at her watch. 'I must go; I've got a mid-day meeting. And Beth, I'd appreciate it if you kept this between us, do you mind?'

'Of course not Joan. We've all been to the place where it all gets a bit too much to bear. Just between us. Alright?'

Joan straightened herself up and placed her half-empty coffee cup in the sink as she left the room.

I sat back to finish my coffee. Joan breaking down, Eddy being professional, what was happening today? These people had shown me sides of their personalities that I would have sworn did not exist. They just wanted to do a good job; in fact they were desperate to do a good job. How sad that they had so few opportunities to do so. I took out my notebook and scribbled, *'We all want to do a good job.'*

Chapter 6

I was still thinking hard about doing a good job in the spare half hour before I was due to brief the Admissions team on the new system. The more I thought about the new system, the less I felt able to keep the good ship Admissions afloat. I made a few notes about my reservations on the project, but the list I'd written just looked like the results of a bitter and twisted woman's encounter with a gin bottle.

Patient service will deteriorate
Fewer patients will get their lifesaving surgery
Doctors will be angrier
My staff will rebel
More complaints
More frustration
And last but not least, I will have to pick up the mess.

Phew! Not a happy list, I was certainly not being my usual upbeat self. Was this the final straw? The extra bit of lunacy that would finally force me to agree with Max and give up this challenge? While I sat thinking about my own list I decided to take a break by emailing my sister-in-law in the States to find out what my nephew Josh wanted for his birthday next month.

I absolutely love my sister-in-law although we do not get to see each other as often as we would like. Max and his brother Harry are not actually talking at the moment so it's up to us girls to act as peacemakers, not a role we relish. However, buying presents for my three nephews and one niece is completely free of family politics and it is one of my great pleasures.

The last time they visited us we sent them home with sports jerseys and they proved a great novelty amongst their friends. I knew Josh was into football, sorry soccer, so now I just needed to know what team was in vogue.

I rarely send personal email from work but this time I thought, what the hell? Considering the way I was feeling about my job this would be cheap medicine at ten times the price.

To: theseagerfamily
From: bethseager@nhs.uk
CC:

Subject: Birthday boy - again!

Hi guys,

Gone are the days of secret phone calls to Harry and Sarah to find out what my nephew wants for his birthday! Josh if you read this drop me a line either here at my work address or at home to let me know what you would like. I'm presuming it's a soccer shirt, but somehow I don't suppose that Portsmouth United will do!

I'm having a really bad day at work today, hence the email from work, it would be good to hear that there is life outside this hellhole. I thought I'd cheer myself up by dropping you a line and reminding myself that there are some places in the world where life is still fun.

If you read this before lunchtime at your end please write back. I will certainly not object if you sent me something funny attached to the message to cheer my day up, as long as it isn't smutty!
Love to you all,
Beth

44

I hit the send button and felt much better and returned my attention to THE PROJECT. After stepping out of the lunacy of the Health Service, even for a short time, I could feel my sense of humour returning. I could almost hear my participation in THE PROJECT as a movie trailer, being narrated by that irritating man with the double bass voice who tries to persuade you that the film will make you check under the bed before you go to sleep.

I smiled as the imaginary voice in my head boomed IT WAS THE PROJECT TO END ALL PROJECTS. WOULD THIS BE THE END FOR BETH SEAGER?

Of course it wouldn't. I loved a challenge and I was buggered if I was going to let this one beat me. Not to prove Fran wrong, or to help poor Joan who was destined to make a mad lemming-like dash over the cliff edge, but for our patients. Someone had to be their champion so why not me? I had nothing to lose and, as my husband Max so often reminds me, there are plenty of other industries that could use me if I failed.

I straightened my back and began to prepare to face the troops to give them their briefing when my computer pinged with an incoming mail. I opened my inbox and saw a message from my brother-in-law Harry. Strange, why would Harry be writing? I'd written to their home email address. I opened the mail with mounting curiosity.

To: *bethseager@nhs.uk*
From: *Harryseager*
CC:
Subject: Bad day eh?
hi beth,
just checked our home account and found your message. i'm between meetings in colorado. sorry to hear that you're feeling so down. what's the problem? Harry

This was not what I expected, no funny cartoons, just a question. What's the problem? Where to start? Do I have time? I decided to unburden myself on Harry. What harm could it do? Just one more email and who knows, I could feel so much better talking to someone outside the Health Service. Not that he would understand. I hit the reply button and began to type.

Hi Harry,

What a surprise. The world certainly is shrinking. What's the problem? Have you got all day?

Well......... as you know I manage the Admissions into the hospital. At least I thought I did. We are officially running at 98% capacity (way too high) and constantly have to cancel patients due to the lack of beds. We are over-run.

We do our best and now the powers that be have announced a new project. We are going to be managed by senior nurses.

On the face of it the idea has some merit. They should be able to prioritise the patients clinically better than us mere clerical staff. But I just don't see how they can improve things.

I have to brief my staff in a few minutes and I am dreading it. I know it won't work and that the project will cause no end of problems but I have no choice. If I don't co-operate to protect the patients I expose myself to the wrath of my line manager and if I co-operate I will spend my time babysitting my staff. Who, believe me, will come crying to Mommy! Just another day in the wonderful British National Health Service.

Anyway Harry, just ranting about it makes me feel better. I think this little therapy session has done me good. Enjoy your meeting.

Take care,
Beth

Writing the email really did make me feel better. I hit the send button and spent a few minutes gathering myself to meet the troops when I heard another ping from my computer.

beth,
you still there? don't go and talk to your staff yet. hang on.
H

What was going on? Hang on? For what? I sat down and stared at the screen for a while. This was silly. Harry is thousands of miles away and I'm sitting here like an obedient dog waiting for a tasty reward. Another ping, another message from Harry.

Beth,
I am dictating this to my secretary. She types much faster than I do.
Will you do something for me? Go tell your staff about the project as best you can but please keep it factual. Then ask them what they think. Go around the room and ask them in turn to comment on the project. Just one comment at a time. Keep it snappy. Write down what they say, then email their responses to me.
Please do this. I am sure I can help you.
Try not to get into a discussion about the project. Just ask them to give you a little time to consider their reaction to it and get back to me. I'll be here. I'll take you through the next step.
Please Beth.
Harry

Don't discuss it? Why? I was confused until I remembered how many times I'd had to do this before. A project is announced with very sketchy instructions and I try to figure out what our department needs to do to make it work; pass it on to my staff and bingo! Within a few weeks the project's originator makes changes that we're not prepared for and my staff turn on me like rabid mice muttering about my shortcomings.

Perhaps Harry had something here. If I just tell them what I know and ask for their opinions, then perhaps I can adjust our practices based on ideas from the staff. That way when it falls over they will be partly to blame. Sounds good. I decided to try it.

To: *Harryseager*
From: *bethseager@nhs.uk*
Subject: Bad day eh?

Harry,
I'll give it a go .... Is this what you do when you say you CYA?
I'll get back to you later but don't hold your breath. Reactions to projects like these from my staff are about as cheerful as the British weather.
Beth

I grinned as I hit send. This sounded the perfect way to cover your ass. Bless him. He was obviously trying to introduce tough American management techniques into the NHS. Still it will make a change and I had nothing to lose.

I picked up the copy of the email from Joan and walked into the outer office. All four of the staff were chatting as they sat at their desks, but they tried to look busy as soon as they saw me. I could never see the point in this. By the afternoon most of the elective work had been decided so for the rest of the day we revert to being reactive and respond to the needs of the Emergency Department.

If they are quiet it means there are no sick or injured people. This is a good thing, but no matter how many times I explain this to my staff they never seem to understand. As long as they have caught up on their work and are ready to respond to a call then I'm happy. These *down times* happened so infrequently

48

of late that I want them to appreciate them and use the time to relax. But the 'if I don't look busy I'll be in trouble' mentality was so hard to break. As they all turned to fiddle with whatever paperwork they had to hand I announced the start of the meeting.

'As you are all probably aware, the way the beds are managed is going to change from Saturday. I'll tell you as much as I know and then I want to hear your thoughts.'

My four usually attentive staff suddenly adopted the type of facial expression usually reserved for stunned fish. I grinned inwardly and wished Harry was here to see them, this was certainly a novel way to start a meeting!

I gave copies of Joan's email to Eddy and Sal, and then to Tracey and Linda, my girls. I could tell instantly that Eddy was not happy with this. I could read him like a book. Why was I including the girls in this? Surely this was above them. He is such a snob! I read the email out loud:

Clinical Bed Management Team - the way forward

Presented by Joan Norman - Director of Nursing

In an effort to overcome the bed shortages at Hartford Infirmary the following plan will be implemented from Saturday 6th July.

The Clinical Bed Managers will visit each ward at the start of the early shift to ascertain how many beds would be available that day.

They will then meet in the Admissions office to review the expected list for the day and will allocate beds on the basis of clinical need.

They carry bleeps 3001 and 3002 and should be contacted for any issues relating to bed allocation.

A second ward round will take place after lunch and any beds identified on this round will be allocated to ED patients.

Any questions should be directed to the Senior Clinical Bed Manager - Tessa Pringle.

'And...?' asked Eddy

'And what?' I replied

'And what else is there? What do we have to do?'

'Exactly what I said at the beginning of the meeting. Tell me what you think about it. Single sentences only. Take turns. Sal?'

'Er, okay, if the early shifts starts at 7:30 and they're gonna visit each ward, what time will we know about the beds?'

'Thanks Sal. Eddy?'

'How many of them will be going to the wards? Because if there's just one then it will take ages, but if there are two of them, then one could do surgery and the other medicine, but if...'

I interrupted 'Single sentence Eddy, not an essay. So you are asking "How many managers will be on duty? Yes?'

'Yeah, I suppose...'

I jumped in before he could start again. 'Thanks. Tracey?'

'How long will this last? They keep doing these things and then they change them and then...'

'Tracey, single sentences remember. Are you asking how long the project will last for?'

'I suppose.'

'Okay. Linda?'

'How will this overcome the bed shortages? Are they bringing in more beds?'

'Which is it Linda? Are they bringing in more beds?'

Linda was the most junior of the staff and was yet to be fully ground down by the system. I was surprised at her clarity of thought. Even I had not thought to ask that simple, but very relevant question.

'Yes, if beds are short are they bringing in more beds?'

Itching to exercise his expertise Eddy jumped in uninvited. 'Of course they can't. We don't have the space, unless they're going to convert the labs on the eighth floor like they've been planning to for years. Perhaps that's what this is all about.'

'Eddy,' I managed to grab the reins away from him, 'we are commenting on the plan as it states in this email. Nothing more or less. So for now we must assume that there will not be any more beds. Sal, your turn again.'

'Hey, I get it, this is like a game, cool. Okay, I want to know who will allocate the beds. Do we have to wait for the managers to tell us or can we offer beds?'

'Good point.' Yet another that had escaped me.

'Eddy.'

'Um. What will happen if we have rolled patients and the managers don't tell us if there are beds available early enough in the morning for us to get them in?'

'I think we've covered that one with Sal's first comment. Perhaps we should phrase it in such a way as to make it clear to everyone. How about, 'Will the managers be able to find beds as quickly as we do?' How does that sound?'

'Okay I suppose, because you know they won't, don't you? We can do it much quicker over the phone and by the time they visit every ward...'

'Yes Eddy we get it' I cut him off again. 'Tracey?'

'Well, I know I don't work on the bed board, but I often overhear the ward staff saying things like, "Don't tell Admissions about that bed yet," will that change?'

'Where did you hear this?' I snapped before I managed to bring myself back to the process. 'Sorry, ignore that Tracey. Are you asking if the managers will be able to stop the wards hiding beds?'

I was livid. We all knew that this practice took place but I'd never heard first hand experience of it before, and to think that the ward staff had said this in front of one of my staff. They could not have realised who she was or they would never have said that within her hearing. This stuff is dynamite!

'Yes, I suppose I am.'

'Thanks. Linda?'

'It says in the memo that beds found in the afternoon will be for the ED patients. Does that mean that we won't be admitting patients to the wards from the Emergency Department in the morning?'

'Good Question. Sal, you again.'

'If they do that and all the morning beds are used for elective cases, the long trolley waits'll go through the roof.'

They were really getting into the swing of this exercise now. 'Eddy?'

'As we always suspected Tessa as being the worst Ward Manager for hiding beds, will she be able to catch out the wards, or will she be on their side?'

'Tracey?'

'Who will be our boss? You or them?'

The room went silent. Eddy sat back and folded his arms defiantly. It was obvious that he had loaded the gun and Tracey had fired it. So much for him not talking to the staff about the project.

'I'm the manager of this department,' I answered calmly. 'You work for me and answer to me. As always our role is to support the medical staff and any changes in practices will have to be ratified by me. Is that clear?'

I knew deep down that this was bull. The project starts in four days, a Saturday. I would not be working, but Eddy would. He would be running around the new Bed Managers attending to their every whim, hedging his bets and trying to make himself indispensable. But they were telling me what they needed to know and there was still time to impose my rules on this project. 'Linda, your turn.'

'Will we continue interviewing the patients before they get a bed?'

'I'll let you know about that one as soon as I've worked through all of the other questions. Sal, anymore?'

'Nope. If you can get answers to that lot we should know what to do, but I don't like it Beth, it feels as if the patients will be getting another bum deal.'

Eddy dove in, 'You don't know that Sal, we've been saying for years that we need more clinical support and now we are going to be getting it. It has to be better.'

His voice was almost whining. He really did care and was as desperate to find an answer as the rest of us. Perhaps there was something I was missing, something better on the horizon and I had not seen it yet.

I thanked the staff and as I did the phone rang. It was the Emergency Department wanting three beds. They had more chance of winning the lottery.

'Back to work everyone. All systems go,' I said, as I returned to my bubble and brought up my email.

To: *Harryseager*
From: *bethseager@nhs.uk*
Subject: Re: Bad day eh?

Harry,
Are you still there?

The most amazing thing just happened. They did my job for me. It will take me a while to get the list sorted but thanks for the suggestion. I didn't realise they knew so much.

I'll send the list later.
Beth

I hit the send key then turned to the list trying to sort out their comments. I was still scribbling when the email pinged. It was Harry.

To: *bethseager@nhs.uk*
From: *Harryseager*
CC:
Subject: Bad day getting better?

beth,
don't be surprised. we always underestimate our staff. the trick is trying to release the knowledge in their heads.

made your job easier? welcome to the world of real management. makes a nice change from fire fighting?

do what you have to do at your end but send me the list as soon as you can - then i'll show you another trick!
must go now.
H

I laughed out loud, causing Eddy to look suspiciously into my office. The cheek of the man! Real management! Firefighting! He may be good at managing factories, but that was a different world from the life and death environment of a hospital.

I sat back and looked at the list. It was obvious that my list of questions for Tessa would virtually write itself following the session with the team. I decided to take the list home to work on that night. With Max away it will give me something to do after I walk the dogs. Real management indeed! No wonder he wound Max up.

Chapter 7

As I pointed my trusty Ford Focus towards home, I mused over Harry's input and the list my staff had drawn up. It would have taken me ages to put a comparable list together from the seclusion of my bubble and I was eager to work on it and send it to Harry. I just wished the new system was not due to start on Saturday. I was contracted to work Monday to Friday even though my department operated around the clock. I didn't want to work over the weekend, but I was worried what Eddie would get up to in my absence.

Max would blow a gasket if I went in to work, despite the fact he's been out of the country on work all week. Besides it would be more ammunition for his argument that my job was taking over my life. What with Harry's comment about *real management*, I was starting to feel bullied by the Seager boys. I supposed that by *real management* Harry meant that I could manipulate my staff from a distance so I should not work extra hours. If only I could persuade Eddy to be a good boy. Hmmph! I tried to imagine Eddy doing as he was told for once as I pulled into the drive. Fat chance! I was just as likely to manage to get in the house without being covered in hair by the dogs.

Many people find it hard to understand that our scruffy mongrels are our family, hairy substitutes to the normality of children. We had decided to wait until we felt a strong urge to inflict our genes on future generations and we manage to enjoy our freedom too much to notice the gap in our family. Between our niece and nephews and the mutts we currently have enough to fulfil our parental destiny. However, whilst our dogs don't keep us up at night teething or playing loud music, they do make coming home in work clothes an interesting experience.

I flung open the door to be greeted with the joyful exuber-ance, not to mention wet noses of Winston and Maggie. The names stem from Max's love affair with the UK. I wanted to call them Bud and Weiser, especially as Maggie is the more in-telligent of the two, but Max wasn't having it. He liked the thought of having Winston Churchill and Maggie Thatcher ly-ing at his feet in the evening.

I quickly led the run through the house to the back door where I was able to divert their attention to the squirrel that was happily scoffing food from the bird table. The dogs never get close to him and he often appeared to tease them by sitting on the fence close to the conservatory window. As the dogs amused themselves by running through Max's flowerbeds I dug around in the freezer for an instant meal.

When Max was away I made my life as easy as possible. I pierced the film lid and threw it in the microwave. The dogs had grown tired of being humiliated by the squirrel and were now playing tug-of-war with one of their toys. I ran upstairs to wrig-gle out of my nasty synthetic uniform and into more comfort-able, dog hair friendly, clothes. By the time I got back to the kitchen the microwave was reminding me that my supper had been sufficiently zapped and the smell of food was enough to prompt the dogs to scratch at the backdoor. Within five minutes we were all tucking into our food and I was opening an email from my nephew Josh.

Dear Aunt Beth,
Thanks for your message and the invitation to decide on my
Birthday present.
As you know I've been following the fortunes of Manchester
United and although they are going through a bit of a rough
patch at the moment I think they are a really cool team. Would
it be OK if you got me their new shirt? It would be really neat if
you could. No one's heard of Portsmouth United around here!

I think I will need a large one this time. I've grown since we last saw you and I'm now taller than Dad!
Love
Josh

I smiled, the email was positively chatty for Josh. I logged onto the Man United website, found the shirt Josh wanted and within minutes it was bought and destined for the U.S. Now this is the way to shop!

I was a little disappointed to see there were no more messages from Harry so I turned my attention back to the list. After a few drafts the list read:

1. *How many managers will be on duty at one time?*
2. *How long will the project last?*
3. *Are there going to be any more beds?*
4. *Who is going to be allocating beds?*
5. *Will the managers be able to find beds as quickly as we do?*
6. *Will the managers be able to stop the wards hiding beds?*
7. *Will Emergency Department beds only be allocated in the afternoons?*
8. *Will we continue interviewing the patients before they get a bed?*
9. *Would I still be managing the department?*

I didn't like it. There were so many unknowns, even worse was the fact they were all valid. I decided to send them to Harry along with a copy of Joan's project brief.

Harry,
I've attached the list and I find it disturbing that so many questions have to be answered before I can start to prepare my department for the new project. Did I mention that it is due to start this Saturday, my day off? Crazy!

I've also attached a copy of the project brief.
Without going into reams of detail, which I can do, I am eager
to find out what your next trick is. What should I do now?
Beth

Within an hour I had enjoyed the falling July sun and all
the squirrels in the local woodlands were now relaxing after
being chased by Maggie and Winston. However there was no
time for me to unwind as I had a reply from Harry.

beth,
that's a really good list. you were right not to send me reams of
detail. it would not mean much to me and you're the one with
the problem to solve and the intuition on how to do it. the trick
is, sorry i really should not have called it that, the next step is to
turn these questions into statements.

to do this try to imagine the project is a sick patient and the
statements are ways of describing his symptoms.

e.g.: **There won't be enough managers to look after the project**

give it a try and don't worry if the statements sound very gen-
eral, they need to be for the next bit to work.

send me the list as soon as possible and be bold. really go with
your gut feel.

i was a little shocked at the project brief is that all you have?

i'm in the airport departure lounge and my flight has been de-
layed so you have my undivided attention, if not my correct
punctuation!
H

I sat staring at my list for a while. How did Harry get *There*
won't be enough managers to look after the project from *How*

many managers will be on duty at one time? Eventually I thought I saw the link and tried it on another of the questions.

How long will the project last? = The project will not last.
Are there going to be any more beds? = There will be no more beds.
Who is going to be allocating beds? = Bed allocation will be taken away from Admissions.
Will the managers be able to find beds as quickly as we do? = CBM's will be slower than Admissions.
Will the managers be able to stop the wards hiding beds? = Wards will still hide beds.
Will Emergency Department beds only be allocated in the afternoons? = ED patients will wait longer for beds.
Will we continue interviewing the patients before they get a bed? = Admissions operational policies will have to change.
Would I still be managing the department = I might lose control of my department.

This turned my list into:
1. *There won't be enough managers to look after the project*
2. *The Project will not last*
3. *There will be no more beds*
4. *Bed allocation will be taken away from Admissions*
5. *CBM's will be slower than Admissions*
6. *Wards will still hide beds*
7. *ED patients will wait longer for beds*
8. *Admissions Operational policies will have to change*
9. *I might lose control of my department*

I sat back and stared at the list and Maggie took the opportunity to plonk her head on my lap.
'Hey, Maggie, I can almost feel the statements connecting to each other,' I said as I stroked her silky ear. It was a good thing I said that to a dog and not a human, or it would be a first class

ticket to the funny farm for me. But the more I looked at them they really did seem to join up, I just wasn't sure how.

I re-read Harry's email. Symptoms; if the project is a sick patient list the symptoms. I tried to imagine that I was presenting the symptoms of this particular sick patient as I had heard cases presented so many times on the wards.

Here we have an immature project that is trying to tackle a mature system that is suffering from overload. The presenting symptoms include a severe lack of resources whose experienced operatives are being taken away from it. The new operatives are too few in number and do not have the experience to operate it effectively. External forces are hampering improvements in the system and the disease it carries is expected to infect other systems in the hospital. As manager of the old system I will not be allowed to treat the patient whose prognosis is not good and could well be terminal.

That's how they link up. It makes sense! Yes the system is sick, but at least we are aware of it so we can treat it like a critically ill patient. We know the little tricks that are needed to keep it alive although the patient's vitals get pretty thready at times. But we keep it going. And now new managers are going to have to go through an extremely steep learning curve to manage it as well as we do. To cap it all, if I help the new managers I could well be rewarded with being taken out of the game. Charming!

I cut and pasted my revised list and my mock presentation of the patient's condition into an email and sent it to Harry.

Harry had already replied by the time I made a pot of Earl Grey tea and settled back at my computer.

beth,
talk about a quick study! Your list is great and your presentation of the patient's condition is bloody marvellous, as you brits would say. ever thought of writing for dilbert?

*the next step of the process i was going to tell you about joins
up the dots, but you've already done this. not quite the way i
would have shown you, but you are almost there.*

*however, I would like to show you how to do it properly, if you
are up to it.*

*take two of your UDE's (the statements you have written are
UnDesirable Effects that your system is suffering from, or about
to suffer from - we call them* UDE's*), that seem to belong together and add a because. like this:*

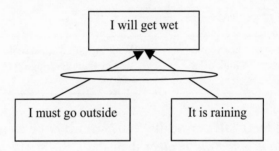

this reads: If I must go outside I will get wet because it is
raining. *it can also be read:* If I must go outside and it is raining
I will get wet.

the UDE's here are I must go outside *and* I will get wet. *the because is* It is raining. *try it on a couple of your UDE's.*

*if you do this in a word document via the drawing tool bar you
will find text boxes and arrows along with a function to draw
circles that you squish down. this makes the equivalent of an*
and, *we call them banana's for no other reason than they look
like them. try one and get back to me.*
H

After fiddling with the drawing toolbar I managed to produce the framework Harry suggested, but the hard part was deciding which two UDE's formed the best fit. Eventually, I decided that *There won't be enough managers to look after the project* and *CBM's will be slower than Admissions* seemed like a pretty closely linked pair. I typed them into the boxes:

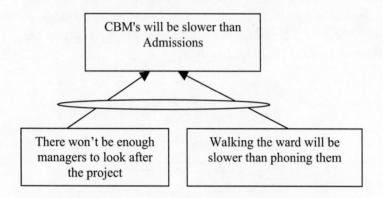

I read the UDE's critically. If *There won't be enough managers to look after the project* then the *CBM's will be slower than Admissions* because *Walking the wards will be slower than phoning them.* I was pleased to see that it worked, but I tried it the other way to make sure.

If *There won't be enough managers to look after the project* and *Walking the wards will be slower than phoning them* then the *CBM's will be slower than Admissions.* It made sense. I liked it. Even better, it only took me 10 minutes to put together. So what was next? I emailed my masterpiece to Harry and he replied immediately.

beth,
this is great. just one thing. try to be consistent in your language and clarity. i suggest a slight amendment:

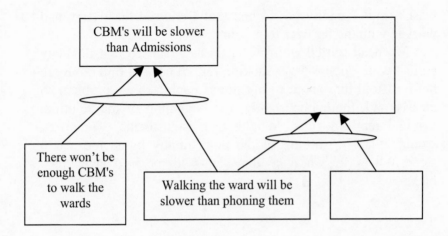

so now it reads: If There won't be enough CBM's to walk the wards *and* Walking the wards will be slower than phoning them *then the* CBM's will be slower than Admissions.
how does that sound?

I cackled at the question. How did it sound? Bloody marvellous!

...ok beth now the next bit. try to hang the other UDE's off these. use the same If, then, because process and check them by saying them the other way around; If, and, then. keep it coming!

i've given you the next couple of boxes, but there does not have to be a regular pattern - by sharing and linking the entities you will eventually build up a series of pictures of all of the things that bug you about the project and how they relate to each other. go for it!
H

Before I knew it, midnight had come and gone. There were breaks in the flow of email as Harry finally boarded his flight and eventually checked into the next hotel. Time seemed to stand still although my brain was rushing round faster than a sample in a centrifuge. I finally tried to slow down the whirring at 12:30 and we agreed to pick this up at the next opportunity. It wasn't until I finally got to bed that I realised that Harry had worked with me for over four hours.

My head started whirring again as I realised that this may be just what The Prof was looking for. I'd have to find out more before I told him about it, but now I could see the problem so clearly and, more importantly, the beginning of the solution. Could I really do this? Would they listen to me? Tomorrow would tell. The snoring of the dogs finally lulled me off to sleep. When Max was away they slept with me, he'd have a fit if he knew!

Chapter 8

I have more need for beauty sleep than most people and when the alarm crudely shattered my rest I discovered I had a nasty case of grasshopper eyes. My dreams were full of UDE's and the frightening vision of Fearsome Fran marching through the wards wearing an army uniform. As a result, I spent the night ferreting about like an excitable nerve. Every time I blearily squinted at the clock the dogs bounced around gleefully thinking I was going to get up. The last time I looked at the clock it was almost five o'clock in the morning. Now, just an hour later I felt as though I could sleep till noon.

I escaped the soothing clutches of my duvet and stumbled towards the shower. I stayed under the invigorating water for at least 20 minutes, my mind whirring faster than the water escaping down the plughole. Gradually, as the minutes passed, my thoughts began to clear and I began to get excited. If the work I had done with Harry was right I could achieve so much!

Eventually, I stepped out of the shower to be greeted by the forlorn and confused faces of Maggie and Winston. Normally, I would never shower before letting them out into the garden. They must have spent the past twenty minutes trying to cross their legs as they listened to the noise of the water. I threw my robe on, wrapped my hair in a towel and went downstairs to let them out.

Coffee! I needed coffee, tea just wasn't going to do the trick this morning. I put the percolator on and cautiously entered the study. What a mess! Max's flip chart was in the middle of the room surrounded by a yellow sea of discarded sticky notes. I quickly cleaned up and stood back to read the night's work.

If this worked I could retain control of my department *and* put systems in place that would react to the needs of the CBM's. Just yesterday these two objectives were poles apart but now, here it was in black and yellow. I tore the sheet off the flip chart, took another sheet for luck and carefully rolled them up and secured it with a rubber band and printed out copies of last night's email.

By 7:15 I was in the office and feeling revitalised. The temperature was minus 42. Better, but not good. By 7:45 the gang had arrived and my face was on. After going through the morning ritual I told the staff I did not want to be disturbed and shut myself in my bubble. I sat back and reviewed exactly what Harry had helped me to achieve last night. The most obvious achievement was completing my very first Current Reality Tree. That's what Harry said the sticky notes on the large sheet of paper were called. It seemed a very apt description. I had never seen a problem so clearly stated before. And even more exciting Harry had convinced me that a single simple action would dissolve all of yesterdays' problems. Could this really all be true?

I unrolled the tree and stuck it to one of the internal windows of my office. I could see Eddy trying to read what was on the paper, not to mention keep an eye on me. However, I knew that all the staff would be able to see were the arrows and bananas that joined the UDE's together. The UDE's themselves were written on the sticky notes so there was no way they would be able to decipher them from the outer office area.

Gotcha Eddy! I smirked as I pondered how long it would take before his curiosity forced him to find an excuse to come in to see what was happening. I taped the extra flip chart sheet above the first one so I could use it to cover the evidence.

I sat back to read the tree again before turning to Harry's email from yesterday.

beth,
you've done really well, don't beat yourself up about not being able to connect all of the UDE's. you are not supposed to.

eventually, you will find that there is a UDE at the bottom of the tree that appears to come from nowhere. this is the one we are looking for, it begins to tell us what the root cause of the problem is.

Harry had been right. Once I had got the hang of the rules of tree building I wanted to make everything fit, but I could not get the one final one to fit anywhere, but at the bottom of the tree; *CBM's don't know Admissions.* It fed into so many of the other UDE's but had nothing feeding into it. It hung there like an odd sock on a washing line.

the core problem of the project plan is that the Clinical Bed Management Team does not know how the Admissions Department works. you've found it beth! now you know this and the effects it will have on the project you have the upper hand. you and you alone can control it.

the next step is use what we call a cloud *to represent the core conflict or core problem. as you have to devise a strategy quickly I've drawn the outline of the cloud for you and filled in a couple of boxes.*

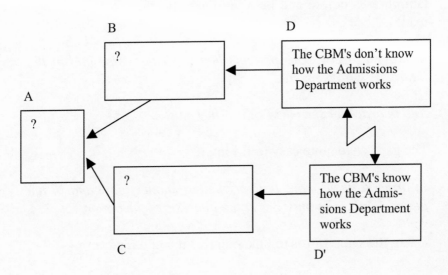

A = What you are all trying to achieve, both parties, Admissions and the Bed Managers
B = What you need to achieve for your department
C = What the Bed Managers need to achieve
D = What want of your department is under threat
D' (we call this d prime; the opposite of D) = what want of the CBM's feels like a threat
D and D' must be in direct conflict with each other, hence the bolt of lightning between them.

what you need to do now beth is fill in the three empty boxes. start with A, it's the easiest.
H

Easy, huh! After half an hour and some guidance from Harry I had whittled it down to we were all trying to do; *Treat More Patients Better, Sooner, Now and In the Future.*

It was quite a mouthful and seemed far too grand an objective for this doomed project, but Harry reassured me that the objective had to be robust enough to apply to any project the Health Service undertook. So I agreed.

The next two boxes were not that difficult to figure out once I knew the rules. To read this diagram I had to place certain phrases before and between them. So the top of the cloud read:

In order to treat more patients better, sooner, now and in the future the CBM's must...

And in order for the CBM's to...They must...

The gaps were quite easy to fill in:

In order to treat more patients better, sooner, now and in the future Admissions must act in the interests of the patients.

Using the same words to link A and D it could read:

And in order for The Admissions Department to act in the interests of the patients the Admissions staff want to use their existing expertise.

I moved to the other side of the cloud:

On the other hand, (another phrase given to me by Harry), in order to treat more patients better, sooner, now and in the future the CBM's must improve on the existing system.

In order for the CBM's to improve on the existing system the CBM's want the Admissions Department to implement the new plan.

With a little tweaking of the words my final cloud looked like this:

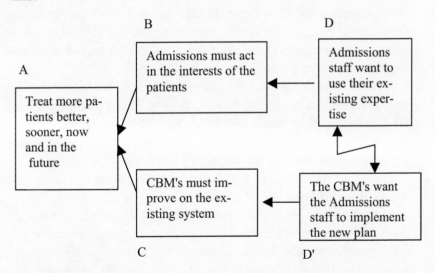

Harry had given me some more *checks*. The first was to make sure that D and D' were direct opposites. They sure were. The next was to make sure D and C were incompatible. I reasoned that as it stood, the CBM's sure as hell would not be able to improve on the system if they thought that doing away with my teams' expertise was the way to go. And finally, I had to make sure that A and D' were incompatible. At that moment the CBM's didn't even seem to know what their plan was let alone prove that they knew how to improve on our performance.

The next step was to find out how best to attack the problem. Harry showed me how to challenge the assumptions I had made when I put the cloud together. As with all of the work we had done so far it was lots of little steps that went to make up the big picture and very soon I had a list of reasons or *becauses* relating to the cloud. The one that really stuck out from the list was the *because* that said...

If the Admissions must act in the best interests of the patients then the Admissions staff must use their expertise because... the CBM's do not know how the system works...

The answer to this, which was in fact the direct opposite of the nasty bit I had just found, was simply, *The CBM's know how the system works.* So simple. If they knew how it worked then they would realise how weak their plan was and they would not want to run roughshod over our department and would need our support to devise a sensible solution.

Harry had congratulated me on attacking the conflict at the best possible place, on the conflict arrow. If we could make the CBM's realise they needed to know how the system worked, all of the other potential problems we faced would soon fade away. It made so much sense they couldn't disagree.

Just when I thought I had reached the pinnacle Harry sent me another email;

...almost there beth. we are not going to have time to prepare a full Communication Current Reality Tree, the one you use to tell other people about your findings, but there is another small exercise you can do that will really help you sell this to the CBM's.

use the list of becauses, to construct your presentation to the CBM's. Don't assume anything. You may end up saying something that to you seems so obvious that you might think that it

does not need to be said, but it could well be the missing piece
your audience needs to complete their understanding of the
situation. and try not to over sell your position. as soon as you
have agreement stop, get your audience to confirm their under-
standing then leave it well alone and what ever you do don't
show anyone the cloud.
H

By this time I was tired and ready to give in, but to please
Harry I gave it my best shot, or at least as good as I could at
midnight the previous night.

When I'd finished the final exercise, sent my thanks to
Harry and wished him good night, I was buzzing and fit to drop
at the same time—a strange experience that was the obvious
cause of my sleepless night.

Now, in the cold fluorescent light of my office I was so
pleased Harry had put me through the final exercise. If I had
gone to Joan and Tessa without completing the list of *becauses,*
I would have looked a complete idiot. They were vital, they
gave the plan credibility.

I began to type out what I would say to them. Harry had
warned me not to show Joan and Tessa the cloud, and I could
see that while the clouds can make you feel clever, they can
make the other side feel manipulated. The resolution discovered
by the clouds needed to be presented in a seemingly unstruc-
tured way, in a normal conversation. It was this imaginary conversation I had to write now.

As I typed the first word there was a knock on my door.
Without looking at the door I stood and pulled the cover sheet
over the decision tree on the window and called out, 'Come in
Eddy, what can I do for you?' Poor man, he had withstood
thirty minutes of burning curiosity for no satisfaction. I smiled
as he entered the room, eyes swivelling madly around the room
like a cross-eyed chameleon.

'Um, just thought you would want to know that both Tessa
and Joan will be attending the eleven o'clock meeting,' he said
without looking at me once.

I smiled sweetly, thanked him and sent him packing. Whilst he had obviously used his information as an excuse to nose around my office, he did give me the spur I needed to write my script. Thank goodness for spell checking, there was no time for perfect English.

Chapter 9

I had imagined talking to Joan and Tessa alone, but as they would be in the department in less than an hour I had been gifted the opportunity to present Harry's theories. By discussing my proposal in front of my staff as well as Joan and Tessa I could kill two birds with one stone.

My plan needed the open co-operation of everyone involved for it to work and what better way to earn it than to get them to agree on the spot how we would move forward?

Within half an hour I had written my script and, heeding Harry's warnings from last night, I read and re-read my notes until I was clear on the order. As a final safeguard I wrote six keywords on an index card and put it in my pocket. I was just gathering myself to leave when the phone rang. I was tempted to leave it but I picked it up anyway.

'Ah Elizabeth!'

Ouch! Only Fran the Fearsome could put that much venom into the use of someone's full name.

'Glad I caught you before your meeting. I just wanted to stress how important this new initiative is, especially in the light of your last unfortunate outburst.'

This time I had no trouble in keeping quiet I was grinning too much to be able to speak.

'I am hoping that this time you will step up to the plate and start the ball rolling so we can solve the Admissions problem through team work. I'm afraid I must warn you that senior management are keeping an eye on your behaviour.'

It was a classic Fearsome Fran speech, full of business bullshit and not much else. However, I did notice that Admissions was suddenly responsible for the lack of beds.

'Beth? Are you there?' Fran's acid voice suddenly sounded uncertain.

I was tempted to quietly put down the phone and leave, but that would only lead to further recriminations, after all, the *senior management* are watching me.

'Yes, I'm here Fran,' I replied lightly. 'And don't worry, I've got everything sorted to get that team working and the ball rolling.' I put down the phone and quickly escaped from my bubble where I just had time to get a briefing from Eddy and Sal on the current situation before the entourage came into the department for the meeting.

'Good morning Joan, Tessa,' I said warmly before adding, 'Congratulations Tessa, and welcome to the wild world of management. I hope you're going to enjoy it.'

Tessa looked stunned. She had obviously heard about my initial reaction to the plan, no doubt from the Fearsome One. I knew they were friends as they often shared a lift to work and I wasn't going to give either of them any more ammunition. Before the visitors could say any more than, 'Good morning,' I continued. 'All of us in Admissions have been giving your plan serious consideration and after the meeting I would like to have a ten minute get together with you and my staff to outline our contribution to the plan. Would that be alright?'

I always find it amazing how my staff can monitor other conversations while they are deeply engrossed in their work. They certainly managed this time as the whole office fell silent as they waited for a reply. Tessa managed to compose herself quickly and was the first to speak.

'Of course Beth, I look forward to it,' she said, flashing a bright smile that almost looked genuine.

Tessa is a strange woman; athletic with a dangerous edge that may cause some men to fear meeting her in a dark alley. She is tall, approaching 5' 10", and her slender frame is covered in well-defined muscles. This gave her a very masculine silhouette, despite her long chestnut hair, but this was balanced by large, dark eyes and wonderful teeth that could produce a radiant smile when she wanted something. She was perfect for those cheesy toothpaste adverts and even more annoyingly she could pose without a scrap of makeup. She had recently taken up kickboxing and rumour had it that she was not beyond using her new skills to put men who like a challenge in their place. Considering her swift recovery from my verbal onslaught I made a mental note to be careful with my verbal sparring.

The meeting started and I let Eddy represent Admissions at the bed meeting, which yielded its usual mix of successes and failures.

Tessa noted the proceedings with interest. As a recent ex-ward manager this was the first time she had seen the decision making process that affected her wards. Her eyes darted around the room trying to follow the rationale behind the decisions. Her body language was confident, but her frown suggested she found the process confusing. No doubt it was moving too quickly for her to fully understand. Perfect! This was just what I was hoping for.

Eventually, the meeting broke up with the usual promises to do everything possible to find beds for the sickest patients and I offered coffee to Joan, Tessa and Eddy as the room emptied.

They sat in silence, watching my actions as if I was putting on a private performance for them. They were waiting for me to start the floorshow, but this was not the right place or time. I needed them to be relaxed and in the middle of the Admissions Department.

I handed them their drinks and asked them to move out into the department. I pulled the chairs out to make a circle and asked the rest of the staff to listen in.

'For the benefit of everyone here I want to go around the room and ask everyone to introduce themselves and say a little about their job. Eddy...'

I called upon each of my staff in turn who relished the opportunity to over emphasise how important their jobs are in front of the new managers. Joan was happy to continue the exercise and when she had finished her contribution I was pleased to see that Tessa had lost a little more of her composure.

'Tessa, would you do the honours?' I asked, making an effort to remain as neutral as possible.

'Of course,' She replied briskly. 'As you all know I'm Tessa Pringle, I am a Senior Sister and have been a Ward Manager for the past year. I've spoken to you all on the phone so I know your voices, as I am sure you will know mine, but it's useful to put faces to your names.'

She was into her stride now, but her arms and legs were still firmly crossed. She was still mentally shutting us out.

'I have recently been investigating how other hospitals manage their admissions and have been asked to head up the Clinical Bed Management team to tackle the problems we have here.'

I could see Eddy was itching to start asking her questions so I quickly responded before he could muddy the waters.

'Good to have you on board Tessa. I'm sure that together we can make a difference. Now I know you all know me, but to keep things professional I will introduce myself as well. I am Beth Seager; I'm the manager of the Admissions Department. I have a staff of 20, who are made up of full and part-time staff. We operate around the clock, 24/7 as the saying goes. I work normal office hours and I'm responsible for making sure that all of my staff know what to do where and when.'

'Now that you all know my role, I would like to give you some feedback from my team. Yesterday I held a brainstorming session with my team...'

Eddy was now leaning back in his chair basking. His boss had just told him he was a brainstormer.

'...and we came up with a number of ideas and questions we need to discuss, but before we go down that route I need to lay some groundwork. Alright so far Tessa?'

Tessa had not moved her eyes from me and was oblivious to Eddy's posturing. She nodded. Good. I was still in control.

'Right. The Admissions Department is a strange one. We are unique in the hospital. We are like the hub of a wheel and our workload fluctuates with demand. We perform a delicate balancing act trying to meet the demands of the whole hospital, while at the same time acting in the best interests of the patients. We have to be accurate, fair and decisive. We cannot put off jobs until tomorrow. We have to do everything immediately. We do not have the luxury of an in tray, an out tray and a pending tray. We cannot dictate our workload.'

I paused and pulled my card out of my pocket. The room was silent. They wanted more. I wondered how long Eddy would take to form a coherent response to my sales pitch, but decided not to risk it for too long. I'd covered another 3 *becauses* in that short speech. I continued.

'We operate within a very complex system to meet the needs of the patients and the demands of the medics. To achieve this we have numerous systems that have been tried and tested over the years.'

I desperately wanted to say 'that work' at the end of this, but realised that the whole object of the new project was to improve the system. No matter how much I wanted to defend the current system I could not afford to alienate the CBM's.

'I would like the Admissions department's initial contribution to the project to be an orientation programme for the new Clinical Bed Management Team. After all, none of us can afford for the system to falter, least of all the patients. We have to keep it going if we are going to improve it. Don't you agree?'

Wham bam. Go on Tessa...agree!

'Thank you Beth.' Tessa said. 'Yes, I agree the current system has to keep going until we find a better way.' She paused as she contemplated her position.

I was ready to jump all over her but just managed to hold myself back. I knew they couldn't improve on 98 per cent, but someone on high obviously thought they could. Keep quiet Beth! It was Tessa's time to speak.

I looked around the room and realised that all eyes were on Tessa. How right Harry had been. If I had shown the cloud it would have been too tough. I had what I needed, their attention. I didn't need to beat them into submission.

'Beth I would like to take up your offer on behalf of my team,' Tessa continued. 'I agree that we need to know what happens here before we can introduce any changes. I did not realise that this department was so involved, so complicated. Thank you for such a thorough introduction.'

YES!... I wanted to jump for joy. At last someone was listening to common sense. Finally, I could be understood. The Prof would be proud!

'Wonderful,' I replied warmly. 'In that case I suggest that Eddy start the process on Saturday as he will be on duty and knows all of the procedures to a T.'

I turned to Eddy. 'Please will you show the Bed Management team as much as you can on Saturday? I think you will agree Tessa, that until the team are up to speed with our systems it would not be fair to start throwing our questions at them?'

'Yes Beth,' Tessa agreed. 'Let's get to grips with what happens now before we start trying to change things. Eddy, I will be on duty on Saturday with another of my team. We'll see you bright and early.'

The meeting broke up and people dispersed to answer phones and bleeps. A couple of the staff crowded around Eddy congratulating him and he took the attention like a cockerel accepting the preenings of his flock of hens. I started to put the chairs back under the desks when Joan clutched my elbow.

'Beth, got a minute?'

She motioned towards the coffee room and once we were inside with the door closed she let forth a torrent of verbal diarrhoea.

'How on earth did you do that? It was amazing. Tessa has been manic ever since Fran forced me to appoint her as the lead on this project. She hasn't listened to a word I've said and in less fifteen minutes you've got her eating out of your hand. Did you drug her coffee?'

I was peaking on a rush of adrenaline and burst out laughing. 'No, Joan, I just used common sense. I worked on the premise that we all want to do a good job, Tessa included. I just pointed out that she couldn't do it alone and that any rash changes would in all probability damage not only her, but our patients as well. She just needed a chance to do it right and I gave it to her.'

Joan flopped into a petrol green chair that by chance matched her suit exactly. The blush pink of her blouse soon matched her face as she joined in my mirth. Eventually she caught her breath.

'Well done Beth, perhaps you can help me control her,' she said with a broad grin that finally let her wonky teeth out into the open. 'Be her joint keeper as it were. We are going to have to keep tabs on her and her team and it is good to feel that I am not alone. Thank you.'

'No problem Joan, between us we can teach these rookies what Admissions is really about. I'll try to make sure they don't show you up.' Another *because* done and dusted.

We sat quietly for a while. In my mind I was going over my *because* list. I pulled the card out of my pocket. I'd only used about half of them and those I did use did the job brilliantly.

Joan eventually spoke. 'I've been thinking about the conversation we had the other day. I've checked out the curriculum of my course and there is nothing in it about pure decision-making. And that got me thinking. If the course I am on is designed for Hospital Managers across the country then the subjects we are being taught should be useful in any hospital.'

Joan hesitated so I jumped in, 'From your hesitation can I assume that they aren't?'

'This is where I'm baffled. We have courses on Benchmarking and on Modelling but...'

'It's not enough is it Joan?'

'No it's not. What I can't get my head around is where these high performing strategies come from. The ideal models of service delivery? Who dreams them up? How do they make them work?'

'Joan, if I know the Health Service, these pinnacles of performance are the survivors of a thousand failed projects. We both know that very few models that work in other hospitals actually work here, how many have we tried over the years?'

'I stopped counting years ago Beth. But what I am trying to understand is why doesn't my course show me how to devise our own solutions rather than trying to force us to try other people's methods that will not work for us?'

All of a sudden I could see exactly what Joan was talking about. Two similar hospitals could be suffering from similar symptoms, or UDE's but if the core conflict is not the same in both places then the right solution for one would be the wrong solution for the other. It was so clear. But how could I tell Joan this? I struggled to find the right words and decided to leave them well alone. The work I was doing with Harry should be able to make it clear for her, but I needed to do much more and she was looking for an answer now.

'Joan, I'm not sure but I think I'm getting closer to an answer to that question,' I said slowly. 'When I get there I'd love to share it with you.' It was the best I could offer.

Joan looked perplexed, 'Come on Beth, do you really understand what I mean, because I don't. Tell me.'

I dipped my toe in the mental waters and tried not to shiver. 'I think it has to do with defining the problem clearly. We tend to assume that all hospitals that are having bed problems suffer from the same underlying problem. Sorry, I'm not making much sense. Let me try again. Many hospitals have difficulty in managing their bed stock. Am I right?'

'Yes...'

'But what if the conditions that make this job difficult are not the same in every hospital? What if they are different in each one?'

'They will all need different answers,' Joan said abruptly.

'Absolutely, but what if we're not able to identify what the different problems are? We're going to be left still desperately looking for an answer.'

'Then we will try what the other places have tried until we find the right one,' Joan reasoned.

'Correct. So does this explain why we try so many solutions that were devised elsewhere and why they do not work?'

'Yes it does Beth. But this isn't good enough. How do we find out what our own problem is and find a way to fix it ourselves? That is what I mean! How do we learn to look after our own problems? That is what isn't in my course. All we do is try other people's solutions that are no good for us. It's pointless Beth.'

I sat back and considered Joan's point. 'I agree Joan. We waste so much time and energy on benchmarking and modelling that we don't have the time or the energy to sort ourselves out.'

'Oh Beth, it is good to hear someone saying that out loud. So what do we do about it?'

I was so close to trying to explain to Joan what I was doing with Harry. I just wanted to blurt it all out, but I knew I wouldn't be able to do it justice. I needed to learn more before I could even begin to teach it. I managed to hold my enthusiasm in check.

'Well, Joan it's a long story that starts with a Man United Shirt and a puzzle and ends with a cloud. When I understand it more myself I'll let you in on it. But I'm really not good enough at it yet to pass it on. As soon I master it we'll have to get together for a couple of hours.'

Joan's bleep went off diverting her attention from my mystical comments. She checked it and turned to me with a curious look.

'Right you are Beth, I'd like that. Don't forget. In the meantime keep up the good work. Must dash; Trust HQ are pulling my chain. Bye.'

As soon as I walked back into the department Eddy was in my face.

'Beth, are you serious about me teaching the bed managers? Shouldn't you be doing it?'

The phrase that immediately sprung to mind was, 'Why keep a dog and bark yourself?' but I was on a roll today and managed to resist the temptation.

'Eddy, you will be on duty on Saturday. I won't. You know all of the procedures. I know you can show them how it all works so why shouldn't you? But and this is a *big* but, Eddy. Stick to the procedures. Don't start asking any of the questions we listed yesterday, they aren't ready for them. Do you understand?'

'Umm, I guess I do but...'

'No *but's* Eddy. This department runs well. We cannot afford for the new managers to make changes until they know what they are changing. Got it? Tell them what we do. Don't ask questions. Can I trust you on this?'

'Of course Beth. Of course.'

I slipped back to my bubble and glanced at my notepad. My final bleary-eyed scribbling from last night was there in front of me.

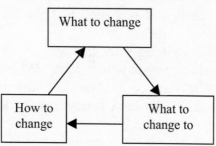

I typed a short email to Harry.

Harry,
We have lift off. What to change is under way. No hitches. Only used half of my becauses. Thank you. Ever in your debt.
Beth

I was very amused a few hours later when Harry made my computer ping again. The sun had reached American shores and Harry was probably up to meet it.

beth,
atta girl! told you.
get ready to start making a new list of UDE's as your current reality changes. begin to prepare for the next constraint. it will come.
keep me updated!
adios fire fighting. hola real management.
H

Chapter 10

The new potential of Harry's TOC kept swimming around my head as I tried to convince myself that it could actually help to solve our problems. However, I had run out of time to think about it now so I tried to convince it to get out and towel itself off. I was in danger of being late for Independence Day.

Being married to an American gives me the perfect excuse to have a few more parties in the year. July 4th becomes more than just another rainy summer's day and Thanksgiving ushers in an early Christmas. However, the 4th of July was doubly special for Max and I. Not only was it a treasured occasion in the American social calendar, it also marked our anniversary.

Normally we would take the day off work and indulge in a little *us time*. We would spend the day browsing around quaint English villages, a pastime that still gave Max a thrill after all these years. It's strange how wonky oak beams and straw roofs can cause such excitement in a grown man. Our day would end with a romantic dinner and fond discussion on how we first met, 15 years ago today in New England.

It seemed such a long time ago now. I was seeking some excitement before I settled down into a nine-to-five existence so I escaped to America and spent a year working as a nanny for a wealthy Boston family. A couple of months after I arrived, the family decided to visit their grandparents in Maine for a long weekend leaving me with the daunting prospect of four days alone in a foreign country.

I quickly ruled out a visit to New York, it may be only a train ride away but I knew I wouldn't feel safe alone. I poured over my Rand McNally atlas of the US and noticed some familiar names in Cape Cod, Massachusetts. Names that I recognised from childhood holidays spent caravanning in the South West of England. Truro, Taunton and Falmouth held many English bucket and spade memories for me so I decided to visit the American equivalents.

After a few calls I found a motel in Falmouth and the landlady assured me it was a safe place for a young English girl holidaying alone. It was peaceful, had wonderful beaches and a great Irish bar where I would be made welcome. So I went for it, packed my bags and drove out of Boston for my first solitary adventure.

The landlady, a bubbly Scottish woman called Eileen greeted me like a long lost relative and even put a proper teapot and some Tetley tea in my room. Falmouth turned out to be the ideal holiday spot and on Independence Day Eileen encouraged me to visit the Irish bar to hear the live music and to try their famous crab cakes.

It took a lot of courage for me to enter the bar alone, but I did it, I walked right in and ordered a beer. I was immediately identified by the landlord as Eileen's border and before the beer hit my hand I had been introduced to the locals.

Within half an hour I was relaxed and enjoying the craic as some of the older locals teased me about attending a ceilidh later on in the week. I discovered that ceilidh is pronounced *kaylee* and heard claims that Shane MacGowan is the greatest poet ever born. In fact I learned a good deal about Ireland, a country less than 100 miles from my front door, from people living thousands of miles away from their spiritual home.

Of course, not everyone was Irish; I was also introduced to a group of students from Boston. They had escaped from Boston for the weekend and were using the freedom to be liberal with their alcohol consumption. They managed to stay just on the considerate side of raucous and they were great fun, but one guy at the back of the group started to make me feel slightly uncomfortable. He had been staring at me for almost an hour before he finally stepped forward and introduced himself.

Max Seager was polite, almost chivalrous, but he had a predatory edge. He was tall, well over 6 foot, with dark hair and an accent slightly different to the rest of the gang. His witty remarks made me laugh and his close attention made me feel special. I had found my future husband thousands of miles from home, next to a plate of crab cakes.

We dated back in Boston and the rest of my year in America sped past at frightening speed. After drowning in tears at the airport we struggled to keep a long distance relationship going for what was the slowest year of my life, but we both needed personal contact. Just when we were facing up to the hopelessness of the situation, Max managed to talk his way into a job in the UK.

I had no idea about his career move and was extremely surprised when an air ticket landed on my doormat. My arrival at Boston Logan International Airport was incredibly emotional and I knew we couldn't let our relationship just disappear.

I was trying to verbalise my feelings when Max told me about the job offer and proposed in one long, breathless sentence. I accepted on the spot and immediately phoned home with the news. That was in the spring and on July 4th of that year Max's parents, brother, sister-in-law, nephew and niece flew to the UK to attend our wedding in my hometown.

With all this history it was natural for us to celebrate the 4th of July, but things had changed this year and my new mantra of 'we all want to do a good job' had a lot to do with it.

In January Max succumbed to a job offer that had been loitering on the table for the last six months. Max liked to say he was headhunted, but he was shrewd enough to know that his new employers wanted the knowledge inside of his head and not Max's head per se. He decided to take the job when the financial package became just that 'little too big to ignore'. The bit that was a 'little too big' eclipsed my entire salary.

There is no doubting Max's ability and desire to do a good job, but I still don't fully understand his job, even after all these years I really should know, I've heard him feed the same lines at parties for years.

'I sell money to people who are trying to sell an idea.' If the recipient of this pearl did not glaze over, he goes on to tell them he is a 'venture capitalist with a heart.'

These last three words became a necessary addition after a colleague's adolescent son accused him of being responsible for the Third World's debt at a rather elegant cocktail party. Max found this 'with a heart' addition to his job title led casual conversation toward the many inventions his firm had invested in and how they could eventually benefit mankind.

In short Max was pestered by people with a business project that was deemed to be too risky by the high street banks. The money he sold was not cheap and often his decision on whether to invest was founded on instinct. Sure, his company did the math, as Max would say, but he was responsible for deciding if the inventors themselves were a worthwhile investment.

Max's new employers agreed to pay an extortionate amount for his success in this ethereal field. As he said, 'They believe in my ability to find the right people to believe in.' This sounded more like a method of picking the winning racehorse than a business decision to me, but who am I to question it? It would only degenerate into a *discussion* that I would never win. After all, Max's income provided us with a lovely home and financial security. So much so that I do not have to work, but thankfully Max understands that I *need* to work.

Unfortunately, he could not understand why I was prepared to 'put up with so much crap' for the paltry sum my job paid and this has recently become yet another taboo subject. With Max worrying about living up to expectations in his new job and me fretting over shoe horning patients into unavailable beds, the lists of taboo subjects seems to be steadily growing.

This is the first time we have not taken a day off to celebrate our anniversary as Max had been out of the country all week and was only due back mid-afternoon. If I had taken the day off I would just get in the way of the cleaner who *did* for me twice a week. We decided to have a low-key celebration and Max invited some of his American colleagues from his old job round for a barbecue.

The extra holidays are not the only bonus to marrying an American, there's also the laid-back attitude to entertaining. Max loves to barbecue and the relaxed atmosphere is a stark contrast from the interminable dinner parties my friends are often asked to host by their husbands. With Max there was no wrestling with tortuous recipes; half a cow and a crate of beer in a rubbish, sorry, garbage bin full of ice and the party was set. I only hoped Max's flight from Belfast was on time so he'd had a chance to prepare the steaks.

I breathed a sigh of relief as I swung into the drive as Max's Jag was facing the front door. Normally he took great care to reverse his car ready to leave the next morning, but when he was running errands he drove straight in. This meant he was probably on top of things.

This turned out to be an understatement; he had set up all the garden furniture and the beer bin, laid out the steaks in the kitchen and filled the fridge with salad. What a complete star! All I had to do was get in the house without the dogs covering my uniform in hair.

Using my briefcase as protection I managed to reach the bedroom in a relatively hair-free state and was greeted by a half-naked husband and the blazing fiddles of the Irish band that were playing in the pub 15 years ago.

'Hi, Hon,' Max hopped over to me with one leg in his favourite Docker pants to plant a kiss on my cheek.

'Hey, they're playing our song!' I responded with a wry grin, the music was about as suitable for smooching as Zippidy Doo Dah was for funerals. 'How was the flight?'

'Good, we got away from the meeting early for once and managed to catch the earlier shuttle. No one in the US office appears to be working today so I thought I'd come straight home. How about you? How's your week been?'

'Don't ask,' I replied rolling my eyes as I struggled out of my clothes and headed for the shower. 'I'd better get ready. Thanks for getting everything sorted, I'll be down as soon as I can.'

Chapter 11

A relaxed evening with friends is the perfect antidote to stress, especially when you don't have to choose what to wear. Jeans and a sweatshirt fitted the bill and our friends Frank and Cathy arrived just as I was going down the stairs.

In a few minutes everyone had a drink in their hands and Max was doing a grand tour of the garden. Max loves his garden even though his sole input is buying the plants. He can't resist any plants he thinks would suit the perfect *English garden* and the borders are groaning with roses, hollyhocks, dahlias, marigolds and foxgloves. Fortunately, we have found a gardener who comes in twice a week to keep it all in order and repair the damage done by the dogs.

I laughed as our friends instantly ribbed Max about his *English* garden. Frank and Cathy are another Anglo-American couple and Cathy and I often escape from the boys when their constant longings for real apple pie and baseball get too much.

As soon as the tour was completed, Max fired up the gas barbecue and the conversation turned to work.

'How's your job going Cathy?' I asked. 'Still hatching that plan to take over the entire retail industry?'

Cathy is a distribution project manager for a huge supermarket chain and we always wind her up about their plans to take over the world.

'Huh, no such luck!' She exclaimed. 'Our chairman quit today, that's the third in three years. The boardroom's turned into a merry-go-round. I've had so many new bosses I email my reports to 12 people in the hope they will get to the right person! It's absolutely ridiculous.'

'I know just how you feel,' I laughed, after all soon I would be reporting to Joan and Tessa as well as a whole gaggle of Associate General Managers. 'Didn't you apply for your boss's job? How did you get on?'

'Don't get me started! They've only gone and brought in a graduate, haven't they? Would you credit it? I've been doing the job three years and they bring in a novice to tell me how to do it! I despair, I really do.'

'You're kidding me Cathy? Sounds just like the Health Service. They've doubled the management at our hospital in the past five years and most of these new wonder managers seem to come straight from University. They don't have a clue what they're supposed to be doing. Hey, it looks as though we're facing the same problems, even though we work in very different fields.'

I looked across at Max who was deep in conversation with Frank as he flipped the chunks of dead cow on the barbecue.

'Sorry Frank can I interrupt a second? Cath and I have just discovered that both our employers are hiring graduates into management positions. Do your firms do that?'

Max looked bemused. 'Well, we try to get the best graduates, but they don't go straight into management, they have to learn the business first. Why do you ask?'

'Well, it just seems strange that's all. Who knows? Perhaps it's a British thing.'

'Oh no! Not that again!' Max retorted as he grinned at Frank. 'Hey, do you remember that conference in Canterbury when we caused mass offence by listing the differences between the Brits and the Yanks? Jeez, they sure got mad at us. It seems the girls here are just beginning to realise we *do* do business differently.'

'How can I forget?' Frank chipped in. 'Cathy I'm surprised at you. When I told you about it you insisted that we're no different. Has the penny, or should I say the cent, finally started to drop?'

Cathy's face instantly flushed bright red. 'Frank, if you remember that discussion as well as I do, you spent ages telling me that Brits are too uptight to succeed in the modern business world. I'm never going to agree with that, we have different cultures so we are bound to be slightly different to you colonials. I just don't see how it affects our business acumen.'

I grinned. The evening was turning out as expected, drink, banter and a mock battle between the cousins from across the pond. I handed out some more beers to cool the situation, but the line of questioning was starting to intrigue me.

'I'm serious about this guys. Can you explain why you think we're different? One of our consultants is South African and he's been asking me some strange questions about what makes us tick and I can't figure it out.'

Frank was not going to waste an opportunity like this. After all this is the man who successfully spun a tale to our local vicar about choirboys in Washington DC being frisked for machine guns before they entered the church!

'Well, everything is so *small* here!' He crowed. We all groaned and Cathy threatened to throw her empty beer bottle at him.

'Oh relax,' he said grinning inanely. 'I'm not talking stereotypes here. I'm talking real estate. Your houses are smaller, but they cost more than a much larger one does in the States. You have so little land in comparison that the value of property is forced up.'

'But how does that make us different?' I urged.

'Well, apart from whinging about the weather, all you Brits care about is the value of your home and how much space you own. You're obsessed with it. People think we are mad when they find out we are renting. It's as if your whole identity is wrapped up in the house you own.'

Max chose this moment to declare that the steaks were ready so I had a bit of time to think about Frank's comment. When we were all attacking our loaded plates I set the ball rolling again.

'Alright, I'll give you that one Frank, Brits place a high priority on home ownership and territory. What else?'

Max pulled a face as he chomped on a piece of steak. 'Well, you talk funny, but you can't help that!'

'Look who's talking!' Cathy quipped.

'But seriously, it goes further than real estate,' Frank continued. 'You're obsessed with status. The schools your kids go to, the cars you drive, where you take your vacations. In my work I meet a lot of Brits who have severe cash flow problems but they seem more concerned about how they appear to other people than the hole in their wallets. Yeah, I'd say that status is very important to Brits, more so than us.'

'But surely this happens in any western society?' Cathy queried. 'We work hard and want the benefits.'

'I think it goes beyond that—both of our societies will jump at an improved job title even if there's little or no financial reward. There's the old joke about calling burger flippers in fast food joints Nutrition Technicians, but I reckon the Brits have put a new spin in this behaviour.'

'What are you talking about Frank?' Max chipped in. 'We're all the same aren't we?'

'Kinda, but I've noticed a difference here. It's subtle, but it is a difference all the same. Look, everyone craves a good job title. How can I explain? Ah yes. When I first arrived here in Blighty I devoured the news programmes to try and get a feel for the place. I saw one of your MP's being interviewed and he was asked how important his job title was to him. He gave the most incredible answer. He claimed that he, like other men, valued himself according to the job he does. He even went as far as to say that something was missing if he couldn't tell someone in one or two words what he is. It was as if he didn't represent anything anymore.

'I was gobsmacked. Okay, forget he's a guy in a high status job. I noticed this attitude when I arrived here from people at all levels, but the really strange part is that he did not mention success.'

'I think I agree with what you are saying,' I replied thoughtfully, 'but what's the difference? Or is the beer dulling my senses?'

'Well, this guy is saying that his whole identity depends on his title. Not if he is good at the job. He's not saying "I need to be a successful MP to have any worth", just "I need to be an MP".'

I paused, I couldn't see how this could make sense. 'So you're saying that our titles are important, but we don't care if we are good at our jobs! No Frank that can't be true! We all want to be good at our jobs.'

There was the phrase again. It seemed to be a permanent part of my vocabulary now. However, I was more intrigued with my inability to take offence at Frank's analysis. In some strange way he'd beaten me to the punch line. Or had he? I suddenly thought of the new Clinical Bed Management team.

'But what if people who aren't trained to be managers have the chance to call themselves managers?' I asked. 'Do they, or should I say we, put our careers on the line for a title even if we don't know how to do the job?'

'Damn right you do!' Max exclaimed. 'What about our neighbour, Beth? The one in local government. She was such a calm lady until she got promoted to a managerial position. Now she's a wreck. Only last week she was nearly in tears when I asked her how it was going. I never thought her stiff upper lip would crack, but she really was in a state.

'Can you believe that she had no training for her new job and now her bosses are really riding her for not performing? When I asked her why she took the job she said it wasn't for the money, she just thought that at her time of life she should be a manager! I was amazed.'

'But this is just one example. It could be an anomaly. Frank, if you are right then there must be more evidence. I don't mean anecdotal tales of managerial incompetence, I mean hard evidence that people are being promoted beyond their abilities.' Max had thrown a challenge to Frank.

'You and your evidence, I swear you should have been a cop. Okay, how about this. How many people have you heard of or dealt with who deliberately down grade their job?'

'Opt out you mean?' I asked 'Like those TV shows where people liquidate their assets and buy a Finca in Spain and grow their own food, that kind of downgrade?'

'I suppose that is the extreme version of it yes. But there are much less drastic moves that people take to disguise the fact that they are not up to the challenge of their job.'

I couldn't help it but I snorted while trying to swallow a mouth full of beer. When I finally managed to recover and speak over the laughter of the group I was incensed 'Do you really think that!' I began to stutter 'Ddddddo you really think that we Brits opt for the simple life as a way of avoiding being crap at our jobs?'

Frank was relishing the reaction he was getting from Cathy and me. She was brewing up and her face was growing redder by the second. 'You've got to be kidding us Frank! Are you seriously trying to tell us that you think Brits wimp out and opt for a better life in Spain than face up to your ludicrous idea that we are not hungry enough to be successful?'

Frank looked relaxed as he leaned back in the lounger. Cathy and I sat on the edges of our seats and Max, who was positioned side on between us, was doing a great impersonation of a tennis umpire. Now he was glaring at Frank to see how strong his next volley would be.

'Think about it.' He said calmly 'The exodus of people on pension income I can understand. It's no different to our Snow Birds migrating to Florida but much younger people with families are emigrating in higher numbers than ever before. Why would they do that? Why would they leave a perfectly safe and civilised country to bring their children up far away from family and friends unless they were certain that they will be more secure, safer elsewhere?'

'The sun,' I replied.

'I know you Brits are obsessed with the weather but that one won't work on me. There is no way parents give up security and family support just to move to the sun. Remember, most of them can't even speak the language of their new home country. Why would they put themselves at such risk?'

We were all silent. Why would they? Friends of ours had done it, we all know people who have sold up and set up home on the Continent and further a field. But why?

I finally found my voice again, 'Alright Frank you are looking too smug. Tell us your loopy theory as to why these people move abroad.'

'With pleasure. Let's see if you can follow this. We all work to gain more security. We save, we buy property, we raise a family all in the fervent hope that by the time the kids are independent, the mortgage will be paid off and there will be enough in our savings account to retire on. Am I right? It's a juggling act that takes thirty years to come to fruition. Right?'

We all nodded, Max included. I realised that he was as fascinated by Franks' theory as Cathy and I were which surprised me.

Frank continued, 'With the increases in living standards we are all fighting to keep up with the game. To have a fighting chance we have to earn more so we need promotions in our jobs. We all chase them, hard, and when we get them we breathe a little easier, we are that little bit closer to achieving the dream.'

'So, what's wrong with that? asked Max. 'We all do it.'

'Nothing, but here is where the two cultures diverge. At home we are taught from an early age that if we work hard enough we will succeed. Am I right?' Max nodded. 'But here you grow up with the idea that there is a finite amount of almost everything.'

My puzzled look, first at Frank and then at Cathy prompted Frank on, 'Beth, you live on an island. Land is finite, it is expensive. You live in a so-called classless society but you are just kidding yourselves. Why are all the tabloids and magazines full of stories about the aristocracy and celebrities? And why are these publications always trying to do these people down? You see success in this country and you take pot shots at it!'

Ouch, that hit a nerve and Cathy and I both knew it. We looked at each other. She spoke first. 'He has a point. As much as I hate to admit it we are a pretty cruel bunch when it come so success.' I could only nod in agreement.

'But do you know why you are like this?' Asked Frank.

'Not really,' Cathy admitted rather reluctantly

'Here's the rest of my theory. You are so conditioned into thinking that resources are finite, like land, that you extend this to success and power AND money. You are all afraid that there won't be enough to go around.'

Cathy burst out laughing, 'You are kidding aren't you?'

Frank obviously wasn't. 'No, I'm not. Think about it, if you thought as we do, that there is enough money and success to go around, then why would you despise anyone else being success-ful and rich? Why would you put yourselves through hell to keep up the appearance of success when you quite obviously are not? And why are you so quick to cash in when you are success-ful? Because you know it can't last!'

I was amazed. Frank had hit so many buttons my mind was reeling. I looked at Cathy, she looked as stunned as I felt. I tried to talk.

'But, but………' I took a deep breath, 'But what has this got to do with being good at our jobs?'

Frank stood up and moved to the beer bin. As he handed out fresh bottles he began his summation.

'Why would anyone promote someone who isn't up to it?' The penny or cent dropped with an almighty clang.

'That's an easy one to answer Frank,' I said. 'His or her boss was probably frightened of the competition. They assumed that if they promoted someone smart they might steal their job and being Brits we all know that plum jobs are finite! I'm right, aren't I? I see it in the Health Service all the time. Promote someone to their level of incompetence to keep your own job safe.'

'You must be kidding!' Max exclaimed. 'Surely the bosses' job is to improve the organisation. How can they do that by promoting idiots?'

'Oh Frank, you've made me feel so much better.' I laughed.

'How so?'

'Well, I had a run in with my boss this week. I've not had a chance to tell Max about this yet, but I had a really rough day on Monday and to top it all, my boss said I would never get a promotion. She must be frightened that I would do her job better than her!'

'Definitely running scared,' Cathy agreed.

'You're far too good for that place. I wish you'd get out,' concluded Max

'Don't start on that again Max, you know I love my job. I may suffer a roller coaster ride each day, but I'm not ready to give up yet. Then again, considering that Cathy didn't get her promotion either we must both be brilliant managers!'

We were saved from a public discussion of one of our taboo subjects by the phone clamouring for attention. I dashed inside to grab it before the machine answered it.

'Beth, its Sarah. Just thought I'd call to wish you both a happy Forth of July, not to mention anniversary.'

'Hi! It's lovely to hear from you. Your husband is officially my favourite man in America!'

Sarah laughed. 'He told me he has been teaching you in the ways of TOC. How's it going so far?'

Her question snapped my thoughts away from the discussion that was still going on in the garden and back to today's success in the office.

'It's just amazing, I'm finally feeling I have a chance of persuading other people to use common sense!'

Sarah laughed again. 'Sounds like you are enjoying it.'

'I am but I'm not sure how far it will take me.'

'Stick with it Beth, you may be surprised at what you can achieve. What are you folks up to today, or should I say tonight?'

'We're having a BBQ with a couple of friends. Max is out in the garden doing his caveman bit as usual.'

'Glad to hear my brother-in-law is keeping up the stars and stripes traditions,' Sarah laughed. 'I won't keep you long, but we were wondering if we could come to visit some time in the fall? We are a bit more flexible now the kids are almost off our hands.'

'Sarah, that would be marvellous, but just the two of you? I can't believe the kids have nearly flown the nest. We would love to see you, when are you thinking of coming?'

'We are thinking of two weeks from the end of August. The kids will be away with friends for a break from their summer jobs before going back to school. We're hoping to tour England then spend a few days in Paris before heading home.'

'Sounds wonderful, but how can you take such a long holiday? Let alone plan it so far in advance? How can Harry be sure he will be free to take time off work?'

'Well, he's head of his division now and he feels confident enough in his staff to book time off in advance.'

'Wow, I never thought I'd see the day, Harry actually planning to take time off! What have you done to him? Don't tell me it has something to do with this TOC?'

Sarah laughed again. 'You could be right there.'

'Can you two teach me how to get Max to do the same?'

'Well I'm not sure we could, but we know people who can.'

'You've intrigued me now. You're not pulling my leg? You actually sound serious about it.'

'Sure am, but it's too complicated to tell you about over the phone. We'll have a long chat when we get there. And by the way I know you say it's okay, but after that last little spat between Max and Harry, I will understand if Max isn't quite so accommodating. We can always stay in a local hotel if it's going to make things awkward.'

'Don't be so silly Sarah, of course it will be alright. That was just a spot of sibling rivalry. You and I can get them over it and your holiday will be the ideal time to do it. I really can't wait to see you both again, but I should get back to my guests. Email me your itinerary and I'll book time off and I'll try to get Max to do the same. Love to everyone.'

'Love to you both and the dogs. See you in the fall.'

I hurried back to the garden to find that the subject of the conversation had changed everyone was discussing Max's new job and Frank was in full flow.

'You really hit lucky there Max. Why did you finally decide to make the move? You know old Johnstone has been hell to live with since you left us.'

'I can't help that Frank,' Max replied with a wry grin. 'You know how he used to keep on at me to write a paper on how I could sniff out a good investment? Well I did and he was far from happy. I wrote a perfect paper in Return on Investment, Capitalisation and Risk Management, but he wasn't remotely impressed by it.

'He said he wanted to know the real formula for my success. He got really mad when I said that if I could put it on paper I'd be worth ten times what he was paying me. He suggested that I should find someone else who would pay for my inflated ego if that was my attitude, so I did.'

'But Max, you must have some kind of formula that you work to,' Frank urged. 'It can't just be luck. You hit the mark so many times it can't just be chance.'

'Well, I'm sorry to disappoint you Frank, but that's a trade secret!'

'Aw, come on, you're among buddies here. We aren't in competition. How do you do it?'

I noticed that Max was starting to look uncomfortable; after all, he makes money from his special ability, should he really have to pass it onto his friend? I felt I should jump in and change the subject, but to tell the truth, I was just as intrigued as

Frank and waited for Max's answer. It was an evening of home truths and I wanted to hear one from Max for a change.

'Honestly? I can't say for sure, but it has something to do with picking inventors who are in love with their project enough to give it everything they've got. They also need to have the ability to make changes in their plans.'

'What do you mean?' Frank was starting to get persitent.

'Well our clients are usually very passionate about their project or their *baby*. That's just great, but they can't be so in love with it that they are not prepared to rethink their plans if something changes.'

'What kind of changes?'

'Markets for example. Some of these people have a very fixed idea about who their markets are. If the market changes they have to be prepared to change as well. That's it in a nut-shell, plus of course the Old Max Moneymaking Magic!'

'So, you're saying that after all the number crunching you test them by finding out if they love their project more than money?' Frank was obviously not impressed.

'That's about it. They have to keep their eye on the target. If their target is their *baby, by that I mean their product or service,* and not money I won't go with them.'

Frank sat back and looked at him with obvious disbelief and a silence rolled across the group. Enough was enough.

'Alright, so who's ready for dessert?' I asked lightly.

'I certainly am,' Cathy chipped in on cue, she looked as un-comfortable as me with the situation, but Frank had returned from his thoughts.

'You're pulling my leg!' he accused. 'It can't be that simple or we would all be doing as well as you.'

'Oh, didn't I tell you about my sixth sense?' Max quipped, trying to lighten the tone. 'I use that as well.'

'That's nearer the truth Max,' Frank smiled. 'I don't know about a sixth sense but I reckon you know exactly what you are doing, you just don't want to share it with me.'

'Would I be that mean to my buddy?'

I was suddenly struck by Max's expression as he grappled with his friend. It was very similar to Joan's just before she admitted that she didn't have a clue about how to solve the bed crisis. It seemed a good time to escape. I motioned to Cathy and we hotfooted it to the kitchen to *prepare* the dessert.

Cathy had brought along a selection of gateaux, from her supermarket naturally. As we started removing the packaging I tried to explain to her the problems between Max and his brother.

'It was really stupid. Max got uptight because Harry was trying to tell him the secret of his successful promotion. He claimed to use a theory he had picked up at a seminar and for some reason Max just blew his top. It soured the rest of the holiday and Max just refused to listen to Harry. I just couldn't work it out. His kid brother was doing well and Max was putting him down, even though the evidence of his success was there for all to see.

'Finally on the plane on the way home I got it out of him,' I continued. 'Max considers himself to be the business brain of the family. Harry chose to specialise in engineering. And Max had some strange notion that Harry should have turned to *him* for advice.'

'That's some ego!' Cathy laughed.

'Max got really angry when Harry started to tear down almost everything he was saying about business. Max was quoting great passages about efficiency and accounting but Harry insisted on discussing bottlenecks and constraint management. Oh!'

Wham! It suddenly hit me. The stuff that Harry is teaching me, it was what he was trying to explain to Max! I nearly dropped a Black Forest gateau with 25 per cent extra whipped cream on the floor.

Cathy looked at me with concern. 'Are you okay Beth?'

I snapped back to the current situation. 'Sure, I'm fine. Sorry, Cath, I suddenly remembered something from work.'

'So what happened?'

'Happened? With what?'

'Between Max and Harry, dummy!'

'Oh, it turned into quite a blood bath. In the end they agreed to disagree, but they are both still sore over it. I only hope that they can come to some sort of understanding.'

'Do you think they will?'

'Well, Sarah seems to think so. Harry seems to have total control of his job now; they are even able to book holidays in advance.

'Huh! Sounds good to me,' Cathy said as she thrust the wrapping in the bin. 'Frank is so stressed we can't even get away for a weekend and he brings so much work home that he might as well spend the evening at the office. They say they do it because they enjoy it, but I don't believe that for a minute. He's scared, scared that someone else will out do him, that he'll be overlooked for promotion if he doesn't keep performing. I guess he's becoming more British all the time.'

'Wouldn't it be wonderful to have a husband who can take proper holidays, to places where there is no Internet or email access and where the mobile phone won't pick up a signal?' Cathy sighed. 'Remember last year? Frank cut his holiday short leaving the boys and me alone for the second week of our holiday in France. Perhaps I should have a chat with Harry when he gets here as well.'

'I'll tell you what,' I declared as we gathered up the plates. 'We'll have a get together and pump him for information and advice. The boy's won't know what's hit them!'

With that we waltzed out into the rapidly cooling evening air with the desert and coffee.

As Max got up from his seat to help me hand out the plates and cups I took advantage of my newfound optimism. 'Max, the call I took earlier was from Sarah,' I said, loud enough for the others to hear. She called to wish us a happy July Forth. Apparently they're planning a trip over here in autumn. She wanted to know if they could stay here for a few days.' I can be very sneaky at times. This way he was forced to agree to his brother's visit. It also meant that he couldn't duck out of it later as I could produce witnesses.

Frank pricked his ears up. 'Hey Max, isn't Harry the kid brother you were telling me about? The one who's doing really well in manufacturing?'

Max pretended to busy himself with his passing round the coffees and didn't answer. 'Yes that right,' I replied on his behalf, 'and it appears he's just got another promotion and is planning a trip to Europe in the autumn.'

'There must be something about you Seager boy's, both of you making it against all odds,' said Frank. 'Are you sure that Seager doesn't mean magician in another language?' I watched as Max disappeared into his own thoughts, but Frank was not to be denied.

'Max? I said, does Seager mean anything?'

Max shook his head as he replied. 'I don't know Frank, I don't know.'

Chapter 12

I woke with a relatively clear head, grateful that our guests had excused themselves at a reasonable time due to it being a weeknight. I cuddled up to Max, trying to ignore the strident claims of the alarm clock, but it was my turn to walk the dogs. I slid gracelessly out of the bed, pulled on some old clothes and a hat to conceal my messy hair and stepped out into the fresh air accompanied by two frenetic mutts.

I do a lot of thinking on these early morning walks and today I was thinking about me and Max. For someone of his stature and intelligence, he could be incredibly shortsighted. I knew he would be sulking after my sneaky tactics last night, but he will eventually realise he has to deal with his issues with his brother.

Our marriage was built on moments like this. Times when one of us became lost in our own world and the other had to break in with some straight talking. Neither of us likes to admit we're wrong so we put this little game down to the simple fact that two heads are better than one. This means we can usually bash our heads together to unravel any problem, I say usually, this brotherly spat was loaded with family politics and I was wary of overstepping the mark. However, Sarah's positive news had given me enough optimism to try and soften Max up before their vacation.

When I returned home, I was surprised to see Max was dressed and ready to go. Normally, he stayed in bed until the last second before hurtling round the house like a whirlwind on steroids.

'Hi Hon,' he said with a smile. 'You got time to sit down for breakfast this morning?'

Perhaps I hadn't overstepped the mark after all. Five minutes later we were sitting in the conservatory munching toast and watching the dogs hunt for the scraps of last night's steak Max had thrown around the garden. Breakfast is the only time Max and I fail to bridge the Atlantic gap. I drink tea and he savours his coffee. We don't usually share this moment during the week and I was enjoying the companionable silence when Max shattered it with an accusation.

'You were dead sneaky about Harry and Sarah last night,' he said attempting to feign a degree of anger, but failing miserably. I could be in the clear after all.

'I wasn't trying to be,' I said radiating innocence.

'You know what I mean Beth. Harry's been insufferable since he got into his strange business theories. I'm not sure I want that garbage rammed down my throat again.'

'Max, don't be such a baby! Harry is doing well. So are you. Why miss the chance to spend some quality time with your kid brother? You know you get on well really. Why are you jealous of his success? Are you turning into a Brit?'

'Tell me about your week,' Max said. 'It sounds as though you have had a rough time.'

This was a classic Max manoeuvre and it meant I was off the hook. No retort, just a side step. If Max had wanted to argue nothing stopped him. But he would not admit defeat either. So a side step in the conversation meant my comments were filed for further analysis. New subject, please.

I told him about the Monday morning meeting and Fran's comments about me never getting a promotion and he listened carefully, but his response was the same as always, 'Why bother? Get out.'

'Max the conversation last night was very helpful to me,' I retorted. 'This week has been hell, but I think I'm beginning to understand what's happening there. Everyone wants to do a good job but something's stopping them. I can't even think of leaving this job until I know what it is. Can you understand that?'

'You and your damn puzzles,' Max said with a resigned shake of his head. 'What's with you? I know you'll walk barefoot through hell just to figure out what's wrong and I applaud your tenacity, but, Beth, promise me one thing. Don't let it get to the situation where it's affecting your health. It's not worth it. There are other industries crying out for your skills.'

I raised my teacup and chinked it against his coffee mug. 'It's a deal.' I agreed.

He understands and he does care. He loves a cryptic challenge just as much as me, and he does have a point. A number of my colleagues have been so badly affected by long-term stress and illnesses that they are no longer able to work. I've told him about enough of these people for him to have genuine concerns.

We returned to watching the dogs as they frantically sniffed out the remaining few scraps. It is amazing how quickly your lovable pet pooch can display their wild genes if juicy bits of steak are on offer.

'Beth, I've been thinking about what you said last night'

'Oh, about Harry?'

'No, the jury is still out on that one. I mean about the differences between the Brits and us.'

I smiled; I was an honorary American in Max's eyes. 'What part in particular?'

'All of it really. If I could understand the Brit's better it might help me out at work. Let me know if you come up with something.'

'Certainly.' I glanced at my watch. 'Now get a move on or we'll be late!'

In fact I was only a few minutes later than usual and the drive was made more enjoyable with the realisation that Eddy would not be in work for the next two days, as he would be working over the weekend.

I went through my normal routine of face painting and fact-finding. Thursdays and Friday's were usually quieter than the rest of the week because so few surgeons operated at weekends and true to form the bed temperature was minus 29, the best it's been for months. However the Emergency Department had admitted a lot of patients overnight and the severity of the surgical cases quickly deflated my optimism. The situation was not helped by the surgical teams trying to bring in patients early for surgery on Monday.

They would rather tie up beds for four days to make sure their patients got in but I had seen through their ploy. My first task of the day was checking whether the patients really needed to come in early. I knew what the doctors would say. 'We need to run tests prior to surgery.'

What they didn't know was that we hold these patient's notes in the Admissions Department ready for distribution to the wards. I pulled the medical notes of the special early bird patients and took them into my office. After so many years of talking to the medics it was simple to make sure that the pre-admission checks had been done, x-rays, E.C.G.'s, bloods. All present and correct for each patient. By the time I'd tracked down someone from each of the surgical teams involved and flattened them with my bed blocking evidence I felt like an absolute heel.

They all fought so hard to justify bringing their patients in sooner than was necessary, but I had proof to the contrary right in front of me. I would have loved to have turned a blind eye and let the patients in, but I had the rest of the hospital to consider. The system would get even more constipated with patients if the teams thought they could get away with it. Even so, it can be very frustrating being the sole voice of reason when everyone was so desperate to do a good job.

I had just finished heading off the last potential bed blocker when there was a knock at the door. The sight of The Prof put me immediately on the defensive, I didn't want him to use our new found friendship to try and influence me.

'I'm sorry Prof, but if you've come to plead the case for bringing in patients early you've had a wasted trip', I said hurriedly.

The Prof's eyebrows beetled up his forehead as he shot me his mischievous grin. 'Ach! Don't worry Beth. I knew it wouldn't work but my juniors got so excited about discovering a loophole that I'm afraid I left them to it. I knew you would find them out. I've already passed a few deflated egos tramping around the corridors this morning.

'I especially like the way you insisted they phone the patients to tell them they would not be admitted until next week. I am sure they would have tried to palm that job off on me even though I warned them to consider the consequences of their actions.'

'What a relief,' I said. 'I thought you were here to try and pressure me into backing down.'

John laughed. 'Good God! I wouldn't dream of it. From what I've seen recently you are doing perfectly well without my interference. Ach, and another thing, please call me John, Prof. is far too formal.'

I smiled, as I knew that his killer secretary Marge was expected to call him Prof.

'Well...' John paused, unsure how to continue. 'I think I may have something and I'd like to discuss it with you.'

I cleared the paper mountain off my visitor's chair and invited him to sit. 'Strange you should say that. I think I have something as well. But you first.'

'A-ha! Intriguing. I'll tell you mine then you'll tell me yours eh?' John laughed. 'Firstly, can I ask you a few more questions about your wonderful bed board? They will probably seem obvious to you but I want to try and get the process straight in my mind.'

'Feel free,' I laughed. 'However, I should warn you that you can't make beds appear by staring at it. We should know, we've tried it before.'

John smirked. 'I bet you have. So you use this colourful contraption to plan all the day's admissions?'

'Pretty much. Along with the patient lists your secretaries put into the computer.'

'But why haven't we all got access to this information? From this board we could develop some really good reasons to shoot the magicians.'

'Pardon? It's not a game of dungeons and dragons John. What do you mean?'

John looked sheepish. 'Sorry, Beth, it was a slip of the tongue. As you know, and can plainly see from the evidence out there, the medics are taking over the hospital. Medics and surgeons don't make comfortable bed mates. We feel the surgeons do the real work while medics work on the periphery.

'I know it's not a fair analogy, but I prefer the certainty of surgery as compared to the test, try, test, try routine of medicine. This is why I refer to the medics as magicians; it's a bad habit I picked up at med. school. Most of my students agree with me, apart from the natural problem solvers who defect to medicine'.

'I like it John,' I laughed. 'The medics expect *us* to perform miracles, they're always asking us to produce beds out of thin air. Perhaps they could teach us a few tricks?'

'That's unlikely Beth, but they are masters at making beds disappear, at least from our perspective.'

John's eyebrows were slowly knitting together and I could tell he was drifting off into his own thought processes.

'Please continue John,' I said gently.

'Ach, I was thinking about your bed board.' He said briskly. 'Why is this bed board still manual in this computerised age? It holds information we could all use every hour of the day, yet so few people know about it.

'Here's what I've been thinking. What if we could use some software to put this information onto screens throughout the hospital? We could use it to police the admissions of patients.'

John was in full flow now. His concept of a real time computerised bed board knocks down so many of the problems we were facing, but I had an uneasy feeling that I tried carefully to define.

'I agree the free flow of information around the hospital would help John, but once the novelty wears off the doc's would bat the decision making back to the non-clinical managers. If the computer guys deliver what you're suggesting we would get every doc in the place trying to play chess on it. Once they realise it doesn't actually produce any more beds, or allow any more patients through the system, they will become frustrated and bored. They would hand the decision making back to us, or the managers, and the outlay for such a system would be yet another expensive half-baked solution that is left to wither.

'Don't get me wrong, John, the idea has merit. It makes sense but alone it isn't enough. It needs something else; a firm foundation.'

John had listened intently to my speech and seemed to be constructing a counter argument behind his customary thinking frown. After a few seconds of silence I was becoming distinctly uncomfortable. When he eventually spoke he surprised me.

'You are right. There is merit in it, but the idea is incomplete. You always seem to be able to grasp the bigger picture. I'll keep working on it and see if I can't polish it. What have you found? What's your answer to this mess?'

I began to tell him the chain of events that led to yesterdays meeting. As I spoke I showed him the Current Reality Tree but I heeded Harry's warning and kept the cloud back.

'So as you can see, Harry has shown me a way to pick through problems I would not normally have tackled. Instead of letting the project drift and picking up the pieces. Now I actually feel in control for once.'

John was lost in the tree, his eyes flicking over the branches. Suddenly he leapt to his feet.

'But Beth, how did you find your solution? It's not on here. Where's the bit showing you how to handle Tessa?'

'John, if I tell you, you must promise to keep it to yourself. Will you?'

'Of course, surgeon's honour!'

'Okay, it's called a Cloud. It's used to state the problem clearly. Here it is.' I laid the sheet of paper on my desk.

'Harry talked me through it. The single box on the left shows what we are all trying to achieve.'

John read it out loud. *'"To treat more patients, better, sooner, now and in the future"* You'll get no arguments from me on that point. It's what we all dream about doing. Ach, the more I think about it, the more accurate it looks. It's bloody spot on Beth.'

'Actually John I thought it was a bit pretentious, but you're right. It's what everyone in the Health Service wants to do. We all want to do a better job for our patients.' John's validation of the goal of the Health Service gave me the confidence to talk him through the rest of the Cloud.

'The next box on the top shows what we need to do here in Admissions, to contribute to the project. Otherwise they won't know what they're changing and we've already seen the wheel reinvented so many times I feel we are stuck in the Stone-age.'

'Tell me about it,' John smirked. 'I've seen more abandoned systems re-emerge than there are patients on my waiting lists. How do you get from that box to the next one?'

'This is what we want to do. We want to contribute our expertise.'

'Ach, I see what you mean. It's all very well us dreaming up bright ideas but we can't demolish systems that work just to implement them. We need other people's expertise to make these things happen.'

'Exactly, this is why we must take their intuition into account. That is what the bottom of the Cloud covers.

'The CBM's have been given the task of improving the Admissions process. They want to do well, but to do this they must know how the current system works. How can anyone improve a system if they don't know what they are improving?'

'Yep, I like it Beth, it is crystal clear. But what is the bolt of lightning?'

'The lightning bolt is the conflict coming out of the Cloud. It's the best place to attack. Look, my solution was to find a way to make Tessa recognise the need to learn about the system before she even contemplated changing it. To do this I had to list the *becauses*.'

'Becauses?'

'Yes, look here. Between *We must improve on the existing Admissions process* and *The CBM's must know how the current Admissions systems work*. If you read it *In order to improve on the existing Admissions process, we must get the CBM's to know how the current Admissions systems work because:*

They don't want to make the system worse

They need us to support them

Their bosses need a successful project

The patients need a better system

Etc...

'None of these things will happen if they don't get it right and they can't possibly get it right if they don't know where they're starting from.'

John sat back in the chair. His shoulders sagged and he suddenly looked tired.

'Beth, I can't tell you how relieved I am to see this.'

I smiled as I realised the look on this face was relief not exhaustion.

'You've got something real here, tangible. You've taken those thoughts that hover in peoples' minds, the ones that make them angry and frustrated, and put them into words. And you know what the crazy thing is? Once they are down on paper they look so bloody simple, so easy to rectify.'

'Well, John it's worked so far, but I get the feeling this is just the beginning. This problem was easy to solve, but I suspect the next one will be a bit tougher.'

'What do you mean?'

'Harry told me to keep making lists of UDE's, you know the undesirable effects. And my list keeps on growing. I have to leave Eddy to start the project with the CBM's and I'm seeing monsters under beds that are already full of patients!'

'Ach, I get the impression this method of problem solving might unearth some pretty scary skeletons Beth. But imagine what we could do with this! It would be bloody amazing if we could figure out what was really making the Health Service sick and treat the root cause, not the symptoms. If we could identify the culprit we could cut it out!'

'Spoken like a true surgeon John. But what if surgery isn't indicated? What if the answer is a form of medicine? Say training, or rehabilitation? How can we do that?'

'Don't tell me you are trying to turn me into a magician Beth!' John roared with laughter. 'Now that I won't stand for!'

We buzzed on our excitement for the next half hour until John had to return to his day job and I promised to ask Harry to bring him into the game. I emailed Harry as soon as John left my office.

Harry,
I have just spent the last two hours discussing our work with Professor John Summers. He's a consultant surgeon here who is as anxious to find answers as I am.

I feel awful asking but would you be prepared to guide him through some of this? He's got some great ideas and he's a good ally, but I don't feel confident enough to help him and he's keen to start.

If you don't have the time I understand but if he could work on the problems from the perspective of the medics and I can do the managerial side of things, we might actually come up with something.
Beth

By the time the 11:00 meeting was over Harry had replied. I was amazed; it was still only 6:00 in the morning.

beth,
you caught me before an early round of golf.

i'm delighted that you have a champion so soon. of course I will
help him just let me have his email address and i'll get him
started as soon as I can.
H

    I still felt guilty about pressing Harry into helping John but if he was prepared to help John with TOC who was I to stop him? We had nothing to lose but time and so much to gain.

    I sent John's address to Harry and relished the feeling that something was actually happening.

Chapter 13

Ouch! I was only a few hours into the day and my brain was already close to saturation point. Not with real hospital work, but with TOC. I kept hearing John yesterday saying, 'If we could figure out what was really making the Health Service sick, treat the root cause, not the symptoms, it could be wonderful.'

Could we? Could we really do this? So many people were working on the problems of the Health Service—bright, intelligent, well-educated people. Who were we to think we could do it where everyone else had failed?

Thank Hippocrates it was Friday, the quietest day of the week. I vowed to use it to achieve our next step of Health Service reform.

I looked out of my bubble and saw the ever-dependable Sally calmly talking on the phone. We had no empty beds and very few patients due in so she was quite capable of working the Bed Board alone. I left her and the girls to it and locked myself in my office. Apart from a few calls and email to respond to I almost had the day to myself.

Whilst closing out the rest of the world was easy, finding a suitable starting point proved to be extremely difficult. Newton was fortunate enough to be clouted by an apple before having his Eureka moment. I was stuck in a featureless office where even the light was artificial. Forget the boy in the bubble; I was the manager in a bubble. I found myself paraphrasing Julie Andrews, 'Let's start at the very beginning, after all it's a very good place to start'.

New medicines are launched all the time. If I classed TOC as a new treatment, which it was as far as this sick hospital was concerned, then why couldn't I set the medicine in motion? Think big. The goal of the Health Service was big. Treat more patients, better, sooner, now and in the future. That was definitely big and hairy enough to scare the bejesus out of me. Assuming that a big problem needs a big solution, I needed to find a solution big enough to make an elephant resemble a cute mouse with a big nose. So just what is the core problem of the Health Service?

After ten minutes of staring at the wall it was obvious that my big solution was not going to simply clout me on the head. I decided to start with the UDE's and was just finding the right piece of paper when I was distracted by the ping of my email. It was Harry.

beth,
i've started john off. he's picking it up real quick and seems like a real bright spark, but it's hard to tell by email.

he mentioned the two of you are aiming to sort out the health service. not too ambitious eh?
if you are thinking of tackling a larger problem i can show you a quicker way of finding out what the Core Problem is. are you interested?
H

Was I interested? Is a stethoscope cold?

Harry,
I've just written a heading. The UDE's of the Health Service. There's nothing else yet. Of course I am interested!!

Help!
Beth

beth
ok calm down!
i've attached a form for you to fill in. pick three UDE's, the
three that bug you most in your job. forget the big picture and
pick the three that really, really get under your skin. fill the
form out and when you have your consolidated cloud get it back
to me.
h

I opened the document and printed it off:

CONSOLIDATED CLOUD

UDE One _____

UDE Two _____

UDE Three _____

UDE ONE: Storyline

_____

_____

_____

_____

_____

_____

_____

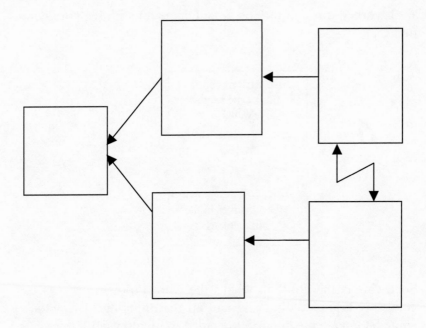

There were three pages like this. One for each UDE. They looked very useful but which three UDE's should I pick? After a few false starts I whittled it down to:

- *Too many improvement projects fail to deliver the expected results*
- *Potential negatives and objections are almost always over-looked*
- *Rank and file staff have seen it all before*

I worked through the forms and came up with the core conflict of

So if this is the conflict, what's the Core Problem? It was no good, my brain was buzzing and all that thinking of Newton's apple had made me hungry. I decided to give myself a treat and escape from the hospital for lunch. I walked to the local deli and bought an exotic sandwich and some apple juice and walked to my favourite part of town, an old blacksmith's yard and found a seat. If people used to spend their days here shaping and twisting metal then surely I could force my thoughts into some kind of order.

According to Harry, the Core Problem has to apply to every level of the organisation, a disease everyone is suffering from. Was I infected? A definite 'Yes' with bells on. I was fed up with having to furtively change my bosses' plans because I knew they wouldn't work. I laughed to myself, I was so infected they should put me in quarantine!

Yeuch! I nearly dropped my sandwich as the joke turned sour. If I was infectious was I passing the disease on to my staff? I remembered Harry's words, 'Everyone must be suffering from it.' Was I doing this to my staff?

I felt sick and pushed my sandwich away. Was Eddy's insubordination caused by me forcing him to do things he knew wouldn't work? The revelation that Eddy might be right was enough to put me off my juice. He was stubborn, irrational, a right royal pain in the butt. Surely he couldn't be right?

I binned the remains of my lunch and stumbled out of the blacksmith's yard in the direction of the old part of the town. Built in the days of Dickens, the old tumbledown buildings now housed specialist shops and Max and I often spent an afternoon here on the weekends. It held a sense of history, maybe even knowledge, but today it made me feel claustrophobic. I started to feel like Ebenezer Scrooge in Dickens' *A Christmas Carol*. He spent years grumbling about other people's failures until he was given the chance to fix his own shortcomings. I winced at the image of the Ghost of Admissions Past showing me all the times I forced Eddy to make wrong decisions. I rushed through the crowds until I got to the Georgian square beyond and found an empty park bench.

Think, think! When Eddy comes to me with his moans and groans what do I do? Listen? Perhaps half of the time. Do I ever act on his recommendations? Hardly ever. Why? If Harry was right, and he had been so far, I should be using Eddy's knowledge and intuition, not dismissing it. Do I dismiss him?

Of course I did! Over the years Eddy's plans had become increasingly outlandish. Whose fault was that? He saw problems and tried to devise solutions, but they were unworkable. As time went by I just fell into the habit of nodding politely and then ignoring him. Oh my goodness, my bosses did the same to me! There was a pattern. We were all doing it. Every single one of us!

Then another metaphorical apple landed. No wonder Joan was so pleased after that first Admissions meeting with the new team. For the first time a subordinate had actually done something she needed, something she didn't know how to do. I'd broken the pattern.

No wonder it felt so good. I had been the exception that proved the rule. This was the first time I really understood what that phrase meant. I dashed back to the office to write it all down and by the time I arrived I was hot, bothered and excited. I was surprised to find that Sal was as anxious as me.

'We were gonna send out a search party,' she said with relief. 'You forgot your bleep. Prof. Summers is after you, said it was urgent.'

'Thanks Sal. I'll call him,' I said nipping into my office to ring the number Sal had left on my desk.

'John, sorry, I went out. What can I do for you?'

'Book yourself on the EPR demonstration next week,' John replied briskly. 'There's an email floating around. Part of our answer may be there.'

'What are you talking about John?'

He took a deep breath and started again. 'Next week there are demonstrations by various software companies who are tendering for the Trust's contract to upgrade the Electronic Patient Record software system. There is a demo of a bed management system on the agenda. I think you should see it. Can you go?'

'I expect so. I'll book myself in.'

'Great! Oh, and another thing, the work with Harry is going great. I hope to have my CRT done by next week. It's a real eye opener Beth. Amazing! Stay well.'

He hung up before I could reply. I checked my email and opened the invitation to the demonstration. Places were limited so I replied immediately.

Phew, panic over. However, there was more stress to come. I needed to find out if I was infecting my staff with the Core Problem and I knew Sal would be straight with me.

'Sal… can I ask you something?'

'You're the boss. Fire away.'

Hmmm, not the best start. 'Sal, when we get a new project we tend to pick it over and do what we can, don't we?'

Sal paused, 'What, like the last one?'

'No, not the last one, I'm talking about previous occasions.'

Sal looked puzzled. 'You do Beth, not us. That's your job. You tell us what to do and we do it. Why?'

'Do I ever listen to your ideas?'

'Do you what?' She hesitated, 'Sometimes, when you're stuck but no, not really'.

Sal was blushing now. Why was she embarrassed? 'What's up Sal? These are simple questions.'

'It's just that, well you're paid to sort out problems. It's your job. I come in, try to keep the system ticking over and nick off home. To be honest, I like the fact that I'm not expected to be a problem solver. Don't get me wrong, if you told me that barking at patients made them recover faster I'd do it. Anything to avoid cancelling these poor people's ops, but I don't really come here to think, just to do as I'm told, so why should I tell you what I think?'

'Thanks Sal, you've really helped me, don't worry about this and do me a favour. Forget we ever had this conversation.'

Sal grinned and simply replied, 'Woof, woof.'

I laughed as I returned to my office, but the laugh soon faded away as I now had proof that I was suffering from the same sickness as everyone else. My analysis proves that our staff have both the knowledge and the answers and we don't listen to them. Why don't we listen? The answer is simple: we don't know how to. And in Sal's case, I have not given her the inclination to even talk to me. I went back to my office and emailed Harry:

Harry,

I'm attaching my Consolidated Cloud.

I've just had a very disturbing time. If I'm right and this analysis holds true for the whole of the Health Service then I've discovered the Core Problem. We don't listen to our staff, or should I say we don't know how to listen to our staff? And this includes me!

Let me know if I'm right?
Beth

I've never felt so down and excited at the same time. I kept fluctuating between elation and despair. If I was right I was a lousy manager but at least I knew how to solve the problem.

I tried to concentrate on some of the paperwork in my in-tray, but my attention span was not up to reading more than two lines of text at a time. Finally my ears detected the ping they were listening for.

Dearest Beth,

You've done it. You've found the Core Problem. I know exactly how you feel. Realising that you are part of the problem is the hardest thing to take. But don't despair, I know it sounds corny, but to be part of the solution you need to be part of the problem. It is very tough to influence a system you are not part of.

Now on to the next bit! Saying you do not listen to your staff is not enough. You need to work this up to a statement that is true for everyone in your position. Work on it and try to depersonalise it. Try to find a generic phrase that will be clear to everyone in your position. This will help you understand that you are not the problem, just that you are forced to act in a certain way because the system does not allow you to work any other way.

Give it a go. I am working from home for the rest of the day and Sarah is typing this for me. Can you tell? We are here for you. Try it.

Love

Harry and Sarah

I wondered why Harry had suddenly rediscovered punctuation! It was good to know that both he and Sarah were at the end of the line helping me along. I prepared myself for some serious word arranging and after a while I came up with:

There is no mechanism by which negatives can be raised and effectively addressed.

I toyed with a few variations that included junior staff and subordinates, but they just caused complications. I emailed it to Harry and Sarah. Their reply was swift.

Beth,
Good work! We agree there may not be a mechanism by which negatives can be raised and effectively addressed, but aren't you missing something?

It's all very well having the mechanism in place but will the staff feel confident or safe enough to raise negatives?
H&S

They were right! Before the negatives could be addressed there had to be a safe way for the staff to raise them, a way they can bring them to their bosses' attention without feeling threatened. There were regular cases in the news describing how Health Service whistle blowers were being ostracised. There had to be a safe platform for these discussions to take place. That was it! I quickly emailed the States with the revised statement. *There is no platform or mechanism by which negatives can be raised and effectively addressed.* Harry replied immediately.

Beth,

You've got it! We are sure this is the Core Problem of the Health Service.

Can you imagine what would happen if the managers in the Health Service were trained to listen to their staff and work their ideas up into sound, practical solutions?

Think on it over the weekend and give yourself a well-earned break. You must have worked really hard this week and you should take some time out. Enjoy yourself and we'll talk more next week.

H&S

Hmm, I wasn't sure I was ready to stop the process yet, I seemed to be making so much headway. I decided to review my week's activities and write a brief summary:

1. *My briefcase is about a pound heavier with all the extra notes I'm carrying around.*
2. *My head is fit to burst with concepts that were totally alien to me at the beginning of the week.*
3. *My department is actively participating in a new project rather than being a passive follower.*
4. *My staff have really come through with the goods at the bitching and moaning session. Their list would make next week so much easier.*
5. *Eddy might behave himself now I've given him some of the responsibility he so badly craved.*
6. *John Summers is fast becoming my partner in what could become the beginning of the rescue of the Health Service.*
7. *I appear to have discovered the Core Problem of the Health Service.*
8. *If I know the Core Problem of the Health Service then it's conceivable that it can be cured. Ergo the patient is still critical but if the diagnosis is right there is hope.*

This last sentence made me laugh out loud. Who was I to think I would be able to make a difference? The British Health Service is a huge and impatient patient. Max told me that it is the largest employer in Europe. So here I was in an 8-foot square glass bubble of office, a minor manager with delusions of reforming the Health Service. Delusions that I could some-how ease the pain and suffering experienced every day by our patients and staff.

After spending some time questioning my abilities I ration-alised the week by adding one more item to my list:

9. *I've found a new puzzle game and it's fun.*

I decided to focus on the last statement. If I'd truly found a solution to the ills of the Health Service then I needed to con-tinue with the puzzle. If I was wrong I would still learn some-thing along the way that should make me a better manager. Af-ter all, if Harry was anything to go by I couldn't lose.

Yep, that was a good enough reason to carry on.

By four o'clock I was beginning to wind down for the week-end. There was no more I could do this week. Or was there? There was no way I could take these findings to the senior man-agement. 'By the way Mr. Chairman the reason this hospital can't cope is because there is no platform or mechanism by which negatives can be raised and effectively addressed.' I would be laughed out of his office.

So what could I say? 'I've realised how much we can im-prove if we could teach people in the Trust to listen to the peo-ple on the ground. They are in the ideal situation to advise on what systems will or won't work.'

But if I start spouting this phrase around the hospital I'll lose any credibility that I've managed to build up over the years. But wait! That is exactly what's happened to most of the managers.

They had Silver Bullet solutions and tackled problems by launching ambitious plans, but these plans were not complete. No matter how loudly the people on the ground grumbled about the shortcomings they couldn't find anyone of influence to listen to them. When the projects failed to deliver, the personal credi-bility of their originators was left in tatters and the ground troops laughed off yet another disaster and returned to their old ways.

There's so little respect in this place but there is no punishment for failure either. The Powers That Be must have very short memories, or perhaps they just get fired up by the next wonder scheme. Either way, the disgraced managers were often promoted after their projects had failed. I knew of at least four who were now working at Trust level having left a wake of failed projects behind them.

Suddenly, Frank's words from our 4th of July barbecue were ringing in my ears. 'They just want the title—they don't want to be a successful manager.'

Somehow this did not ring true. If they wanted to be managers so badly, surely they wanted to be successful at their jobs? But if Harry was right, it was the faults in the system that forced them to act like this because they had no chance of success, no matter how good their ideas were. The house would win every time. It was a real live crapshoot.

But to hang onto a top-flight job didn't one have to be successful? Of course, but successful at what? The day job, or the politics? Which was more important? Being good at the job and getting tangible positive results or playing the political game and learning how to dance around land mines? This would take same serious thinking time. Before I went home I decided to send one last email to Harry:

Harry and Sarah,

Thank you both for your help today. Finding the Core Problem was a really marvellous revelation. I know you suggested that I take time out but I can't stop thinking and I need just one more piece of advice.

Where do I go from here? I know what needs to be changed and I'm sure that figuring out what we need to end up with will not be too difficult to establish, but how do we get there?

I know I will need to convince others for any progress to be made but how do I do that?

I guess I really have two questions for you.

1. *How do I get the message across?*
2. *How do I make sure that it is the right message, one that they understand?*

I will find it really difficult to leave this hanging over the w/e. So if you could give me any ideas to mull over I'd be grateful.

Thanks again to you both.
Love,
Beth

I was back to waiting for my computer to ping. After running a few errands I returned to my office to close down for the day and to take a final look at my mailbox. Sure enough, there it was a response from my mentors.

Beth,

We've been extravagant and enjoyed a family business lunch!

Can't let it go can you? We don't blame you, we were the same when we first started using TOC. How about this?

First of all you are right. The Consolidated Cloud is not sufficient to relay your message to other people. Remember I told you it was a short cut to find out what the Core Problem is? Well you will have to do the Current Reality Tree before you can clearly communicate your findings to other people. Yes, this is going to be huge and this is normally a task that you would do under direct supervision, but I guess we can try to do it over the net.

Secondly, you will need to learn how to bring people along with your thinking. To do this we use a simple method to track people's buy-in. *It's called the Six Layers of resistance. I've attached a copy of them.*

Why not read these over the w/e and try to get them into your head? The tree will be a huge job, and after the week you've had, you need a break. But try to study the six layers and we will discuss them next week.

Max always said you were a swot at school. Now we believe him! That will be more than enough homework for the w/e.

Talking of Max, what does he think of your newfound management skills? Harry would love to know.

Take care and remember to relax,

Sarah & Harry

PS. The typist gets top billing when the author has had a few glasses of wine!

I grinned as I read the email. It was obvious that Sarah was completely up to speed on this TOC lark as well. I printed off the attachment and stuffed it into my bag as I said good night to the evening staff and left the hospital for the weekend. When I got to my car I turned on the radio only to hear that the city centre traffic was solid. Why rush? I took the sheet out of my bag.

The Six Layers of Resistance
0.   I don't accept your agenda...
1.   I don't agree that the problem is what you are saying it
*   is...*

2.   *I don't agree that the solution you are presenting is go-
     ing in the right direction to get us to a workable an-
     swer....*

3.   *I don't accept that the benefits you claim your solution
     will bring will actually materialise...*

4.   *I think there are possible negative side effects from your
     proposed solution...*

5.   *I don't think we can overcome the obstacles your pro-
     posed plan will encounter on the way...*

6.   *I said "yes" but I won't move—we have an abused past—
     "who the hell are you to talk to me about my area of ex-
     pertise"*

I read and re-read the list. The points made sense but why I
was not sure. I needed to try these out. If I could find a problem
and a solution to test them out on then I might understand why
they felt right.

As I sat in the car park I thought about Harry's last email.

'Talking of Max, what does he think of your new found
management skills? Harry would love to know.'

Max! I hadn't even told Max I had been in touch with
Harry. Let alone the fact Harry was coaching me.

I had been so caught up with my progress that I hadn't even
contemplated telling him what I was up to. Max would freak if
he knew I had gone to Harry for advice and not him. I had finally discovered that managers don't listen to their staff and I
hadn't even tried to listen to my husband!

Oh boy! I had a major problem and it was right under my
nose. If Harry sent an email to our home account and Max got
there first I would be branded a scarlet woman. My life would
be hell and it was all so innocent. I started the car and ploughed
into the traffic jams, my mind running riot as I sat trapped in a
queue of metal. I tried to run through all of Max's possible reactions and each one ended with his anger at me consorting with
the *enemy*? I had no choice but to tell him what was going on
and I had to be quick about it.

Chapter 14

I swear I heard my tires squealing as I hurtled into our road, but my manic driving was in vain. Max's Jag was parked on the drive. I couldn't believe it. Max was home early! He was bound to be working on the computer. I gingerly put my key in the front door wondering if I would be greeted by a frosty silence or furious insults.

It was silence, not frosty but complete. No energetic doggy welcome and no sign of Max, angry or otherwise. I looked at the coat rack and noticed the dog leads were gone and breathed a sigh of relief.

I dumped my bag in the hall and dashed through to the study. I needed to delete the email from Harry before Max got back. I skidded to a halt the moment I saw his open briefcase on the desk. He must have already seen the email! Perhaps that's why he's taken the dogs out; to fume and let off steam.

The sound of Maggie whimpering brought me out of my panic. I nipped into the kitchen and saw Maggie and Winston gazing through the conservatory windows, their backsides a blur from their vigorous tail wagging. My heart stopped as Max walked into view. He looked mad. Very mad. The scowl that was plastered across his face made John's frown look like an inane grin. I was in so much trouble.

The dogs sped in to the kitchen as Max let them in and covered me with equal amounts of affectionate love and dog hair. I wasn't expecting the same from Max.

'Darned dogs!' he ranted. 'I take them out for a special walk and they go AWOL chasing rabbits. Took me ages to get hold of them. Just what I didn't need it at the end of the day. Dammit! Everything's gone wrong. I escaped from work for some peace only for the damned PC to keep crashing. Couldn't even get a connection to the Internet, let alone email anyone.'

He paused for breath and I could have jumped on him and hugged him. With a bit of careful planning I could be in the clear.

'You poor love,' I said sympathetically. 'Sounds like you've had an Italian day. Why don't you run yourself a bath and I'll bring up a bottle and some glasses.'

Max smiled, kissed me on the cheek and went upstairs. An 'Italian day' is our slang for a monstrous, toe-curler of a day. One so bad that you don't just want a glass of wine, you want the whole bottle. This is the perfect occasion to open a bottle of Italian red because no matter how well you re-stopper the bottle, it never seems to taste as good the next day. In this case it was also the perfect distraction for me to try and erase Harry's messages.

I was just about to boot up the PC when I had a nasty thought. Harry might send more email to check on my progress. Should I tell him not to email me at home just in case Max read the messages? I would then have to explain that Max didn't know what I was up to. No matter which way I skinned the rabbit I had to tell Max before he found out about it himself. It was time to face the surgeon's knife. It was a scary thought, but at least I could ask for his help at the same time.

I had a quick read through Harry's six layers of resistance as I opened the wine. Layer 0. *I don't accept your agenda.* Poor Max was certainly going to start with that. I took a couple of gulps of wine to steady my nerves before joining him in the bathroom.

I felt a pang of desire as I handed Max his glass of wine. His broad shoulders filled the bath and his warm smile had returned to his face. I resisted the temptation to jump in the other end of the bath and plonked myself on the chair that always ends up covered with damp towels.

'So what went wrong at work today?' I asked.

'Oh nothing and everything,' Max replied, carefully taking a sip of his wine. 'One of my projects is flunking and I can't work out how to solve it.'

There was a pause as I summoned enough courage to dive in. 'I've been solving a few problems recently,' I said cautiously. 'In fact I think I might have found an answer to the difficulties I've been having at work over the past few months.'

'At last! I knew you had something on your mind. Don't tell me, you're gonna resign?' Max's face was flooded with relief. This was not a good start.

'No, Max. I'm not giving up, quite the opposite. I want to make things work. I want to be a better manager'.

'But you're constantly battling and you're getting no place,' Max argued. 'What makes you think you can do anything to improve that dinosaur?'

'Max, I need you to understand where I'm coming from on this. I need to try. I need this challenge.'

'But why Hon, we don't need the money! People will be hurling jobs at you with your skills. You know that place is using you. Why put yourself through more agony? It's just not worth it.'

'But that's where you're wrong Max. It is worth it.'

I was struggling to work out how I could explain it to him. He was so focussed on goals and success and the Health Service just bumbles along from one bad press report to the next. It was so big, how could I get Max to understand my need try to make it better?

Max exhaled a deep breath. He was moving into his exasperated teacher mode and this meant a lecture was coming.

'I've been thinking about the Health Service since the other night and I've come up with something that might help you understand the futility of your job.'

Futile eh? Is that how he saw my job, a waste of time? Thanks for the support! I was bursting to tell him about our cancer patients, about lives devastated by a system that the staff so desperately wanted to change. About their good intentions and how they differed from his money grabbing cronies who were just out to make a buck. But I knew this was like opening our bottle of wine. Once you start you have to finish and I needed him to listen to me rather than argue with me. I almost bit the edge off the wine glass and forced myself to listen.

'Beth, the Health Service is a monster. It's out of control. You know why?' He answered before I could unclench my teeth from my glass. 'Of course you don't, how could you? I'll put it as simply as I can, so you will understand.'

He was in full flood now. I could have cheerfully thrown the contents of my glass at him but decided the only thing it would achieve was turning the bath water pink. I drained my glass and poured another. I needed all the fortification I could get.

'The British Health Service is unique, well almost. There are very few centrally funded health services in the world and the Brits certainly have the biggest. It employs the highest number of university graduates of any single employer in the world. Do you get the significance of this Beth?'

This was new to me. Of course I worked with qualified staff every day. But I hadn't really thought about the size and scale of it like this. Not that I was going to admit I had over-looked this fact. 'Yes I do. The British Health Service must have the highest collective IQ of any organisation in the world. That's what you are saying aren't you?'

'Yes, Beth. Now think of this. The British Health Service is immune to the perceived laws of economics. Yeah, it ebbs and flows with the economic tides like every other organisation, but when the going gets tough it's the financial managers that get going, straight out of the door. The organisation is untouchable. Do you follow me?'

'Not really,' economics talk always bored me and Max knew he had the upper hand.

'Okay. Think of it this way. How much was your Trust overspent last year? 10, 12 million? How many organisations can operate with such huge losses?'

'But they are not losses, Max, that's what it costs to deliver the service. We all cut back as much as possible and that's what it cost us. We didn't lose that money, we really needed it.'

'That's exactly my point. Why didn't the Health Service go bust? Why was it allowed to operate with such huge losses?'

'But Max you're comparing the Health Service to a commercial organisation. It's different. We are different. We're not in business to make money, we're there to provide a service. We're there to treat more patients, better, sooner, now and in the future.' There, I said it; I'd finally managed to get a point across. How would he react?

He calmly took another sip of his wine before answering. 'You're right. That's what you're there to do, but at what cost Beth, at what cost?'

I was amazed. Max had accepted my analysis of the role of the Health Service without question. He accepted it as a given and I was too stunned to answer him.

'Beth, tell me at what cost?'

'Well, the cost has to be measured in terms of patients not money.'

'In an ideal world I would agree with you. But this is not an ideal world Beth, it's pounds and dollars that count and this is where the British Health Service *is* different. For political reasons it cannot be allowed to die in its current form so it will never be allowed to go bankrupt. It would be political suicide for whichever party is in power. It survives in a bubble, in an artificial world, where the managers can play at managing without any real recriminations. Beth, it's fake, it's not real. Can't you see that?'

I felt deflated. Max was right. The Health Service was too big, too powerful. How could I expect to be able to tackle its ills? I was back to being a manager in a bubble.

Maggie chose this moment to push her way into the bathroom to join us. Winston would never enter under his own steam as he associated the room with his own bath times. Maggie was much more like her namesake, she wasn't scared of anything and Max turned his attention to stroking Maggie until I was ready to continue.

'Max, if you're right and the British Health Service employs more graduates than any other organisation in the world *and* if it cannot go bankrupt, why can't it get it right?'

'Welcome to my world Beth! These are just the problems I've been struggling with today. On paper all the elements stack up, a bright committed workforce, you've shown me that, money to do whatever needs to be done and still you come home with horror stories about patients being cancelled, about unacceptable waiting times, about an organisation in crisis. What's missing? That's what you're asking, right?'

'Yes, what do you think is missing?'

'Well, I think it's the management, not money. Oh I know you'll say if we had more money we could have more beds, more doctors, more nurses, new equipment. But that's not the answer Beth. You know how much Health Service funding was *not* used last year? Millions! Over 50 at the last count. And why? Because the managers could not figure out how to spend it, at least not the way it was intended to be spent.

'These pots of money were put aside for new projects and initiatives and the criteria for accessing them were not met so they just sat there.'

'But that money was impossible to access. We tried Max! We needed more beds and they wouldn't buy us any. This extra fund of money is an urban myth'.

'No it's not Beth.'

'How do you know?'

'Because I got my hands on some of it. I co-wrote a proposal with one of my clients. We agreed to match any investment pound for pound they could get from the Health Service and they got it. Believe me Beth it's not a fantasy. It's just your managers don't know how to get their hands on it. Their ideas and plans just aren't good enough.'

'So are you saying the problem lies with the management of the Health Service?'

'Absolutely. Once I looked at the figures it was obvious. Each Trust is allocated funds calculated on the size of population it has to serve. A few manage to perform to very high standards with the money they receive, but others fail. The variation in population size does not fluctuate enough from year to year for the funding figures to match the inequality of performance. In short, if some Trusts can perform on their allocation and others can't, there must be something wrong inside the organisations, otherwise there would be no winners.'

'So it must be the management, or at least how they perform. Are we agreed?'

'Completely. See you *can* understand my theories. You really are wasted in the Health Service Beth, so what were you saying earlier about finding an answer?'

He didn't miss a trick. But that made two of us. He had just confirmed that he's got past Layer Zero. We agreed that the management of the Health Service needed a serious shake-up. But the next layer would be tougher. How could I get him past 'I don't agree that the problem is what you are saying it is?' I laughed at Maggie's bedraggled ears and Winston's worried face peering round the door and with a deep breath I returned to the fray.

'Max, we seem to agree that the Health Service has problems but I'm not sure the management is solely to blame. Can I run something by you? Pick your brains?' I knew how far a little flattery would go and Max was happy to oblige, but his face still said, 'I'll keep it simple.'

'The British Health Service is over 50 years old. It's a big lumbering creature that cannot be killed, but has difficulty fending for itself. It's sick; it's not the healthy, lean organisation you're used to dealing with. Would you agree?' Max nodded.

'As such it's the biggest institution in the UK. And, as we know, institutions tend to develop their own way of operating, they have their own culture, their own ethos. This particular ethos is undoubtedly noble, providing cradle to grave healthcare free at the point of delivery, but it's failing many of it's... shall we call them clients?' Another nod. Using Max's language seemed to be helping.

'Well, this institution is so big that anyone coming to work in it takes time to adjust. That goes for the government ministers as well as us in the trenches. We need time to acclimatise to the working practices and the way the organisation reacts and performs. No one person is responsible for the paradigm of the Health Service it just is. It exists in it's own right. We all have to give in to it. Do you agree?'

'I suppose I do. I guess it's like one of those ocean going tankers that take miles to turn and even further to stop.'

'If we accept that the Health Service has a life of it's own then we must accept that the people working within it are almost powerless to change it. They can no more steer it onto a new course than a rubber dinghy can make a tanker change course.'

'Sounds reasonable.'

'Okay, so if this is the case how can we blame the managers? They're very small compared to the size of the organisation and they're forced to work a system they have very little hope of ever changing.'

'You make a good argument Beth, but you can't blame the system. In every organisation the buck has to stop somewhere. Who is the captain with his hand on the wheel? He's the guy who should be steering a better course. That's where the problem is.'

'Max, this is what everyone's been saying for years. But it hasn't worked. Think about it. How many times have I told you that a new government initiative has been launched and how many times have I told you why it won't work?'

'I've lost count and, to be honest, I stopped listening. Sorry Hon, but it gets a bit boring after a while.'

'That's exactly my point Max. If you're bored with it, just imagine how we feel. We're trying to make these unrealistic plans work.

'We are completely cornered. Do we do what our boss wants? Or what we know will work? Even though it's not what our bosses want? And why do we wrestle with this every day? Because we want to make things better, even though we know we're wasting our time. We live in hope that one day someone will actually come up with something that will work.'

'So what are you saying? The guy with his hand on the wheel doesn't know which way to turn?'

'Exactly! He relies on information being passed up the chain of command and the information he gets is conflicting. All he is doing is trying to slalom through the disasters. The boat is rocking so hard no one knows where it's supposed to be. We know where we want it to go, but getting there is making us all seasick!'

'Interesting analogy, Beth. But where does this leave you?'

'As I said, the information is being distorted as it's passing up the line. We need to listen and act at a much lower level. As managers we need to make better use of the knowledge our staff have locked away in their heads, we need to manage better. This is what I'm trying to do.'

'Sounds admirable, but how the hell are you going to attempt it?'

My heart skipped a beat. Was that an acceptance of my understanding of the problem? I needed to check.

'Do you understand what I am saying Max? I believe that the closer to the problem the staff are, the better understanding they have of it, and therefore they should know how to put it right. Providing their solutions can be polished and are practical, their theories should work much more effectively than the vague instructions we get from the top. I want to release and use the intuition of my staff to achieve the targets I am charged with.' A thought hit me at the same time it hit Max.

'Does this mean you would refuse to participate in projects you feel have no value?'

It was time to commit. 'Yes, if necessary.'

'You really have been working on this haven't you? But I don't get where all this is coming from. Where have you picked it up from?'

I took a big gulp of wine. I was now in deep water, much deeper than the warm, soothing water in Max's bath.

'This is what I was coming to. Now, Max, promise me you won't get mad?' He nodded slowly.

'I've been in contact with Harry. It was unintentional. I emailed Josh to ask what he wanted for his birthday and Harry replied to my email. I'd mentioned having a bad business day, an Italian day, and he wrote back asking what was wrong and things kind of snowballed from there.'

'Harry!' Max exclaimed sitting up in the bath and sending water slopping over the edge. 'What the hell does he know about the Health Service?'

The combined effect of Max's shouting and the water was too much even for Maggie and she shot out of the room. I was tempted to follow her.

'Nothing,' I replied as calmly as I could. 'That's what I'm trying to tell you. You know this management method he's using? Well he's been guiding me through some exercises this week and I've learned more about the Health Service in one week than I have in my whole career. It works Max and I'm sure I *can* make a difference.'

Max stared at his wrinkled toes in silence. 'Do you mind leaving?' He said quietly. 'I want to get out now.'

I was just about to try and reason with him but I saw the cold look in his eyes and left him to it. With hindsight the bathroom was a bad venue for such an important discussion. I had blown Max's trust in me and he was hurt and confused. It didn't help if he was naked and vulnerable as well. I pulled the layers of resistance list out of my bag and checked it. Layer 2. I was presenting the solution and Max was not with me. The real issue was how far away he was from me. I dried Maggie's ears and waited for the inevitable row.

When Max finally came downstairs the coldness in his eyes had taken on arctic proportions. 'So you've been exchanging email with my brother all week and you haven't told me,' he said bitterly. 'Was that what your little speech at the barbecue was all about, pumping me for information? And tonight, pretending you wanted my input when all you really wanted was my blessing for you to work with Harry?'

'That's not true and you know it!' I shouted. 'You're just getting paranoid.'

'Paranoid?' Max laughed coldly. 'So why didn't you just tell me? Why did you have to play this game? You don't want my input at all. You just want his wacky theories. Well, if you're crazy enough to fall for his brand of management then be my guest, but don't expect me to pick up the pieces'.

'Max, you are wrong!' I objected. 'Yes I want you to be alright with this, but I need your input as much as Harry's.' I took a deep breath and tried to calm down. 'You've really helped me tonight. I have learned so much about the financial side of the Health Service, I would never have worked that out on my own. Won't you help me with this? I really need to solve this and I need your help.'

'Beth, you know how I feel about this TOC thing. It works in a factory. Harry has proved that, but beyond that environment it's just another fad. He got lucky that's all. In the real world it's the money people who drive the ship. Not the bleeding heart liberals who think the world can be put to rights by talking and understanding. Don't get sucked in Beth. It won't work.'

'But if the moneymen can't make the health service work, and you agreed that it can be made to work. Who else can do it? The top managers? They've failed, so the only other option is the people on the ground. People like my staff and me. There's nowhere else to go. I need this Max and I need you to support me.'

Max looked at me with contempt and picked up the dog leads he had left in the conservatory.

'Where are you going?' I asked. 'You've already taken the dogs out tonight.'

'Perhaps this time they'll catch the damned rabbit,' Max snarled as he stormed out taking two ecstatic dogs who couldn't believe their luck. 'And by the way, I'll be sleeping in the spare room tonight.'

'Well the bed needs changing and you can bloody do that yourself!' I shouted after him but he didn't even break his stride.

Chapter 15

Monday morning approached with the speed of an arthritic sloth. The house was laden with tension despite the fact that Max escaped from the house for most of the weekend. Max is able to out-sulk even the most hormonally charged teenager, but this time it was different. On the few occasions that our paths crossed he repeatedly refused to discuss the issue and simply radiated the self-righteousness of a monk. I just couldn't get out of the house fast enough and as I sped my way into work I even savoured the fact that Max was disappearing on a work trip to Paris later that morning.

As I screeched into the car park I tried to lower my stress levels so I wouldn't enter the office spitting fury at the staff. I reminded myself that Max's extra golf practise over the week-end had left me plenty of time to work on my UDE's. Even storm clouds have silver linings, it's just a shame they soak you in anger and guilt.

When I got to my office I saw a large brown envelope lurking on my desk bearing my name in Eddy's infantile scrawl. It was too thick for his resignation so I decided to delay opening it after I had taken the temperature and fixed my face.

At this time of year the schools were beginning to start their summer vacations. This leads to a downturn in throughput at the hospital as the surgeons took time off to be with their families. As I suspected our elective surgery list was reduced by about 25 per cent but the Emergency Department was still heaving with patients. The resulting temperature was minus 59.

In a way this was worse than last week. At least we could cancel elective surgery, but with more patients coming through the ED, this Monday would be tougher than last week. I gritted my teeth as I packed away my cosmetics and prepared to open Eddy's envelope. The top page was typed in Eddy's poorly scripted form of English:

TO THE ADMISSIONS MANAGER
FROM THE CLINICAL BED MANAGEMENT TEAM
SUNDAY 8th JULY

FIND ENC. REWRITTEN PROTOCOLS FOR THE
ADMISSIONS DEPARTMENT AS INSTRUCTED BY
TESSA PRINGLE, NURSE IN CHARGE OF THE CBMS.

Bzzzzzzzzzzz! Was it only a week ago that I blurted out to Fearsome Fran that I 'did not understand?' I seemed to have travelled so far since then, but the words on the envelope told me I was still on the starting line. I winced as I flicked through the rehashed copies of my original protocols. My fists clenched tightly onto the offending documents as I heard the door open. If Eddy had entered the office at that moment the bed temperature would have been increased by one, and he would have needed an intensive care bed. Luckily it was Sally.

'Hiya Beth, nice weekend?' She asked with a smile.

'Not particularly' I snapped, glaring at her over my rewritten protocols. Sal's smile froze and she calmly turned on her heel and took up her place at the bed board.

Shit! 'I'm sorry Sal,' I called out to her. 'I've just had some bad news. I'll be with you in a while. The board is straight but I suspect that 23 and 15 are holding some beds back. Can you see what you can find out?' Sal just nodded, smiled and slipped on the headphones.

I took a deep breath and prepared myself for the worst. It was a deep breath well spent. I opened the protocol file on my PC to discover that Eddy had changed all my documents without saving the originals. The idiot hadn't even changed the issue dates! I summoned up the courage to check my email and was relieved to find there was nothing in the Inbox, but the Sent Mail box was full of trouble. The revised Admissions protocol folder had been sent to everyone in the new CBM team. Or at least I assume that's who the recipients were; I had not been informed of the complete team yet.

Could he have done any more damage? Could he do anymore? I flipped through the pages of doom and quickly assessed the damage. It soon became obvious what he had done. He had added Tessa's name and her email address to every protocol where it was required that a figure or information be reported to me. At least he hadn't removed my name completely. It was time to unleash my storm cloud.

I opened my office door still clutching the amended protocols and looked around for Eddy. I saw him trotting up the corridor and deciding to catch him off guard I burst through the doors to confront him in the corridor. However, he obviously didn't notice my expression as he still managed to get the first word in.

'Hi Beth, the weekend was really good,' he yapped. 'I showed Tessa and the team all of our systems and they picked them up straight away, no problems, we got all but two patients in and this week will be quieter so we should be ahead of the game and...' Eventually he noticed my fiery expression and paused for breath.

'Eddy, what the hell have you done?' I shouted loud enough for most of the floor to hear let alone the people now gathering in the department. Eddy's expression changed completely.

'I, I, I...did what you told me,' he stammered. In the few seconds it took him to respond to my outburst he moved from deflation to belligerence.

'I did what you told me to! I showed them the systems then amended the protocols to include them in the system. It's what you told me to do!'

'That is not what I told you to do,' I snarled walking towards him. 'I told you to *tell* them about the systems. Not to change anything!'

Eddy was starting to back away, but I continued to walk into his personal space. 'Not to revise our protocols, not to send *unauthorised* revisions around to all and sundry,' I continued as Eddy retreated down the corridor. 'Not to work on my computer, *not* to ruin *my* protocol file. *Not* to use my email account.'

My words were now white hot with anger and I realised I was almost whispering. Eddy's eyes were bulging as he continued to retreat and he was staring at me so intently that he didn't see the porter pushing the large oxygen cylinder across the corridor. He backed into it and tumbled gracelessly to the floor, his big flappy feet smacking against the wall.

I desperately wanted to laugh but I was too ashamed. There was me trying to solve the problems of the Health Service and I was practically assaulting my staff. I helped Eddy to his feet; assured the porter that it wasn't his fault and quickly led Eddy outside. He was rubbing the back of his head; he must have taken quite a blow. It had certainly stunned him into silence.

We ended up in Smoker's Corner, a small garden wedged between two towering buildings complete with a distasteful sprinkling of cigarette butts and a lonely bench. Eddy lit himself a cigarette and pulled deeply on it making the tip glow bright red.

I was disgusted with myself. I had snapped at Sally for no reason a few days after asking why she didn't feel able to make suggestions to me. Now I had humiliated Eddy when according to my theories I should be asking for his input. It was time to make amends, and hell it was going to be difficult.

'I'm really sorry Eddy,' I said sincerely. 'I shouldn't have lost my temper, it was unprofessional. I've…' There was no way I was going to admit to Eddy that I was having marital problems, even if I was responsible for sending him arse over tip in the corridor. 'I think we need to start again.'

Eddy was staring at me as he sucked hard again on his cigarette. I couldn't tell if he was going to fight or cry.

'We don't get on very well,' I continued, 'and this may be due to a personality clash or the difficult situations our work puts us in. I am hoping that with a bit of effort we can resolve both of these issues.

Eddy crossed his free arm across his chest, he was still in defensive mode but this could easily change into attack. I had to be careful so I motioned Eddy to sit beside me on the bench.

'Eddy. How many projects have you seen come and go in our department?'

'A few.' He was reluctant to talk, for once.

'How many last month?'

'Three or four.'

'And the month before that?'

'About the same.'

'Alright, so we agree that our department is often used to launch new projects, yes?'

'Yes, but...'

'Not yet, Eddy. How many of them have worked?' I could see he was regaining some confidence.

'Umm, the new discharge system wasn't a complete failure and the ...'

I cut him short. 'Wait. What are we trying to do?'

'What do you mean? We are trying to run an efficient department.'

'No Eddy. Not just us, not just our department. All of us. What are we trying to do?' Harry's list of the Six Layers of Resistance kept running through my mind. I had to get Eddy to agree to my agenda.

'What are you talking about?' He said as he blew out another lungful of smoke.

'Alright, let's start at the beginning.' I decided to keep it simple. 'We're just a small cog in a big machine. The hospital is a big machine. What does the machine do?'

'Treat's patients.'

'Good. So what are we trying to do?'

'Umm, get a better rating from the Government?'

'No, simpler than that? To get a better rating on performance we need to do what?'

'Treat more patients—make the waiting lists and times shorter.'

'Right! Now, we know we want to treat patients quicker, but how many do we want to treat?'

'Anyone who needs treatment.'

'Right again. So is that less or more patients than we treat now?'

'More of course! There will always be more than we can treat.'

'Good. Now do we want the standard of our services to slip just so we can treat more patients?'

'No, of course not.'

'So do you agree that we need to treat more patients, better and sooner?'

'Of course.'

'Alright, we are nearly there, Eddy. If we find ways to treat more patients, better and sooner, do we want these brilliant ideas to be just a passing phase or do we want to keep making the systems better?'

'Keep making them better of course, what a daft question!'

'Is it Eddy? Let's recap. We want to treat more patients, better, sooner now and in the future. Yes?'

'Yes. So what's your point?'

The magic yes! He agrees with the goal of the Health Service. Layer Zero achieved. We are on the launch pad!

'The point, Eddy, is this. All the projects we have participated in over the years have not achieved this goal so what do we do about it?'

'But this might work!'

'Yes it might, but you agree that things are getting worse not better, don't you?'

'Yes they are, which is why we have to act fast. We have to do something now!'

'And by doing something now you mean changing the protocols?'

'Yes, we've got to move fast'

'That is where you're going wrong Eddy. We have to take it slower. We have to do it right this time. We have to do it different. Last week you said that we will finally get the clinical input we need to help us make decisions. You may remember that we've had this before when the Exec of the Day project was launched and where did that get us? Be honest Eddy, how much better did that make the system?'

'Not much. The doc's stopped shouting at us and shouted at the Exec of the day, but it didn't get any more patients in.'

'So, what's going to be different with this project? How is it going to help us get more patients in?'

'The CBM's should find more empty beds. That should help.'

'Should? Eddy I want to make sure that they do. I don't want to work with *ifs*, *buts* and *maybes* anymore. I want guarantees. Don't you?'

'Yes, but what has this got to do with the protocols? I don't see the connection.'

Layer One. He agrees that these projects are too flimsy, too weak to work. Now onto Layer Two... I need to present the solution...

'The connection Eddy is that by speeding into new schemes we are letting people try out their own half baked ideas. Ideas that we know will not work. The CBM's don't even know how the system works as they only saw a small part of it in their previous roles as ward managers. We are in the fortunate position of being able to see most of it, and this is what we have to teach them. How can they improve a system they don't understand?'

'Okay, if I'm getting you right you're saying that before they can see if their ideas will work, they have to find out how *we* work. Then examine whether their ideas will fit or if things can be changed to fit. Is that right?'

'Kind of. Look it's like a triangle. First of all they need to know what has to change. Once they know how we work we have to figure out what the ideal situation would be, or what we should change to. Do you follow? The final side of the triangle is that we all need to know how to change. Does that make sense?'

'Yeah, I guess so.'

Layer two home and dry. He's accepting that we are going in the right direction. Now for layer three...'So do you see why I was so mad at you for changing the protocols without authorisation?'

'Umm, we missed a step. We went straight from what to change, to how to change. We missed the bit in between. What to change to. We just bent the old system to fit.'

'Exactly. Who is to say that the system won't change beyond recognition? And you have sent out revised protocols that may only last a week or two. What does that remind you of?'

'All of the projects we've been involved in over the years!' There was a glimmer of understanding in Eddy's eyes.

'Right. But this time I want to do it right. I hope the whole department wants to do it right. This time we have to take our time and really make a difference!'

'Okay, but if we do take this one a bit slower and get a clear picture of where we're going before we decide how to get there, what guarantees can you give that we can do it? That we can find a way to really make things better?'

'That's where we all have to work together Eddy.' This was really going to stick in my throat but I had to say it. 'This is where I need your input Eddy, and not just yours, Sal's, the new Bed Managers, everyone's. We have to devise a clear, practical workable plan. But we have to do it together. We must work as a team. Before we try anything we have to make sure that the people who will be working the system think it will work. Even more than that, we have to get them to agree that it will work. I don't want to launch yet another doomed project. It's got to be tough, robust. Do you follow me?'

'Yeah Beth I do. But why didn't you tell me this last week? I'm not stupid! If you'd told me this last week I wouldn't have changed the protocols.'

Eureka!

'So, are you saying that if you'd known you would be getting a say in what changes were going to be made, you would not have gone against my instructions?'

'Umm, not so much that, but I would have told the CBM's that they had to learn the system before they started to make changes. I would have told them why they had to learn it.'

So this was it. Eddy had been forced into a compromising position and changing the protocols was his get out.

'Uh-huh, tell me what happened.'

'Umm, Tessa was okay on Saturday. She just sat, observed and asked questions. But yesterday, Sunday, another Bed Manager was on, do you know Jane? The one who used to run Day Surgery? Umm, she kept on and on about the power of information and how she would not tolerate Admissions being 'precious' about keeping information to ourselves. She was insisting the Bed Managers should be 'fully appraised' of the bed situation at all times and that we should not do anything without their knowledge. I just thought including them in the information loop would keep them off our backs a bit, that's all.'

'And was Tessa aware of this change in policy?'

'I guess not. But it got Jane off my back.'

'Alright Eddy, now we have to do some damage limitation. I understand why you did what you did and it wasn't your fault. You were under pressure. Jane had no right to push you to do something that had not been agreed between Tessa and myself and I will make sure Tessa is aware of this. But in future, if you feel this pressurised again, call me. You aren't paid enough to take that amount of flack. I am. Remember that won't you?'

'Okay Beth. I will now I understand where you're coming from. But do you really think you can make this work? Do you really think we can make a difference?'

He was in Layer Three! He wasn't able to accept my claims that I could find the solution. Truth be told neither did I yet, but for once we were on the same page. Boy, this was a weird feeling. I still didn't trust him but we had made a start.

We completed our surreal alfresco meeting by agreeing that I should email the recipients of the rogue email asking them to ignore it. The plan was to tell them it was only a draft document. We hoped that would work, after all, who has time to read a 30-page attachment if they are told it is not relevant?

Chapter 16

I just about made it on time to the Monday morning catastrophe meeting, but I was too late to grab a seat, let alone my favoured position at the back of the room. As I snuck in, I was relieved to see that Fearsome Fran was not chairing the meeting today. I certainly didn't need another confrontation so soon after my bust up with Eddy. I leant back against the wall, locked my knees and prepared myself for some more bad news.

However, the moment the depressing discussions started my brain unhinged itself and took itself for a walk through the recent events. I relived Eddy falling over the gas canister in slow motion, his shocked expression etched on my brain.

I couldn't believe I'd got myself into that situation; I had all but assaulted him! But who would have believed that Eddy's unfortunate trip would put him on my side for once? I was sure this would only last a couple of days, but I desperately needed some allies. I was at war with both my boss and my husband and I still had enough patients needing beds to fill an extra hospital wing.

I tried to tune back into the meeting but my brain kept escaping from the choreographed, yet muted hysteria of the meeting to TOC theories and Max's sulking. My mental health seemed to be on a mission to book itself into the Emergency Department, it was time to try and slow things down, to find a little perspective.

I wanted to placate Max, but his self-centred stubbornness just kept putting me on the attack. I know I betrayed his trust, but it takes two to have a screaming match and he was not interested in how, or why, my work with Harry had turned my business life around.

I was brought back to the meeting by a sudden outburst between the Max Fax and Trauma teams who were practically clawing each other to reserve a bed for their patients. I wanted to crawl quietly away. I didn't have time to listen to these fire fighters squabbling over who gets to hold the hose, even if they were fighting for such good causes.

It felt like I was having a secret affair, an opportunity to step out of real life to enjoy the pleasures reserved for those who cheat the status quo. Yet the steps of TOC seemed so logical, perhaps you needed to bunk off life to accept them?

Suddenly, the spat was put on hold and everyone was looking at me, waiting for my report. I wanted to scream that we shouldn't be arguing over individual beds, but working on solving the inherent problems of the system. However, I knew that wouldn't help the poor patients desperately waiting by their phones. I presented the report as normal and it brought the typical Pavlovian responses from my colleagues.

I was struck by the way the room was filled with finely honed presentations conducted in stilted *lawyer-speak*. My colleagues had obviously been watching too many law television programmes. A man from the Urology Team leapt to his feet.

'We have a patient who is already travelling all the way from Plymouth for surgery,' he declared, his arms crossed defiantly. 'He is having a minor op, but we simply cannot cancel him, he has been waiting far too long and has made numerous arrangements. He can only have his operation at the beginning of the summer because he is a college professor and needs the summer to recover.'

I half expected him to blurt out, 'I rest my case!' as he took his seat, but he simply resolved to finger pointing as he was drawn into a frantic discussion with the Max Fax team. As the arguments crashed around the room I was reminded of the TOC work I had struggled over during the weekend.

My colleagues were debating how to schedule the treatment based on the patient's postal address, whilst also considering their social circumstances. One of the pages in my briefcase was headed *Private Treatment vs. Health Service* and I could predict exactly the outcome of this patient irrespective of what was said in the meeting.

The patient would have been sent a letter telling him to phone the hospital before leaving home to check whether a bed was available. I would have bet Maggie's whiskers that he had left home to travel over 100 miles without making the phone call—a fair distance for a wasted trip.

All admission letters told the patients they would be admitted in the morning when, in fact, we wouldn't know if we would have any empty beds until well after midday. For more than a year I have been asking the medical teams and the Duty Execs to change the letters to match the reality of the situation. Unfortunately my pleas had the opposite effect.

Some months ago I resorted to sending an email to all of the teams showing the standard letters we sent out on behalf of each department. I was trying to persuade them to improve their letters, but I had not considered the impact of the teams analysing each other's letter templates. They discovered that the various departments requested their patients to come in at different times. The teams who had previously asked their patients to arrive later on the day of admission decided that this later arrival was causing the cancellation of so many of their patients. Through twisted logic they concluded that their patients would get a bed if they came in earlier!

This type of Health Service logic is known in Admissions as *magic*. I was gobsmacked when the teams informed me of their intent to attempt to admit all of their patients in the mornings. I felt like curtsying and saying, 'Your wish is my command master.' There was absolutely no thought as to how this particular brand of magic would work and I was stonewalled whenever I tried to discuss possible solutions. The people with the authority to change the system simply brushed me off with comments like, 'That's not my concern, just do it Beth.' I was firmly stuck in a lose-lose situation with absolutely nothing up my sleeves.

The meeting dragged on and I was horrified to feel my head twitching as the Orthopaedic team gave an extended rendition of their patient histories. How could I nod off when these patients were in such pain? The answer was simple, far too much detail. So why were we being drowned in data when getting hold this type of information is usually more difficult than pulling teeth from a tetchy alligator? It was madness.

If I thought it was madness, how were the new Clinical Bed Management team faring? I scanned the room and spotted Tessa and Jane the ex-manager of Day Surgery who had twisted Eddy's arm over the weekend. Tessa looked as though she was having as much difficulty following this meeting as the previous one in Admissions last week. Jane was whispering in her ear and showing her some notes, but Tessa swatted her away like a fly as she tried to follow the proceedings.

Tessa and her team were currently stuck at the bottom of the Admissions learning curve. As previous Ward Managers they had to manage people, information and systems, but all their functions had been defined and agreed upon eons ago.

Take one patient with an inflamed appendix; keep the patient nil by mouth until theatre, post-op treatment ABC. With enough protocols in place to detect signs of infection, this end of the Health Service was system driven, plain and simple. But Tessa was now facing the challenge of making decisions without protocols and political decision-making was a whole new experience. I was fascinated to see how she coped.

I couldn't detect any other new faces so perhaps Tessa had taken my advice to find out how things worked before launching radical changes. I certainly hoped so, but I wasn't in the mood to challenge her about it. As the meeting finally finished I took advantage of my latecomer's position to nip out of the door and escape to the relative safety of my department.

I completed the journey back to Admissions in record time and blasted through the doors to find Eddy and Sal in the middle of a discussion. They almost jumped apart when they saw me, so I guessed they were discussing my crabby behaviour this morning. I smiled to myself, I couldn't blame them for that, I left for the weekend relatively normal and returned fuming like Cruella DeVil.

'Hi Eddie, Sal,' I said rather breathlessly after my exertions. 'Before we get stuck into the rest of the day I would like to apologise for being so short with you earlier. It's not fair of me to take my problems out on you and I'll do my best not to do it again.'

Sal just smiled at me as she retook her position at the bed board and Eddy? Well, his expressions are often hard to read, but I think he was going for nonchalance. He may just have been suppressing a persistent fart; it was hard to tell.

I escaped into my bubble to revisit the reality of a Monday morning. My bleep had 12 numbers crying for my attention and I had suddenly gained about 30 new email messages. I checked on Eddy and Sal, but they looked in control out there so I lifted the receiver and started on my bleep list.

I was just finishing my last phone call when I was distracted by a very loud, self-important voice booming through the department. I was surprised to see that it came from a short, aloof man with an excessively neat beard. Thankfully the visitors can't just walk into the department, we have a small reception area that opens through a hatch into a waiting area. All the noise was coming from someone who was actually standing in a different room.

'I tell you, I am booked in for an operation today,' he boomed, fixing Eddy with a haughty stare.

'I'm sorry sir, but you should have phoned us this morning to check that the bed was available,' Eddy replied, he was on automatic pilot; he could have this conversation in his sleep.

'So I have been told young man,' the man continued, 'but I have travelled over 100 miles to be here. Perhaps you would be so kind as to tell me how I was supposed to check whether my bed was ready at six am? Because that was the time I had to leave to make my arranged appointment. I did indeed call, but I was greeted by an answer phone message. As far as I was aware, it did not inform me that my bed was unavailable.'

A simpering woman with unfeasibly blonde hair had attached herself to his shoulder and she started to giggle and glance down at him in adoration. I quickly finished my phone call and groaned.

'I'm sorry sir, but we will not know if there will be a bed for you until after lunch,' Eddy continued, word perfect with the script.

'But I have an appointment! I have been waiting for months for this operation. I have to have it now, otherwise I will have insufficient time to recuperate.'

'I'm sorry sir but these things are beyond our control,' Eddy continued. 'We...

The man drew himself up to his full five feet and two inches and rather foolishly attempted to look down his nose at Eddy, an impossible feat considering that gangly Eddy was a full foot taller than him. 'Do you know who I am?' He demanded.

I knew who he was. He was the professor they were discussing at today's meeting. I wondered if he would be so pompous if he knew he was fighting for a bed with patients with broken limbs, poor souls with excruciating Crohn's disease and cancer patients.

I closed the door and tried to return to my work. I knew this professor would eventually wear Eddy down into explaining the system to him. Yes, ideally we should have a bed, but the patients in the Emergency Department take priority and the flow of incoming patients is as unpredictable as the weather. There would be no way of knowing his chances of admission until the doctors finished their ward rounds and declared all the discharges.

This would keep him quiet for a while, but during his hours of anxious waiting he would work out that the doctors were the real owners of this ludicrous system. So he would be tempted to try and bypass this inept administration system by speaking to a doctor. Eddy would stall him and persuade him that the best course of action was to leave the doctors to continue with their ward rounds, so they could discharge patients and empty some beds.

I heard Eddy running through this very conversation and I tried to divert my concentration to my email. By the time I had noted down my ridiculously long to-do list the department was relatively quiet again. Eddy had performed his calming role, but we all knew it was only a matter of time before the patient returned.

In fact he returned sooner than most. He was obviously not used to being kept waiting. He was also no stranger to bullying tactics, after being unable to intimidate Eddy he made a blatant attack on Sal.

'This is quite ridiculous,' he bellowed as he waved his Admissions letter. 'It says quite clearly on this letter that I will be operated on today so either you find me a bed or I will have to speak to your superiors.' Sal didn't flinch, but then again she didn't make any effort to pander to him.

'I'm sorry sir, but as my colleague has already explained, we will not know whether there is a bed for you until the doctors have completed their rounds.'

'This is just not good enough,' the professor complained. 'I demand to see your superior, it is my right. After all I pay a ridiculous amount of taxes to fund this dump.' His wife nodded her head proudly at his outburst. They were going to fight this together.

I saw Sal glance towards me and noticed that Eddy was advancing on the whinging professor with a look of blatant menace. I decided to jump in; after all I owed them both after my outbursts earlier in the day.

'Excuse me sir,' I said, all smiles and politeness. 'I am the manager of Admissions, can I help you?' He looked at me with doubtful scorn, taking in my polyester uniform and the tiny office I appeared from. Eventually he decided that I was worth being rude to.

'I have a complaint to make,' he boomed.

'You had better come into my office,' I said and let him into the department and showed him into my office, clearing my visitor's chair so he could sit down. He strutted behind me following the lead of his impressive beer belly. He resembled a squat bullfrog, a resemblance that probably explained the volume of his voice. His adoring wife who struggled to carry his heavy overnight bag followed him closely.

He tried the same speeches he had used on my staff and I gave him the same responses. Suddenly he lowered his voice and leaned towards me. I knew what was coming next.

'I can pay, you know,' he whispered 'pay for a bed.'

Discussing the concept of paying for beds is a common tactic at this time and it all depends on the wealth of the patient. Those who cannot afford to pay for private treatment start to assume that private patients were being given priority. Occasionally this frustration would boil over into accusations that we were admitting private patients ahead of them.

I looked at the professor and paused and he wrongly assumed I was considering the offer.

'Money is not a problem, just find me a bed.'

'I am sorry sir, but there are no beds.'

'No beds!' He exclaimed. 'There must be beds! How can a hospital operate without a buffer stock of beds?'

If only he knew how close to the edge we operate, but I will not allow my staff to pass on this information. If a major incident did occur, such as a large transportation accident, we would identify pre-operative patients and send them home to make way for casualties. Then the doctors would trawl the wards to identify anyone that could possibly go home to free more beds. We would press other hospitals to take postoperative patients, even private hospitals and nursing homes, anywhere. Thank goodness we have not had to resort to this, at least, not during my time.

I politely stonewalled him, watching as his threats turned to desperation and self-pity. I wish patients wouldn't take their anger out on my staff, but I do understand their frustrations. As I showed the defeated man out of my office I hoped I wouldn't be telling him in a few hours that his operation had been cancelled. It is always my job to cancel patients face to face. My staff are not paid enough to take that sort of grief.

I have all the responsibility for the system when it fails, but no authority to change it to stop it failing in the first place. I sat back and flicked through the morning's events to see if there were any other links with my homework from the weekend. I was immediately struck by the prolonged speech from the Orthopaedic team, it was such an unhelpful tactic, but they must have thought they were gaining something from it. Perhaps they were just showing off?

'We know our patients better than you know yours so you have no right to meddle with them.' Or perhaps they were constructing a smoke screen designed to blind those powerful enough to take their precious beds away? Put up enough obstacles and hopefully the duty Exec, or now the CBM's, will leave them alone.

I had learned through bitter, not to mention boring, experience that the trick with those meetings was to spot the gems among the detritus, those rare *light bulb* moments when someone reveals a preciously guarded piece of information—the one-liner that completed a small part of your personal managerial jigsaw.

Newcomers to this game stood out like a bloody nose. They scribbled notes like crazy and were the first to ask questions. Their naivety made the old hands smile and offer tarnished pearls of advice at the inevitable post meeting mêlée. The length of time a newcomer withstands these mobile lectures is a measure of how much of a threat they will be to the current members. In fact many people seemed to spend so much time measuring this threat that I often wondered how they managed to get anything constructive done.

My thoughts crossed over to my homework and I grabbed a note from my briefcase. Titled, *Information as a Weapon.* I had scribbled it down after Max had been around long enough on the weekend to throw a petulant fit. It left me wondering why he was so opposed to me learning something new. Who was he to decide what theories I could learn?

If I separated the issue of Harry, I could not find a relevant reason for Max's attitude. It was not as if I'd had an affair with his brother, he just passed on some business advice. Was Max's childishness just another example of information hogging? I was used to it in the Health Service and after my recent soul searching I was painfully aware that I wasn't guilt-free either. But why?

I had withheld information from Eddy last week and that certainly caused its share of problems. Luckily I was able to right the wrong and limit the damage reasonably easily, but what happens when the effect of information hogging surfaces in another time and place, away from the originator?

I bit the end of my pen as I concentrated. I knew I was a victim of this situation. The failed projects that Eddy and I discussed before the meeting were perfect examples. Leaving aside the failure to properly plan many new projects I could attribute many project failures to lack of information. Why? What was so precious about information that it was being held back?

I winced as I bit through the end of my pen and tasted the bitter ink, but I scribbled down my conclusion before my thought process was broken.

Information is power and in large organisations power is equivalent to currency. We all protect our information until we need to throw an opening bet on the table. Not too much, just enough to catch the eye of the person holding this month's project budget.

If they wanted more they would have to entice you to show your hand. However, we only did this when the rewards were big enough, if they made it worthwhile. A slight increase for the departmental budget, an extra member of staff, maybe even promotion. Then there was the example of today's orthopaedic team, the reward of retaining beds, which in today's Health Service were the most valuable possession of all.

I checked my face in my compact and wiped off the traces of ink that clashed with my lipstick. This was turning out to be an interesting day.

Chapter 17

My day suddenly became even more *interesting* when my computer pinged and I was looking at an email from Jane, Tessa's eager terrier.

To: Beth Seager; Tessa Pringle; Fran Whitcombe; Joan Norman
From: Jane Graham; Eddy Garcia
Subject: Processes and Procedures for the CBM's

Dear all,
Over the weekend I worked my first shift as a CBM and am pleased to be able to report that considerable progress has been made to bring the Admissions reporting processes and procedure in line with the objectives of the new team.

A revised copy of the department's policies should be in your in-box and I encourage you to check the changes made, which I am confident will go a long way towards breaking the stranglehold that currently restricts the information we currently receive.

I will forward other revisions and upgrades as we achieve them.
Jane

'Oh, shit!' I said out loud as I flopped back into my chair holding my head in frustration.

Where are you now Harry? I've got a stonking great fire to put out and I've already doused it once. So much for, 'Hola Real Management!'

I stopped my brain whirring and forced myself to calm down and evaluate the situation. Jane was accusing my department of hogging information, the very thing that led to my recent mini eureka. I looked at my notes again. She was right! Then again she was also wrong, very wrong.

Was Jane assuming that I was withholding information for some sort of Machiavellian reason? For a power kick? Perhaps she thought this was the disease that was causing the current ills of the hospital? It seemed a harsh assumption, but why else would she go for the jugular of the department?

Over the weekend I had planned to take a few days to compose my list of questions for the CBM's from my Admission's staff meeting. Now it was imperative that I quashed this before Jane caused an infection of her own. At least I had sent out my email rectifying Eddy's mistakes several hours before Jane's mail hit the circulation.

I sat back and tried to imagine how I would react to receiving the three email. I would have left the original amendments to read later and then ignored them after reading the second mail. However, Jane's mail would have raised my curiosity enough to go back and check the amendments. I slapped the table in frustration. My only hope was that the recipients had sent the revised protocols to the delete bin before their curiosity was aroused by Jane's message? But how many would have done that? Perhaps half? Hmm…maybe.

Alright, so the situation was bad, but it would be worse if Jane's mail was directly contradicting my mail rectifying the amendments. I re-read Jane's mail. The wording suggested she hadn't read my mail so this was not a full-scale conflict. Well, not yet anyway. But the moment Jane realises I have trashed the revisions she will use it as confirmation that Admissions are information hoggers of the highest order. She may even accuse me of being obstructive and insubordinate.

The key to this particular puzzle had to be speed, but my response has to allow everyone to have a get out, a way to rationalise their actions. I took a deep breath and started on my response. Information hogger eh? Well get a load of this!'

Dear All,

As you are all aware the launch of the Clinical Bed Management Team took place two days ago.

In line with the agreement made between my department and Tessa, Eddy took time to inform the CBM's on duty how the Admissions department operates.

Those of the CBM's who have yet to spend time with us can expect the same level of attention from my staff as they become orientated with the finer workings of the department over the coming days and weeks.

I know that we are all keen to start making improvements to the operational procedures surrounding hospital Admissions and to this end Tessa and I have devised an outline of a plan on how to achieve this.

The first step is to ensure that all of the staff involved has a clear understanding of how the processes operate now before we start devising changes to the system. I anticipate that this process should not take too long and have already started compiling ideas and suggestions from my own staff on the areas that need scrutinising.....

That last sentence gave me, what my Grandmother would have called, a funny turn. Just re-reading it made my stomach flop around uncomfortably.

I knew it wasn't true, I had a whole list of reasons why the process wouldn't work, but I had to stay ahead of the game and declare my department's willingness to participate. Otherwise I would lose all control over the changes that were destined to happen. I saved the half written letter as a draft and took out the list I had sent to Harry:

1. *There won't be enough managers to look after the project*
2. *The project will not last*
3. *There will be no more beds*
4. *Bed allocation will be taken away from Admissions*
5. *CBM's will be slower than Admissions*
6. *Wards will still hide beds*
7. *ED patients will wait longer for beds*
8. *Admissions Operational policies will have to change*
9. *I might lose control of my department*

Nothing on the list had changed over the weekend, each UDE was still valid, but the reality surrounding them had shifted significantly. What had changed? It was obvious from Jane's message that the CBM's needed to justify their existence. By claiming to own the information, the CBM's gained the perception that they are in control of my department. However, I knew better. They would only confuse matters and start the *try this till it fails* style of management. Just the thing I was so desperate to avoid.

I had to find a way to prevent this happening. But how? It was like the riddle of a locked room with a murdered body inside. I needed to find the key to unlock the mystery.

I took out my cloud from last week. It had helped me make so much progress last week; perhaps it could help me locate the key. As I puzzled over the *becauses* I had the nagging feeling that I was missing a vital clue.

The CBM's need to learn how Admissions works because:
The CBM's don't know how large the department is

The CBM's don't know how to disseminate information to my staff
The CBM's don't know how much our jobs overlap and are interchangeable
My staff don't realise how valuable they are
We have to react quickly, fairly and decisively
We are part of a very complex system
We all want to do a good job
We don't want to lose our status as an effective department
Changes must be in the interests of the patients
Personal politics must not interfere with patient's interests

Something was definitely missing. I thought back to that Admissions meeting. Harry said that a UDE was something that made you feel uncomfortable, an action or situation that did not feel right. So what else had not felt right at the meeting?

Bingo! The one thing that I struggled to stop myself blurting out loud, our system already works!

'We operate within a very complex system to meet the needs of the patients and the demands of the medics. To achieve this we have numerous systems that have been tried and tested over the years.'

Oh how I wanted to add 'that work' at the end. Tact forced me to hold held back from aggravating Tessa by not claiming that my department is already a success. Operating at 98 per cent capacity was a huge success to anyone's reckoning. This is the only thing my department have to hang onto when things got tough. We knew we couldn't do any more to help the patients. This is how Sal manages to remain so calm. She doesn't feel she should question the system; she takes the baton in the morning and runs like hell all day until she passes it on at the end of the day. We do our best; it was the others who would have to change.

When is a UDE not a UDE? Is being too successful an undesirable effect? It was time to check with Harry. I saved the partially written email and returned to my inbox to find a message from Harry already waiting for me.

hi beth,
got a strange message from max yesterday. he asked me how much work i had done with HMO's and when did healthcare become a production line.
strange. can you throw some light on this?
H

Oh, oh! It was time to face up to my tutor.

Hi Harry,
Confession time. Things moved so fast last week and Max was away on business that it was the weekend before I finally got around to telling him that we were working together. He was not impressed. Max still has this idea that TOC is just for manufacturing and not for health management organisations. He's still smarting from our last visit to you. You tried to dislodge so many of his sacred icons, yet you continued to be successful so he has had a hard time rationalising your success. I think you bruised Max's ego when you tried to teach Big Brother how to make money!

When I told him that I was using TOC to try to improve my own management skills he went off the deep end. It soured our weekend but I suspect it may have improved his golf handicap...I'm not sure how to deal with him at the moment. You know how he can sulk. I'll probably just let him ride it out but any advice you can give would be useful.

On to work. Can I ask a stupid question? When is a UDE not a UDE? Or to put it in English - If something is a success can it be an undesirable effect?
Take care,
Beth

I turned my attention back to my day job until the computer pinged some thirty minutes later.

beth,
so sorry to hear max is upset. i have a confession to make as
well. i remember your visit well and realise that i made a huge
mistake with max. remember the 6 layers of resistance? my
mistake was thinking that max would not suffer from them be-
cause we are brothers. i suppose i just wanted to show off to my
'hero' that I had made good as well. i didn't use TOC to explain
to max what I had done, i just assumed he would be so pleased
with my success that he would instantly buy into the way i work.

big mistake on my part. its strange because just yesterday
sarah was talking about the bridges i need to build with max
during our holiday. i swear she is psychic!
i know he'll take it the wrong way if i try to do this by email so i
promise to use the holiday to try to patch things up. i just hope
you guys manage to survive until then and, beth, if you want to
drop this just let me know.

now on to your question. first of all there is no such thing as a
stupid question, just stupid answers. if you don't know some-
thing that you need how can a question be stupid?

the one thing that TOC does is make people realise that there
are things they don't know. i think that this is its real strength.
after all, how do any of us know that we don't know things?
once we realise where the holes are in our knowledge we can
really begin to move forward.

so, in answer to your question, yes, a UDE can be a success.
particularly if this success is blocking improvement in other ar-
eas.

*I have also attached something that will help you summarise
your findings. We call it the five focussing steps, have a go at
them when you have the time!*

hope this helps.

*if i don't speak to you again please take care and remember,
what we do during the day is only a job. they can be replaced;
spouses are tougher to find...*
H

I must have read that email a dozen times. Harry was right.
He'd taken Max straight to layer 4 or 5 and had expected him to
applaud Harry's success, which according to Max's financial
sensibilities had been founded on quicksand. No wonder he was
annoyed. He was scared that his kid brother was heading for a
fall. Typical Max, ten steps ahead of the game and jumping to
conclusions. I realised that I would have to work on him before
Harry and Sarah's holiday. I had to get him to talk to *me* first
though! I shrugged and turned my attention to Harry's answer to
my 'not so stupid' question.

A UDE can be a success if it is stopping progress. I could
almost hear the klunk-click as the puzzle fell into place and I
added the tenth UDE to my list.

1. *There won't be enough managers to look after the project*
2. *The project will not last*
3. *There will be no more beds*
4. *Bed allocation will be taken away from Admissions*
5. *CBM's will be slower than Admissions*
6. *Wards will still hide beds*
7. *ED patients will wait longer for beds*
8. *Admissions Operational policies will have to change*
9. *I might lose control of my department*
10. *We already operate at 98 per cent capacity*

Then I dived into my email and added:

Dear All,

As you are all aware the launch of the Clinical Bed Management Team took place two days ago.

In line with the agreement made between my department and Tessa, Eddy took time to inform the CBM's on duty how the Admissions department operates.

Those of the CBM's who have yet to spend time with us can expect the same level of attention from my staff as they become orientated with the finer workings of the department over the coming days and weeks.

I know that we are all keen to start making improvements to the operational procedures surrounding hospital Admissions and to this end Tessa and I have devised an outline plan on how to achieve this.

The first step is to ensure that all of the staff involved have a clear understanding of how the processes operate now, before we start devising changes to the system. I anticipate that this process should not take too long and have already started compiling ideas and suggestions from my own staff on the areas that need scrutinising.

I am sure that everyone involved in bed management is acutely aware of the problems our patients suffer from each and every day and that the hospital is already running at 98% bed capacity. In order to improve on this Tessa and I have agreed that it is imperative that the level of service we currently offer must not suffer and to this end we will be working together to ensure that any changes we make are for the better.

Once all of those involved in the improvement programme are familiar with the current system I hope that we will start to pool our resources to devise solutions.

Regards,

Beth Seager

I sat back and surveyed my handwork. It justified my move to trash the revisions and asserted my authority over the department. It also bypassed Jane's maverick attitude and gave Tessa a reason for shelving her actions, if she chose to do so.

It felt right. No gut wrenches here and I could defend my actions in both composing the message and sending it to everyone involved in the project. I hit the send button and it was off. Chasing the other thousands of messages that sped around the hospital each day.

I glanced at the clock and was shocked to discover it was after three. Lunchtime had arrived, failed to divert my attention, and sulked away to hide. After flip-flopping around responding to my instincts, my stomach was now shouting for food. I left my bubble and quickly checked on my staff and was amused to see them all reading my email.

Eddy looked up as I left but it wasn't until I was approaching the coffee shop that I realised he had passed on a compliment. 'Nice one boss.'

Short yes, but fatteningly sweet after our recent troubles. I beamed at the coffee shop assistant. I had dug my way out of a difficult situation and Evil Eddy had complimented me. Things were looking up.

Chapter 18

My stomach was complaining again just half an hour later. I was too late to grab a sandwich; all the coffee shop could offer me was a cold pasty. The combination cold pasty, meat and potato, had agitated my stomach so much that I was forced to rummage through my less than organised handbag to find some antacid tablets.

My grumbling stomach aside, the day had calmed down nicely and the whole administration side of the hospital seemed to be releasing a huge sigh of relief. We even managed to find a bed for our arrogant academic. The morning's fires had been extinguished, or deferred to the next day, and we knew how many beds we had for the ED patients. There were never enough, but nothing more could be done.

The only department still suffering the indignity of passing on bad news to patients was the Emergency Department and their staff are so adept at dishing out bad news that it was second nature to them. It was this time of day that we roving managers returned to our foxholes to retrench for tomorrow's battle and to catch up on the day's events. I had just located my antacids when the phone rang.

'Hello Beth, it's Joan. I've just read your email. You've done it again!'

'Eh?' I said, struggling to free a tablet.

'You've corralled the CBM's for me again. I was worried they would try to overrun your department. When I saw the policy revisions I thought they had succeeded.'

'Oh, that. Yes I had a bit of a barney with Eddy this morning. He'd given in to Jane's demands over the weekend, but the poor guy had been bullied into it. I had a long chat with him this morning and I'm sure it won't happen again.'

'Well, you've certainly set the tone for this project. I have been discussing it with Fran we have agreed to back you up and make sure that the CBM's include your department in the plans for the project.'

Fran backing me up! This TOC is starting to work bloody miracles! 'Thanks Joan,' I said keeping as calm as possible. 'I was a bit concerned that we would not be kept in the loop. Can you give me any hints on what they plan to do?'

'I would if I could Beth. Do you remember the chat we had about finding models from other Trusts? Well they have short-listed a few, but they are still deciding which one to go for. I would really appreciate your feedback and I must say, Fran is surprised at your level of co-operation. She was grilling me to find out if I had been working on you. I didn't tell her it was the other way around!'

I laughed. 'Thanks for sticking up for me with Fran, Joan. We aren't on the best of terms at the moment. Who knows? I might be able to remove myself from her hit list. Thanks again and see you soon.'

I was so surprised and happy that I felt like jigging around the room. This stuff was dynamite! I had befriended Eddy, re-gained some control over both my department and the dreaded new project and Fearsome Fran was actually sticking up for me. What a day!

The computer pinged as if it was trying to gatecrash my private celebration. It was an email from Sarah entitled, *The curse of the old clunker!* What a perfect time to be sent a joke.

Dearest Beth,

Harry told me that you have both been making confessions and that you are in the doghouse with Max. Well, it's now time for my confession. First though, I should warn you that TOC can be both a blessing and a curse. It can solve so many problems, but if it's not used properly it can cause just as many personal problems. Just remember the old saying – No-one likes a smar-tie-pants!

Before Harry discovered the wonders of TOC our marriage was entering rocky waters. He worked such long days that I hardly saw him, hell you know all this, but there was a definite crunch point—a vacation. I stupidly thought that a long weekend in the great outdoors would give us some quality time. Huh! Poor Harry was loathe to leave work and was in a terrible hurry to get to our hotel so he could, wait for it, check his email!

We were travelling with our friends from the next block as Josh is buddies with their two boys who are a couple of years older than him. We made a three car convoy, us Seagers minus Josh in front in Harry's Jag, followed by our friends in their flashy new car (I've no idea what it was, but it was blue and real shiny!), with the sons following behind in a beat up old Honda Civic. Of course, Harry sped off and our friends struggled to keep up with us, the boys fell way back as their old clunker struggled whenever there was a steep hill.

I started to get worried when the kids disappeared from sight, so we stopped and waited and eventually they re-appeared in a puff of exhaust fumes, all grins with the adventure they were having. We set off again but the same thing happened, we were getting nowhere fast.

Harry wanted to know why their car was so slow and opened the trunk to find it full of fishing tackle and beer! Not popular! Anyhow, Harry transferred it to the Jag and we set off again, this time with the kids in the middle so our friends could make sure they hadn't got into difficulties.

However, it still wasn't working as our friends were worried about getting lost and kept calling Harry on his cell phone asking him to wait for them. Harry was real pissed! He stopped

*and waited and made all the kids except the driver get out of the
old clunker and squeeze into the other cars. Then he made the
poor kid drive the banger first with the rest of us behind until
we reached our destination.*

*The strange thing was that Harry went silent once we tried this
final strategy, (apart from when he was giving the kid directions
over his cell phone that is!). Even though we spent the rest of
the journey clouded in noxious fumes. You see it had solved his
major problem at work....*

My giggles stopped as I devoured the rest of the email and I
realised why Sarah had sent it to me. Cogs started whirring in
my brain and they didn't stop until after the panic meeting the
next day. Then the nerves set in. I had a theory, a mad, insane
theory, but it was solid. Very solid and boy was it going to be
unpopular!

I sped through my daily tasks after the panic meeting finished. I was on fire. My staff were looking at me with bemusement and were visibly relieved when I told them I would be out
of the office for a while. I reminded them to bleep me if anything cropped up before I almost sprinted out of the door. I was
surprised to see Eddy bounding along behind me.

'I take it you mean that you want to know if the CBM's try
to change anything?' he whispered, brimming with conspiracy.

'That's right Eddy. Just do what we do best and let me know
if they try to change anything.'

'Okay, boss. I understand. I'll clue Sal in, see you later.'

Eddy was loving this. For the first time in years he was be-
having himself. It would take time for me to become comfortable with this newfound enthusiasm. After all, I was expecting
his loyalties to change at any given moment, but for now it was
working and it was a mighty good feeling.

My heart was playing an intricate percussion in my chest as
I zoomed down the corridor. I was risking a new and valued
friendship here and all because of a smoky old banger. I knew

from the recent panic meetings that John Summers' operating list had been halved for the morning. Barring emergencies he should be coming out of theatre very soon.

I arrived breathless and hot at the security door of the operating suite just as the porters were wheeling a semi conscious patient through the large double doors. I held one door open for them and we exchanged pleasantries. Just like us they are doing a difficult job and we always swap a bit of banter when our paths cross.

Once inside the suite I checked the whiteboard to find out what John's schedule was for the morning. There it was, just one operation and the porters had already wheeled out today's lucky winner. John should be emerging soon. I collapsed onto one of the chairs by the administrator's desk and waited for him. Ten long minutes later John put his hand on my shoulder.

'Hi there stranger, when did they let you out?' He asked with a waspish grin.

'Morning, John,' I smiled. 'I hope you don't mind, but I checked your schedule and thought that you might be able to spare me a few minutes.'

'A few minutes? Ach, my operating schedule has been butchered and I'll do anything to avoid catching up with paperwork. Hell I can give you the rest of the morning if you can use it.'

'Yes please John. I've come across something that may really help us, but I need a consultant's perspective. I'll take as much time as I can get.'

'Sounds interesting Beth, much more interesting than being bullied by Marge. By the way how has my bullish secretary been treating your staff recently? I had a word with her, but I suspect it missed her ears completely.'

'No complaints so far. But you never know with Marge, she's probably chewing somebody else out. Where shall we go?'

'Well, my office is out of bounds. The Marge dragon doth lurk there. How about the medical library? Finals are over so it should not be infested with students.'

'Sounds good.' As we started to walk off I noticed that John appeared to be limping. 'Are you alright John?' I asked. John laughed. 'Ach, not you as well. I had a slight surfing accident.'

He looked so sheepish that I had to probe further. 'Go on.'

'I was having a go at windsurfing,' he said with a mischievous smile.

'Doesn't sound too dangerous, what happened?'

'Ach, I was surfing at the same time, I was attempting to surf on a windsurfer. I had what the youngsters call an "awesome wipe-out".'

I just couldn't help laughing at the thought of John being pulled out of the water by a crowd of young, trendy surfers and I didn't stop until we reached the library. The quad in the middle of the library block was deserted and an enormous tree shaded an empty bench. We decided it was an excellent spot and John started to tell me about his work with Harry.

'He's quite a taskmaster your brother-in-law. I have not been getting to bed until well past midnight; my social life has gone out of the window.'

'Not you as well! This work is really getting to me, but now I'm in the middle of it I can't stop. I'm even starting to feel more energised on less sleep. I suppose it's because I now feel there are answers out there. We just need to find them'.

'You are obviously a few steps ahead of me Beth. I'm up to my eyeballs in entities and bananas. Makes a change from entrails and biopsies I suppose. But what are these answers you are talking about?'

'Well, I want to tell you a story and need you to tell me if I'm on the right track.'

'No problem, fire away.'

'I haven't had time to script this so bear with me if I ramble a bit. Right, you know we've just had a new Clinical Bed Management Team thrust upon us?'

'Yes, we discussed it at the last directorate meeting and I must admit I was surprised at the level of support they got from my colleagues. Pulling senior nurses away from key operational areas just doesn't feel right to me. What do you think?'

'The very same. I will work with anyone if they can improve the system, but surely depleting senior nursing staff from the wards goes against Trust policy? We're always hearing about the trouble we have recruiting and retaining good ward staff and then they take them from the wards.

'Anyway, I should get back to the point. My gripe is that the nurses have very little management training. I'm not saying that nurses make bad managers, they manage their wards well, it's just that managing well-established procedures is very different to devising new ones. Especially ones with far reaching effects throughout the hospital.'

'So is this your revelation?' John asked quizzically. 'Nurses won't make good policy setters?'

'No this is just the beginning. I've been using TOC for just over a week now and I think I have the CBM's where I need them. I've been working on my Current Reality Tree or CRT, whatever Harry calls it, as well and as long as I stay focussed on what I think the core problem is, I reckon I can train them as we go along.'

'You've found your core problem? Ach, what is it? Tell me!' John was all eyebrows and eagerness.

I laughed. 'Sorry, John, I've promised Harry not to reveal this until you've found yours. I understand you are working on the Surgeon's dilemma, is that right?'

'Yes, but I am progressing so damn slowly. I just wish Harry was here and not on the end of an email. My typing is so slow. Surely it would be easier if he passes on more advice? All this cloak and dagger rigmarole is stretching my patience.'

'I'm with you there John,' I replied with a laugh. 'But I've been thinking about how we hold on to information a lot in the last few days and I know Harry must have a good reason for not giving us the whole picture. After all, it would make life much easier for him just to drown us in theory.'

'Fair enough,' John conceded reluctantly. 'I'll accept Harry's advice, but if you know your core problem, you should be on the home stretch.'

'I wish! I've found the core problem and I'm working on it like mad, but the CBM's are gunning to find quick answers. I'm petrified they will launch half-baked ideas that will just create more work and send us off in the wrong direction.

'Let me explain. I've got a really silly story to tell you. It's something that inspired Harry when he was trying to sort out the problems in his manufacturing plant.'

'I always said this place was a glorified factory, go on, I'm intrigued.'

I started to explain about the mismatched convoy and John chortled as I described Harry's frustration building up to boiling point.

'So he has reduced the banger's load even more and put it at the front of the convoy,' I concluded. 'This way they all travelled a bit slower but at least no-one gets lost and there's no need for time wasting catch up stops.'

'Yes, but I don't see how this relates to the hospital.'

'Well, the old banger was the weakest link and as you know a chain is only…'As strong as the weakest link,' finished John. He was just starting to get impatient.

'Exactly. Now, I've found my core problem and it relates to the way Harry managed his convoy, but his problem was trying to find the constraint and breaking it so he could achieve his goal of reaching the hotel in time to deal with his business issues'.

The Prof suddenly perked up. 'So, let me check this. You have figured out how to get people to do what you need them to do, but you are not sure what you want them to do. Am I right?'

'In essence yes, but I'm sure the answer's in the story. Look, this hospital is running at 98 per cent capacity! We've got no more slack, but we desperately need to find some. We need to lighten the old banger's load so we can move patients through more quickly. Does that make sense?'

'Perfect sense. But what is your concern?'

'My concern is that the CBM's will not recognise the banger. They will play with different parts of the system and leave the banger still struggling as much as he was before.'

'Ach, I get the impression you have identified the old banger of this hospital. Am I right?'

'Yeah, but...' This was the bit I was nervous about; luckily John sensed my reluctance and encouraged me to name the culprit.

'Come on Beth you are among friends, or at least one. It is impossible to offend me after all the work I've done with Harry. I keep upsetting myself by realising how I contribute to our current despicable system. Let me have it.'

'Alright, but let me do this my way. No short cuts.' 'You are the boss,' John grinned.

'Before the bed crisis, each of the consultants had their own wards. You would visit them first thing in the morning and do your ward rounds. By 11:00 we knew exactly how many patients you would be discharging for the day. We could then plan to use those beds and our job was practically completed by midday. Sure we would still have to cancel some patients, but nowhere near the numbers we do now.

'Then we hit the *winter pressures*. We threw patients anywhere to get them out of the Emergency Department. Medical patients ended up on surgical wards, trauma on urology and you know the rest. 'Tell me John what had happened to your ward rounds?'

John's eyebrows beetled together as he considered his answer. 'Ach... since last winter I have to split it. Do some in the morning and the rest in the afternoon. On some days I can't make the afternoon rounds so I let my team take the strain.'

'Why is that John?'

'You know the answer Beth. This place is so big that just the effort of physically getting to all the wards to see my patients is like walking a marathon. It takes too much time. We have to split them.'

'And what happens when your juniors see the patients instead of you?'

'For the most part they are fine. When they are foxed by a tough case they ask me to see them the next day, so I adjust my round accordingly.'

'But what would have happened if you had seen those tougher cases the day before?'

John's face lit up, 'Goddamn it! They would have started my prescribed treatment sooner! Beth, have you any idea of the numbers involved here?'

'No John, but my hunch is that our discharge times should improve dramatically if we reduce the time it takes for the senior doctors to do their rounds. It works in the ED. Admissions fall significantly if a consultant is on. If it works at that end of the process it must be the same throughout. Do you agree?'

'So, I'm a bloody old banger! I've been called many vulgar things in my time Beth but never an old banger!'

'I'm sorry to whack you with this bad news John, but this is where I need your input. If the Consultants are the old bangers and the ward rounds are your boot full of beer, how can we lighten the load?'

'The answer is obvious Beth! Bring our patients back to a single location so it is easier to monitor them, just like we used to.'

'I'm glad you said that John, that's exactly what I wanted to hear.'

'Well, let's bloody do it then! You told me you can track all the outliers on your bed board, all we need to do is juggle them about.'

'That's easier said that done. From your point of view it's simple, but the porters and nursing staff will tell you that moving a patient involves a lot of work. Work they just don't have the time and resources to take on. Their attitude is "they are in a bed, let them think themselves lucky!"'

'But if we can speed up the process it has to be worth investing in more staff!'

'Exactly, but where will the money come from?'

'Ach, you are right. How about keeping the patients in the ED until the right bed comes up?'

'Tried that John, we hit so many 12 and 24 hour trolley waits that we were told to put them in any bed, just to get the Department of Health off our backs.'

'Right. Another tack. Cancel elective admissions for a week and take time repatriating the patients. If what you say is true, and I've no doubt that it is, we should make up the time in a matter of weeks.'

'Sounds better, but there are still obstacles John. It would work for surgery, but the medics have so few elective patients these days that their emergency admissions would take any beds that you free up.'

'But you said yourself that ED admissions fall if there is a Consultant on duty!' John urged, standing up in his excitement. 'We should insist that the heads of the magicians work in the ED and suspend elective surgery for a week. That should do it!'

I laughed at his enthusiasm; this was what kept my brain whirring most of the night. 'I agree, that was the same conclusion I came to, but how do we do this? Can you imagine the uproar if the Surgeons told the Medical Consultants they have to work in the ED? And can you see the Board suspending surgical electives when the DOH is breathing down their necks to increase throughput? Then there's the indignation of the patients and their relatives when we start wheeling them all round the hospital. No John, I'm sure it's the solution, but how the hell can we make it work?'

John sat down again wearing his finest frown. 'I see what you are saying Beth and as always you are right. So how do we achieve this miracle?'

'Sorry to disappoint you, John, but I haven't got that far yet. I only started working this up last night and I was just looking for validation on what seemed like a pretty wacky midnight idea.'

'Ach, I'm not disappointed, Beth, far from it. I think there might be a light at the end of the tunnel and hopefully it's not an express train. As you said it's early days, let's both work on it and get together again and discuss it. Are you going to the EPR demonstration on Thursday?'

'Yes, I managed to snag one of the last places.'

'Excellent, here's a deal for you. You keep thinking about how to implement this project and I'll finish off my CRT. We'll talk again on Thursday and see what we can come up with. In the meantime keep the CBM's in check and if you need any support call me. I'll back any decision you make. Between us we can stop them from doing anything too drastic until we can devise something that will actually work. Deal?'

'Deal.'

'I'd better start my afternoon ward round. Good talking to you Beth, as always. Keep up the good work. Stay well.'

In a flash John was gone, his brain already digesting what he had just heard and despite his limp he seemed to have a spring in his step. He left me feeling stunned. It worked. John bought it. This was moving fast, perhaps too fast, but this was just what I wanted. There was no way I could stop now.

Chapter 19

I was still fired up when I returned to my office and after sorting out a few immediate issues I returned to answering Harry's last email.

Dear Harry,
Thanks for your email. Your take on the Max situation seems to be right on target. I used the 6 layers with him when I started explaining the work we have been doing together. I had him right with me until I mentioned your name. So I know that taking him through the layers worked. It was only when we hit another layer zero—working with you—that he got annoyed. I don't think I can do too much about that, as it will make Max think I'm taking sides, so that will be your holiday task, if you feel up to it.

I don't want to stop doing this; in fact I don't think I could stop. But I will tread carefully with Max on this topic until your visit…!

Back to work: I've identified our old banger and maybe a way to speed him up. Unfortunately, there's more than one of them, but I have been using those five focusing steps you sent earlier. I've been focusing on Identify, Exploit, Subordinate, Elevate and Repeat and they really helped! Let me know what you think.

Identify: *Our old bangers are our consultants. They carry a huge load. Over the last few years the system has loaded them down so much that we couldn't even see what effect the load was having on the rest of the hospital—until now!*

Exploit:

Being a teaching hospital the junior doctors need the support of their superiors to get the patients through the system as quickly as possible. This support is in the form of access to the senior colleagues to make decisions, e.g. making changes in treatment regimes. The less time they have with senior doctors, the longer the patients will be occupying our finite resource of beds. We are already at 98 per cent capacity; so without changes in the way the senior doctor's work we cannot exploit them any more. This is the next thing we have to do.

Subordinate:

To subordinate the rest of the system, thus lightening the consultant's load, is going to be the tough part, but John and I are going to work on it together. We need to make sure that every other system in the hospital is ready to react to the instructions of the senior doctors. We have ideas but they are very rough at the moment and will take a lot of polishing. We have to make sure the rest of the hospital recognises that the consultant's time is the most precious resource we have and everything else has to fall into line behind them.

Harry, a little note here for clarity. I don't know if it is the same in the States but here the consultants are often referred to as God or the Boss. They have built a reputation over the years as being dictators. The really astonishing thing is that we need them to fulfil this dictator role. If they speak, the rest of the place should jump. It used to be like this but we managed our way out of a system that worked—at least we did here! But this time we need to make the consultants a little more user friendly.

Elevate: *If John and I can get a good enough plan to-gether we should be able to make sure that this particular old banger's habit does not remain our constraint for long. We need to devise a way to keep a close eye on the consultant's work pat-terns and make sure that they are not forced to slip back into old routines.*

Repeat: *If we can do this, I have no doubt that the con-sultants will not be the old banger for long. Finding and dealing with the next constraint should be simple after this one—if we make it!*

Have I interpreted this correctly? It feels as though I have, but I'd value your view. I do have one worry. You've been telling me that for an analysis to be right it should apply to the whole Health System. I'm not sure this does. I'm giving myself mixed messages. Help!
Take care,
Beth

Harry's response was cryptic.

beth,
*you know the **core problem** of the health service. there is no platform or mechanism by which negatives can be raised and addressed. this, from what you are saying, is the sickness that the whole health service is suffering from.*

the way the system has been forced to work, because of this problem, and the effect it has on the consultant's time is the constraint your particular hospital is suffering from. other hospitals will be suffering from the same core problem but their constraints will be different.

don't confuse the two, or take your eye off either of them.

your interpretation of the 5 steps is more than good enough for this stage of the game but keep refining them.
write soon!
H

Hmm, I was starting to agree with John's frustrations about Harry's coaching methods. I wanted answers and I needed them now! My grumblings were stopped by the shrill ring of the telephone. Seconds later I was in full fire fighting mode and it took me most of the afternoon to take control of the flames. It was no good; I couldn't cope with running the department as well as planning how to solve the problems of the entire Health Service! I was having trouble shaking off the feeling that dealing with the minutiae of hospital life was all a huge waste of time. Especially after discovering that the only way we could hope of improving the situation was to work on the old banger.

I looked out into the department at Eddy who was shooing the girls out of the door as he followed my orders to ensure no other little sparks could set off the next inferno. Could I trust him? I shuddered. I had very little choice. I leant out of the door.

'Eddy, can you spare me a few minutes?'

'Sure Beth. What do you want?'

I decided this was an ideal opportunity to apply the five focusing steps to me so I slotted myself into them. I also cleared the visitor's seat for Eddy. The look of surprise on his face was comically evident.

'Do you want me to close the door?' He asked.

'No, it's alright, this won't take long.'

Eddy's look of surprise faded, he was obviously hoping for a conspiratorial briefing on how we were going to out manoeuvre the CBM's. I decided to have a bit of fun with him and started to use military slang to keep his interest.

'Eddy, I have to prepare the next stage of the operation. To do this is I need to offload some of my duties to free up time to work on it. How would you feel about representing the department as my lieutenant at the 11:00 meetings this week?'

'On my own?'

'Yes, can I trust you to do it?'

Eddy sat to attention, 'Of, course you can.' I would not have been surprised if he had snapped off a salute in his eagerness.

'Now, remember Eddy, stick to the current rules. Do not bend, amend or alter them in any way. The CBM's are still in the learning phase and we cannot afford for them to start a counter offensive before we are ready. And report back to me after the meeting. Nothing fancy, just a brief summary, enough to keep me up to speed, and to pass on your perception of the CBM's understanding of the system. Can you do this?'

'You bet. Report the bed situation at 1100 hours; report back to you on the Bed Sit along with a reconnaissance on the CBM's position on the learning curve. You've got it boss.'

I smiled, his eagerness was catching. 'Alright, Eddy, no heroics, remember, this is a covert operation and if anyone asks I'm busy working on a request for some stats from the surgical consultants. That should keep them at arm's length. I'll also be diverting the general enquiries to you and Sal, as much as I can, including a few of my email, alright?'

'Good thinking. I'll make sure they leave you alone. Umm, one last thing though, do you want my help with *The Plan*?'

I had not reckoned on this level of support from Eddy and my first reaction was to dismiss his offer of help, but I checked myself when I remembered the core problem. Once I had devised a plan I would have to present it to the team so they had the opportunity to raise their negatives. To use one of Fran's many clichés, I must walk the talk.

'Not at this stage Eddy, but as soon as I have it roughed out we'll get together, okay?'

'Great! Go get em!'

Eddy's support was unnerving and comical at the same time. I was still dubious of his long-term loyalty, but what were a few missed meetings compared to trying to sort out the problems they had been struggling with for years?

I had identified that time was my personal constraint so to exploit it better I had to offload some of my tasks. If I subordinated the rest of my duties to devising the plan I should be able to release enough time to work on the plan during work hours. This prevented me taking it home and annoying Max. After evaluating the value of my time, both at work and home I decided it was time for me to start building bridges, especially as Max returned from Paris that night.

I knew Max's trip had gone badly the moment I saw him. He was settled in an armchair staring blankly at the news on the TV. He didn't even notice my arrival despite the usual ruckus from the dogs and he only looked round after I had been looking worriedly at him for several seconds.

'Hi Hon,' he said without much enthusiasm. 'Look, I know we have a lot to talk about, but I don't think I can face it right now. Can we take a time out for a few days?'He looked up at me with the same sort of expression the dogs use when they think they are going to miss out on a walk.

'That's fine with me,' I said graciously as I tried to cover my relief. 'Can I just say one thing before we lay it to a temporary rest?'

'Oh Hon! Please don't! I have had such a terrible trip, I really can't face anymore stress.'

'I'm not going to cause any stress,' I said, determined to at least soothe one factor of the argument. 'Just let me say it and I'll get us some dinner and we can curl up on the sofa in front of the TV.'

'Oh man that sounds good,' Max sighed.

'Well?'

'Okay Hon, do your worst.'

'All I want to say is that my acceptance of Harry's kind offer to help was in no way meant to cause any offence, nor does it mean that I do not want your advice. In fact I'm going to need to pick your brains a lot over the next few weeks.'

'But...' Max faltered, he really looked exhausted and was obviously in no state to have an argument. He looked at me and smiled. 'Fancy a bottle of Italian with our meal?'

I smiled. Max's deft side step may have deferred our problems to a later date, but we had made the first hesitant steps towards reconciliation. I knew the following steps would be harder, I had never seen Max looking so stressed about work. I presumed it was just a combination of fatigue and a bad flight home. We needed to take a breather to make sure we made it through Round Two without a knockout blow.

Chapter 20

I thought things were going too well. Eddy was doing well with his extra responsibilities and Max and I were enjoying our truce. Now I found myself yawning through the first presentation of the EPR demonstrations that was as useful as a split colostomy bag. When it finally finished I joined the mad dash to leap on the coffee and doughnuts and bumped into John and his particularly unimpressed eyebrows.

'Ach, this is horseshit, it's a total waste of my time.'

'I know what you mean John,' I could be fighting for a bed for that poor thyroid patient. What's the next presentation?'

John consulted the thick agenda, 'Inventory tracking; a paperless system.' We've got more chance of finding a whole ward of empty beds back at the Infirmary than finding anything of use here. I think I will just sit at the back and polish up my logic tree.'

'Have you finished it then?' I asked.

'Just about,' he grinned. 'I can't seem to leave it alone though. Anyway you should know what it is like. I've emailed it to you. Haven't you read it yet?'

'No John. I've got it but haven't opened it.'

'Ach, too busy eh?'

I took a deep breath. I found it hard to put John in his place. 'No, John. Remember the instructions from Harry? It's your work, you need to check it. There's no point me imposing my opinions on your work. I don't have your intuition for your subject. If I start making alterations it will lose its punch. You will have to present it to me.'

'But if I read it to you I'll sound like Data from Star Trek. If, then, because. I'll sound bloody stupid! Also when are we going to get the time?'

I paused. I felt like a school kid planning to skive off double maths. 'Why don't we hang back here? The next session really isn't relevant to us.'

John's bushy eyebrows beetled up to his forehead in surprise.

'You really are starting to be a bad influence on me Beth.'

Ten minutes later we had the breakout room to ourselves, not to mention a belly full of doughnuts. It was time for me to have another go at persuading John to present his ideas to me.

'Remember John, the object of this exercise is to persuade other people that you're an expert in this area,' I cajoled. 'It's the same when you teach. You're the expert. You can move around your subject smoothly. If you want people to believe that you know what you're talking about, you need to know this subject as well as you know surgery. Go on, give it a try.'

'Ach, I suppose you are right,' John murmured. 'If I think of the, the wotsits? The entities, as prompts from my lecture notes...' John paused as he tried to gather his thoughts. It was strange to see such a clever man struggling to verbalise his thoughts, but I completely understood his uncertainty. 'Dammit! Why is Harry so strict about this?' He asked.

'It's not that he is a masochist,' I grinned. 'This is the way he was taught to do it. He says it's the best way to check the logic.'

By the look of John's famous frown he was obviously unconvinced. I tried a different tack.

'Saying it out loud is very different from reading it to yourself,' I reasoned. 'How often have you experienced niggling doubts when reading a paper that discusses a novel topic? It seems to make sense on the surface and you can't place what you don't like about it. After all it could be something as simple as the style of the author's writing.

'When this happens to me I often don't have the confidence in the paper to fully support it. Then later on, perhaps in a meeting, I may be asked for an opinion, but I'm reluctant to be critical. What if it's just me not understanding the new concept? I bet you could identify what's wrong in an instant if the paper covers a specific surgical procedure. But when we're not sure of the subject we keep our heads down because we don't want to look stupid. Then bingo! Another daft project is launched.

'What we're trying to do here is tackle an area that no one appears to understand. We are trying to become the experts and if we can't fully understand the subject how can we expect anyone else to take us seriously?'

'I see what you are getting at Beth, but there are thousands of so called experts in this field, not to mention yourself, you are a manager. Why do I have to go through this rigmarole? I thought I could just give this to you and leave you to work on it.'

'Perhaps I could,' I replied with a smile, I was flattered that John assumed I would instantly be able to follow his logic. 'But I really think we should do it the way Harry suggests. After all, I want to really understand the medic's problems. How often do you consultants complain that the managers just don't understand them? Well, this is your chance to finally get at least one manager to understand. Go on give it a go.' John's frown slowly unravelled. I had used the right tactic at last.

'Okay Beth, I accept your challenge, but you may not like what I am going to say. Just in case you never want to speak to me again I will take this opportunity to stress that it's been good working with you!'

'Don't worry about offending me John,' I laughed. 'It's your turn to get your own back after I accused you of being an old banger. Do your worst.'

John grinned mischievously. 'You are right. It is payback time. If you are sitting comfortably I will begin.' His grin disappeared as his concentration kicked in. 'As doctors we have to take the Hippocratic Oath. There are two mainstays to the oath. We have to undertake to give patients the best medical treatment possible and we have to agree to give medical treatment to anyone in need. I am sure good old Hippocrates meant well when he first drafted this but it's not so simple now.'

John stopped and his frown started to return. 'I've strayed already. I'm not supposed to say that last bit yet.'

'This is why we have to read it out loud,' I reassured him. 'You have just added more clarity because you intuitively felt the listener would not make the desired connection. Don't worry about it, carry on.'

'Ach, okay. This is the easy bit. I have to fulfill my oath and to do this I must give my patients the best treatment possible. So I must give my current patients the best I have available to me. Okay so far?'

'Yes, no problem with that.'

'We should be able to determine who gets what treatment based solely on medical considerations. To achieve this we should be looking at the big picture, like your bed board and treating patients on the basis of most clinical need.'

I nodded again; this sounded just like what I wanted to hear, someone speaking with clarity at last.

'But on the other hand, to fulfil my oath I must give treatment to anyone who needs it. This means I must give the best treatment to all patients, mine and those of my colleagues.'

'The magicians you mean?'

'Not just the magicians, I should help my fellow doctors to achieve the same. But here's the rub; the cost of medical treatment keeps increasing to such an extent that the budgets are being used up too quickly. When you put these two together we are all forced to act within the budgets.'

'I completely agree. Modern day medicine meets the optimism of Hippocrates.'

'Exactly!' John beamed; he was obviously beginning to feel more comfortable with the process. 'We are increasingly being forced to compromise on medical considerations because of budget constraints. Can you see where I am coming from?'

'Yes, but this has been going on for years,' I cautioned. 'There isn't a doctor in the world who isn't caught in this dilemma; too many patients, so much treatment and too little cash to do it all. John, it's the times we live in. Come on, tell me more.'

'But, it shouldn't be like this Beth. Can you really believe that this is as good as it gets? I can't.'

My attempts to process a response to John's comments were scuppered by a rhythmic screeching sound emanating from the corridor. It was nearly matched in volume by a constant stream of rhetorical conversation. The noise got steadily louder until the source shuffled into the room.

A large metal catering trolley entered the room followed by two extremely bored looking catering staff. The first woman to enter the room was providing the commentary and she instantly reminded me of the dinner ladies from my school days. Those thickset, no-nonsense women who coasted towards retirement on a sea of 'I remember when all this was fields,' and 'a good dollop of lard never hurt anyone'.

Those dollops had taken their toll and were currently stretching the lady's uniform, but her chunky forearms suggested she could wrestle an ox. Not someone to mess with. Her colleague was the complete opposite. A sullen, silent teenager, her eyes carefully plastered with mascara and eye shadow to achieve the desperate drug addict look. The screeching stopped the moment the trolley came to rest, but the dialogue was harder to quench.

'I told 'em we'd be late clearing up,' the dinner lady prattled. 'I mean what do they expect? We can't be two places at once, now can we? We're not super heroes now are we?'

This monologue would have gone on for much longer had the narrator not turned to see us sitting in the corner.

'Oh, hello dears. Your not attending your little talk?'

'Indeed not,' John replied with a smile. 'We are having a private discussion.'

'Oh don't mind us dear,' the lady replied as she swung the trolley into position. 'We would have been here earlier, but they told us to go the long way round. Told us to pick up some dirty crockery on the way.' She pointed a stubby finger at a small pile of coffee cups on the bottom shelf of the trolley. 'Not really worth the trip if you ask me, but who am I to reason why? Eh?'

She started stacking cups and plates with the kind of volume that only real experience can achieve.

John and I exchanged glances; it would be impossible to work here. Our catering friend noticed the looks.

'I'm sorry dears, but we're going to be *working* for sometime here. Why don't you continue your *private discussion* on the benches outside? It's a lovely day, I'd sit outside if I could, but there's me stuck in here with work to do.'

We needed no further invitation. We collected our papers and tried to keep a straight face as we walked out of the room. We could hear her prattling on as we escaped down the corridor.

'Sitting inside on a day like this. These health workers don't know their arse from their elbows. Ha! Get that Sandra, don't know their arse from their elbows? I should hope they do eh? Wouldn't want them to operate on me otherwise. Isn't it funny the silly things we say? Anyway, my Harold is still on the waiting list for his hip replacement, four months it's been, criminal it is...'

Chapter 21

We couldn't control our laughter as we escaped into the fresh air. 'She was priceless!' I gasped.

'More than you know,' John grinned as we took a seat on a bench under the reach of a magnificent horse chestnut tree. 'She's just reminded me of something. A part of my work that does not seem to fit my tree, it's the bit I'm still working on.'

'Now you've intrigued me John.'

'Okay, I'll try to explain, but remember this is not part of the CRT yet, perhaps you could let me know how you think it fits?

'Sure,' I said with a smile. John was really getting into this.

'Now imagine you are walking through the hospital what do you hear?'

'People asking for directions?'

John grinned mischievously, 'I hadn't thought of that, but you're not really trying. Think of what we just heard.'

The penny dropped. 'People complaining!'

'Exactly. And how do they do this?'

'What do you mean? Just like the tea lady back there, they have a good moan.'

'Yes, you're right, but let's think of it in a different way. How many patients make official complaints compared to the number of moaners?'

'Well, there's been more official complaints recently, but I think I see where you are going with this. We had a college professor causing a rumpus the other day, but he didn't take the matter further. Almost everyone complains, but relatively few put in official complaints. Am I right?'

'You are nearly there Beth, but why do so few make an official complaint?'

'I don't know. British reserve? Not wanting to rock the boat? Although in a way I wish they would complain. It would make our lives easier if the top management got to hear more of these complaints. I know the number of complaints have increased, but that's because the Health Service have issued a press release asking people to complain if they were not happy with the service. However, we still don't get anywhere near the amount we should according to the amount of complaining I hear as people walk around the hospital.'

'My point exactly.'

'Which one?'

'Ach, we have both staff and patients complaining as they roam the corridors, yes?'

'Yes, I've overheard complaints from both.'

'Okay, let's look at the patients first. By far the majority of them cannot afford private health care so we are their only real option; they have to come to us.'

'Yeah, but...'

'So, you accept their layer zero?'

'I didn't know Harry had introduced you to the six layers!'

'Well, now you do!' John grinned. He obviously enjoyed keeping me on the hop. 'Layer one is that the patients see a problem and leap to conclusions about the source of the problem. They blame the government, health ministers, anyone in authority and they do this because they do not want to blame the people who will eventually be delivering healthcare to them.

'This is perfectly understandable. After all, they are trusting their welfare, hell, sometimes their lives, with Health Service staff, so they don't want to even think these people can be responsible for the mess the service in. Thankfully, this assumption is usually correct. Our medical staff are great and very professional when it comes to medical issues, but when it comes to management, well that's a whole other story.'

I nodded as I remembered Joan's confession about her lack of management training.

'As a result most of this public pressure is directed at the government,' John continued, 'Relatively few complaints are directed at us and when they do they tend to be related to clinical issues.

'Now on the other hand, if a patient complains to a manager, such as yourself, you have a greater understanding of the source of the problem; the system. You are able to explain the problems of the system to the patient so they leave with the impression that only really big changes in the way the service is run can prevent the problem from happening again. Am I right?'

'Unfortunately, you are John. I do this all the time, but I stand by it. I'm telling the patients the truth'.

'Ach, I'm not disputing that Beth, but do you agree this is the reality from the perspective of the patients? Very few patients lodge written official complaints because the way the Health Service staff respond to their verbal complaints leave them feeling small and powerless. And to compound this they have no choice; they cannot shop around for an alternative, so they just accept the situation. Am I right?'

'Absolutely. They are firmly stuck in layer one. They perceive that the source of the problem is at government level. However, if we are so bad at managing the service, no matter what the government does, or how much money is thrown at us, it will never get better until we manage it better. But that is the last thing the service is going to admit.'

'Yes,' John agreed, 'but there is something not quite right here. Harry has shown us how to take complaints and see them as undesirable effects, the UDE's we have built our trees from. We as managers are not doing the service any favours by defusing complaints as they come in. We are stopping the senior management from seeing what is really happening. They will never see the UDE's that we do. And to make it worse, those that do make it through to the rarefied heights of top management are used as a tool to beat the managers with. Don't you agree?'

A subdued laugh escaped from me as I realised that the whole basis of TOC, the UDE's were not even being recognised as having the value that John and I knew they have. They were the pearls that this work depended on and they were being discarded while the managers played with the oysters. I tried to formalise my thoughts.

'No wonder nothing changes. Even our current reporting structure does little to help the system. The reports that do the rounds following a formal complaint are focused on the symptom. I've yet to see one that even comes close to trying to find the root cause.'

'So you see what I mean?' John said as he returned to his notes. 'Trying to slot this into my tree has been a bloody nightmare, but it's not over yet, let me tell you what I found out about the staff, this should give you an even bigger laugh! I hope you are sitting comfortably.'

John picked out a few pages covered with the illegible scrawl that only someone who has taken the Hippocratic Oath can produce.

'Okay, we've discussed the patients, let us move on to the staff. Think back Beth, think of a recent conversation you overheard in the corridors between staff members. What did they talk about?'

'I don't really know, I tend to ignore it, it's just gossip.'

'Maybe, but let's return to our mad tea lady. What was she moaning about?'

'The fact that she was late because she had to walk the long way round.'

'Exactly. She was trying to improve things.'

'But there were so many other things she could improve! Why did it need two of them to fill a trolley? Why didn't she get someone to fix that squeaky wheel?'

John laughed. 'My thoughts exactly. Let's return to the hospital, what do they moan about there?'

'Well, there is the odd personal gripe about someone.'

'Okay, what else?'

'Well... they might ...' Finally the penny dropped. 'I'm with you John. We all want to do a good job and we should listen to our staff.'

'Pardon?'

'Sorry John, our trees have crossed that's all. You're trying to tell me that the staff are motivated to help solve problems and we should listen to them.'

'One step ahead of me as usual,' John grinned. 'I want to return to gossip, well, to be more precise, the inverse Pareto rule of hospital gossip.'

'Now you've lost me.'

'You know Pareto? The guy who recognised that 80 per cent of the wealth resides with 20 per cent of the population? In this gossip scenario we bitch and moan about a problem for 20 per cent of the conversation, while the remaining 80 per cent of the time is used to try and figure out a solution.

'There's so much goodwill in the health service Beth. Why can't we tap into this to make the systems work better? That's what I'm getting at.'

'I agree John, and I think your strange rule explains why so many people stick with the jobs they have,' I conceded. 'They're all living in hope that one day things will get better. We must be a nation of optimists.'

'Ach, don't fool yourself Beth, I haven't finished the main feature yet, but bear this in mind while I run through it.' John leafed through his papers before continuing with his tree. 'We've agreed that we doctors are being forced to go against our oath because there is not enough money to do what we want. Yes?'

'Yes.'

'By being pulled between these two poles we are forced to compromise. We are forced to act against everything we believe in, everything we signed up for. Our vital interests if you like. Without these we are lost and as scientists and professionals we need to know we are in control. It's tough.'

'But, John surely, if you feel that strongly, you will fight having to make compromises.'

'Welcome to the game Beth! That is exactly what we do. We fight like hell to maintain the standards we signed up to. So how is our goodwill gauge looking now?'

'Oops, it's taken a real dive. But where do you go from here? Tell me you have an answer.'

'Ach, don't be too optimistic Beth. Let's continue. Would you say it's true that when we are forced to act this way we become blind to the interests of others?'

'Ye-es.'

John was really getting into his presentation now. His confidence was growing, his eyebrows were becoming more animated and I realised he was beginning to use his teaching voice to encourage me.

'Okay, put it another way, how much tunnel vision do you see each day?'

'Plenty according to the Bed Board. Each team fights to get their patients in regardless of the other patients we have to accommodate.'

'Sorry Beth, but it's worse than that. Let me move on to the next bit. We all know that the budgets for health care are fixed. It's a pie that has to be divided up. If we win, someone else loses. But if we tie this with the fact that we are all becoming less and less sympathetic to the interests of our colleagues, and there is less and less compromising going on, all we can expect is increased friction between departments and units.'

'But John, management have a big say in where the money goes. Surely it's up to the units to plead their cases before management cut up the pie? If one unit submits a proposal that is weaker than another, where should the money go?'

'When did doctors have to become bloody accountants?' John snapped, his face folding instantly into an ugly frown.

I looked away towards the ornamental pond in the centre of the garden area. I had found a chink in his presentation and he didn't like it.

'Let's go for a quick stroll,' I suggested. 'That always helps me get the logic juices flowing.'

We gathered our bits together and walked down the path towards the pond. I could almost hear John's brain whirring as his face scrunched up in concentration.

'I'm sorry,' he said. 'I didn't mean to snap at you. It's the system.' As we reached the pond he took hold of the protective rail and stared at the brightly coloured fish darting around the murky waters. 'Do you remember a few years back when the consultants had their run-in with management? Single page submissions were being made for funding by the consultants, but management were refusing to accept them because they did not contain enough information to let them differentiate the varying needs of different departments.

'The Consultants thought this *less is more* tactic was a masterstroke that would force management to go along with them. Unfortunately, there wasn't enough money to go around and as management had no way of comparing the claims, they had no choice but to keep the budgets the same as the previous year. This lead to the consultants complaining to the press that the hospital management were stopping vital groundbreaking work. No one won.'

'Ah-ha! I remember that, but those of us on the shop floor never really knew what was going on. Now it makes sense, but John, you are doctors, how are you expected to produce business plans when you have so many patients?'

John's eyebrows perked up. 'Interesting that you call them business plans. They are called all sorts of other things in this profession. Why do you use that name?'

'It's my husband's influence,' I admitted. 'He's a venture capitalist, not in the truest sense. He's not squandering our life savings on risky ventures. He manages a fund that invests in projects that can't find money elsewhere. They are high-risk projects, but by picking the best he makes millions for the fund holders. He always has a fistful of business plans in his case and occasionally he asks my opinion on one, particularly if they concern medicine or health management.'

'Ach, I see. But who writes these plans?'

'Max says that the best ones are those written by the owners or the inventors themselves. These show their passion for their project, or so he says, but an accountant almost always countersigns the financials. Just to show they are realistic expectations of the business.'

'I thought so,' John mused. 'We don't have that luxury. We have to write and submit all our own business plans and we are sick of being rejected, or being asked to re-work things. The infighting became so bad that we resorted to citing our Hippocratic Oath as the reason why we would not make decisions on budgets that would have life and death consequences. John suddenly reached into his case and pulled out a piece of paper.

'Ach look at this! We are back on track,' he cried. 'If medics are increasingly forced to compromise on medical considerations due to budget constraints and if the goal of a medic is to fulfil the content of Hippocrates' oath, then medics regard the demand to compromise on the moral code of their profession as a threat to their vital interests.

'If these people think their vital interests are under threat, they try to fight with all their might. So when medics are forced to compromise on the moral code of their profession, they try to fight it with all their might.

'See this is the next page!' He declared. 'But I've explained using only one example. What I've written down here is the reason why it happened. Beth do you realise that this sheet of paper explains almost every conflict the medics have ever had! I didn't see it before but I've written the generic reason for the problems. I was just following the rules Harry sent and I've really come up with something!'

'John, this was what I was trying to tell you an hour ago,' I said with a smile. 'Your intuition is strong. If I had just read it I would have missed out on the examples you've given me that makes this so real.'

John's mischievous grin reappeared. 'Ah, I'm with you now. Can I continue?'

'Be my guest,' I laughed.

He consulted his notes eagerly. 'Well, as I said, when medics are forced to compromise on the moral code of their profession, they try to fight it with all their might. And when people fight something with all their might they tend to become blind to the interests of others. And if we are forced, more and more, to compromise on medical considerations due to budget constraints, then as medics we will concentrate more and more on the interests of our kingdom, to the extent that we become blind to the interests of others!'

'Doesn't exactly sit well with helping each other as professionals, does it?' I chipped in.

'No.' John said bluntly. 'Do you know how I came to this? It was when I didn't stop my team from pressurising you to bring our patients in early. I see now that it added stress and work to your day and I apologise.'

'Thank you,' I said with a smile. 'Apology accepted.'

'Ach, let's get through this… So with that statement in mind and not forgetting that budgets are becoming more of a constraint, then there is less and less acceptable compromise in allocating the budget.

'Add that to the growing interest in protecting our kingdoms and the fact that the overall budget is a fixed amount then the only thing that can happen is an increase in the friction between the units. If this happens and the budgets are doled out according to decisions made by top management, then even more walls of distrust are being built, not only between the units, but between the units and management as well.

'Now bear with me as we are getting into your territory Beth. Just remember that this isn't personal.

'It is obvious that the medics are going to put more and more pressure on top management to increase their share of the budget. As there is no more money to go around, the managers are going to get more and more frustrated with the medic's refusal to accept that the hospital is really between a rock and a hard place.

'After all, the medics accept that the managers control the money and they see it being *wasted* on other units that they see as less worthy of the cash allocation. So the managers are constantly reminded that they are the only ones who can do anything about it. They are the only ones that can alleviate the budget constraint.

'But there are lots of managers and they represent certain units, so they are under pressure to fight with their bosses to get more money for their area. But their bosses tell them to use what they have to find more effective ways of using the money they do have. So unless they can find different methods of attracting money into the system they are stuck.

'Eventually the managers reach the stage where they feel the medics will not listen. So a very tempting way to prove a point is to hand the problem over to the medics, to let them take a shot at fixing the problem. The managers become increasingly tempted to devolve the tough budget decisions to the medics, so the complainers get a taste of what is it like to try to make the books balance.

'This move gains credence from another quarter. The medics get sick of trying to get the money they need and they are convinced that they can't do any worse, so demand the chance to prove that the managers are not doing the job properly.'

'I agree with your analysis John,' I butted in the moment John finally drew breath. 'We've seen this oscillation of budgets for years now. They are the *hot potato* that is constantly bounced around the hospital. But that can't be the source of the problem. Remember, Harry told us we are looking for a single common cause and I can't believe that bouncing budgets are the cause of all the problems, otherwise someone would have fixed it by now. After all so many people have had a go at them.'

'Ach, you are right. Who manages the budgets isn't the source of the problem,' John agreed, 'but it is a contributing factor. Now we need to climb another branch of this so-called tree.'

John's thoughts were interrupted as he spotted some of the delegates escaping from the building for a break. The presentation was obviously over. 'We had better save the next bit of tree climbing until another time,' he suggested. Do you think they missed us back there?'

'I doubt it, but I'd like to find out what they are saying about the presentation. How about circulating and trying to gather some more info during the break so we can compare notes afterwards?'

John flicked through the itinerary and winced. 'I don't suppose the next session on data archiving will be riveting, do you? Shall we duck out again and continue our brainstorming?' I laughed. 'Now who's leading who astray?'

Chapter 22

Despite our advances with John's logic tree I felt guilty about bunking off the presentations so I milled around the room trying to make up for lost time. I jumped on the people I knew and tried to collar some of the reps who were doing the presentation, but I was unable to get the information I wanted. I could see John doing the same and by the way his eyebrows had snuggled together at the bridge of his nose it was obvious that he was faring no better. We met up again just as they were starting to herd back into the auditorium.

'Find out anything useful?' John asked.

I shook my head. 'I asked if anyone had seen anything that would allow the hospital to actually treat more patients and all I have heard so far has been hot air. How about you?'

'I've been asking about the cost of the system, but no-one will even give me a rough idea. However, I did notice that the Chief Exec of the Trust is here so I will try and grab him before we go.'

'What are you going to say to him?' This was suddenly getting serious and I felt my heart quicken with alarm.

'I will just ask him the two questions we just mentioned. Anyway, that is for later. You must help me get my tree sorted out first.'

We returned to our bench under the horse chestnut tree and John dug his papers out of his case. 'So where was I?' He asked as he prepared himself.

'We had agreed that all medics are defending their castles from the evil managers not to mention each other, to the extent that they try to disarm the *enemy* by trying to take control of the money.'

'Ach, a fair if somewhat whimsical summary,' John admitted with a grin. 'Let's move on. As we know, there are many processes in hospitals that require collaboration and synchronisation between units. It's very rare that a patient requires the services of a single unit. But these units have many policies and procedures that are peculiar to them, so it is a fact of life that the way they operate will have an impact on the way other units work. Do you agree?'

'Do I ever! Working the bed board is a minefield. Even wards under the same speciality have different policies. Sometimes we forget a certain policy and offend a ward manager and boy do we suffer for it! I really agree with this point.'

'So, working up another branch using what we have already discussed, we find that the managers are pressing for a more efficient use of the budgets. If this is to be achieved the policies and procedures have to be re-examined. If these two entities are combined the pressure to re-examine policies and procedures gets stronger and stronger.'

'I agree John, but the worst part is the way each unit expects the other to change. They push the problem onto someone else.'

'That was my conclusion, but I've worded it a bit differently. I've come up with; *In more and more instances, policies and procedures that were determined in one unit, are suspected of jeopardising the efficiency of other units.*'

'Yes, that's a better verbalisation at this stage because the suspicion always precedes any action, as you have just demonstrated.'

'So the result of this is that walls of distrust are built, higher and higher, between levels and units.

All of a sudden I just couldn't stop myself from grinning. John was not impressed. 'Beth why are you smiling? It's not funny.'

'You will think it is when I read you my tree. I guarantee it!' I chortled.

'Ach! You didn't tell me your tree was finished. You could have gone through this agony first. I'm beginning to feel like I've been conned here,' John said with a twinkle in his eye.

'Oh come on John!' I retorted. 'You're enjoying this as much as I am.'

'I must admit it feels good to actually find some reasons for our depressing current situation,' John admitted.

'I don't know about you, but I'm beginning to think we can find a solution to this mess,' I said. 'I'm slowly entertaining the thoughts that these problems can be overcome.'

'Oh to have your optimism!' John teased. 'Even if we discover the reasons for the Health Service's decline it is going to take some fancy talking to get managers, medics and staff to buy into it.'

'You've already started that particular ball rolling but first things first John,' I scolded, 'I don't want to derail our momentum so let's return to your tree.'

'Okay, let's start with another part of the tree. No wait a minute! I'm beginning to realise something here. Normally when we work through a problem we think in straight lines. I'd never have thought of trying to join the dots up before the way these trees do.'

'You've lost me John.'

'How can I put it? If I was writing a report on how I want my department to run I would never think of quoting the same cause more than once, but we do it all the time in medicine. A solitary condition can cause a ripple effect through a system. I just never thought of an organisation in this way. I always thought that management was linear but it's not. Am I making sense?'

'You have just said what I have been saying for years. I've always felt that writing a report is like trying to produce a 2D version of a 4D system.' I paused. 'You will probably think I'm mad, but recently I've been thinking of the Health Service as a ball of problems. Like a globe. No a better example would be the sun.

'You know the pictures of the sun they've taken through telescopes that show huge flares leaping up off the surface? These flares are the problems we have to fight everyday, but the driving force of these problems is hidden deep inside the core. I'll only be happy when my imaginary globe is made of clear glass and I can see the real problems right in the middle, like the coloured bit in the middle of a huge marble.'

John's eyebrows were having a conference in the middle of his forehead.

'Now you really think I'm nuts,' I added.

'Ach, not nuts,' he reassured me. 'Perhaps a little ahead of me on the thinking, but not nuts. I'll get back to you on that one, particularly the 4D bit. Shall we return to earth now Spock or should I call you Janeway?'

'Neither,' I said with a laugh. 'You know the more you understand, the cheekier you get. Come on, I want to hear the rest before we are over-run with people again.'

'You're a hard task master,' John laughed. 'We are on the home stretch now. Remember earlier I said that a way out of the financial dilemma is to increase income and the pressure to do this is increasing all the time?'

'Yes.'

'Well, if we accept this we must recognise that increased income is usually only achieved through investment.

The old *speculate to accumulate* adage. However, there can be situations where we are prevented from getting hold of money because the budgets can't stretch to the initial investment to get the project up and running. I expect you can guess what happens next.'

'The walls of distrust are built even higher.'

'Correct. There can be a lot riding on these projects so now not only are the medics fighting for money to do their day jobs, their research or career prospects are stymied too. This is where it gets nasty. You should never come between a medic and his research. It would be easier to take a bone away from a rabid wolf.'

'These walls are getting pretty high John. How many more courses of bricks are you going to put on them?'

'Just one. Now as you know we do have some sources of extra income so it's not impossible to get new initiatives going because people can be very resourceful and occasionally an inventive proposal is approved. But what happens then? Add this new income to the needs of the assorted medics all vying for extra funding and lo and behold what happens?'

'The extra income is swallowed up into the central budget, into the pie, not to the unit generating it?'

'Got it in one! Another layer of distrust.'

'John, do you mind if I have a stab at summarising your tree?'

John looked surprised. 'You are very confident for someone who has not made any notes, but be my guest.'

I took a deep breath, 'Here goes. If people fight something with all their might they tend to become blind to the interests of others. And medics are forced, more and more to compromise on medical considerations due to budget constraints. And when they are forced to compromise on the moral code of their profession, they try to fight it as hard as they can. Then medics concentrate more and more on the interests of their kingdom to the extent that they actually become blind to the interests of others.

'If they are blind to the interests of others and if there is increasing pressure to become more efficient, then they all blame each other and the mistrust starts growing.

'Also, if they are blind and they are forced to make clinical decisions based on financial constraints, they will try to remedy the situation by increasing their income, which leads to the inevitable brick wall growing day-by-day.

'Now I need to tie in the budget bit. Oh I know. If they are blind then there is less and less chance they will agree on a compromise over budgets. Another brick in the wall.'

'Very good Beth. I wish my students would learn such a complicated concept as easily.'

'It's not complicated John. It's complex, but not complicated. Remember, I just think of my globe and wrap the problems around it. That way I find it easy to see the connections. But judging by the look on your face I'm not getting an A plus am I? What am I missing?'

'The most frightening bit of all. Let me just top it off for you. We have our brick wall, which from time to time we try to scale, but as it gets higher and higher we get more frustrated and when we fail, time and time again to get anywhere, this frustration leads to apathy. Who cares anymore? Ach, why bother?

'The end result is that the budgets are used even less effectively than before because we have all run out of energy to fight the system. So with so many people giving up we hit another round of tough decisions and so the crisis deepens. Finally, if you add the fact that the units have to work together despite the distrust, we see that the budgets are hit again.'

I thought hard for a while. There was something missing. 'John, if this were all true then the wall would stop growing and we could chip away at it. But it's not, so there must be another negative loop that is fuelling the growth of the wall. Where is it?'

'You are right. It has to feed back into the kingdom protection element. Do you agree?'

'Sounds about right to me. So what's your root cause?'

'The entity that says that, *When people fight something with all their might they tend to become blind to the interests of others.*'

I sat back to absorb this last point. 'You know John. I really expected your tree to be radically different to mine, but it's not. I need to show you mine, but I've got some more work to do on it.'

'I thought you said it was finished?'

'It is, but my precious brother-in-law is insisting that I will have to present it in reverse.'

216

'You mean to say I've done it the wrong way around?'

'No John. You were presenting it to a friend who understands what you are doing. If you were presenting this work to a TOC novice the last jump from the top of the tree back to the bottom would blow your whole case. This is why Harry says it has to be done backwards to communicate the concept. This creates the crescendo the audience is waiting for.'

'I think I got off lightly,' John decided, his mischievous glint returning to his eye. 'When you are ready I'll make time to hear it. I'm really intrigued to hear what you have found out.'

The door behind us flew open and our thoughtful oasis of calm was ruined by the footsteps of legs in need of stretching.

'Here come the sheep again,' John said. 'Can you send Harry's email on to me if there's nothing too personal in it?

'I've already sent this to you.'

'Of course, but we'd better join the throng and try to pick up a feel for what happened in there. We may be asked questions later.'

'Forget answering questions Beth, we've got a few to ask ourselves!' John said with a worrying hint of malice.

Chapter 23

John was cranky as we sat down to watch the final presentation of the day. He had been unable to get the Chief Exec of the Trust's attention in the final coffee break and he was making intricate plans to grab him before he left.

We had made great progress on John's tree but our, or more especially my, brains were hurting so we decided to attend the last session as it promised to include electronic wizardry designed to manage bed occupation. At least this looked like it would be the most useful presentation of the day.

John had grabbed us a couple of seats near the exits. In fact it was the exit he knew the Chief Exec would be using as he was seated on our side of the auditorium. As we sat down together I noticed a few people glancing our way and started to wonder whether they thought John and I were having an affair or something.

I shrugged my shoulders. They could think what they liked. I turned my attention to the leaflet describing the imminent presentation, but I still had the uncomfortable feeling I was being watched. I leaned forward to glance along our row of seats and there she was. The source of my discomfort, just a few seats away, wearing a designer jacket and an evil glare; Fran the Fearsome. I gave her a little nod and smile and quickly pressed myself back into my seat.

She may have given her backing to Joan and I but it was obvious that she still hated me. Either that or she objected to me spending my precious time at a corporate presentation.

'Oh, shit!' I whispered.

'The presentation hasn't started yet, give them a chance' said John

'Fool! No, it's Fran. I didn't think she was here, but she is sitting just down our row, glaring at me. If looks could kill I'd be in the morgue with a label round my big toe.'

John leaned forward and caught Fran's attention with a particularly charming smile. 'I've press-ganged the Admissions Manager to join me for this presentation. I need an expert interpretation.' John said as he jerked his thumb in Beth's direction.

Fran's steely gaze melted away and she gave John a half smile before sitting back in her chair.

'What did she say?'

'Nothing. Why should she?'

'We don't exactly get along and I know she's desperate to find ways to neutralise me.'

'Ach, don't worry. Just tell me if she comes for you. I quite like Fran, she has spirit. We just need to make sure she uses her energy to attack the right people.'

'Spirit? She's poisonous!'

'Schh...' John grinned. 'They are about to start.'

A well-dressed presenter approached the podium as the intro music faded. As he did the screen behind him changed to an animated logo of the company he was representing.

'Impressive,' John said with a smirk.

'Smoke screen,' I replied. 'They'll be offering popcorn next.'

'Good afternoon ladies and gentlemen. For our fourth and final session today we are going to demonstrate how our system links theatre schedules to the resource schedule, an area close to many of your hearts.'

His accent was so much like Max's that I re-examined the leaflet and discovered that his doctorate was from MIT in Boston. No wonder it was familiar.

We listened and watched intently and eventually the slick screen presentation moved on to the bed management section of the program. I was hoping to see a giant representation of the bed board, but all the program showed was a representation of the fictitious hospital's bed stock in the same way as my computer shows my files. To determine which beds were vacant you had to drill down through the many layers. The only attempt to personalise the system to hospital bed management was the replacement of the little icons showing folders with icons of tiny beds. By double clicking on a bed an imbedded screen would show the occupant's details.

I winced as John dug me in the ribs. 'That is horseshit Beth. It would take hours to get any useful information from that.'

'You're telling me John!' I replied. I couldn't believe they had come up with something so cumbersome.

'And as you can see this system shows you everything you need to know about your bed stock and allows you to allocate beds up to three months in advance.' The presenter said with a flourish.

The poor man was so confused by the laughter that followed that he checked his autocue as if he was searching for the joke that was not there. A quick look at the audience told him he was either about to be laughed off the stage, or his flies were undone, but being the consummate professional he pulled his jacket across his front and continued with the presentation.

The audience soon settled down again and ten minutes later the chairman thanked him for his entertaining presentation and asked for questions from the floor. I yelped as John dug me in the ribs again,

'Come on Beth! You can't have people thinking this crappy system is an improvement on what you have.'

I reluctantly raised my hand, but John pushed my elbow so it shot up and grabbed the presenter's attention.

'The lady at the back, please stand, tell us who you are and ask your question as soon as we get the microphone to you.'

I stood up and took the microphone, trying to ignore Fran's fearsome eyes boring into the side of my skull.

'I'm Beth Seager and I manage the Admissions Department at the Infirmary.'

I gave a little smile when I heard the audible intake of breath and noticed some of the audience folding their arms as they settled back into their seats. They were obviously predicting some entertainment.

'My question is a simple one. Can you show us a single screen that shows current bed occupancy, predicted movement, and patient's details?'

'We sure can ma'am.' The techno wizard positioned at the side of the stage started to manipulate the program. In quick succession it showed three screens. The first was showing a series of graphs, the second what looked like a project plan and the third the details on one of the patients.

'No, that's not what I meant.' I said quietly. My heart beat accelerating with every passing second.

'Sorry ma'am, I didn't quite catch that, can you repeat it?'

'That is not what I mean. Our current system shows all of the information I need at once. Can you show me all of that at the same time? And not just one patient's details, all of them?'

'What, all 500?' gawked the presenter.

'Yes.'

'Well now ma'am I hate to disagree with a potential client, but there isn't a system around that can do that.'

The condescending tone of the presenter was helping my bravery stand up and be counted.

'Yes there is,' I insisted. 'It is in my office and as yet I have not seen anything in your demonstration that comes close to being as effective.'

There was a murmur in the audience as they started to warm to the volley taking place between the now rattled American and their homegrown contender.

'Are you telling me you have a programme that can do all of the things you are asking for?' the presenter challenged, shooting a worried glance at his colleagues.

'I never said it was a programme. It's manual.'

'Well, there you are then if it's not electronic what is the point?' The presenter cut in.

I almost missed the return, but rallied just in time to reply.

'The point is obvious. If the computerised system forces us to take a retrograde step why would we want to take it?'

The presenter was lost for words, but another question was asked before I could continue and the microphone was rudely snatched from my hand.

'Ach, nice try Beth,' said John as I sat down. 'These people obviously don't want to listen, we may have to use some shock tactics.' I hardly heard him as I was trying to hear the rest of the questions over the whispered comments from the people who sat around me.

'Nice one Beth.'

'That told him!'

I looked up the row at Fran, but she looked right through me before turning coldly away. The presentation was being swiftly wound up and people were just starting to gather their things together.

John leapt to his feet. 'Time to rattle a few cages,' he said to me before grabbing the microphone as it was being taken back down to the podium.

'If I could ask just one more question,' he said as he strode forcefully down the stairs. 'My colleague Beth just asked a very pertinent question that was for some reason shrugged off when it should have been given careful consideration.'

The presenter froze on stage from the glare of John's eyes and a few people stopped their badly camouflaged rush to leave.

'However,' John continued. 'I have two questions that may have a more basic influence? And I wonder if I could ask them to the Chief Executive of the Trust?'

These words stopped everyone and I felt myself shrinking down in my seat. What on earth was John up to?

John was now standing opposite the Chief Exec, with nothing but the microphone between them. The Chief Exec smiled warmly at him.

'Good to see you taking an interest in this project John.' The Chief replied with a perfect, manufactured smile. 'I would be happy to answer your questions, but perhaps you should adhere to the normal protocol and introduce yourself before you ask the question?'

'Thank you Giles,' John replied politely. 'I am Professor John Summers and I am a consultant surgeon. I have a couple of questions for you Giles, questions that I am sure everyone here would like to know the answers to.'

'Fire away John, that's what I am here for.'

I was amazed at how coolly the Chief Exec was handling the situation. After all, this was nothing short of insubordination. It is amazing what a spin-doctor can teach you.

'Once we have decided on a system, and it is installed and working, how many more patients will this super computerised patient record system allow us to treat?'

'Well, you've raised an interesting point there John. We anticipate that the new system will give everyone faster access to patient's records and we will be able to track their progress through the system much faster.'

I winced. A reply like that was like dabbing vinegar on a mouth ulcer.

'That's not what I am asking.' John replied. 'The Board must have an idea Giles. How many more patients will a computerised patient record system allow us to treat?'

'We anticipate that the new system will free up some medics time by allowing them to access patient's notes much faster.'

'But Giles, medics aren't responsible for finding patient's notes, so how much time will it give us? More to the point, how many more patients will it allow us to treat?'

'Well John, you know as well as I do that our paper system is a mess and that, this will really help.'

There were cracks starting to form in the Chief's warm expression. His eyes darted around him but his senior colleagues had all shrunk away.

'But, how many Giles?' John persisted.

By now John had grabbed the attention of everyone in the whole room. There was complete silence as everyone watched the Chief Exec being pushed to answer a direct question.

'I appreciate that I am putting you on the spot here Giles,' John continued as he saw the Chief start to falter. 'But I have patients who are dying of cancer, patients who are waiting their turn to be wheeled into an operating theatre that is not being used to its full capacity. Not only do I have to tell these people to wait their turn, I also have to try and explain why they have to wait to their relatives, their husbands and wives, mothers, fathers, even children! If I have to do these despicable acts, surely you can answer my question?'

The Chief Exec crumbled in front of this considered request. The genial bluster on his face tumbled into defeated resignation. His shoulders drooped, but still he forced himself to look John in the eye.

'The Board recognises that although the new system will free up some doctors time it will not be enough to allow us to treat any more patients.'

There was a gasp from the crowd, but this was soon quelled as John took a breath to speak again.

'As I suspected Giles, it's good to hear that the Board are being honest about this.' John paused just long enough for his comment to sink in. He was not blaming the Board rather he was congratulating them. The crowd looked puzzled, but I knew what John was doing. He was trying to show both Giles and the assembled masses that the Board were being forced into commissioning the new EPR system.

'Now, if I may ask just one more question.' John continued. 'How much is this going to cost us?'

This question commanded even more respect than the first one.

The silence was solid. You could have cut it up and built a wall out of it.

While Giles was inhaling a deep breath, the Finance Executive who stood to his right took a half step forward. But before he could speak Giles held his forearm and said, 'It's OK Nick I can field this one.' Nick looked at Giles with a pleading look on his face as if to say, 'Do it right or we won't get out of here alive.' 'As part of the national modernisation programme it is estimated that the tri Trust, of which we are a part, will need to invest somewhere between fifty and eighty million pounds in this project,' he said sadly.

A gasp was emitted from every mouth in the room except those belonging to the few Board members present. This was obviously old news to them.

John was the first person to regain his composure and before the masses started chattering he formed a simple statement that echoed all of their thoughts.

'So we as an individual Trust are going to be forced to spend anything up to, let's say £30 million, on a system that will not allow us to treat anymore patients? Correct?'

All eyes were on Giles. John had drawn first at the OK Corral and the bystanders were waiting to see if he had got his man.

'It's not that simple John, but yes. To comply with the modernisation plans, this Trust will be spending a considerable amount of money to upgrade to a system that we do not anticipate will allow us to treat any more patients.'

Bullseye! John had got his man. However, he didn't stick the knife in any further.

'That was a brave thing to do Giles. You told the truth. You proved to the people here that the system forces even you to do things that are not right. Well done and thank you.'

John offered Giles his hand and the two men looked at each other as they shook hands.

The crowd suddenly found their voices and the chattering reached a crescendo. The Finance Executive, Nick had an urgent conversation with his number two, a look of panic etched across his face. He quickly steered Giles out of the room, talking into his ear all the way, but it was evident that Giles was not listening. His thoughts were far away, perhaps, in his head he was already looking forward to his retirement, planting seedlings in the land surrounding his villa in Portugal.

John returned to me and steered me to the door. I was still in shock and it wasn't until I reached the fresh air outside the auditorium that I finally caught my breath. John's eyes were alive in triumph.

'John!'

'What?'

'You know what!'

'Tell me, what have I done?'

'You....you....you....'

'I forced the person with the ultimate responsibility for running this Trust to tell the truth.'

'But, but.....'

'Ach, don't worry Beth. He'll get over it. I have to do that every day. As I said, I have to deliver bad news to patients. I have to tell them they are dying. For once Giles did the right thing, just as we do every day. The only difference is that no-one is going to die.'

After a few minutes silence Beth spoke. 'But it seemed so hard on him. He may have made some dodgy decisions but he is a nice guy. Did he deserve that?'

'Beth, it was the ideal opportunity, one I could not afford to miss. If another consultant had been here, and I see that they are conspicuous by their absence, they would have done the same. It's the business we are in Beth. We deal with facts not spin.'

'But what will you do with this information? It will be around the Trust faster than my bed temperature.'

'That's the idea Beth, and now I can report back to my Directorate that I had it straight from the horse's mouth. What better way to start to demolish our walls than with the truth?'

Chapter 24

The final day of the week in Admissions was quiet, too quiet. Despite a worrying rise in the bed temperature, the 11:00 panic meeting completely failed to live up to it's name. The attendees seemed desperate to leave as soon as possible, although they all passed on effusive good wishes to me as they left. However, very few of them managed to keep eye contact and they all had a strange smile, as if they knew something I didn't. My paranoia really set in when I returned to my bubble to find Sal smirking at me at me as well.

I nipped out to the toilets to check my appearance, but I couldn't see anything wrong. My make up was fine, all the buttons on my tasteful spotty blouse were in the correct holes and my stockings were free of ladders. As I stared hard at my reflection in the mirror I decided that everyone's strange behaviour must stem from my questions at the EPR. I even found myself wishing that Eddy was working today. He would be bounding into my office to gloat about the gossip. Perhaps I shouldn't be so mean. Eddy had surpassed himself in the last few days and Sal was calmly coping with anything that I dropped into her lap.

I grinned. That was it! I could ask Sal about my special reception today. I strode back to the department and noticed that Sal was attempting to placate an irate patient who was very loudly claiming his right to have a bed that day. I slipped a quick U-turn as I decided to leave Sal to it and went to visit the wards to collect the data for my weekly reports.

The warmth of the ward manager's welcome always depends on the severity of the bed situation. If a ward is having problems, I can either expect to be grilled or, even worse, to receive a heartfelt plea from the ward managers to intervene and help solve a particular situation. Today was different. Today I was greeted with a politeness that bordered on being formal, with an unhealthy edge of displeasure. Reports were handed to me at arms length while *urgent business* cut their conversations to a minimum. I was being hustled. Was I too dangerous to know? Didn't they want to be seen talking to me?

It wasn't until I reached Short Stay Surgery and was greeted by Niamh's wonderful Irish brogue that I realised the extent of the situation.

'Here she is, the heroine of the hospital!' she cried. 'Well done Beth! And may I be the first person to welcome you to the dark side.'

'Dark side! What are you talking about Niamh?'

'From what I'm hearing, you've joined the good fight and are standing up for the rest of us mortals.'

My face must have reflected my confusion as Niamh continued with a broad smile.

'Ah c'mon! The EPR presentation yesterday! You blew the Chief Exec out of the water!'

'Me! No Niamh, you've got it wrong. It wasn't me!'

'That's not how I heard it Beth, the rumour flying around this place is that you primed Prof. Summers to have a showdown with the big man himself. Don't tell me you didn't do it now. You'll be disappointing me'.

'Oh, that. Sorry Niamh, but John managed to do that all by himself. I just happened to be sitting next to him.'

'Now, now, Beth. I know that the Prof is a bright spark but you can't tell me as that he actually managed to figure out what a negative impact this EPR will have on the hospital?'

'You underestimate him Niamh. He's made it his goal to understand how this place ticks.'

'How in God's name has he managed to do that? We both know the medics don't give two figs for the administration of this place. All they want is for us to pander to their every need throughout their working day. I thought they only got involved in things that hit their pay packet and the EPR will have little or no impact on that! It's us, the nursing staff and your admin bods that will have to suffer the consequences of a new system, not the medics.'

'But it will affect them Niamh. That was John's point in a funny sort of way. We all know that so-called *extra money* will be found by the government for this project, but John was trying to make the point that even if the money is extra to our budget, it will not significantly improve matters. Don't you agree?'

'Agree? Is the Pope catholic? What I want to know is how is the Trust going to announce this to the public?'

I paused, Niamh's question had fired off some new neural pathways in my brain and I struggled to force my thoughts into words.

'If this Trust is forced to spend £30 million on a new computer system it will have to become public knowledge, after all it will be taxpayer's money. And if the hospital continues to perform as badly as it has in the past, the local population will be justified in demanding that this money be spent on improving services not buying a new fangled system that will not help them.'

I looked at Niamh's surprised face. 'Does that make sense?' I asked.

'Make sense!' Niamh retorted. 'You've just said what of the rest of us have been trying to figure out all morning. So what do you think will happen?'

'Hmm…I'm not sure'.

'Ah c'mon Beth! You seem to have this pretty sussed, tell me, how can the Board justify this?'

I remembered John's words from yesterday.

'The only way they can justify this after John's outburst is to admit that government policy is forcing them to do it.'

'But the press will have a field day with this Beth! How are you going to cope when the news leaks and you're still being forced to cancel patients? You'll be needing to wear a bullet proof vest, so you will.'

My knees suddenly sagged as I was hit by the widespread impact of this project. It was bigger than anything else I had experienced in the Health Service. Hell, it was the biggest showdown I have ever faced in my life. If this project was handled as badly as all it's predecessors, and both Niamh and I knew it would be, we were heading towards a medical and PR catastrophe. Only this time it would be me that the patients would be gunning for.

I began to shake involuntarily and I flinched as Niamh placed her hand gently on my arm.

'Beth, are you ok?'

I managed to pull myself back from the mental precipice I was teetering over and refocus on Niamh.

'Yeah, I think so. I've just seen the future and I think you're right. It is the dark side.'

Niamh looked at me with a half quizzical, half professional eye. 'Do you need to sit down? A glass of water?'

'No, no I'm fine. Do you have the weekly figures for me?'

'Sure, here you are.'

Niamh passed me a sheet of paper, which I put inside of the folder I had been clutching to my chest like a shield. As I looked at the plastic cover I could see impressions of my own sweat in a handprint.

'Thanks. Have a good weekend. See you next week.' I said, returning to normal conversation to try and slow down my thudding heart. Just as I turned to leave the ward, I stopped and called back to Niamh. 'Hey, is this all around the hospital?'

'You bet. It flew around faster than the temperature! Keep up the good work Beth but make sure you don't hang yourself out to dry. It can get pretty lonely out there in the dark side.'

I returned to my office on shaky legs. What a week! Thank goodness Niamh was the good friend I always knew her to be. She was the only Ward Manager who would be honest with me. I could almost feel some of John's brick wall being built around me. But these people didn't seem to realise that I just wanted to do my job and do it well.

Once back in my office, I tried to concentrate on compiling my ward reports, but my mind kept slipping back to that conversation with Niamh. When my phone rang I jumped so much I almost knocked over the mug of coffee on my desk.

'Hello, Admissions department, Beth Seager speaking,' I answered as calmly as possible.

'Ah, Elizabeth.'

It was Fran. My heart thudded into overdrive and I could feel beads of perspiration emerging on my forehead.

'I need to see you,' Fran barked. 'Next week will be soon enough, my office, Tuesday at mid-day. See you then.'

'Alright Fran, but can you tell me what this is about?'

'As if you need to ask,' Fran spat and the phone went dead.

I felt very small and alone as I quietly put the phone down. This was just what Fran had been waiting for and she was going to do her best to make me suffer. She had given me three and a half days to mull over what was going to happen at the meeting and she was banking on me worrying over the weekend. I kept reminding myself that I just wanted to do a good job and I had done nothing wrong. Then I remembered John's offer of support and quickly rang Marge, his secretary's number.

'Professor John Summer's secretary, department of surgery, how can I help you?'

'Hello Marge, its Beth from Admissions, is The Prof around?'

'Yes, but he's busy, can I take a message Beth?'

Before I could answer John had obviously taken the receiver from her and I could hear Marge saying that he should not be interrupted with trivial matters and that she could handle me.

'Beth, how are you?'

'Not good John. We whipped up quite a storm yesterday.'

'Ach, did we ever! I've been talking to some of my colleagues today and they are in agreement. We cannot let this project proceed until more fundamental problems within the Trust are addressed.'

I felt my hand clenching around the receiver. 'Hang on John. Slow down!' I almost shouted into the receiver before I dragged myself back into control. 'It's great that you guys are all talking and are in agreement, but we have to do this right. We will be just like them if we rush into something without properly thinking it through. Can you hold fire on this until we get some more input from Harry? He's already told me that we have a lot more to learn before we start devising solutions. Can you wait a while?'

'Ach Beth, you are right as usual,' John replied, good-naturedly. 'How has your day been? Any good feedback?'

'Good! You are joking aren't you? It's been a nightmare. Anyone would think I was carrying the plague. I am *persona non grata* to most of the staff and as I predicted Fran is gearing up to tear strips off me as well.'

'What? I thought that the reaction from the staff would have been good.'

'In principal it is, but they do not want to be seen associating with a troublemaker. I get the feeling they just want to stand back and let me perform for them. They do not want to get involved. I guess they think the fallout will be too much to handle.'

'Ach, that's really awful Beth. Are you okay? Is there anything I can do to help?'

'Well, for one thing we have to start building a solution to this whole mess as soon as we can. At the moment all we can do is prove where the problems are coming from. Not how to solve them. Until we can do that I think I will have to keep a low profile.'

'Sounds sensible. I'll email Harry now for the next step and I'll work on it over the weekend. But how about you, what's this about Fran?'

'She's summoned me to her office at mid-day next Tuesday. I'm not sure what her game is but I expect she is counting on me reconsidering my position as a team player by then. She will probably be expecting an apology.'

232

WE ALL FALL DOWN

'Like hell you will!' John fumed. 'You did nothing wrong. You were acting in the interests of this hospital and the patients, you have nothing to apologise for.'

'Thank you for the vote of confidence John, but I know she's gunning for me and she is one determined lady. To be honest, I'm not sure how to handle her. She is my boss after all.'

Admitting that I did not know how to react to Frans' summons somehow made it seem a little less daunting, but only a little.

'Beth, don't worry. I'll figure something out. Fran and I have always got on rather well. Now go home, have a relaxing weekend and I will work on some solutions over the weekend. Oh, by the way can I have your home email address? I may want to ask you a few questions over the next couple of days?'

I gave him the address and then instantly regretted it as I had vowed to have a TOC-free weekend to concentrate on building bridges with Max. Too late. We said our good-byes and promised to touch base on Monday if not before.

I'd had more than enough for one week and after checking that all was alright in the department I prepared myself to face another confrontation, this time with Max. I knew I should really spend the weekend working on a solution to the problems we had unearthed. There was no way I could relax knowing that I would have to face Fran the Fearsome unarmed on Tuesday. I desperately needed to take something into the meeting that Fran needed, but what?

Chapter 25

By the time I got home I realised I just had to bring Max up to speed with the recent chaotic events at the hospital. He was not going to like it, but after realising just how vulnerable I was at work, I really needed to have my loved one alongside me. After all, if I could heckle a presenter in a high-powered presentation I should be able to point out a few home truths to my husband. He may be reluctant to hear about my work with Harry, but I could not get through the next week without his support. It was my need for back up versus his obstinate pride. It was going to be an interesting encounter.

It was a perfect summer's evening, the sun was just starting its descent and the garden was alive with chirruping birds and the spectacular acrobatics of energetic swallows. I sorted the dogs out and sent a quick email off to Harry before I prepared enough goodies for a leisurely barbecue. I was counting on him being home within the hour so I chilled a decent bottle of Semillon chardonnay and had a quick shower. A perfect evening to unwind and relax, the worst possible setting for a blazing row.

He arrived over an hour late and I had worked myself up into such a state that I nearly jumped out of my chair when the dogs started barking. He looked tired and drawn, but he did manage a genuine smile as he fought off the attention of the dogs to say hello to me.

I lit the barbecue and slapped on some lamb cutlets and Max changed into shorts and a T-shirt and came out to join me, armed with the bottle of wine. He poured us both a glass and we slumped down in the chairs, fighting off the attention of the dog's eager noses. I took a deep breath and jumped straight in.

'So are you able to tell me about the Paris trip now?' No warm up, no opening gambits, I simply offered him the opportunity to brain dump his problems on me.

'Kinda, yeah I suppose, but I warn you, it ain't pretty.' Max said, taken aback by my abruptness.

'Try me,' I smiled. 'You never know, I may understand.'

Max settled himself in his seat as he prepared to tell his tale. 'I've been working with a small software company, a bunch of really bright guys and for once, at least for this sort of business, they're not too precious about their software. They are great programmers and have developed some really neat packages. But their real passion is their ability to get to grips with a client's needs and develop innovative solutions quickly. The standard of their work is superb.'

'Sounds good. So how many of them are there?'

'Five, three guys and two girls, all in their mid twenties. They were at university together and really gelled. So much so that they have followed each other from job to job, picking up some really great experience on the way. What really struck me was the balance they have. They each have terrific programming skills, but it's more than that. They have complementary business skills as well.

Gilly, the youngest girl is a whiz at presentations, not just on the computer, but to clients as well, a real sharp communicator. She could sell ice to Eskimos. Two of the guys work in complete synchrony. One analyses the client's needs and the moment he has finished the other guy is churning out chunks of programming to meet those needs. A lot of what they provide for clients is off the shelf stuff, which they tailor to make custom made packages.

'The eldest is a natural leader. He's heading up the business and is their negotiator and quality control man. The fifth member of the team is Anna, she's the mother of the whole bunch and her fine-tuning on the programmes is astounding. I've never come across such a well balanced team, not in all my years in business.'

'Sounds like you have really taken a shine to them, but what happened last week?'

'I flew to Paris to attend a presentation of theirs to a potential client, a French chain of hotels. This chain have just diversified and bought some holiday sites. You know, a mixture of static trailers, chalets and campsites. They were looking for a quick and easy way to centralise their booking system; a kind of one stop shop for all types of holiday accommodation that they could offer online. The kids did a great job and I was there as their potential saviour. They have put everything they have into the business and are really up against it. Venture capital is their last chance. But obviously I have to be really sure.

'My investors are dead wary of businesses run by people so young and this lot had the extra stigma of being associated with the Internet. The mere mention of the 'I' word sends my investors almost apoplectic. But I really believe these kids can make it.

'I agreed with the Board that I would go to the presentation and check on a few key points. If they failed on any of them our answer would be no. I was so confident that they would come good that I really stuck my neck out for them.'

'Wow Max. I've never heard you talk about potential investments like this. You really do believe in them don't you?'

'Yeah, I'm a fool!'

'Why, what happened?'

'Well, I spent the first part of the week monitoring their progress at various technical meetings and did some background checks on the Hotel chain. If this is going to be their biggest client I needed to be sure that our investment would yield a good return. No problems there, everything was fine. Then I attended their final sales pitch to the Board in the guise of their financial backer. We were so close Beth.' Max hung his head. He suddenly seemed deathly tired.

'Tell me, what happened next?'

'They did their presentation and it went down a storm. The Board appeared to have made up minds in our favour but then their web development director asked a question that scuppered the whole deal.' Max sighed and took a sip of wine.

'What was it?' I almost shrieked. I knew Max was tired, but dragging the story out like this was as much agony for me as it was for him.

'The web development guy asked who would be producing the French version of the web site.'

'So?'

'So! They only forgot to include the cost of the translations in the costings. And even worse, I had overlooked it as well! The whole deal fell apart. The Board would not pay extra for the translators and the deal could not go ahead without it. They talked for ages.

'I tell you Beth they worked their socks off. I've never seen such skilful negotiating. But they lost the contract when they had to admit they could not cut the costs any further. Then the Board starting talking in French and none of them had a clue what was being said. It was obvious they would have to bring in outside help and without the extra charges they were stuck.'

'Oh Max! What did you do?'

'There was nothing I could do. They knew how much we were prepared to invest and I knew they couldn't get more funds from anywhere else. Why else would I have been there?'

'Nothing! You couldn't do anything?'

'No Beth. I had no choice but to leave and catch the next flight back.'

'What's happened to them now?'

'I had to tell them this week that we would not be investing in them. I felt wretched, but I had no choice. I really think they could have hit the big time and to make matters worse I missed those damned translation costs in their proposal as well. I behaved like a rookie and I let those kids down.'

'No wonder you've been feeling so bad. No doubt they think you're a hard hearted capitalist.'

'Yeah I guess, but I had no choice. I could not have salvaged anything with my investors. I had nothing to take back but a list of no's to their questions. So that was it. Finito, nada, nothing.'

'So what will the kids do now?'

'Get jobs I guess. They all have huge debts and have borrowed heavily from their families. They will be working a long time to pay everyone off.'

'That's such a shame'.

'Yeah, I know.'

Max heaved himself up and turned the cutlets over on the barbecue. He looked back at me with a thoughtful expression.

'I suppose you want to discuss your involvement with Harry's barmy schemes now?'

There was no way I was going to react to that bait. He could call Harry's TOC whatever he liked, as long as he listened to it first.

'I *would* like to talk about what we have achieved at work,' I replied lightly. 'After today you may have your wish and see me leave the Health Service.'

Max frowned. 'Are you saying they're trying to kick you out?'

'Who knows what will happen,' I replied 'but we have certainly stirred up a right kerfuffle.'

'These are just about done,' he said transferring the cutlets to a plate. 'Shall I bring out the salad so we can eat out here?'

He disappeared inside leaving me to fume that he had once again sidestepped the conversation. I waited for us both to load our plates before I returned to the attack, but Max beat me to it.

'Are you saying that my kid brother has put you in danger of losing your job?' Max was scowling and I noticed he was gripping the cutlery much harder then he needed to.

'No!' I cried and then stopped and thought for a few seconds before adding, 'Maybe.' It suddenly struck me as very funny and I started to giggle. Max's face was a picture of astonishment, making the situation even more absurd. The giggles burst into laughter and soon tears were tricking down my cheeks. Max finally started to smile and soon he was begging to hear what had been going on.

'I'll tell you what's been happening,' I said when I had finally recovered from my fit of giggles. 'But you have to separate it from your spat with Harry. John and I managed to get ourselves into this pickle all by ourselves.'

I told Max the story of the EPR presentation the previous day. I left out the bit about John's tree and just told him about the bed management programme and mine and John's questions. By the time I had finished he was actually laughing.

'You? You actually did that? And this John guy, what's he? Another manager?'

'No Max, he's Professor John Summers, a consultant surgeon.'

'A professor? Asking sensible business questions and more to the point getting truthful answers! I don't believe it. All the medics I've ever dealt with are too obsessed with their own work to fight for anyone else. Perhaps there is hope for the health service. This guy must be really smart. I'd like to meet him.'

This was my chance. Max was open to our discussion. I decided to take the plunge.

'He is smart Max, but he's had some help'

'Who from?'

'You know who.'

'Harry?'

The look on Max's face was amazing as he tried to digest this astonishing news. 'Harry? My kid brother Harry? Are you sure?'

Max fell silent as his digestion returned to his recently finished meal. Maggie broke into his thoughts by grabbing some bones from his finished plate that he had stupidly left on the ground. She dashed off and tried to hide in the dahlias, hotly pursued by Winston and Max who started to chase the mutts around the garden trying to take the offending treats from them.

The play soon degenerated into a mock battle on the lawn between the three of them with the dogs staying just out of Max's reach. Eventually with the bones safely in the bin, Max joined me back at the table for coffee with grass stained knees and muddy feet. The dogs were exhausted and flopped at his feet.

Max turned to me with a smile and asked. 'So my kid brother is teaching a professor?'

I knew then that Max had found a new respect for his brother. The fact that I had been working with him was almost forgotten. If Harry was working with a professor and he was successful, then he must have something that Max was not aware of and in typical Max fashion, he just had to know. I was out of the loop; this was between Harry and John.

We talked for ages and I brought out John's tree and talked Max through it.

'Are you telling me that Harry taught John how to do this purely by sending him email?' Max asked scratching his head.

'That's right. And I've been doing the same,' I confessed.

'So where is your, what do you call it? Tree?'

'It's not finished yet.'

'Why not?'

I laughed. Give me a chance Max!

We decided to call it a night, but Max spent the next day asking me questions and looking through the trees. I could tell he was still trying to prove it wrong, but he listened to everything and accepted my logic. By the evening he was with me all the way. Strike! All six layers done and dusted. Max also helped me devise a plan to handle Fran. We were back. The TA team as we used to call ourselves. Trans Atlantic not Territorial Army!

The only low point of the day was when I asked Max to email Harry. He replied that he'd rather not let Harry know that he was in the loop, not just yet. But on the whole I was happy that I could handle Fran and anything else the hospital could throw at me. The rest of the weekend was ours and we took it.

Chapter 26

Monday came and went with the usual problems and a freezing bed temperature despite the heat wave outside. Eddy hadn't caused too many ripples over the weekend and the CBM's were beginning to learn the system and ask sensible questions. Between them they had started to make a list that looked very similar to the one that my staff had given to me at our private meeting. That meeting certainly seemed a long time ago.

I was being pushed along on the regular tides of email that flowed across the Atlantic. I had progressed my ideas for applying TOC to our problem, but I had not had time to work on anything apart from my Communication Current Reality Tree, or CCRT – the tree I was going to use to explain my theories to other people. It was becoming obvious that as a lone TOC'er I would not be able to develop a rescue plan. I needed much more input from the people around me, but the method of gaining this help was way beyond me at this stage. I decided that I needed to talk to Harry directly and arranged to phone him the following evening from home.

I was so preoccupied that I had not given my meeting with Fran a second thought until Tuesday morning when I was getting ready for work. Max had taken the opportunity to work from home and he offered to meet me outside the main entrance at one o'clock and whisk me away for a quick lunch.

The morning passed in a blur of fire fighting, but all the time I was aware of the nagging worry about what Fran would hit me with this time. I arrived at the Fearsome One's office on the stroke of mid-day and was firmly told to wait in the corridor by her secretary. All of a sudden I was back at school, waiting for the headmistress to dole out a punishment.

Ten minutes later and Fran still hadn't acknowledged me. I knew this charade was all done to intimidate me and I was annoyed to find it was working. I could feel the tension inside me start to build like the fizz under a Champagne cork.

Finally, at twelve minutes past the hour Fran opened her office door and invited me in. Her look was cold and as hard as I've ever seen it. I swallowed hard and braced myself for the onslaught as I took my seat and waited while Fran took her time to elegantly arrange herself behind her desk.

'That was quite a show you put on last week, Beth. Do you have any idea of the ramifications your outburst has caused?'

Her words were hard but her face had changed. She was grinning at me like the Cheshire Cat from Alice in Wonderland. The mixed messages were confusing to say the least. Before I could reply she had resumed talking through what appeared to be a state of rictus, a strange forced smile that made her look distinctly evil.

'Of course you haven't, how could you? Now before I bring you up to speed I must congratulate you on your work with the CBM's. Joan has been telling me how well things are going with them and I expect to see some favourable results soon. Just make sure you don't hold them back?'

The mismatch between her words, her plastic smile and the expression in her eyes made me quickly scan the room for a camera. Was this conversation being taped? I couldn't detect anything that looked suspicious. I decided that Max's advice to keep quiet until I was asked a direct question was the best tactic I could adopt. I could take being shouted at, I would really appreciate some praise, but this schizophrenic mood clash was putting me even more on edge.

Joan had obviously spoken up for me. She was a complete star and I would have to thank her later. I wondered whether Fran was wary of me making friends in high places and had summoned me to her office to put me in my place. It was possible, but it was an extreme approach, even for the Fearsome One. There had to be a catch. I kept silent. No direct question.

No answer. The silence between us lasted a few seconds before Fran started talking again.

'Your, or should I say Professor Summer's, questions have got the rumour mill working overtime. I have been deluged with requests from various directorates for presentations on how we manage the bed situation. I would do it, but the timing is inconvenient as I am going on holiday for the next couple of weeks. And, as I am not prepared to put the CBM's onto this yet, you will be required to step up to the plate.'

This was followed by another silence that gave me a chance to make a quick dissection of Fran's little speech.

1. Fran thinks that I put John up to asking the questions.
2. This is another friend in a high place, making me more of a threat to her.
3. She had no chance of doing the presentation. She knows next to nothing about the system she is responsible for, so her holiday is a convenient excuse.
4. Joan has taken the stance that the CBM's do not know enough about the bed management system yet to do the presentation.
5. Last, but by far the most important, is the win-win situation for Fran. If I do these presentations while she is away she can claim ignorance of any problems and collect any praise on her return.

Still no question. So I saw no reason to speak.

'So?'

I was just about to formulate a reply when there was an urgent knock on the door.

'Enter!' snapped Fran. I was surprised to see John's head pop through the open door.

'Are you busy Fran, got a minute?'

The sight of John prompted Fran to jump to her feet and launch into an automatic grooming routine. She smoothed her skirt with one hand while attempting a careless flick of her long, blonde hair over her shoulders with the other. It was quite a comical sight and my inner tension evaporated.

'Of course Professor, please come in, we are nearly through.'

'Ach, hello Beth, how nice to see you again!' John beamed. His eyebrows feigning total surprise. 'Actually Fran it was Beth I had come to see you about, so meeting like this is quite appropriate.'

Fran was completely confused and her face showed it. Her eyes darted between John and me as if she was trying to figure out what was going to happen next. Fortunately, she obviously realised that I was as surprised as she was.

'Please come in, take a seat,' she purred. 'Do you want Beth to stay?'

'Yes, I don't see why not. What I have to say is for her as well.' John smiled at me, but I was still confused.

'Please continue,' said Fran

'Ach, I just popped in to congratulate you on your staff, Beth to be more precise. She was a great help to me last week at the ERP presentation and I just wanted to express my thanks. That's all really.'

'Thank you Professor, we are here to help.' Fran's smile was more genuine now and she sat back in her chair before continuing. 'As AGM for surgery I try to ensure that my staff assist the Directorate whenever possible. I am glad that Beth managed to hit the floor running, in fact she will be helping out a bit more soon.'

Fran went on to explain to John that I would be deputising for her with the Bed Management presentations to the various directorates. She ended her announcement with her first direct question to me.

'You will give the medics a clear understanding of the current bed management system won't you Beth?'

'Of course,' I replied.

'Good, this will be an excellent grounding for them before we start to implement the changes the CBM's are planning. Hopefully Beth's presentations will pave the way for the improvements. Won't they Beth?'

I found myself trying not to smile at the syrupy, condescending flow of words. 'Yes, of course.'

'I won't detain you any longer Beth, just liaise with the relevant secretaries to get slots at the directorate meetings. 15 minutes each should be enough and be sure to compile reports on
any feedback from the doctors for when I return from my holiday. Okay?'

'Yes.'

'You can go now.'

'Thanks.' I stood to leave and John stood as well.

'Was there anything else I can do for you John?' said Fran
with another deft hair flick. She was obviously trying to find a
way to keep him in her office.

'Ach, I'm afraid not Fran. I'm due in theatre soon so I must
dash. I just like to give credit where it is due. Stay well and
thanks.'

I followed John out of the office and we remained silent until we were outside of the building.

'Ach, either I was in the nick of time or you two enjoy sitting and staring at each other!' John smirked as he finally broke
the silence.

'Is that what you were doing?' I laughed. 'That was very
sweet of you John, but I could have handled her, I think. I just
gave her a good listening to. I don't think I spoke more than ten
words. I was expecting a fight and she's asked me to do these
presentations. I'm more than happy to do them but I still suspect
her motives.'

'You two are really building walls aren't you?' John quipped
with a mischievous grin. 'Well at least you now have the perfect
opportunity to present your tree to all of the doctors. You have
to go for it Beth!'

'What? My tree? No way! She only told me to tell them
about the Admissions systems.'

'Ach, Beth, you and I know both know that the Admissions
system is not at fault, it is the way the medics are forced to
work. You must present your tree, you simply have to.'

RESOURCES ARE Ru
Bottle Neck

I was stunned. For once I was slowly creeping back into Fran's good books and here was John inciting me to rebel. I felt a hand on my shoulder and saw John take a step back.

'Hi Hon.' I spun around and looked up at Max. 'Hi there, you're early.'

I turned back to John noting how much shorter he looked standing next to Max. I also noticed Max's questioning stare so I broke the ice. 'John, I'd like you to meet my husband, Max.' 'Max, meet Professor John Summers, Consultant Surgeon and apprentice white knight.'

'Good to make your acquaintance,' said Max as he extended his hand.

John took it and said. 'Ach! The Venture Capitalist who helped us learn to look at the problems of the Health Service in terms of business proposals.'

Max looked stunned and quickly glanced at me and I smiled back.

'You Seager brothers seem to have been born with business acumen. You have also solved another mystery for me. The fact that your wife is able to understand my English so well, you are from another old colony I take it?'

'Yeah, the States, try as I might I can't shake the accent. And you, Jo'burgh, I seem to recall Beth telling me?'

Soon they were talking about far-flung places and comparing cities. I was almost forgotten. The beeping of the crossing lights reminded them that they were standing in the way of the crowd of people trying to make their way to the main hospital building.

'Really nice to meet you Max,' John beamed. 'I have a suggestion. It's the Summer Ball soon and I get free tickets, one of the perks of being a professor. How would you and Beth like to be my guests? Should be an interesting night.'

'Sure,' said Max. 'Let Beth know when and we'll be there.'

John strode across the road and Max began to follow him before realising that I was not with him. He quickly leapt back onto the pavement to find me.

'What a nice guy!' He said. 'That should be a really good night. You okay Hon?'

'Me? Oh don't mind me! How many years have I asked you to go to the Trust Ball and how many times have you made excuses? Honestly Max.' I feigned anger but he could tell I was joking.

'It will be fun won't it? And I didn't realise that you work with such interesting people. We'll go, yeah?'

'Alright, but for that you can buy me a proper lunch and I'll tell you about my meeting.'

Chapter 27

Before I knew it I was standing up in front of a room full of very bored looking surgeons who started checking their watches the moment John started to introduce me.

'Please welcome Beth, our wonder manager of the Admissions Department,' John said grandly. 'She is going to tell us how to we can solve the core problem of the Health Service.'

There was an impenetrable silence that was broken by someone giggling at the back. This set someone else off and the giggles evolved into laughter. Soon the entire audience was openly laughing at the claim. Tears were tricking down cheeks, sides were being held and the volume of laughter was deafening.

I was left standing there in my nasty synthetic uniform, a dejected object of ridicule. Then Fran appeared from the back of the room. She fixed me with an evil glare that was so powerful that it set off the fire alarm. The alarm mingled with the laughter but suddenly someone was gently shaking my shoulder.

'Beth, it's okay, it's just a dream!'

I opened my eyes to see Max's concerned face and realised the fire alarm was actually our alarm clock. I breathed a huge sigh of relief. This presentation was really getting to me.

Everything had moved so fast following my summons to Fearsome's den. I was only given five days to prepare for the first presentation and they were all packed into a fortnight. Luckily John insisted that I give the first one to the surgeons so he could give me some support, but that hadn't stopped me spending the whole night fretting about it. Now I was only hours away from a performance that could make or break my career. I was more nervous about this than I was for my wedding!

One of the difficulties was the fact that Harry had persuaded me to present my work in reverse order to the Current Reality Tree. As usual his logic was spot on and after hearing John's tree I knew that presenting it from the bottom up would earn more enemies than friends. I had to gently lead the audience to a place where I could start gathering support for training, not only myself, formally, with TOC, but for my peers and line managers as well.

I knew what I had to do, but that didn't make it any easier to work the tree in reverse. How could a message so full of accusations and finger pointing read any better backwards? Did I have to build a foundation? Get an agreement on the Goal of the Health Service first?

According to the Six Layers of Resistance I would have to get them to agree on the problem before I could start explaining the causes. I had to do the same with the surgeons that I had done with Eddy. That hadn't been too difficult, in fact it had been really straightforward, which, considering our past history was miraculous. Eddy and Max had agreed on my definition of the Goal of the Health Service on the first pass, so there was no reason why the surgeons would be any different, was there?

Harry had stressed that my work should read like a conversation, not a presentation so this is how I wrote it. I even left spaces where I was hoping for nods or murmurs of agreement. This was very important, as the audience should not be expected to take anything on trust, everything should be as clear as possible. So I had to set out my agenda first and get them to agree on it.

Layer zero states that you need to get the audience to agree with the agenda. The agenda is quite clear. Let's all do better. I knew I could state that clearly enough, but Layer One worried me: Get agreement on the problem. Luckily I had Harry's email to refer back to.

beth,

once you have got agreement on the Agenda you have their at-
tention. it is likely that your audience have never heard such a
clear explanation of what they are trying to achieve. they will
be interested. they will want to know more.

here's the tough part. you have to take them through the journey
you have been through but don't reveal the Core Problem until
the end. you need to pile on the agony. tell them about the
problems they face every day, make them realise that you are
the expert they have been waiting for. to do this you need to
keep the UDE's as generic as possible. remember, you are go-
ing to present this to all different types of people in the service
and they need to see that they are not alone in suffering the con-
sequences of the system, and it is the system that is sick!

while presenting your work you are offering them a way out, an
escape, and at the same time you need to unite them. you will
not achieve this if your presentation gives them ammunition to
point the finger of blame at other people. you cannot give them
an easy option and blaming individuals is the easiest option of
all. you have to unite them against the system and then make
them realise that they are the owners of the system and that they
are the only ones who can change it.

give it a go and send me your work. i'll do my best to be your
sounding board. if i can understand it, anyone will! good luck.

H

Huh! I knew people were trying to wish me well, but the
phrase 'good luck' implies that you're going to need it. As I
waited in the surgical directorate training room, trying to talk
calmly to John as the room slowly filled with surgeons, I tried

to forget about the well educated brains that would pool their grey matter to shoot me down if they didn't agree with my logic.

'What on earth are you doing to us today John!' Boomed a voice with a heavy Welsh accent. It was Euan Griffiths, well known in the hospital for his boorish tendencies, fascination with rugby and his ability to down a pint of beer in less than three seconds. I tried to stop myself shrinking away, but John stood up for me as always.

'Ach, just take a seat and listen Euan,' he replied with a waspish smile. 'I can assure you this will be of interest to you and everyone else here. In fact, there is more chance of the Welsh beating South Africa at rugby than there is of you leaving here uninspired.'

Euan bustled off to the back row sending back good-natured insults and complaining to everyone he met how he had 'seen all these silver bullet theories before and none of them had managed to nail the werewolf.'

Someone replied to him that at least it should be entertaining, good for a laugh.

I remembered my dream with a jolt. I felt as if I had just drunk a pint of cappuccino, my heart was racing, my knees felt weak, and I was desperate for a pee. I tried to talk to John so I could excuse myself, but my tongue had suddenly swollen to twice it's normal size and I wasn't sure that I could form any words at all.

John took my aborted attempt to communicate as my desire to start the presentation. Before I could stop him he had introduced me and I was left standing in front of a mass of faces that ranged from expectant, through bored to hostile.

I forced myself to open my mouth and thank John for his introduction. I was relieved to find that my tongue was capable of forming words albeit with a slight lisp, but with every word the lisp became less noticeable.

'I am speaking today about the work that I have been doing to try and improve the situation in this hospital. To start with, I will try to summarise the problems we are facing.' I said before pausing to check the audience.

'Oh come on Beth!' Euan boomed. 'We all know about the problems, just tell us how you think *you* can solve them.'

I could feel my tongue inflating again. How could I stick to my plan if they didn't want to listen? I was saved by Lucy, another of the surgical consultants. She was a very serious looking lady with bright auburn hair and an impressive array of freckles.

'Euan Griffiths!' She exclaimed loudly. 'As one of a number of people here that has had the misfortune to hear your rugby songs I would kindly suggest that you sit down and listen to what Beth has to say.'

The room rippled with laughter and agreement and I forced my tongue to behave and launched into my script. 'The British National Health Service was established to provide cradle to grave medical treatment, free at the point of delivery to the population of the United Kingdom. For over 50 years it had struggled to achieve this, and now more than ever it is feeling the strain of demand.

'Whilst those of us working within the service have a clear personal view of what we would dearly like to be able to achieve, we have no single agreed statement of what we are actually striving for. I would first of all like to try to do this as I hope this will give a clear reference point for the subject matter I want to discuss with you.' The audience had stopped fidgeting and were obviously listening to what I had to say. I started to get into my stride.

'We are currently trying our best to reduce our waiting lists. Ideally we would like to see no lists at all. We would like to think that patients would never have to wait for a bed on uncomfortable trolleys in the Emergency Department, and to complete the trio of of things we want to eliminate, I am sure you will agree with me that we all want to see an end to cancelled operations.'

My overhead showed:

Primary Measurements
1. Length of the time patients wait for treatment
2. Length of time patients have to wait, on a trolley in the ED, for a bed on a ward
3. The number of sechulded opearations that are cancelled

'Hear, hear!' Euan boomed sarcastically, a big grin on his face. He was determined to misbehave so like everyone else I ignored him.

'Looking at this wish list in its simplest form, the first thing we have to be able to do is to find a way to treat more patients.

'I don't think that anyone would disagree with this as an opening statement of the goal of the Health Service. Do you?' This statement was met with nods all round.

'So *Treat More Patients'* is our cornerstone. On its own this is not a sufficient goal to meet the challenges we are facing. We also have to throw a few more elements into the mix.

'With the evolving field of medicine we have new treatments being introduced all the time. As more treatments are found, our potential client base, the number of patients we are able to treat grows almost daily. Our already overstretched resources are being spread thinner and thinner as time goes by. However this does not mean that we do not want to treat them. Wouldn't it be wonderful if we could find the funding, personnel and equipment needed to treat all of the ailments our expanding knowledge will allow us to?' I looked up to view a sea of nodding heads.

'So are we in agreement that we would like be able to offer our patients better treatments as soon as we can? If we add this to our first statement it now becomes *'Treat more patients better.'* But to make this statement really represent what we would like to do it still needs some clarification.

'We also need to reduce the time it takes for them to get treatment so I suggest that we expand the statement to read. *'Treat More Patients, Better and Sooner.'* Does this sound right?'

I was greeted with nods again with the added benefit of a few smiles. 'I think there is still something missing. When do we want this ideal world to come about? Ten years time, twenty? No, ideally we would all want this to happen now. Tomorrow. As soon as possible. So should our Goal read '*Treat More Patients Better, Sooner, Now*?' The audience silently agreed.

'Still not complete is it? We don't want another here today gone tomorrow solution. We've all seen these come and go...'

'Hear, hear!' Euan interrupted again.

'What we really want is a sustainable improvement in the services we offer,' I continued. 'So why not expand the Goal to read '*Treat More Patients, Better, Sooner, Now and in the Future*?' 'Idealistic? Yes. I know what you are thinking. It would take a bottomless pot of money to achieve this and I agree with you. 'If we accept this as the Goal of the Health Service you will initially say that we will never achieve it. 'But let's read it again. '*Treat more patients better, sooner, now and in the future*'.

'It's not saying that we should aim to perform miracles, just improve a bit each day, each week, each month, each year. 'By adopting this as our goal we should be able to focus on making sure that each decision we make is for an improvement not a retrograde step. Do you agree that this is what we should be doing?'The nods were now accompanied by a low murmur of agreement.

'In medicine we will always have tough choices to make but it is how we make those choices that interests me, and I hope you too. 'This is where our stated aim of '*Treating more patients, better, sooner, now and in the future*' can help us decide how to give better value for taxpayers' money. 'Do you think that we can we do better than we are now?'

The audience gave more murmured affirmations and while I could see Euan making side comments to the people around him in the back row, I could tell they were ignoring him. 'I don't know of anyone working in the Health Service who is satisfied, who is confident that it is as good as it can be. Why is this? We all instinctively feel that inefficient processes and systems are failing us. We all know of areas in the service where it seems to be haemorrhaging cash. But it is never in our department. Why is this? We have all asked the question, 'Why does XYZ get funding when ABC does not?'

'Whatever our feelings about money, we work in a uniquely funded organisation. How many times have we heard about overspending? How many times have we been forced to work with reduced budgets? Many. But how many times has the Health Service made staff redundant? How many times have hospitals been forced out of business due to bankruptcy? Never?

'We all know why. Whatever the political climate the government of the day could not retain its power if it applied the same rules of finance to the Health Service that businesses have to adhere to. The Health Service will not be allowed to go bankrupt.

'Let's take a minute to think about the British Health Service. As the largest single employer in Europe and one of the largest in the world, the British Health Service has the highest proportion of graduates of any employer, anywhere, ever. We are a smart organisation.

'We all know and complain bitterly about the rates of pay in the service and we all consider life outside of the service and the financial rewards that we could reap, but we stay. Why? For the most part it is because we believe wholeheartedly in what we are doing. 'We are smart and we are dedicated and at the end of the day we are protected from financial ruin, so why can't we get it right? 'This is the heart of what I want to discuss with you today. 'How to make the best decisions we can on behalf of our patients. 'To begin to understand what the Health Service should invest in, we need to get a clear picture in our minds of what we do now.

'We have to understand *what we do now* before we can decide upon *what we should be doing in the future* and until we know this we cannot possibly know *How to change.*

'We could get into a huge political debate about healthcare funding, but in reality it's the everyday decisions that you and I make that affect patient care. It's how we deliver the service on the ground that determines the patient's experience of the Health Service.

'To prove this I would ask you to consider a simple scenario.'I paused to take a sip of water and the room remained silent as they waited for me to continue. Harry's method seemed to be working, it was actually working!

'You all have plans, ideas, and fantasies, call them what you want, about how you would like your departments to operate. I have no doubt that most of you think that it's a lack of funding that stops you from making these dreams reality.

'Along comes a genie, your wish is granted. Your budget is huge and you set about spending it. So what do you spend it on? More beds, where do you put them? The building is full and although your budget is many more times bigger it is not big enough to finance the building of another wing.

'More doctors perhaps? Only the best will do so where would you get them? Other Trusts who are desperate to keep them? Abroad, where they are needed by their own people? Sponsor more places at Medical School and wait years for graduates who might be enticed away by better salaries?

'How about more equipment? State of the art? Who will operate it? How long will it take to train these new people? 'My point? Long-term investment in people, resources and equipment is needed but we need answers now, this week, this quarter.

'It is more important that we understand what we need to do now. Given the current state of the health service would you be confident that any future investment would not be wasted? I wouldn't. Why? Because we can't make the system work now and unless there are some significant changes in the way we operate what hope do we have for the future?

'Those of us working at an operational level are the people who are charged with making things happen today. And so far we are not achieving the targets we have been set. 'We try, we try very hard but somehow so few of these targets are met. To understand why we are unable to meet so many of them we need to understand what we actually do. If we do not fully understand what we do, how can we even begin to understand how we can improve what we do on a day-to-day, month-to-month, year to year basis? How can we begin to meet our previously stated aim of treating more patients, better, sooner, now and in the future? Do you agree?'

The audience broke their silence as the word 'yes' was peppered around the room. I noticed several consultants looking at each other and nodding. I had grabbed their interest and their trust, it was time to move on.

Chapter 28

'Let's try and establish a really clear picture of how we currently respond to our commitments in the Health Service,' I continued. 'At this moment in time we have three very clear and prominent measurements that we are all measured by. They are: The length of time a patient has to wait for a consultation with a specialist; the length of time a patient has to wait for an in-patient bed in the Emergency Department and the number of elective scheduled operations that are cancelled.

'Would you agree that these are the three main or primary measurements that we are currently forced to work to? Our current *Primary Measurements*. Yes?'

I was greeted with more nods.

'Of course over time these may change but I think you will agree that whatever *Primary Measurements* are the *dish of the day* we are all forced to respond to them as quickly and effectively as possible. Yes?

'Alright, so what happens when one of these measurements is out of step? When they are too big to be acceptable, to us, the patients or to the government?' The audience was silent, waiting for me to tell them the answer.

'First of all the warning bells start to sound. Through data collection techniques someone, somewhere identifies a problem. Eventually, someone with enough authority will get to hear about it and will need to devise a solution. Let's call these people the Auditors for the sake of our story.

'Where will they go? The Auditor will try to trace back through the system to find the source of the problem. When they think they have found it they will approach the person responsible for the area where they think the problem resides.

'They will adjust the targets according to the needs of the system. Of course they will tell the Head of the *offending* department/directorate/ hospital or Trust that he or she needs to address the problem and of course, it needs to be done within the current budget.

'At last' thinks the Head, who for the sake of clarity I will call *Head A*. 'I've known that there's been a problem here for ages but until now I have not had the authority to put it right. With this authorisation I can.'

'So *Head A* sets about achieving the new targets. This is too good an opportunity to miss. *Head A* sets about tidying up those nagging operational issues in their own area using the excuse that they need to put their own house in order before they start tackling the problem.' There were a few muffled snorts of laughter at this comment and I looked up and smiled. Obviously, John and I were not the only people to come across this situation.

'After *Head A* has managed to implement some changes and the offending area has improved their operational procedures. The staff go along with the changes as they always do and the internal performance of the department has improved.

'Unfortunately, the *Primary Measurement* has only improved slightly, not enough to satisfy the Auditor. *Head A* tries to understand why. 'If I have improved my area of responsibility and the Primary measurement has not improved as much as we have, then the problem cannot be under my control.'

'*Head A* is finally on to something. Having achieved the authority from the Auditor they start to seek the source of the problem in another area. One day *Head A* identifies where the problem really resides. Over there. It is another department's fault.' The rumble of comments showed that my audience were still with me. 'So armed with the authority given to them by the Auditor, *Head A* arranges to meet with the Head of the other area, *Head B* to discuss how they can improve.

'The meeting does not go well. The Heads get together and are outwardly sympathetic to each other problems, but *Head B's* area is already in the middle of a similar project and they also have authority from an Auditor to improve another of the primary measurements. And as these measurements take equal priority, *Head B* has to dedicate all of the area's resources to solving their own problem not somebody else's.

'*Head A* leaves the meeting annoyed. For the sake of a little co-operation his team could really sort this problem out. *Head B* appears to be stubborn and irrational and obviously resents the attempted interference. They leave the meeting having damaged their working relationship.

'*Head A* faces more dead ends. Eventually The Auditor demands a report: 'I have achieved this, this and this but I could not do as well as you asked because *Head B* blocked me.'

'By giving a clear explanation of the effect of *Head B's* stubbornness, *Head A* pleads for more authority, 'Please will you make it clear to the other area that they have to do as I say? If you do that then I can deliver what you ask.'

'In the meantime the Auditor is also under pressure to deliver and is being pushed for positive results. At the next meeting with his boss the Auditor reports the progress made in the offending area but is unable to report on any great improvement in the primary measurement.

'However, data now shows that the problem has shifted and now lies in another area. The Auditor knows the other area well and is aware of the work being done there to improve another of the primary measurements. At the meeting the Auditor argues that *Head B's* area does not have the resources to tackle two primary measurements at a time and develops arguments for more funding.

'The extra funding is agreed and eventually *Head A* gets to hear about it. *Head A* is convinced that they could have resolved the problem as well as *Head B* if *they* had received the funding. *Head A* feels that the Auditor has lost faith in their ability and begins to resent both the Auditor and the *Head B* even more.

'A final attempt is made to convince the Auditor that the additional funds would be better utilised with *Head A's* team. The plea is ignored as the decision has been made and processed and after all *Head A's* area has improved while *Head B's* hasn't, so the money is needed more there.' I paused. The audience had been quiet for some time now. I needed to know if they were still with me.

'Does anyone recognise this game of Ping-Pong? This goes on all the time. Departments improve but they are punished.' I was met with a rousing affirmation so I knew I could continue.

'But this is just the beginning of our managerial tale of woe,' I said, pausing for dramatic effect. I was met with good-natured groans and I prepared to tackle the next section.

'A few months later, *Head B's* area had improved but they had failed to make anything but minor improvements to the primary measurements, and *Head B* has to ask *Head A* for a meeting. Co-operation is needed to continue improvements. What sort of a response does *Head B* get?'

'Bog off!' Euan boomed from the back and everyone laughed.

'Right,' I agreed with a smile. 'Or rather: 'I don't have the resources to do as you ask.'

'So where do we go from here? The Auditor is still under pressure to deliver and it is obvious that neither Head can provide what the Auditor needs. Some improvements have been made, but nowhere near enough to satisfy the layer of management above. A new plan, a new strategy is needed.

'The Auditor rationalises that if neither Head can resolve the problem then someone with skills that neither of them posses is needed to tackle the problem.' This statement earned some more snorts of laughter from the audience.

'By now the competition between the Heads is getting more and more intense and the working relationship between the areas is deteriorating. So the Auditor decides to create a new post, justifying the expense by the impact on the *Primary Measurements*.'

'Hooray!' Euan shouted, earning himself another laugh. I didn't mind at all, it showed that the audience, not to mention Euan, had bought into the process.

'The Heads both apply for the post, but they are not considered suitable candidates, after all they failed to solve the problems first time round. A new appointment is made. This New Head, who I will call *Head C*, is invariably given more authority; they will need this to accomplish the task. *Head C* is inserted into the hierarchy between the Old Heads and the Auditor.

'This naturally upsets the Old Heads. After all, they claim that they know how to solve the problem, and now someone who knows nothing about their areas is going to tell them what to do.

'But *Head C* needs, somehow, to get up to speed with recent events and operational procedures. *Head C* will ask around, but eventually will have to approach the Old Heads.

'It almost goes without saying that they will not be particularly helpful, after all this is the person who *got their job* and all the benefits that position promised.

'They will be polite, but not particularly helpful. *Head C* will try such tactics as trying to elicit a wish list from the Old Heads to try and get a handle on the problems. But *Head C* cannot ask the subordinates of the Old Heads what is wrong. This would be crossing unwritten boundaries and the Old Heads are saying that 'it's not our fault.' Where does *Head C* go from here?' I paused, but there were no suggestions from the floor. They just wanted to know what was coming next.

'*Head C* got the post because of a track record for solving problems. But so far the problems are masked and the only clue as to where they reside is in the available data. But the data gathering technique on which *Head C* bases the new plan has not changed since the problem was last addressed. As a result of this the New Plan, inevitably looks very similar to the plans from the Old Heads.

'Let's return for a moment to the Old Heads. They have been overlooked for promotion. They feel that their authority has been diluted. They no longer have the ear of the Auditor. They have to report to *Head C* who is being paid more than they are and, is in all probability, better qualified. Also *Head C* is not fully aware of the tremendous efforts that have been made in the areas.

'When *Head C* presents his plan to the Old Heads they are not surprised when it appears to be very similar to the plans they had already tried to implement a short while ago. But they just shrug their shoulders and tell themselves, '*Head C* must know something I don't'.

'They aren't going to help *Head C* succeed where they failed, but they aren't going to disobey him either. So they return to their areas to tell their teams about the new initiative.

'These teams, have, in their opinion, moved mountains, to improve their areas. And now the Head they worked so hard for is telling them that their efforts were not good enough. Not only were they not good enough, they have to do almost the same thing all over again.

'Their reaction? First of all they don't even agree that the problem is in their department. They know from experience that other departments have to improve before they can improve anymore.

'But they don't get an answer when they ask their Head what the other departments are doing. The Heads aren't talking. And their Head sure isn't going to ask *Head C*. So the Head is forced to tell the team that they have to comply with instructions that they don't understand.

'The team, on the other hand, feel that their Head no longer values their input and that they are being treated like idiots. They know that the new plan won't work so they are not confident to drop old practices in favour of the new ones. To protect the system they worked so hard to improve, they effectively double their workload by maintaining the old system alongside the new.

'After all, who will have to clean up the mess when the new plan fails? More to the point, they fully believe they are there to serve the patients and anything that reduces this service must be kept away from the patients at all costs, even the wrath of their Head. This has a devastating side effect.

'Eventually they decide that the cause of their problem is their own Head and they eventually stop sharing their day-to-day problems, preferring to try to handle them alone. More than this, they begin to hide day-to-day problems from their Head because admitting to them would reveal that they are still maintaining the old system.

'Eventually a day-to-day problem becomes too big, or too troublesome to handle and they decide they 'don't get paid enough to put up with this' and throw it at their Head, while it is red hot. This is how fire fighting starts.

'So where are we now? We have teams who do not trust their Heads. We have fires flaring up all around the Head's insubordinate teams and *Head C* who is insisting that they implement plans that will not work.

'This means we have *Head C* who is not getting the results from the plans he had hoped for and to add to his worries the only feedback he is getting is from the Old Heads and it is worse than useless.

'A pattern has been established. A negative loop. This loop appears at all levels and is not confined to the lower operational levels. Where do we go from here?'

Again there was a restless silence, they agreed with me so far and were waiting for my solution. 'Well there is a possible outlet,' I continued. 'The Old Heads begin to realize they have something valuable to offer *Head C*. And in the ensuing chaos they need to score some points.

'They know the obstacles that will stop *Head C's* plan from working. More than that they know when the obstacles are going to become a real problem because they have seen the warning signs before. But *Head C* does not take kindly to warnings from belligerent subordinates. So another pattern has begun to develop.

'The Old Heads fall into the same pattern as their teams and now only hand the problem of the obstacle to *Head C* when it has become a fire.

'Very soon *Head C* realizes that support is needed to put the fire out and support from other areas is sought to protect the precious new plan. And because the problem is a fire by the time it reaches *Head C*, action has to be taken immediately.

'By the time *Head C* needs assistance, there is no one to help as everyone is busy with their own fires. So *Head C* joins the negative loop.

'In the meantime the teams have just about given up on the new plan and have reverted to the old, but slightly improved system. The slight improvements have been made through fire fighting and so an updated new mode of operation becomes established.

'A valuable note to point out here is that some of the new practices adopted from the failed plan do not always make sense. Often these new practices were designed to work as part of a new overall plan and once implemented within the old structure appear out of place and pointless—but the staff were told to do it so they do.

'As time passes each system picks up some of these useless processes that hang onto them like limpets. They do not fulfill a function, but no one thinks to clean them out.

'Eventually *Head C* falls into the same mode of operation as the Old Heads and they now all have more and more projects on their hands. The slight improvements have been sold to the Auditors as the best they could do under the circumstances. Time to move on to the next fire-fighting project.

'Why do I claim this? Because, by now, fires and improvement projects are indistinguishable. And it all starts again.'

I paused and allowed people to fidget as they digested the fact that I had reached the end of the tale.

'Well that is where we are now,' I continued. 'An interesting story? I'm sure that every person working in the Health Service could put names to the people in this story and it would ring true. But it is more than just a story and this is where I prove it to you. This scenario is not just the result of random observation. It is the results of a detailed cause and effect analysis.

'As doctors you are all aware of cause and effect. You practice it every day. You see a patient with symptoms that appear unrelated. You use your skills as physicians to find the root cause, which you treat. Either with medicine, surgery or both.

'The system you work on is the human body. The system we work within is the Health Service. On the face of it, it is suffering from symptoms that at first seem unrelated. As managers we are charged with curing the symptoms. But they don't go away. What does this tell you? 'We are not treating the root cause of these symptoms. Can it be done? Can it be found? 'I believe it can and even better, I believe that I have found it.'

Chaper 29

My last comment had the desired effect and the room was buzzing with side comments and murmurs. I took another sip of water and glanced over at John. I had been granted a twenty-minute slot for this presentation, I had already run over by five minutes and now I had an expectant audience. Should I mention that I was out of time, or take Harry's advice to keep going as long as possible the moment I had their attention?

As chairman of the meeting John was not going to cut me short, but someone else might get annoyed at me taking their time. The audience looked quite eager, but it was hard to judge the best way to go forward. I looked across at John and he motioned for me to continue. I took a deep breath and dived straight in.

'To find out what is causing a disease or medical condition you, as medics, look for symptoms. A certain cluster of symptoms will cause you to test for others and eventually you get to the root of the problem.

'We can do the same with the problems we have here, in this hospital.

'I have already mentioned many of the symptoms we are all suffering from, but for this part of the presentation I'll pick just three of them and try to establish their cause.

'The three that annoy me the most are…'

I pulled up a slide showing the following bullet points and read them aloud.

- *Too many improvement projects fail to deliver the expected results*

- *Potential negatives and objections are almost always overlooked*
- *Rank and file staff have 'seen it all before'*

'Do these annoy you?' I asked.

There was a murmuring of confirmations and the audience scrutinized the slide.

'Let's look at each one in turn,' I said. 'The first one is that too many improvement projects fail to deliver the expected results. Does this ring true?'

I was met with more appreciative mutterings.

'We often see new managers or newly promoted supervisors attempting to instigate improvement programmes.

'Often these programmes are the result of a crisis, or knee jerk reaction to a new situation or an old problem resurfacing. They can also be attempts to streamline systems to try and save money. Whatever the cause they are rarely documented, apart from financially, and are often apparently *off-the-cuff* actions.

'Very little time is taken to fully prepare or even understand what really needs to be done. They hardly ever take negative consequences into account.

'They end up as yet another sticking plaster that will eventually fall off or cause an infection in another part of the system.

'Yes? Have you seen this happen?'

The murmurings had reduced, but nearly everyone was nodding their heads.

'So we have an attempt to improve a part of the system. But today's problems have to be dealt with in order to make this improvement, and in order to deal with today's problems, the person charged with making the improvement has to make changes as quickly as possible. Do you agree?

'However, changes will have to be made in order to improve and they will have a long term impact. To make these types of lasting changes it is imperative to take time to plan them properly to avoid any possible negative impacts they might have.

'So do you agree that the people charged with running these improvement projects are torn?—Torn between making things happen now, and taking the time to plan changes that will not have potential long-term negative impacts. Yes?'

I was greeted by another sea of thoughtful nods.

'Let's move on to symptom number two, potential negatives and objections are almost always overlooked.

'We've already agreed that long term negatives are rarely considered due to a perceived lack of time, but let's look at this a bit closer and see if it gets us any nearer to the root cause. I am sure you will all recognise this scenario:

'Projects are usually *launched* at a meeting where the problem they are designed to overcome is first discussed with the operational staff.

'Those not involved with the *invention* of the solution are expected to participate in its execution.

'More often than not, the inventor does not ask for, or listen to, the potential negatives raised by the operational staff who are expected to manage the tasks.

'The operational staff who raise objections, are often shunned and/or overlooked for promotion.

'So, to summarise, in order to have successful projects we must achieve the projects' goals as perceived by the inventor. And in order to do this we must do exactly as the inventor demands. But there is a flipside to this argument. In order to have successful projects we must also ensure all potential predictable negative side effects are eliminated, and in order to achieve this we must be able to challenge the inventors' plans. Do you agree?

'Do you also see the conflict here? How do we get a successful project if we just do as the project inventor asks without challenging his plans? Especially if we know that they will not work?

'We can't, can we?'

A few quiet no's rumbled out from the audience.

'Good. Now onto the final undesirable effect of our three; Rank and file staff have 'seen it all before'.

'A huge number of projects are launched by new managers that many long serving staff have 'seen it all before'. So many projects have failed that a large proportion of the staff no longer trust anyone who launches improvement projects.

'Because of this they go along but maintain existing systems. They do this because they know that they will be the ones who will have to pick up the pieces when the managers lose interest and try to bury the failed project. Perhaps more importantly, they are dedicated to their jobs and to the patients.

'The analysis of this symptom runs like this; in order to do a good job, and I am assuming here that despite the bad press we have been getting lately, we do all want to do a good job.'

There were a few snorts of laughter.

'In order to do a good job we must prove we are good team players and in order to do this we are forced to participate in doomed projects. But there is another way of viewing this symptom. In order to do a good job we must minimise the damage that will result from these doomed projects. And if we are forced to do this we have to maintain the existing systems. So, yet again, we are caught between a rock and a hard place. We either participate in doomed projects or we maintain the existing systems.

'But we have already discussed this and what happens? A compromise. Both happen at the same time and what is the result? The mess we are in today.

'As physicians would you be satisfied with treating two symptoms if the root cause were equally easy to remedy? No. So why should we put up with it in our management of the hospital?

'This brings us on to the root cause. The part you have all been so patiently waiting for.

'By amalgamating these three symptoms we can come up with a single analysis which will show us the source of the root problem.'

I paused to take another sip of water and the audience paused with me.

'In order to make a positive contribution we must be seen to be good employees of the system, and in order to be seen to be good employees of the system we must do what our bosses think they need us to do. But on the other hand, to make a positive contribution we must also do what actually needs to be done, and in order to do this we are forced to make changes to the boss's plans.

'Does this sound right to you? I know it does to me. So why does this happen? In order to be able to break the conflict between doing what the boss thinks he needs and doing what actually needs to be done, whilst at the same time maintaining the working relationships that are needed to run a hospital, we need to be able to raise our concerns in a productive way.

'Put another way, we must feel that we are able to raise negatives without being threatened by the system.

'Sound too simple eh? Consider this.

'First of all, when was the last time you were asked to participate in the planning of a project before the project manager told you how the project was going to run?

'Or look at it another way. When was the last time you asked your staff to participate in the planning of a project you were charged with running?

'I'm sure this has rarely happened. Why? Because you know that if you asked your staff what needed to be done they would load you down with unnecessary suggestions that would cloud your thinking. Am I right? I know this is true because I have done it time and time again.

'So, the way we currently operate is to deny our staff the platform from which they can raise potential negatives. We do this because if they do offload all of their negatives on us we don't know how to handle them. I know from experience that once this floodgate is opened it is very hard to close it without upsetting our staff. We just don't have the mechanisms to hand to allow us to explain to the people who bring us seemingly irrelevant problems that this is not the time or the place to deal with them.

'Even more to the point, if they insist that these seemingly unrelated problems do have relevance, they are often unable to explain why. They just assume that we can see the connections when often they are the only ones who can. And if they cannot explain them to us we just ignore them, usually at our peril.

'We are lacking a platform where negatives can be raised and we, as managers, are usually unable to sort the wheat from the chaff, which means that we do not have a real robust mechanism to deal with them.

'The core problem of this hospital and indeed the British Health Service is that there is no platform or mechanism by which negatives can be raised and effectively addressed.

'Take a minute to think of a recent problem if you need further proof that this is the root cause of all of our current problems. Imagine what would have happened if you'd had the opportunity to discuss it in an environment that was safe and supportive, with managers who were capable of taking your potential solution and working on it until it was good enough to be implemented?'

The room was filled with silence. It was as if I had asked the assembled audience to pray.

It was Euan who broke the silence. 'Poor old Martin would still be here instead of being branded a whistle blower.'

This time no one laughed at the class clown's latest outburst. The looks of concentration on their faces deepened as they remembered the junior surgeon who was forced to move abroad after he leaked his story of failing surgical procedures to the press. This was an unexpected serious twist to the presentation. They had made a connection with my analysis in a way I least expected.

If I needed further proof that I was right this was it.

Chapter 30

I took a deep breath and tried to raise the sombre tone of the presentation. True, I wanted them to realise the full extent of the problem, but I had to be careful not to avoid blaming anyone in particular.

'So we agree that the fact that there is no platform or mechanism by which negatives can be raised and effectively addressed is the core problem of the Health Service. Yes?'

I received a few nods of assent.

'By accepting this as the core problem I now hope that you will accept the following analysis in the nature in which it is given. Not a criticism, not finger pointing, just a means to an end. A way to identify a practical solution to the day-to-day problems we all suffer.

'Thank you for giving me this platform. Now on to the mechanism.

'Assume that the Health Service is a patient of yours. This inability to raise negatives and address them effectively is the same as asking you to treat a patient while you are at another location with scant communication between yourself and your patient. Much the way NHS Direct works.

'I am sure that all of you are aware of the Telephone Triage service offered by NHS Direct, but I'll just clarify the exact nature of the service.

'NHS Direct is a 24-hour telephone medical advice service. Anyone can call them from anywhere in the UK. Call handlers who take basic details such as name, address, age, family doctor and basic symptoms answer the phones and these details are recorded on a computer system. The call handlers are trained to spot life-threatening conditions and at this early stage of the process will advise very poorly patients to call for an ambulance.

'Once the patient's details are on the system they are called back by an experienced nurse who determines the right course of action for the patient to take by working through a set of questions.

'Often the nurses can give advice over the phone. For example, take two paracetamol, and see your family doctor if the symptoms persist. But more serious conditions need to be referred straight to a doctor or to the Emergency Department so that the patient can be seen by a doctor, in person, before a diagnosis can be made.

'In essence, although the patients are seeking a diagnosis from which they can be advised on a quick and appropriate treatment regime, the service only provides a triage system. It is a stopgap in the process of finding the best entry system into the Health Service where the patient can secure a diagnosis. Doctor's time is the scarcest resource the service has so this system is designed to relieve the burden of time-wasters and patients presenting trivial symptoms. In short, doctors, or in your case surgeons, are the bottleneck of the Health Service.

'In management terms you are the constraint. And the rest of what I'm going to tell you today relates to the management of this constraint and how we can begin to overcome it.'

'Hallelujah!' Euan proclaimed from the back and earned a few grins. The clown was back.

'The management of constraints is not new. It's been happening in industry in many parts of the world for years now. But so far the progress has been slow in medicine. This is because until now the profession has not been aware of the core problem.

The core problem exists because as managers we are not trained to understand that the undesirable effects or symptoms the system is suffering from are just that, symptoms. I know that during your training you spend years learning how to link symptoms back to causes. We have not done this in the management of medicine. We didn't have the diagnostic skills, until recently.

'By teaching the managers these skills we can begin to monitor the health of the service and prepare to start to address the bottleneck. Note I said bottleneck in the singular.

'I'm sure that most of you feel that you have bottlenecks in your area of concern, but think of this. If I could prove to you that there is one deeply embedded bottleneck in this hospital that would alleviate many of the symptoms this hospital is suffering from, how would you react? Wouldn't it be great?

'If we know exactly what it is then we can treat it. Oh, sure there would still be another bottleneck, but once the biggest one had been eliminated the next would be smaller and more manageable. Does this make sense? There will always be a bottleneck, but eventually they will become smaller and smaller and easier to manage.

'So, would you like to know what the bottleneck of this hospital is?'

There were a few murmurs and nods from the audience, but I was after a stronger confirmation. I needed to know if they were still with me.

'Would you like to know?' I repeated.

'Just get on with it!' Euan boomed from the back.

I took a step backwards, I had a nasty thought that I was losing their attention and I started to falter as I scanned for my place in my script.

John stood up. 'If you feel you could succinctly list the problems of the Health Service in thirty minutes Euan, then feel free to come up here. However, I suspect you will be staying put so just hear Beth out. She is trying to explain a complex theory in a short space of time and she needs to know that you are following her logic, so please help her out when necessary.'

I could have hugged John, but I had other allies. Lucy with the auburn hair jumped back into the fray.

'Do go ahead Beth. You are making perfect sense to me.'

This was followed by more confirmations and *go ons* from the audience. I took another deep breath.

'Alright, here goes.'

'As with your diagnostic methods there are certain steps that one must take to find the constraint. It is commonly thought that the constraint lies with the way bed occupation is managed in this hospital and to some extent it is.'

I smiled as the audience began to move about in their seats. After all as the Manager of the Admissions department I was seen as the primary source of bed management in the hospital and I had been prattling on about raising negatives for the last hour. No doubt they thought I was about to confess my sins to them!

'There are five steps, one of our new mechanisms,' I continued and brought up a slide to illustrate my claim.

Five Focusing Steps of constraint management
1. *Identify*
2. *Exploit*
3. *Subordinate*
4. *Elevate*
5. *Start again*

'Now we all know we are desperately short of beds. But according to national studies we have the correct ratio of beds per head of population we serve. In fact we are a little better off than the average, but we never seem to have enough. Would you agree?'

The room was alive with murmurs of agreement.

'So if we say that beds are the constraint, we should be able to exploit them more to give us more capacity. But we are already running at 98 per cent. So we cannot do any more on step two.

'Subordinate. What does this mean? It means that we have to subordinate everything else to the constraint. According to this we shouldn't book elective patients until we know we're going to have beds to put them in. Does this sound right? It doesn't to me. So what is wrong?

'If we have an average population to serve, and according to national figures we do, then the actual number of beds cannot be the constraint. Do you agree? If other hospitals can make this ratio of beds to population work then the constraint must be something else and the good news is that it is inside of our system, where we can treat it. Yes?'

There were no affirmations forthcoming, just puzzled looks.

'Alright, let me ask you something else. A few years ago before we experienced our first *Winter Pressures* how long did it take you to perform your ward rounds? Compare that to now. I know that some of you have had to split your rounds. And I know that some of the medical consultants only visit some wards twice or even once a week.

'As a teaching hospital your junior staff are quite rightly dependent on your input. And if you are expected to make decisions on your patient's care you, being the professionals you are, will want to have sight of your patients before your make changes in treatment regimes.'

The audience was beginning to nod in agreement. The NHS Direct analogy was beginning to make sense. They would no more consider a new course of treatment based on inexperienced doctors' information than the nursing staff would over the phone.

'So the rate at which treatment can be amended for patients with complications has just been extended by the time it takes you to get to see them. Do you agree?'

I was very relieved to see definite nodding from the audience.

'Now we move onto the system analysis. You would not have chosen to work this way so why do you?

'Because the bloody patients are all over the hospital,' Euan quipped.

I nodded and was greeted with more verbal responses.

'We walk miles to see them all.' 'We can't see them all in one day.'

At last I started to feel in control.

'And whose decision was it to spread your patients around the wards?' I asked.

'Management!' chimed three of the attendees at once.

A ripple of laughter rang around the room.

'And why did management implement this policy?' I challenged.

'Because of the pressure to move patients out of the Emergency Department before they hit the trolley wait reporting times,' Lucy replied.

'Thank you, and who decided that the trolley wait times would be implemented?'

'The bloody Department of Health!' Euan shouted.

'Alright, so do you agree that you are not to blame?'

'Yes!' said half a dozen voices at once.

'And do you agree that it is not the fault of your colleagues in the medical directorate?'

More muffled confirmations were given up. 'Suppose.' 'Yeah.'

'And do you agree that Admissions are not to blame?'

I was pleased to receive a more positive, 'Yes' to this.

'And what about management?' I pushed and earned another subdued confirmation.

'Alright, so we agree that the system had forced us to act in ways that are contrary to the way we want to work. Yes?'

'But the medics have at least 30 per cent of our beds!' Someone cried indignantly.

'I'm glad you mentioned that. You all know that medical patients take, on average, longer to treat than surgical patients. Just think of the impact that having medical patients in every ward in the hospital is having on the medical teams.'

'No wonder they are always so pissed off,' Euan quipped and then paused as he realised the breadth of his comment.

Everyone in the room laughed and I was amused to note a nervous edge to it.

'Yes' I said. 'And I take it you have been goading each other into near fistfights over bed occupancy!'

John decided that it was time for him to join in the discussion.

'Ach, I know I've had a go at a few of the magicians,' he admitted. 'I'm sure we all have and Beth has proved to us that they are not at fault, the system is. So how do we overcome this Beth?'

'Well, I've been working on this as well, but first let's just check back with the five focussing steps. Do they work?'

'If your time is the constraint and I think we all agree that it is, then how can we exploit it better? We need somehow to off-load some of your current obligations to allow you to do your rounds quicker. What would be the least productive thing that you would like to shed to make more time for your patients?'

'Wandering around this bloody place like a lost soul!' Euan shouted. He was obviously beginning to enjoy this.

'Alright, so if there were a way that we could eliminate the time it takes you to visit your patients your time would be better spent. Yes?'

'YES!' They all shouted in unison.

'So in order to achieve this we have to subordinate the rest of the system to our plan. Yes?'

'Yes, the whole hospital needs to help,' a lady in the front agreed.

'Good, so what happens when the whole hospital is with us? We elevate the constraint. We look to find more ways to free up your time until you are able to work as fast as your patients can cope with you. Until you are completely on top of your ward workload. Yes?'

'YES!'

'When we reach this utopia we start again, looking for the next constraint that is slowing our patients through our system.'

'That will be pharmacy.'

'No it won't, it will be hospital transport.'

A general discussion was about to break out, I had to regain control.

'Ladies and gentlemen, before you get carried away let's get back to the point in hand. Unless we solve this problem all the others are just minor irritations. Do you agree?'

The hubbub died down.

'So how can we remove the burden of you traipsing around the whole hospital to see your patients?'

'We could repatriate them to more appropriate wards, group each of our patients in one area,' Lucy suggested.

'Yes, we could,' I agreed, 'but how?'

'When beds become available we move patients over.'

'Alright, but what about the patients in the Emergency Department? As much as we would like to, we cannot ignore the poor souls stuck on trolleys for hours on end. As beds become available we have to move them on to start their treatment. Don't you agree?'

I looked around the room to see some of the best minds of the hospital deep in thought.

'How about...no.' Said one.

'I know, said another, 'divert them to another hospital.'

'Won't work,' someone else argued. 'Beth has already said that we should be able to solve this internally and the other hospitals are suffering as much as we are.'

'What's the answer Beth? You must know, come on put us out of our agony.'

'Actually the answer comes in two parts.' I replied and raised my eyebrows to encourage them to field their suggestions. I was really beginning to enjoy this. I looked over to John who nodded indicating that he knew what I was doing. Harry had made it clear; they must come up with the solutions in order to own them.

John decided to prompt them and as he was one of them, this was quite within Harry's rules.

'The two parts Beth's referring to are the ways patients enter the system. Anyone?'

'Through the ED and through Elective Admissions,' came the reply.

'Yes, so...' said John. 'Ach, come on, try thinking laterally, try considering something new. How can we achieve this wholesale reshuffle of patients? Think of it as a board game. To move patients around we need what?'

'Empty bloody beds!' Euan chimed up.

'Right and how are we going to get empty beds?'

'Either by discharging them or...by not admitting them!' Lucy replied.

'Right. So how can we not admit them?'

'We could cancel routine admissions, but this would mess our figures up,' She considered.

'But how long would we need to stop routine admissions for,' John pressed. 'Especially if we would guarantee shorter stays once they are here? A month, three?'

'No, about a week I reckon,' she replied. 'What do you all think?'

'So, if we suspend routine admissions for a week, do you think that we could perform this minor miracle?' John urged.

'Maybe.'

'What doesn't feel right?'

'What if we suspend routine admissions for a week and the medics grab the opportunity to drag in all and sundry?' A lady near the front asked.

'Good point.' John agreed. 'What will stop the medics admitting everyone they see in the ED? Remember, most of their admissions are through that route; their patients are usually different to ours, they are sick before they get here. Most of our routine patients have to be reasonably fit to undergo surgery. Think.'

'Well, as most of their patients come through the ED they need to stem the flow there,' Lucy reasoned.

'And how can they do that? Think back to the NHS Direct example,' John urged.

'They need an accurate diagnosis before they are admitted, not after. That way they might be able to treat and street more patients direct from the ED rather than admitting them,' she replied.

'And how would they do that?'

'By having the more experienced doctors working the ED!' Euan roared from the back.

'I'd like to see that!' Lucy agreed.

'Okay,' John agreed. 'So if the Medical consultants could be persuaded to work in the ED to minimise admissions, and you cancel your routine patients for a week, is that all we can do to guarantee sufficient time to shuffle the patients?'

'We could do more,' said Lucy before looking sheepishly round at her colleagues. 'WE could work there for a while as well.'

There was a minor uproar among her colleagues

'No hear me out,' she argued. 'We all know that our house officers admit some patients that should really have been given outpatient's appointments. They are too cautious, but we have the extra experience to allow us to make the decision. It could be worth it for a week.'

It took a little time for this to sink in but I was delighted to see reluctant agreements popping up around the room.

'So, you are saying that you might be prepared to work the ED in order to reduce the number of admissions for a while?' I asked.

'Maybe, if the medics do it as well and if we can make this plan work.'

'Alright, one final thing.' I said.

John looked at me in surprise. He thought I was done.

'We all know that Monday afternoons are the worst time of the week for admissions. The family doctors send patients in by the truckload. Yes?'

'Yes, but...'

'Exactly. If you are truly going to commit to reducing admissions can't we tackle this black spot as well? If you were present in the ED on Monday afternoons we could eliminate even more unnecessary admissions.'

'I have clinics on a Monday.' Said John

'I know it won't be easy, but if I'm going to work up a plan to do this, I need to have all of your support to do it, right. Will you help me?' The faces around the room were deep in thought. The senior medics gathered here were used to leding their support to various improvement programmes but they were not used to rolling their sleeves up and working on the front line from choice.

Finally the silence was broken by Lucy. 'Seems silly not to do the job right,' she agreed.

There was a period of extended muttering before general agreement was reluctantly reached.

'Alright, thank you.' I said with relief. The show was almost over.

'What's next in your grand plan Beth?'

'Well, I hope that today we have come a long way in understanding what we need to change.'

I put up the What to change, what to change to, how to change slide.

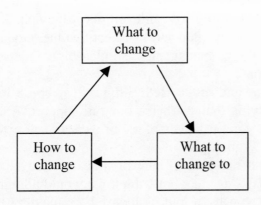

'And what we need to change to. The next step for me is to get the support of the rest of the directorates and then simply to devise a grand plan.'

They laughed.

'Seriously, I have to get the Medics onboard as well as the minor directorates. I will be doing this presentation to them all over the next two weeks. From there I will have to start working on the management. And to do this I will need your support.'

'You've got it Beth.' Euan quipped from the back, complete with a cheeky smirk.

'Sure have,' others agreed.

'But there is a problem you can help me with now,' I continued. 'If any of the other directorates catch onto this plan before I have a chance to present this to them they will feel they are being manipulated by you, the surgeons, and what effect do you think that this will have?'

'They will shut up shop and go home!' Euan laughed.

'Right. So can I ask you all to keep this to yourselves until I am able to get their support? I know it is a lot to ask, but I really need this to have a chance of making this work.'

'Okay Beth, but how long before we can start this? We need it to happen now.'

'This is the difficult part. Remember early in my presentation I explained where fire fighting comes from? Well, we cannot afford for this to become yet another fire fighting exercise. It will be killed before we can even get it moving. It will take time to formulate the plan and I suspect that the toughest groups to move will be the management so please give me some time. Can you do that?'

John stood and spoke 'Beth, I think I can speak for my colleagues in saying that you have our full support. And I would like to thank you on behalf of all of us for such a fascinating presentation. Well done.

'I'm afraid that due to lack of time we will be unable to complete today's agenda, but I think we would all agree that in light of what you have told us today the remaining items pale into insignificance and can be added to next month's meeting. Thank you.'

For the first time in my life I got a round of applause. As the audience got up to leave some of them approached me with words of congratulations. It felt good, but it also felt very scary. How the hell was I going to convince the management? I now knew that the doctors would be easy to convince. But Fran?

I needed to tell Harry about today to get more advice.

Chapter 31

I was buzzing with exhaustion when I finally got home and I was delighted to see Max was waiting at the door to welcome me.

'Hi Hon! How'd it go?' He beamed.

'Better than my dream that's for sure,' I smiled.

'Did they buy it?'

'Yes, I think they did,' I admitted and found myself grinning inanely. It felt so good to get recognition, both at home and work. I gave Max a big hug while the dogs whimpered impatiently as they waited for their turn.

'So tell me all about it then,' Max said.

'Give me a chance! I haven't even changed yet,' I objected with a laugh.

'Heck, you're a woman, you can multi-task,' Max replied with a smirk.

An hour later I had finally told the whole story and we were still in the bedroom. I suddenly noticed that Max wasn't dressed for mooching round the house; he was also starting to be a little edgy.

'Is something wrong?' I said.

'Not really,' he replied. 'But I need to go out this evening.'

'Sounds mysterious.'

'Not really,' he replied unconvincingly. 'It's work, but I should only be an hour or so.' He started to leave the room, but paused by the door. 'By the way, Harry left a message for you. He wanted to know how it went. Can you give him a call back?'

'Max!' I said in my best school teacher voice. 'You're not making an excuse to avoid talking to your kid brother are you?'

'Of course not.'

'So why don't you wait for five minutes while I call him? You can at least say hi.'

Max slumped slightly. 'I'm sorry Hon, but I'm not ready to discuss this with Harry yet. My head is still full of the situation. Can you do me a favour and not tell Harry that I'm TOC's newest recruit?'

'But that's ludicrous!' I objected. 'This is turning into a silly feud.'

'Please Hon, just for me?' Max donned his best puppy face and I laughed despite myself.

'Alright, but only if you promise to speak to him soon!'

'Thanks Hon,' he replied humbly and left the house with deceptive speed.

I grabbed myself a drink and dialled Harry's number, noting with wonder how I managed to be better friends with Harry than his brother.

A gruff voice at the other end said, 'Hi.' It was Josh.

'Josh, how are you? It's Beth.'

'I'm doing great Aunt Beth and thanks for sending me the Man Utd strip. It's real neat.'

I laughed. It seemed a long time ago that I sent the email that started this whole Health Service avalanche.

'No problem Josh, it was our pleasure.'

Before I could say anymore I heard a rousing 'Hi!' coming from Harry and Sarah. They quickly switched the call to speakerphone.

'Hey Beth!' Sarah cried. 'So tell us, how'd it go?'

'Yeah, give us all the grisly details!' Harry added. 'And as it's your call you can take your time.'

I laughed as I heard Josh excuse himself and leave us mad adults to it.

What the hell? I thought. We could afford a long phone call and after half an hour I had managed to cover the whole day. From my dream to the assurances from the surgeons that they would give me time to formulate a plan.

'Sound's like my star pupil did a great job,' Harry crooned. 'I'm sorry, I've got to ask. What does Max think of it all?'

This was the question I had been dreading.

'He's been a great help,' I said 'and he is starting to listen to TOC, but he's not quite bought in yet.' I winced as I said this. Crossing your fingers when you tell a lie doesn't have the same effect when you're an adult.

There was a long pause from the other end that was eventually broken by Sarah.

'Hey, but it's great that he's starting to learn TOC isn't it?'

I readily agreed, but the optimism of the conversation had wilted and died.

'Is Max around?' Harry asked. 'TOC aside it would be great to have a chat with him.'

'I'm sorry Harry,' I said. 'He's not here, he had to go out.'

'Where?' Harry asked, probably without thinking and was promptly admonished by Sarah.

'I don't know to be honest,' I replied. 'He said it was something to do with work.' I obviously didn't sound very convincing as the remark was greeted with another pregnant pause.

'Can I ask you a question, while I've got you on the phone?' I asked, desperate to change the subject.

'Sure Beth!' Sarah replied, perhaps a little too eagerly.

'Today I had surgeons shouting out the answers to questions I hadn't even considered asking a few weeks ago, yet I... well, I still feel very vulnerable.'

'Why Beth?' Harry asked, his attention obviously firmly switched back to my health service conundrum.

'Where to start?' I thought aloud. 'It's all so complicated.'

'No it's not Beth,' Harry chipped in. 'Remember that it may be complex, but it's not complicated!'

I laughed. I had shot myself in the foot and Harry couldn't resist pouring a little salt into the wound.

'Remember Beth, you have done a great job by showing that a change in behaviour in one department can have an effect in another. Sure, the connections are complex but they are not complicated. By the simple fact that, so far, you have not found a department, or person who stands alone from the system, who can adversely affect it without feeling the impact of their actions. It's only when this happens that things get complicated.'

'Yes, I understand that.' I said. 'As long as all of the decision-makers are affected by the problem it's possible to present a rational argument for improvement. Is that what you are saying? Following on from there, if a person or a department are not connected to the whole in some way, they or that department become much more difficult to influence. The problem become complicated rather than complex. Is that right?'

'Yeah. As long as all of the decision makers are in the mix, the job of convincing them might be complex, but it's not complicated.'

'I'm with you on that one. But I have a real complication looming up now. I could be forced out of my job over this and what good would all of this work have done?'

'I guessed this was coming,' said Harry. 'Have you made any more notes on the management UDE's?'

'Hang on,' I said, as I rifled through my bag searching for my notes. 'What I do know is that if I have a constraint on this project it will be convincing the management to sanction it.' I finally grabbed the piece of paper I was after. 'Right, here goes. Let me run through my list and see if you come to the same conclusion that I have:

- *Management is not comfortable unless they have a model to work to*
- *Management needs numbers on which to base decisions*
- *Management does not know TOC*
- *Management are short-term thinkers*
- *Management are always trying to control the medics*
- *Management are suspicious of untried theories*

'That's all I have so far but the 3 UDE Cloud analysis has thrown out this: *In order to exploit our constraint fully we must relocate our patients and in order relocate our patients we must violate the primary measurements for admissions.*

'On the other hand, in order to exploit our constraint fully, management must ensure that our primary measurements are met, and to do this management must support this project.

'So asking the management to support the project and violating the primary measurements are in direct conflict.'

I took a deep breath. 'Do you agree?'

'Sure do Beth,' Harry said. 'The whole crux of the project is getting management to go against all that they hold sacred. It's a tough one but I've seen worse.'

'Ah, but you are forgetting that I'm in the UK,' I said. 'Max is always telling me how much easier it was to persuade management to try new ideas in the US. He describes the UK managers as *belt and braces guys*."

Harry laughed, 'Sounds like my big brother! Don't give up hope Beth. I've got an idea, but I need to work on it. How about reverting to email now, as it will take some time? In the meantime, start working on those *becauses* that you are so good at and I'll give it some thought at this end.'

'It's been great to talk to you Beth,' Sarah said. 'I'm really looking forward to seeing you both in the flesh soon.'

'Say hi to Max for me,' Harry said hopefully.

The moment the phone line went dead there was a canine commotion at the door and Max walked in looking very pleased with himself.

'Harry says hi and he was very upset that you didn't want to talk to him,' I said with a meaningful look.

'You didn't tell him that I was avoiding him?' Max asked, surprise etched all over his face.

'I didn't need to,' I replied primly. 'It was perfectly obvious.'

'I'll sort it out. I promise,' he replied, his smug air quickly returning. 'Now let's get some food together and I can tell you my eureka.'

'What have you been up to?' I asked suspiciously as he walked past me into the kitchen. I caught a whiff of beer as I followed him into the room. 'Have you been down the pub?'

'It's amazing what problems you can solve over a pint of Fursty Ferret,' he grinned.

'You told me you had to go somewhere for work!'

'Calm down!' He laughed. 'Now tell me how it went with Harry.'

I told Max about our conversation and showed him the list of management UDE's I had been working on and he jumped on one particular one with glee.

'You say here that one of the reasons management won't go for your plan is because no one has tried it before. But surely there is a way that you could prove to them conclusively that it would work? Just because it has not been tried before doesn't mean it won't work.'

'That's my big problem Max. You know how long it took me to present to the surgeons. I had a captive audience and they are, by the very nature of their training, willing to accept that problems need thorough discussion and consideration.

'I've got a favourite saying: if you get six doctors in a room they will come up with 12 opinions, especially if they are discussing non-medical issues. They are prepared to look at a problem from all angles. But management isn't like that. You saw the announcement of the CBM's project. If it won't fit onto one page it won't be considered. They are fire-fighters not thinkers.'

'I see what you mean. So what you need is something to grab their attention quickly. Something that will make them think.'

'Exactly, and I know that I can't do that with one sheet of paper. It just won't work.'

'But what would?'

'Well, I had hoped that the EPR might have given us a hand, but the bed management program was just too awful for words so no help there.'

'You mean a computer program?'

'Yes, something dynamic that would be able to show them a speeded up version of the bed board, with the proposed plan working in front of their eyes.'

'So you're past Level One then?'

'What?' I couldn't believe what I was hearing.

Max could hardly control himself he was laughing so much. I had to wait at least a minute for him to regain some sense of control.

'I'm sorry Hon,' he said, wiping tears from his eyes. 'It's just...just so funny. Everything is starting to come together.'

'If you don't tell me what you're up to this very minute I am going to kick your cheeky American ass out into the garden!' I fumed, half joking, but boiling with frustration.

This was a bad move as Max dissolved into fresh fits of laughter forcing me to attempt to carry out my threat. Luckily the dogs intervened in a flurry of barking and we compromised by glaring at each other across the kitchen table.

'I've got a question for you,' Max said mischievously. 'What is the similarity between beds and tents?'

'Max you're talking rubbish. How many pints did you have down the pub?'

'Just the one,' Max grinned. 'Let me phrase it another way. What's the similarity between hospital beds and hotel beds?'

'Hospital beds!' I exclaimed and suddenly I fell into Max's plan. 'Are you suggesting those kids write a program for the bed board?'

'Got it in one! Max roared. 'I was sitting at the pub musing over two problems. The kids I had let down and your battle with the beds. Suddenly it was obvious, the kids had written a program to monitor vacancies in the holiday trade and you needed a program to monitor vacant beds.'

'But...'

'It's not as easy as it sounds,' Max continued. 'These kids have a huge constraint of their own. Money. They haven't got any and...'

'...we have,' I finished. 'Max, this sounds like a fantastic investment!'

'The trouble is that I can't be seen to be poaching investment opportunities from my employers. It's highly unethical.'

'But I thought you said that your firm had closed the book on them. They are on their own. Aren't they?'

'Yeah, they are but I don't know if they will trust me again.'

'Why not invite them over this weekend and I'll do all the talking?' I suggested. 'They can say no if they want, but if they say yes, we can throw them a small financial lifeline.'

'We can talk, but I need to be sure that they can come up with the goods before I invest our hard earned cash in them and I will want a cut in the business.' Max had changed from the fool to the business exec in less than a minute. I knew he would never let us make an investment mistake with our own money.

'Oh Max, I know this can work and we'll be working together. It will be marvellous.'

Chapter 32

By the end of the first week of presentations I was beginning to feel quite schizophrenic. Some of my colleagues continued to treat me like a leper, while most of those who had heard my *Grand Plan* tipped me knowing nods and winks when we passed in the corridors. Eddy had got wind that something was up and flitted between being attentive and dismissive when I promised to tell him all about it on Monday.

It was a bizarre existence and to make things worse I knew that the rumour mill would be working overtime for both camps despite my pleas for restraint. I really had to move quickly or the impetus would wane and I would be branded the mad manager from Admissions.

Max had contacted the programming team, who I was delighted to discover are called 4D Solutions. I looked forward to telling them my analogy of using the sun as a 4D model for the problems we face. It would be nice to be met with something other than a blank look for a change. Max had managed to overcome their initial scepticism and persuaded them to come to our house to discuss a possible commission. It was all set for Saturday and Max promised to take care of the catering which meant we were having a barbecue. I just hoped the weather would hold.

For my part, I had to gather as much information as possible to present to them. I borrowed Max's digital camera to take pictures of the bed board, as it would be much easier to explain how it worked with visual references. I even became a willing IT student for once, listening carefully to Max's instructions on how to use his old laptop. By Friday morning I had three presentations under my belt and a laptop full of information.

By lunchtime I was itching to meet with 4D and was dreaming about leaving early to go home to tidy up my presentation when Joan knocked on my door. She was modelling quite a subdued combination of peach and tan. Unfortunately, her suit was peach and the blouse tan. A distinct visual imbalance and from the look on her face I could tell that her emotions were as unbalanced as her dress sense.

'Beth, got some time? I've got a few questions for you.'

'Sure Joan, what can I do for you?'

With Fran off my back, and the widespread acceptance of my early presentations I was feeling quietly confident about the *Grand Plan*, but I felt my stomach flip-flop when she entered my office, a sure sign of a guilty conscience but at that point I had no idea what I had done to deserve it.

'Beth, I've been hearing some strange rumours about the presentations you've been giving to the various directorates about the Admissions system. I know you are doing us on Monday and I wondered if you could fill me in on it beforehand?'

Oh wow! This was a tough one. If I gave Joan a potted version of the presentation I would be in danger of making the same mistake Harry did with Max. If I gave her too little information her resistance to the plan would be huge and the last thing I needed was uncooperative Clinical Bed Managers. The CBM's were the key to the whole plan.

However, if I brushed her off I would be doing exactly what I have accused other people of, information hogging. I may have been right about making Eddy wait but Joan had stood by me, believed in me. I should have gone through it with her before the first presentation. I had no choice but to go through it now. My early finish sailed out of the window.

'Joan, do you remember a few weeks ago you asked me how I managed to stop Tessa from ripping this place apart? Well, I have a confession to make, not to mention a big apology. I've been testing out a new way of working. It worked on

Tessa and I've been using it around the hospital to test out a plan, a plan that could bring our waiting lists down, reduce the number of 12 and 24 hour trolley waits and minimise cancelled operations.'

Joan's edgy expression dropped into full-blown astonishment. I quickly continued.

'I've had very little time to work on it and I've been using the presentations on the Admissions systems to test out its viability. As I'm due to present to you on Monday I planned to wait until then to fill you in on it.'

Joan's expression changed from stunned to hurt. I'd overlooked one of my best allies, how could I have been so stupid?

'I'm so sorry Joan. I realise now that I should have told you about this sooner. Will you forgive me and let me make amends?'

Joan's expression remained set. 'I can't say I'm not disappointed Beth. I thought we were friends.'

We clearly had some personal constraints to overcome before she would grant my wish.

'We are Joan and believe me I really appreciate the way you have been sticking up for me with Fran. I just got distracted for a while. Look, do you have an hour to spare now? I can give you the full presentation here.'

My offer was obviously not enough to overcome Joan's hurt feelings. She wanted more and I needed her support. Without it the plan was doomed. It was all or nothing. I had taken control away from her and the only way I could redeem myself was to give it back. I had one option and I had to take it.

'Joan, hear me out for an hour. If you're not happy with what I have to say then I won't present it to the nursing directorate on Monday. The decision is yours.'

This seemed to placate her a little and she made a great show of checking her watch and her diary.

'Hmm, you can have an hour, but I'm not sure...'

'Let's go into the coffee room,' I suggested. 'It's much more comfortable and I'll make some tea.' I grabbed the laptop and asked Sal to try to make sure we were not interrupted. As I made the tea I started on the repair job.

'Joan, do you remember the conversation we had a couple of weeks ago about decision making?'

Her face fell still further as she remembered how she had broken down in my office. I had struck a nerve so I carried on before she could speak.

'Don't worry Joan, I wouldn't break a confidence. I have not mentioned that day to anyone but you really got me thinking. Before you left we discussed if there were any operational models that might help us. Do you remember?' I prompted, as I handed her a mug of tea, I needed her to join the conversation. At last she spoke.

'Yes and I've found one that will work,' she replied stiffly. 'I was planning to present it on Monday but I've been hearing that you have been over running your presentation time. That's why I came to see you. To ask you to keep your presentation short so I will have time to present the new plan.'

My stomach hit the floor. Another plan! I had not reckoned on a rival plan. Oh hell! What was I going to do? Parts of my presentation flipped through my head. Joan was a brilliant fire fighter and the majority of my presentation was aimed at debasing her way of working. Here she was about to launch another half-baked plan and I'd been planning to trash her whole way of working.

'Can you tell me about it?' I asked tentatively.

'I don't see why not. It's quite simple really, the best things always are. There is a hospital up North who have had great success with it and I want us to use it here.'

'What have they done?' My stomach was now auditioning for the circus high wire act. Had someone beaten me to it? Had all my work been a waste of time? I had been flying so high with this plan that I forgot the question I kept asking myself a few short weeks ago. Who was I to think that I could make a difference? I felt about three years old and totally helpless.

'They have opened an observation ward close to the ED. This ward allows them to move patients out of the department cutting the trolley wait times dramatically. It has doctors on duty 24/7 and is really working.'

Uh? This was nothing like my plan. In the few seconds Joan was speaking I could tell that the model she was proposing was just a holding bay, a way of massaging the figures, a mechanism to take the patients off the ED clock and hold them while they waited for beds on the ward.

'Joan, can I ask you something?'

She could see that I was unimpressed and looked distinctly bristly.

'Yes.'

'Can you tell me which doctors will staff this unit?'

'The ones on duty in the ED. It will give them a base and they can start treatment before the patients go to the ward.'

'Do you mean treatment or diagnostic tests?'

'Mostly tests I suppose, but it will speed up the process. The unit is used mostly for medical patients, which should alleviate pressure on the surgical beds.'

I could see gaping holes in the plan already. The medics would get more beds, making the consultant's ward rounds even bigger. Even worse, if the unit is staffed by ED doctors it is likely that they will admit even more patients than before as they will have even less support from their team leaders. This would be a disaster!

However, I couldn't say this. Not now. I needed Joan to understand my plan. If she announced more medical beds before I presented to the medics next week I would stand little or no chance of success.

'This sounds like a great idea to investigate. Would you like to hear mine now?'

'It is not an idea Beth. The decision on the finance is being made next week and I am confident that it will be passed.'

I had to move quickly or the observation unit would become reality.

'Great news. More beds, just what we need. Congratulations Joan.' I don't think she bought my far from sincere reply but I had to try and play along with her to make her listen to my ideas.

I opened my laptop and set up the presentation. This was it. The crunch. I may have dreaded presenting to the surgeons but this impromptu presentation would be the breakpoint of the whole project.

Even worse, I wasn't sure that it was in the right order to meet Joan's needs, but if I wavered from the script I would surely miss a vital point. I remembered Harry's words. Keep to the script, don't miss a step! If you miss one they will too and you will lose them. I had to do it as it was written. I knew it would offend Joan but we are here for the patients. I must remember that.

I launched into the first part of the presentation where we established the goal of the organisation. Joan did not appear to have any problems with this.

'I've heard this treat more patients better, sooner now and in the future, a number of times this week. I wondered where it had come from. You can continue.'

Joan's face was hard and as far as I could tell all I had done so far was annoy her.

My next question from the presentation would leave me wide open.

'Do you think that we can do better than we are doing now?'

'Is that a rhetorical question Beth?'

'Kind of, but I can tell you're already ahead of me on this one with your idea of the observation unit. Can I carry on?'

Joan nodded.

By the time I got to the *What to change? What to change to? How to change?* slide I was able to personalise it a bit.

'The first stage of this is what my team have been doing with the CBM's. Does it make sense?'

'Yes, it does,' Joan agreed. 'It has focussed them very well. They realise that we need more beds to get this place functioning properly so it has worked.'

'Tell me Joan. You must have done a lot of research around bed numbers. Can you tell me how we stand in relation to beds per head of population? Are we above or below average?'

I already knew the answer to this, but I needed to stall for a while before launching into the next part of my presentation, the part that challenged the need for more beds.

'Actually we are slightly above average and the new unit will give us one of the highest patient to bed ratios in the region. Why do you ask?'

'Oh, it's just that this next bit is tough. I'm sure it's right but please remember, this is what I've been using to try to get greater co-operation from the doc's. Will you give me a little latitude on this without getting mad at me?'

'Beth, so far I haven't heard anything offensive and your presentation seems to be geared to getting better co-operation among the different directorates, something we have needed for a long time. So go ahead. I won't take offence.'

'Alright, but remember this is what I've been using on the doc's.'

I read through the next part of the presentation about having wishes granted and I skirted around the issues of new beds, burying it in among the examples of more doctors and equipment. Before I could carry on I had to know if Joan was still with me.

'Well, do you agree, in principle?'

'I know where you are coming from on this Beth. The medics think that we in management can wave a magic wand and meet their demands, but we can't so I can see why you put this in. It's really putting them in their place isn't it?'

Joan had placed herself in the medic's shoes. I wasn't sure if this was good or bad. Would she miss the point of the presentation completely? I still needed her to recognise that we are all forced to work in certain ways because of the way the system works. Would she grasp this? I had to carry on.

The section on the Auditors and the warring heads was well received and we even managed to have a laugh over it by inserting some names into the scenarios. But I was still concerned that Joan was not personally connecting with the tale.

By the time we got to end of this section a flicker of doubt ran across Joan's face, but it disappeared almost as soon as it appeared. I remembered the exact time when I realised I was one of the players in this diabolical little performance. It had hit me really hard and I'd had Harry to support me. Could I be the support Joan would need when the truth really hit home?

Before Joan could start asking questions I was not ready to answer I leapt into the section covering the three UDE's. She quickly became a willing participant citing the names of colleagues who had acted in the ways we were discussing. By the time I got to the punch line of the lack of platform or mechanism by which negatives can be raised and effectively addressed, we were almost back to our old selves.

'Beth I can well see why the medics are all talking about you. You've really nailed them. This is wonderful. If you can get them all to realise how difficult they are to work with, our lives will be so much easier. Thanks.'

'I'm not finished yet Joan. That was just setting the scene.'

Joan looked at her watch. With our little diversions the hour had flown by. I could not leave her with the impression that I had constructed a large hammer to beat the medics with. She had to stay.

'Can you stay just a little longer? Please?'

'I suppose so, but half an hour at the most. However, I think what you have told me so far would be sufficient for Monday's presentation. Go ahead.'

No, no, no! I could not let her cut me off, not today and especially not on Monday.

To speed the presentation up I condensed the NHS Direct analogy. Joan was an experienced enough nurse to know that face-to-face consultations are the only way to secure a good diagnosis. She quickly grasped the idea of symptoms and causes, but then I hit her with a sledgehammer blow by stating that as managers we are not trained to spot that the symptoms of the system are connected.

Ouch! I saw that one land as Joan slumped back in her chair.

I carried on and Joan sat up straight in her chair again as soon as I accused the doctors of being the bottlenecks.

'Clever move Beth, deflect the blame, then hit it back at them.'

This was not going the way I needed it to, but I was in too deep now, I had to carry on.

I brought the new slide up on the computer screen and started to explain the five steps as they applied to the bed situation.

'This is good Beth, but you know that it does not apply now. Not with the new beds. You've got three and four the wrong way around.'

Cruel to be kind. I had to be cruel to be kind.

'If what you say is right then the five steps will not work on another possible constraint,' I argued. 'Do you agree?'

'I'm not sure, but try me.'

I read through the section on winter pressures and the docs ward rounds. Joan was comfortable again. I was pointing the finger at someone else. The logic was easy to follow and by the time I got to trying to devise a solution Joan was eager to press on.

'So do you think reducing the time it takes for the consultants to visit patients would be a good idea?' I asked.

'Of course, but how will we manage to do this?'

'This was the amazing part of the presentation. The surgeons came up with a really neat solution all on their own.'

'You mean they thought up an answer without you having to tell them?'

'Yes, would you like to hear it?'

'Fire away, this I've got to hear.'

I went on to explain their solution of stalling routine admissions for a week and their offer to work in the ED while the patient moves were taking place.

'Are you really telling me that they offered to do this? They really offered this on their own?'

'Yes Joan. And this is why I maintain that beds are not our main constraint. They accepted the five steps because it made sense.'

I went on to add the icing to the cake. The agreement to keep quiet until all of the directorates and the management were on board, even the promise to review their Monday afternoon activities to see if they could be subordinated to the plan.

'Joan. I really did not mean to step on anybody's toes with this. When John encouraged me to present this to the surgeons I was sceptical. But they exceeded my expectations as you can see and it kind of snowballed from there.'

She sat back in her chair. Eventually she spoke.

'Do you realise that apart from some overtime for the porters this plan is cheap?'

'I'd already figured that out and that was going to be one of my selling points to management. Look Joan I'm not trying to take the wind out of your project, but wouldn't it be worth giving this a try before we start adding more beds?'

'I'm not sure Beth. I've been working my butt off to get support for the new unit and the funding is almost nailed down. No, we will still need more beds. There is no way this can free up enough bed space to meet our needs. No we need more beds as well.'

'I agree that our plans are not mutually exclusive, but couldn't we try this first? It will take the pressure off now and building the new unit will take time. We do need answers now, don't we?'

'I suppose. I need to think about it, but I wish I had known about this sooner.'

'So do I Joan. As I said, this kind of snowballed almost out of control and I accept that if the majority of the management are not happy with it, it will not happen at all. That is why I need your support before I present it to the medical consultants, let alone the nursing directorate.'

There, I had put the project in her hands. I knew that without her support it wouldn't happen and I knew from experience that if she took time to think about it she would realise that she was part of the system. She would hit the same brick wall of realisation I had the day I was sat outside with my unwanted lunch, feeling like I'd been stampeded over by an invisible herd of destroyed egos.

I could not afford to leave her in limbo like this. An idea struck me.

'Joan, I suppose you heard about the EPR presentation?' she nodded, deep in thought. I could imagine her charging towards the abyss of self-blame. 'Well, tomorrow I'm meeting with some people that might be able to give us what we need to make this work, some computer programmers. We're having a barbecue at my house. We're meeting at mid-day to discuss it, can you come? Have you planned anything for tomorrow?'

'Saturday? Just taking Pepe to the dog groomers. What time did you say?'

'Midday. Your input would be really valuable and you could bring Pepe along. We've got a really dog-friendly garden. You would both be very welcome. Please say you will come.'

I scribbled my address and home phone number on a scrap of paper and gave it to her. She looked at it without reading it.

'Yes, that would be nice Beth. Tomorrow at twelve o'clock. I'll see if I can make it.'

'Good. In the meantime call me on this number if you want to talk. Promise me?'

'Yes. I have to go now.'

Joan was almost acting like an automaton. I was worried, but what else could I do? I just hoped she would accept my invitation.

Chapter 33

It was already 11 o'clock in the morning and Joan still had not called me. I cursed myself for not asking for her phone number so I could check she was alright. I had blitzed Harry's brain last night for advice on how to persuade Joan to buy into the *Grand Plan*, but he had no magic solution for me.

...sorry beth but the best thing you can do is hope that she shows up. if she doesn't you need to make sure she is ok the next time you see her. TOC can produce a brutal reality hit as you well know! i'll offer any support i can, the worst thing you can do is to ignore her. if you do that the whole project would be a bust.
H

I busied myself with fine-tuning the presentation while Max prepared the barbecue. The weather was not brilliant and showers were forecast for later. When I was happy that I couldn't do any more to my presentation I tidied up the lounge and removed the dog toys, ready for a possible hasty retreat if it rained.

At 11:30 I heard the dogs skidding towards the front door. The bell rang, but there wasn't an extra car in the drive. It was probably the neighbour's kids squealing for their ball back before Maggie and Winston punctured it.

I fought my way past the mutts to answer the door. It was Joan.

'Ah Beth, I have got the right place. I know I'm early but I wanted a quick chat.'

I could tell that she had not slept well. Her face looked drawn and tired.

'Joan, so glad you could make it. Don't worry about the time. We're very casual around here. Where's Pepe?'

'He's in the car.'

'Where's your car?'

'Outside on the road.'

'Bring it onto the drive and bring Pepe in. It's far too warm to leave him in the car.'

'If you are sure. He can be quite destructive.'

'So can ours,' I assured with a smile.

As Joan went back out along the drive to move her car I had visions of a miniature poodle or a Chihuahua. I pulled our dogs away from the front door and pushed them out into the back garden so they couldn't overwhelm our canine guest.

I returned to the front door to find Joan standing next to one of the biggest dogs I had ever seen. St. Bernard's are a dominating sight at the best of times, but this one was fresh from what must have been a lengthy blow drying session. His hair floated all around him as if he had just peed into an electricity socket.

I laughed, 'Let me guess. He woke up today and just couldn't do anything with it?'

Joan joined my laughter nervously, 'I know he looks daft, but there reaches a point when I just can't keep up with the hair he sheds. She suddenly looked worried. 'I can take him round the back,' she said.

'Don't be silly,' I said. 'Our two produce enough hair between them to outdo Pepe. I just want to see their faces when they see him.'

I was not disappointed. Maggie and Winston's eyes bulged the moment they clocked this dopey fur monster with its lolling tongue, but Pepe was still in adolescence and eager to play. So within a few minutes Maggie and Winston were cautiously indulging in their usual rough and tumble and the spectacle proved to be the ideal icebreaker.

Joan and I drifted into the kitchen once the dogs were settled in their play.

'Coffee, juice or beer?' I asked.

'Coffee please.'

'So how are you Joan?'

'Not good. What you said yesterday made a lot of sense, but when I got home last night I started thinking. You were talking about me being a bad manager weren't you?'

Joan's words came out in one long stream. She had obviously rehearsed this and wanted to get it over and done with as soon as possible.

'Oh Joan!' I said and gently put my hand on her shoulder.

'Well, now I know it I...'

'I was not accusing *you* of being a bad manager Joan.'

'But I have done everything you talked about yesterday! Weren't you trying to tell me that I'm awful at my job?'

'No I wasn't. I was trying to tell you that we are all bad at our jobs.'

Her face took on a puzzled look.

'Let me explain.'

I went on to tell Joan how I had *found* this hidden truth using the email that Harry had sent me and how hard I had taken it. I explained that if this core problem was true then it had to apply to everyone. It did, and that was why Joan was feeling this way. I very quickly followed this up with the explanation that we are all victims of the system and that we collectively have the power to change the system.

It was a quick and dirty pep talk but I knew our guests would be arriving soon and I needed to make Joan comfortable before they arrived.

Max came into the kitchen and I introduced them to each other. The doorbell rang just as Max began to ask her about Pepe's pedigree. I indicated to Max to stay with Joan. I didn't want her making a run for it.

I ushered our other five guests into the garden and Max did the introductions. He left Joan to last and made a big deal of introducing her, 'and this lady here is the one you need to impress the most. This is Joan, she is the head of nursing at the infirmary. She's a real smart lady so you'll need to keep your wits about you.'

Thank you Max! This was just what Joan needed, a reminder that her opinion is important. Keep it up Max. Flatter those rather fetching red socks off her!

Max played the role of chairman and chef with equal aplomb. He steered me though my presentation, even apologising to Joan for expecting her to sit through it again.

This according to Harry should do the trick. By planting the seed of *we are all victims* in her head a second run through should allow Joan to see the whole presentation in a different light.

The kids soon warmed to the presentation adding names of past employers to those of the Heads and the Auditor. I was surprised to hear that my analysis seemed to work outside of the Health Service.

By the time I reached the stage that Joan had been a party to yesterday the atmosphere was relaxed and friendly. Max served the kebabs and I handed around the bread and salad.

'How are you doing Joan?' I asked again.

'Much better thank you. What you said here really does make sense; I can now understand why you asked me if I had any training in decision-making. I really haven't. I'm sure that if I had attended any lectures that made this much sense I would have remembered.'

'I'm pleased you feel like this Joan. I've been feeling really guilty about leaving you out and then dumping all this on you and only giving you part of the solution.'

'Is that what this crew are here for? I did wonder.'

'Yes, I hope this will be the *coup de grâce*. Let me know what you think after their presentation. And remember you're the tough Health Service manager these kids have to impress so play along alright?'

Joan laughed, 'This sounds fun! Much better than spending the afternoon shopping. And I'm really sorry about Pepe digging up your lovely azaleas.'

'Don't worry, if he hadn't done it I'm sure Maggie and Winston would have!'

The dogs moved from person to person, scrounging scraps of food. When we had all finished eating Max re-opened the proceedings by announcing that the real feature of the day was about to start. This auspicious remark was celebrated by the arrival of fat drops of rain.

We all rushed to move inside, grabbing plates and utensils along the way. Once we were all settled in the lounge I set the laptop on top of the mantle and pulled up the first of a series of photographs of the bed board.

I launched into an explanation of how the board worked and handed out A4 sheets with the rules neatly typed on them.

Joan was scrutinising this while the two lads responsible for the analysis and the core programming asked questions. In a short space of time they had grasped the functions and were answering more questions posed by the rest of the team without my input. Boy, they were quick.

'I'm right aren't I Beth? You have no automatic hook-up to the wards?' David, the analyst of the team asked.

'No we don't,' I replied. 'We can only verify the bed situation by checking on the Patient Administration System. But this system is not real-time. It's updated as and when the ward clerks get around to it so we are reliant on phone calls to the wards for accurate figures.'

'And worse than that we know that the ward managers tell the ward clerks to disguise the true bed availability,' Joan chipped in

'Why do they do that?'

'Because if they declare an empty bed and the next patient on the list does not need their particular specialist treatment, they get sent to them anyway,' I explained.

'So it's all down to who's next on the list? Oh man, that explains why my little brother was put in a ward with old men with catheters when he broke his leg. I thought it was really bizarre, but I can see how it happened now.'

'So what formal processes do wards have to go through to discharge patients?' David continued.

Joan was warming to this rebound of her status from a crap manager back to Head of Nursing. 'There are two main things,' she explained, 'a letter for them to take to their own doctor so if necessary he or she can continue treatment and some medication to take home.'

'Great. Now do all patients get a letter and medication?'

'No some get both, some get only get one'.

'But do they all get one or the other?'

Joan paused, 'Yes, I'm sure they do.'

'I'm guessing that your pharmacy is already computerised because I picked my brother up when he was discharged and the staff checked the progress of his prescription by computer. How about your discharge letters? Are they computerised?'

'No, not yet, but our technical guys are working on an electronic form. We are trying to get all discharge letters and summaries on to email to speed up the process. Why do you ask?'

'This is brilliant! We can hook your pharmacy and discharge letters to the electronic bed board. Every time a discharge prescription is written, or a discharge letter is typed, it can indicate that a bed is about to be vacated on the bed board.'

'You can do that?' said Joan in amazement. 'Beth! This could mean the end of undeclared beds?'

'Yes Joan,' I said beaming from ear to ear as I relished the impact of this simple suggestion. 'What David is proposing is tying the bed constraint back to the discharge mechanisms. It will be *impossible* to hide beds.'

While we had been talking, Mike, the second half of this technical double act, had been tapping away on his laptop.

'David. I think I've got it. The changes to the holiday booking solution will be minimal. In fact, what Beth has shown us uses fewer data fields than we have already accommodated. Can I show you all?'

Mike set his laptop on the mantle next to mine. He flipped my lap top visual back to the bed board. 'We have already developed a program that we can tweak to suit your needs. Here we have a system that shows the available accommodation at different holiday sites. Each strip shows different types of accommodation. Camping pitches, Caravan pitches, RV Pitches, Static Vans and chalets. In each strip are the boxes that are the equivalent of your t-plates or cards. Just the basic information is on view much like your patient details, date of admission and the initials of the admitting consultant.

'By clicking on any one box the hidden information covered by the next card comes into view. On here we have data fields for contact phone numbers, when the booking was made, how the client paid and if the booking is a part or full booking, even if they are moving onto another of our sites.

Also there's ample capacity for additional information. Things like, '*Does the client have a dog?*' And even space for a warning for the next site if the clients are unruly!

'If you think of each of these strips as a ward, we can mix and match the bed type much as the campsites do to accommodate fluctuations in demand. Do you see?'

Joan was the first to speak. 'Amazing! You mean this could become an electronic version of Beth's bed board?' She paused while the team gave her a positive answer.

'But you are only showing 5 *wards* we have 25, how would you manage that?'

Mike pressed a few buttons on the computer and the screen changed to show hundreds of small boxes in columns.

'We have the capacity within this system to manage 1,000 units over 20 sites. How many beds do you have?'

'500, would this be too small to work?' Joan asked with a frown.

'At the moment, but there are ways around this. We could tailor this system to show all of your 500 beds and it would be big enough to be workable just as your bed board is now.'

Gilly rose to stand next to Mike, she was a bit more cautious, but I think this had more to do with being in close proximity to Pepe than her presentation.

'We can install two 48 inch plasma screens that could be operated exactly as the bed board is run now,' she said with a smile.

Their handover was seamless. These kids seemed to be able to read each other's minds. I could see why Max was so impressed with them.

It was Gilly's turn to ask questions. 'Is the information only needed in the Admissions department?'

'No!' chimed Joan and I together.

'We have regular crisis meetings in the board room,' I continued 'and it would be very useful if parts of the bed board could be accessed throughout the hospital by the doctors, especially when they are planning their ward rounds.' I looked over to Joan who was nodding vigorously.

'No problem,' Gilly replied. 'I assume the existing system is networked throughout the hospital? This could be networked as well with users having restricted access to parts that concern them. But the most exciting part would be if we could install a data projector in the boardroom. The whole bed stock could be projected onto a wall and it could be shown in real time.'

Both Joan and I were struck dumb. Images of a giant bed board flashed through our heads. We looked at each other and still could not speak. The silence in our lounge was palpable. I turned towards Max who was indicating to Gilly that she should not speak.

'What?' I asked

Max stood next to Gilly. 'If these guys had a fault it was that they tended to oversell their products. I told them to keep quiet once they hit the *aha* moment. I think you two just had a great *aha* moment, didn't you?'

Joan started laughing. 'Do you realise what we could do with this?'

'Obviously, not as well as you do,' Gilly replied with another smile, 'but all you have to do is tell us what you want it to do and we'll make sure it can do it. That's what we are good at.'

'Good?' squawked Joan. 'It's not good, it's bloody brilliant!'

Three of the kids sat close to Joan and she started to tell them about the plan to reassign patients to the most appropriate wards and how we needed a model of the movement to prove to the rest of the managers that the plan would work. I hadn't even mentioned this obstacle to Joan and here she was trying to find a solution to it.

Max and I slipped out to make coffee. Once in the kitchen we felt free to talk.

'What a buzz!' I said, once I had closed the door.

'Now you know why I love my job,' Max replied. 'Let Joan have some time with them and we can sort out the details later. I think there are some features that you might need in this system that Joan has not even thought of yet and I need to discuss money with the kids, but for now let Joan hold the stage. I think it's doing her good.'

We returned to the lounge and served coffee. Joan's hand was shaking as she took the cup and saucer. 'Beth, I never knew that management could be so exciting, thank you.'

At least she was shaking with adrenaline not fear, as she had been when she arrived. Somehow, over the past two hours her face had changed, she looked ten years younger and even the dogs were getting excited, so Max and I guided them back out into the garden.

An hour later Joan said her goodbyes and thanks and assured me that I would have all the time I needed to make my presentation to the directorate of nursing. More than that she would also attend the meeting of the medical consultants, where she would squash any rumours of more medical beds. They could wait, after all why rush? She needed time to plan the expansion of the bed base properly, like a proper manager.

Pepe, like all young mammals, fell into a deep sleep as soon as he realised the fun was over and sprawled out in the back of Joan's estate car. We waved her off then returned to our young guests.

The rain had stopped and they were all in the garden playing a game of piggy in the middle with our dogs who had yet to tire from the excitement of the day. We wiped the water off of the chairs and invited them to join us.

'Looks like you made a good friend in Joan,' said Max. 'Beth has a few more bits of information for you and then we need to talk money.'

My potted version of TOC was received very well despite my amateurish attempt and they soon grasped the need to track the constraint. We discussed how the newly named TABS system could achieve this. They were even quick at thinking up names! TABS, I was informed, stood for Trust Admission and Bed System. I liked it. We are always trying to keep tabs on the beds and this acronym soon slipped into our vocabulary as we discussed ways of monitoring the constraint. Nothing seemed too much trouble for this team and their enthusiasm was infectious. Soon it was Max's turn to discuss money.

I left them to it. I didn't want to step on Max's toes and there was always a chance of me doing a repeat performance of the last auction we went to. We had sensibly fixed our maximum bid for a particularly nice piece of antique porcelain, but I got carried away during the bidding. When Max realised how much I had paid for it he hit the roof. Luckily for me he calmed down later when he saw how good the piece looked in our dining room, but I was not about to make the same mistake again.

I busied myself in the kitchen and I had just turned the dishwasher on when Max waved for me to re-join them. The danger period was over.

I sat next to Max and squeezed his arm. He knew that I was anxious to know the outcome. 'I'll let Guy explain the deal.'

I turned to the quietest one in the group who until now had not really spoken on the subject of the program.

'Max has thrown us a lifeline and we are very grateful for that. But we are in business, or we would be, to make money. As you know we have all had to take full time jobs to survive, but we kept hoping that an opportunity would present itself and today it has, I've been roughing out some figures and if this takes off, the earning potential for us is huge.'

He paused, I suspected for dramatic effect.

'As I said, we are all in full time employment now, but full time to our employers is part-time compared to how we used to work. Each of us are prepared to put in 20 hours a week to work up the model Joan requested. We reckon it will take us a month to produce the model for demonstration to the other managers. Financing our time is not a problem but the equipment is. So we have struck a deal with Max and I guess yourself. I hope you agree to it.'

I was squeezing Max's arm even harder now. Eager to know how much was this going to cost us.

Max nodded at Guy to continue.

'None of us can get credit. So Max has offered to buy the wide plasma screens and any additional hardware we might need for this project in return for a share of our business. He drives a hard bargain but we are happy for you to own 10 per cent of 4D Solutions for this opportunity. It's a better deal than his venture capital company was prepared to make and we will have to seek development funding if this takes off, but Max has assured us that as a member of our Board he will be able to find it.'

I turned to Max, 'Can you?'

'I'll find it from somewhere. My fund isn't the only one around and I know enough people in the money business to be able to twist a few arms. I'll start with Frank.'

'So we have a deal?' asked Guy.

'You sure do,' I said not having a clue how much the hardware would cost, but I trusted Max as he seemed to be trusting me.

Chapter 34

Just four short weeks ago I attended the meeting that sparked this whole thing off. And now it was Monday again. Only this one had the potential to be more explosive than the first Monday. The hospital was buzzing, not just with the never-ending stream of patients and worried relatives, but with a wave of optimism from the staff. Joan had turned into my groupie and insisted on attending all of the presentations and she was a great help. Last week's presentations to the medics and other director-ates went even better than we had hoped. Everyone knew how much Joan cared for the patient's welfare so her presence helped the audience quickly understand that this was no silver bullet, quick cure.

She was also surprisingly canny and she delayed our pres-entation to the CBM's until the BIG ONE: The presentation to management that was due today. After all she said, they needed to be treated like successful managers if they were to become them and rubbing their noses in their inexperience would not achieve anything.

However, despite Joan's help I was still wary of one factor. The return of the Fearsome One. She was due back from her holiday today and boy was she going to be surprised! The plan was to invite her to the presentation at the Catastrophe Meeting. Joan had kindly booked the lecture theatre and had emailed all of the relevant people to attend. So far the take up rate was good, but we had decided that I should invite Fran personally. This would be my report to her. I had been acting under her in-structions so she should take some of the credit. Joan and I hoped that this would take the sting out of the work we had been doing over the past two weeks while Fran had been away.

The first part of the morning slid by as I prepared for the Catastrophe Meeting and tried to keep myself calm. The bed temperature was getting noticeably colder but that was nothing new and by 10:30 I had caught up with my outstanding email. Most of my incoming mail now was from various people, who had already attended one of my presentations and were eager to see the start of the project. Fortunately, I had kept a record of their questions and was now able to circulate a list of FAQ's and answers. Life was so much easier now that we were all getting behind the same project.

I was distracted from my reflections by a sudden, loud argument that erupted from the outer office. I swung around to see Fran and Eddy face to face, angrily shouting over each other. Fran's face was contorted with anger as she pointed first to Eddy and then to the bed board. There was no choice, I had to intervene.

'What on earth is going on here?' I said as I stepped out of my bubble. This was my territory and I felt confident to make demands on it. 'There are patients out in the waiting room, keep the noise down!'

The whole department fell silent as Eddy and Fran looked at me as if I had two heads. I felt my confidence slip away like a frightened puppy. 'Eddy, please return to the bed board,' I continued with considerably less authority 'Fran, shall we...?' I started to say as I indicated the way to the coffee room.

Fran turned on her heel and stomped into the room before I could say anymore. I could hear her muttering under her breath something about how she knew she shouldn't have gone away.

As I joined her in the room and closed the door I could see the anger continually rising in her face.

'I knew I should not have trusted you,' she snapped. 'I gave you a chance and what do you do? Throw it in my face. Beth, I've had enough of your antics and now your staff are becoming as belligerent as you are. What the hell has been going on?'

It was time to face up. 'I've been doing exactly as you asked Fran,' I replied as calmly as possible. I was on the verge of copying Eddy's tactics of a toe-to-toe row. 'I have been showing my staff and the directorates how the current admissions system impacts on the rest of the hospital.'

She looked confused. 'But Eddy was ranting at me that nothing can change, that the CBM's are a waste of time and money. Who the hell is *he* to tell *me* that? No, more to the point, who filled his head with these notions? He sure as hell isn't bright enough to figure these things out by himself!'

Now I was confused. 'What do you mean Fran? I've never said that the CBM's are a waste of money. If Eddy thinks that, he's expressing his own opinion, not mine.'

Fran drew a deep breath and straightened up. Her face had flushed bright red. For one awful minute I thought she was forming a fist and preparing to throw a right hook. 'That oik questioned whether the CBM's could make a difference when we are already operating at 98 per cent capacity'.

'Oh,' I said. 'If that's what he said then I do agree with him. But I didn't say the CBM's were a waste of money.' Not aloud anyway, I added to myself. 'He's right Fran, but you've only got a fraction of the picture. Please tell me what you've heard so far and I'll try to fill in the gaps. Please sit down. Let's be civilised about this.'

Fran sat and rubbed her face in her hands. Her tan was fabulous and I noticed that she was wearing some new jewellery. The gold looked good on her tanned fingers. As she pulled her hands away from her face she dropped her elbows to her knees and sat forward in the chair. She was obviously trying to decide what to say next. Eventually she spoke.

'I had the most wonderful holiday, inspiring even, and I return to work full of enthusiasm only to be greeted in the most peculiar manner. Doctors have been grinning at me as if I have ketchup stains on my clothes whilst other mangers are scowling at me as if I am public enemy number one. And when I try to find out what on earth is going on I am told to speak to you! You of all people!'

'Ah, yes,' I said as I wondered how best to handle the situation. 'I was going to ask you for some time after the meeting to discuss my presentations. I was rather hoping to surprise you— a welcome back gift.'

'A Gift! I feel like a bloody alien. What the hell is going on Beth?'

I went on to explain that Joan and I had been working with the doc's to devise a plan to free up beds and that we had their support, but that the management would have the final say.

'You mean the doc's are willing to participate?' Fran asked, the shock taking the sharpness out of her voice.

'Yes Fran, if management are willing to help. It's up to you.'

'Up to me?'

'Well, you and your colleagues. We needed to wait until you got back to present to the management. We've got the lecture theatre booked for this afternoon at two. Please say you can make it? All of the other AGM's will be there along with most of the ward managers and managers from IT and most of the support services.'

'What do you mean, up to me?'

'Fran, without your support, not to mention the other AGM's, the plan cannot work. But you all need to be comfortable with it. If one of you decides not to participate, it will not work.'

'What is it?' Fran was slowly starting to soften.

'That's the surprise. And I promise you Fran, you will like it.'

'And you are telling me that all of this has come about because I asked you to inform the rest of the hospital about the admissions system?'

'Yes.'

'I'm telling you Beth, this had better be good. This really is your neck on the block this time, do you hear?'

'Yes,' I replied calmly. 'You won't be disappointed. And don't forget you have the right to veto the whole plan.'

'Hmm, I'll be there, but keep that moron in his place, I will not be shouted at by an oik!'

Fran strutted out of the office shooting venomous looks at Eddy as she left and I dashed back to my bubble to grab my stuff for the Catastrophe meeting. Fran was hurriedly starting the meeting as I arrived and I was just in time to hear the ED representative report that they had three cases of suspected food poisoning that would need beds ASAP.

I gave my contribution as quickly as I could and left the meeting with the usual round of promises. Just as I was leaving the room I saw Joan approach Fran and say, 'She's done you proud Fran, don't be hard on her. You've got a good one there.' The only response I could hear from outside of the boardroom was a 'Humph!' Still I had this afternoon to turn her around.

By the time I had returned to my office we'd had three more requests for beds for patients with suspected food poisoning. Eddy and Sal were already worrying about contingency plans so I quickly rang David in the ED.

'Hi David, it's Beth. What's the story with these food poisoning cases?'

'Brace yourself Beth, it could be a bad one. I think we've nailed the source. The patients all went to that balloon festival in town over the weekend. There must have been a dodgy food vendor there. We'll just have to wait and see but by the early signs I would prepare for an onslaught.'

This was just what I didn't need today. I wanted to present to the managers and we could all be tied up with this problem. I sent an email to the consultants who had already attended my presentations warning them of the possibility of an increase in admissions throughout the day stressing that it was too early to say how many patients would need to be admitted.

I needed to speak to John. If I was going to be tied up with the presentation when more bed requests came in later in the day it would be too late to cancel admissions and we would hit the -100 mark very quickly. I needed my champion to be out there in the field controlling the troops.

I dialled Marge's number but was told in no uncertain terms that he was not available. Damn that woman! She would not even tell me where he was. I placed a call to his pager and my phone rang almost immediately. It was Marge again.

'I've told you he is busy! Try his registrar.' She slammed the phone down on me.

What the hell was this woman playing at? I needed reinforcements.

I called Fran's office number. She answered giving her full name, title and department.

'Fran, it's Beth. We may have a problem.'

'Oh, one you can't handle?' she said sarcastically.

'Fran, I'm not messing about. We've got five bed requests for patients with suspected food poisoning, and we are likely to get many more if the patients go to their family doctors this morning.'

'What makes you think there will be more?' Her concern was genuine and we slipped into the professional mode quickly and easily.

'It seems that the source of the dodgy food might have been a vendor at the festival yesterday. There were thousands of people there. Fran this could be bad, really bad.'

Fran took a deep breath. 'Here's what I need you to do. Cancel all admissions apart from the diagnosed cancers. Cancel them all. I'll come over and direct the teams to identify discharges. I'll see you in a few minutes.'

I wasn't brave enough to disagree with her there and then so I quickly paged Joan and within minutes she was on her way to the department.

I left my bubble to pass the news onto my staff. They quickly busied themselves cancelling as many patients as they could. Fran swept importantly into my office and pulled up a chair at the bed board.

'I need to know how many discharges have already been declared,' she said the moment her bum hit the seat. 'Then I'll send the CBM's to the wards to rustle up some more possibles. Get me a list of the duty consultants. I'll send them where they are needed.'

My staff quickly gave Fran the information she asked for so she could give directions to the CBM's to go to the wards and identify as many discharges as possible. I was delighted to see Joan arrive, red faced and out of breath. At last I had a true ally to persuade Fran to try our new proposed system.

'Now, Beth, Joan,' Fran continued. 'Here's the list of Consultants on duty today. I want you to call them and tell them to get to the wards to get these discharges moving.'

Joan and I looked at each other, both of us willing the other to speak. I took a deep breath and took the initiative.

'Fran, this is not the best use of their time. Let's get them to work in the ED. They will have a much greater chance of stemming the flow of patients into the hospital and the registrars can handle the discharges.'

'What?' squeaked Fran.

'She's right Fran.' Joan had finally found her voice. 'Trust us we know what we are saying.'

'But, they just won't do it!'

'They will Fran, all you have to do is speak to Prof. Summers. Please try it and see.'

Fran dialled Marge's number and listened to Marge's sing-song reply.

'Professor Summers Secretary, department of surgery how can I help you?'

'Marge, it's Fran. Put me through to John.' Fran listened for a while and then spat, 'I don't care if he's rewriting the New Testament, put me through. Now!'

'John, it's Fran. We have a problem that I understand you might be able to help with, though why I'm talking to a surgeon about this I have no idea.'

She went onto explain the problem as two more bed requests were logged. Eventually she put the phone down and turned in her chair.

'What the hell just happened? John said he'd get the senior medics to the ED. Tell me what happened?'

I laughed despite myself, feeling ridiculously proud of our achievements. It was time to put my trust where my mouth was. 'You'll know soon, Fran, I promise. It's too complicated to tell you now. But it's nearly time for the presentation.'

'Presentation! At a time like this!'

'Fran we will be alright. Eddy and Sal can handle things at this end. Can't you?' I said as I turned to them.

'Sure Beth, no problems. We'll run the interview, notes, admit routine if that's all right?'

'Yes Eddy perfect. Sal can you warn pharmacy to prepare for a rush of discharge scripts? They will know what you mean and they will prioritise them. And don't forget to offer to arrange transport for the patients that are being sent home. Not just ambulances, remember to try the patients friends and relatives first, offer them the facility of our waiting room and ask the head porter to make sure someone is on standby to bring patients down to us and to collect their medication as soon as it is ready.'

'No worries Beth. Go to your meeting, we'll be fine.' Sal said as she reached for her headset.

Fran looked at my staff in disbelief and reluctantly allowed Joan to lead her out of the department by the elbow. Joan winked at me over her shoulder.

'I'll see you in the lecture theatre in ten minutes,' she said.

I looked back at Eddy and Sal. More than half of this plan was theirs. It was their idea to bring the patients to our waiting room; it was nearer the front door and the patient pick up point. It was their idea to have a dedicated porter when things got tough. It was their idea to get pharmacy to prioritise these patient's prescriptions, their idea to co-ordinate transport. Every one of the ideas they had worked out with the relevant departments who were glad of the support. They owned it and by God they would make it work.

They were working the phones like demons. Two phones each, a headset and a handset. They were good. They were doing a bloody brilliant job.

It was finally time see if my *baby* could walk alone, time to place my trust in them and leave them to it. Now this was what Alex really meant when he said welcome to real management! The ability to walk away and have the confidence that my staff would be doing exactly what was needed. I knew they would, but couldn't resist one final word to them.

'Don't forget. Bleep me if you need me.'

They turned in unison and laughed as they cried out in unison, 'Yes, Mum!' at the same time.

The rats! They must have rehearsed that.

I grabbed Max's laptop left the office and took the lift to the lecture theatre.

Chapter 35

As I strode along the corridor to the lifts I saw Tessa and Jane coming towards me. They should be heading for the lecture theatre. As they got closer to me Jane was the first to speak.

'What the hell is going on Beth?'

'Walk with me to the lecture theatre and I'll tell you.'

Jane planted her self directly in front of me with her hands on her hips to bar me passing. 'Now you just listen to me Beth Seager. I am sick of you pulling my chain. We get a call from your pathetic little crew telling us to send the rest of the CBM's on a wild goose chase. I won't stand for it! I won't!'

All the time she was ranting Tessa was trying to interrupt her but did not succeed. As soon as Jane drew breath Tessa jumped in.

'Beth, what Jane is trying to say is that yet again we are being excluded from the information loop. Can you fill us in?'

Tessa's tone was much more amenable and although she looked flustered it was obvious that her frustration was the result of trying to rein Jane in.

'Tessa, Jane. We have a possible crisis on our hands, food poisoning. My staff and the medics are dealing with it and my presentation is due to start in five minutes. We really need to get upstairs, now.'

'Presentation? At a time like this?'

'Yes Jane. I take it you've sent the other CBM's to the wards to identify possible discharges? You have haven't you?'

'Yes, but... we need to work the bed board. We are needed to direct them.'

'No you're not Jane. My staff are doing that. You're needed in the lecture theatre. You will be of more use there than in my department.'

Jane looked as though she was about to explode and despite Tessa's attempts to calm her she remained angry as we boarded the lift. For once we were not sharing it with passengers as Tessa continued with her job of placating Jane.

'Jane, calm down. Beth's staff can handle the situation. It's what they do. You have to remember that we are the new kids on this, we are still learning, we can't just barge in and expect to do any better than people who have been doing the job for years.'

Jane was close to tears now as her anger turned inwards. 'But they are hopeless Tessa. They can't get it right.'

Tessa glanced at me and probably expected to see a second angry face in the enclosed space with her. But I was still basking in Tessa's words. She really had taken on board the need to know what to change before barging in headfirst. I just grinned at her and shrugged. It was a surreal situation. Tessa the terrible was now placating a member of her staff in a way that I never thought I would see.

'Let's get this presentation over, Jane, and then we will discuss what has been going on.'

Oh boy! It was so clear. Tessa had not brought her team up to speed and now she was reaping the consequences, just as I had with Eddy. We really were all suffering from the same problem.

The lift doors opened and I immediately spotted the 4D crew. I escaped from Tessa and Jane and made a beeline for them.

'How's it going guys?'

'Great Beth, we are set to go.'

'Now, you know your cue?'

'Ready for lift off.'

'Great. See you in there.'

For once Max had not blown a gasket at me working at the weekend, he had come with me. Along with the kids from 4D we had set up the data projector in the lecture theatre to show our fledgling bed board in wonderful Panavision. It would be projected on the wall at no less then three times it's normal size. A 30-foot wide full colour, computerised real time bed board showing 500 fictitious patients in all their glory!

The guys had done a fantastic job and although they had not yet completed the full *what if* strategic programme, they had managed to animate the board enough to show the managers what a speeded up run through of an idea would look like.

As I approached the lectern I began to realise the enormity of what I had undertaken. The theatre was almost full and among the faces I spotted many that had already attended my earlier presentations. Even Euan was there in the front row within easy heckling distance.

John was waiting for me at the lectern.

'Good turn out Beth.'

'Can I go home now?' I asked through a Fran special rictus smile.

'No way kid. This is your big chance. You can do it.'

I half expected to hear the *ding ding* of a bell and an announcer instructing the seconds to leave the ring. Instead, I heard John's introduction.

'Ladies, gentlemen, members of the Board as you all know Beth and I recently attended one of the EPR demonstrations looking for answers to our problems.'

A ripple of laughter rang around the room.

'We had no luck on that day, but today you are in luck. I give you Beth Seager.'

'Thank you John.'

I was beyond panic. I didn't even need my notes. I knew exactly what needed to be said. My words flowed like they have never done before. I got through the first part of my presentation in less than half the time it took me the first time. I said the phrase 'It's *how we make decisions* that I want to discuss with you today' and the whole auditorium lit up.

There it was. My bed board projected on the wall behind me. I didn't flinch, didn't turn around, just allowed the audience a count of twenty to take it in. As I counted I scanned the audience, which were a sea of swivelling, nodding heads. By the time I reached 15 everyone was talking. I raised my hands and by the time I reached 20 the hubbub had died down. I continued with the presentation.

I had them transfixed. By the time I got to the solution I was ready to turn to the giant bed board to show them what it could do.

'I know that we have tried many, many things to improve the bed situation but now we have the chance to try out our ideas before we affect the patients.'

The board started to move. The clock at the bottom of the screen speed through three days and patients were moved around the wards. As they moved I explained what was happening showing the effect of decisions—cause and effect in brilliant colour, before their very eyes.

'So, ladies and gentlemen, do you think we can afford to listen to our staff now? Can we afford to find out if they have the answers they claim they have? Can we put a stop to bed hiding? Can the medical teams start supporting each other by discussing facts, not rumour? Can we start making sound decisions?'

The room was almost silent. Time for just one more sales pitch.

'Can we work with other hospitals to manage the flow of patients and make the best use of each of our specialists' skills?'

As I said this the wall behind me changed. It now showed three bed boards. Over each one was the name of the hospitals involved in the tri trust tender for a new EPR system. Patients began to move not just from ward to ward but from hospital to hospital. As they moved an animated icon showing a hospital record file with wings flew behind the patient's admission card.

'Now I must warn you that this programme will not move the notes, but that is what you are good at. You sort out the records and this will tell them where to go. Can you do this?'

I knew that this was already in the planned system, but needed to give the managers something to work on while we sorted out the beds. I needed to control the bed project.

Silence.

More silence.

I was becoming embarrassed. I looked at Euan, a sure source of a response. John leapt to his feet and took the microphone, but before he could speak I remembered Max's words. If they hit the *aha* moment leave them, don't oversell. I quickly indicated to John to keep quiet. Putting my hand over the mike I whispered. 'Leave them John, this is important.'

He handed the mike back to me and just stood looking at the audience. After what seemed like an eternity they began to speak to each other and then across rows to colleagues. Eventually the din was deafening.

I took a deep breath and said as loud as I could, 'Any questions?'

The next half-hour passed in a blur. John was acting as chairman and he soon calmed the crowd. I was able to answer every question and eventually they dried up.

'I have two final questions Beth, how many more patients will this system allow us to treat?'

'Initial estimates range from 5 to 15 per cent, but if we can start working with Social Services and the private nursing homes to support their efforts, we could be looking at 20 to 30 per cent more bed capacity.'

'Of course we will have to run the strategies through the system to verify these figures first to make sure that the patients benefit.'

'And my final question Beth, how much will this cost us?'

'As 4D, the company who have developed this software, are looking for a platform to advertise their wares, the cost to us will be based on the success of the system, we will pay them based on extra bed capacity released as compared to last year. About £5 per bed per day. How does that sound?'

I eventually got off the stage and, after many invitations to speak to people I didn't even know, I found Fran. John was already at her side.

'I was just congratulating Fran for accepting the logic with such a limited knowledge of the big picture,' he said with a smile.

'Yes, I'm so sorry I wasn't able to bring you up to speed before,' I blurted out to Fran. 'But I was just doing what you asked. I hope you didn't mind.'

'Not at all Beth. I knew you had it in you. You just needed someone to trust you.' Fran wasn't really talking to me. She was still staring at the bed boards. It was as if she was already rehearsing her report to the board.

John winked at me and I moved on to talk to more people. I found myself facing Tessa and Jane.

Tessa was the first to speak. 'Well done Beth, that was great.' She turned to Jane who appeared to be in shock. 'Now Jane, is that enough information for you to be getting on with?'

'Umm, what? Oh, yes.'

It was my turn. 'In that case Jane I suggest that if you want any clarification on how the admissions system works you go and ask Eddy. He's fully up to speed with this and has helped us develop the programme.'

I turned to leave as my bleep went off. It was Eddy, time to manage the beds.

Chapter 36

On my way back to my office I swung by the Emergency Department. As I dodged a trolley being wheeled into the Major End, I spotted Tracey in one of the cubicles interviewing a patient. She saw me and smiled. She looked calm and in control. Fantastic.

The rest of the department was less calm and the smell of faeces and vomit strengthened the further I got into the treatment area. Health Care Assistants were setting up a trolley with supplies of grey cardboard bowls, wipes and paper gowns. They were obviously expecting more patients from the festival.

I spotted Chris in the cubicle at the far end of the department and passed a number of occupied cubicles to reach him.

'Hi Beth, don't often see you in the trenches.'

'Doesn't mean I don't think of you all in here fighting the good fight.'

'So I hear, and I understand we have you to thank for the appearance of the brass.'

'That's what I've come down to check. How many have turned up?'

'Four! Its brilliant!

'We've really hit lucky with this one. Public Health were able to identify it quickly and advise us. The bug's not too fierce and unless the patients have other medical conditions it is self-limiting. All they have to do is stay empty for 24 hours and it passes.

'The senior doc's are assessing the patients and making sure that their carers know what to do and then get the junior doc's to make them up packages to take home. One of them has even dictated a help-sheet for the patients that our department secre-

tary is typing up as we speak. As soon as she has run off copies
we can hand them out to the first batch and send them on their
way.'

'Surely they aren't discharging all of them? Now that would
be too good to be true!'

'No. So far we are only bringing in three.'

'Out of how many?'

'Fifteen so far. The three we're bringing in either have other
medical conditions, live alone or both. And those that are going
home are agreeing that given the way they feel they would
much rather use their own bathrooms and beds than a bedpan in
here!'

'A good selling point, but what about a back up? What if
they deteriorate?'

'It's all in the help-sheet. Call their own GP or us or just
come back. The GP's have been made aware of the situation and
they are making sure that the Out of Hours Services are fully
stocked with the necessary drugs to get them through the night.
Same with the ambulance service.

'Oh I nearly forgot the real breakthrough; someone had the
bright idea of asking the ambulance crews to call in for advice
on patients presenting with D&V symptoms before bringing
them in. One of the medics has been taking calls for the last
hour from paramedics who are with patients and are able to give
medication on the doc's advice. It's working well Beth. It's a
bloody miracle.'

'And so far just three admissions?'

'Yep. Just three. If the junior docs had been on their own at
least 12 would have been brought in. It's great, but the day isn't
over yet.'

'Are they still coming in at the same rate Chris or have they
slowed down?'

'Well most GP home visits should be over by this time and
the phones are quieter so I'd say that the flow is slowing down.'

'Great, so how many left in department to be seen?'

'Nine.'

'And on the expected list? How many more do we know about that are on the way?'

'Eleven, but the doc's are phoning them as well. As I said because we were able to identify the source of the outbreak so early, it's just a vicious little swine that responds well to medication and starvation. So your next question is going to be how many more beds do we need? Am I right?'

'Yes. What do you think, and be paranoid.'

'Okay, probably three, maybe four, but...'

'How about if I keep six back to allow for any relapses overnight? I'll lock these down for you. How does that sound?'

'Great. I'll let the doc's and the rest of the team know. Thanks Beth. Today has been brilliant!'

'I honestly don't know how you nurses do your jobs. You are up to your ankles in shit and vomit and you're happy!'

'Beth, it depends on the type of shit! This type I'm fine with, it's the bullshit we are expected to take from management I can't take.'

I was just about to say to Chris that hopefully there would be less management bullshit around from now on when the sound of a patient retching in one of the cubicles caught Chris's attention.

'Sorry Beth, duty calls'

On the way back to the Admissions department I was musing on the tasks that nurses undertake without flinching; taking care of their fellow humans in situations that would send the rest of the population running. We are so lucky to have these people and I realised that if I could not even contemplate doing their job, why should I even expect them to try do mine? What right do any of us have to expect these precious people to do the jobs that others can?

As I entered the Admissions department I was surprised to see John and Fran sitting on two of the tatty kick stools that we use to retrieve notes from the higher shelves, in between Eddy and Sal at the bed board. The four of them were deep in conversation that stopped as I approached them.

I was the first to speak. 'Have we cancelled everyone yet?'

To my surprise Fran was the one to speak. 'Not yet Beth, we were waiting for you to get back.'

The surprise on my face must have been evident. 'Oh, I've been talking to Chris in the ED. He reckons that six more beds should do it for today and overnight so we may not need to cancel all of the patients.'

'As I was hoping, so what do you suggest?' Fran was asking me what to do!

'Umm, well get the major cancer patients in ASAP to give them time to settle and we can start to prioritise the rest of them when we know what we will have left. Alright?'

'Fine by me,' said Fran as Eddy and Sal were already talking to their cancer patients telling them to come on in. They weren't going to give us a chance to change our minds and must have had the patients' phone numbers on redial to have got through to them so quickly!

John appeared to be listening intently to the conversations taking place between my staff and the patients when he turned to me and said, 'You know you've got a great team here don't you?'

'Yes I do,' I said, 'All they needed was a chance to use their expertise.' By now Eddy was off of the phone. 'Eddy, did you rig up the phone link between the paramedics and the doc's in the ED?'

'No that was Sal,' said Fran before Eddy could answer.

I was genuinely surprised. 'Sal!'

'What have I done now?' she yelped as she put the phone down.

'The hook up between the paramedics and the ED—what made you think of that?'

'Well not long after you went to your meeting Chris phoned down from the ED to say that the bug was not a serious one and hopefully they could send quite a few of the patients home that they had requested beds for. And that got me thinking. If the patients were coming in for a diagnosis and the doc's knew what they were dealing with, then surely with the paramedics at one end of the phone being able to describe the patient's symptoms the doc's could decide if the patient had the bug or something more serious. The more serious cases would need to come in but the buggy ones might not need to.

Look, here's the analysis, just as you showed us. It turns negative, at least from our perspective when the patients are brought into the ED, and quite honestly if I were a patient with this bug and I didn't know if I were coming or going, as it were, I'd much rather do it at home, so I guessed that coming in here was when the Branch turned negative for the patient as well.'

I had never heard Sal say so much in one go. Even at her interview she spoke in short sentences. It took me a short while to respond and in the time it took Fran had picked up Sal's analysis and was reading it intently, following the lines with her manicured index finger.

'Sal, that was a stroke of genius. Thank you.'

She beamed from ear to ear and before I could say more Eddy had found his voice, 'I talked the doc's into agreeing to talk to the paramedics while Sal sorted out the Ambulance Control end of things.'

'Eddy it was a fantastic team effort. Thank you both and I just have one question for Sal. Since when did you decide to think at work?'

'When I knew someone would listen!'

The bed board phones rang in unison so I went into my office to try to make sense of the day. With so much happening in one day I felt as though I had already done a week's worth of work. I didn't have the energy to talk to John and Fran and instead started to type an email to Harry and Sarah outlining the day's events. Before I knew it my day was over and it was time to go home. I sent the long rambling email to Harry, quickly checked the bed situation with Eddy and Sal who were sitting back in their chairs chatting. Everything was fine and they told *me* to go home. As I left my department I decided to make one last sweep through the ED. The waiting room was almost empty. All the cubicles were full but there weren't any of the usual scenes of hustle and bustle. The department was calm and a few of the staff had time to say Hi.

Driving home that night I didn't recall any of the usual landmarks, the traffic did not bother me and I tuned the radio to the Classical station to avoid the news and harsh music of to-day's popular musicians. I floated home on a cloud—not one containing lightning bolts.

Chapter 37

Every cloud has a silver lining regardless of whether it contains lightening bolts; in this case it was a satin lining and it was nestled inside the glorious dress Max bought me for the Summer Ball. Pampered and polished, I felt like a princess as we entered the marquee in the grounds of Hartford Manor. Max looked fantastic in his tux and his aqua bow tie matched my gown perfectly. We certainly made an entrance as we were stopped at least half a dozen times between the car park and the marquee by people congratulating me on the presentation.

The whole experience was a bit overwhelming and I was pleased when John spotted us across the reception drinks table and waved for us to join him. We took a couple of glasses of bubbly and made our way across the dance floor towards John who was grinning like a loon as he jumped forward to shake Max's hand.

'Ach, the venture capitalist who's found a team to rival Microsoft!' He smirked.

Max laughed. 'Well we've invested in a winner,' he said, 'but they're rapidly emptying our savings fund. Those hardware costs are starting to mount up.'

'Aha,' John explained, 'I was wondering if you would be interested in other investors, I'm looking to make plans for the next stage of my life.'

'What's this John?' I asked. 'Has all this TOC prompted you to solve your own clouds?'

'Ach! My cloud is simple, I want to return to the warm sun of Africa,' he grinned, 'but enough about me, you look stunning tonight Beth, quite the belle of the ball.'

I blushed a deep scarlet. 'It sure beats my hospital uniform. So where's your mystery partner? I can't believe you wouldn't tell me who it was earlier.'

John just grinned, 'Ach, you'll see, she's just walked in the door.'

I span round to see Joan walking towards us, resplendent in a beautifully embroidered oriental gown that obviously satisfied her need for colour.

'Joan!'

Joan treated me to a full beam smile. Her eyes lit up, distracting my gaze from her crooked teeth, she looked fabulous.

'Don't look so surprised Beth,' she said. 'I do venture out on some social occasions. Unfortunately, I seem to have lost my husband already, he was last seen heading for the bar.'

I turned back to see John trying unsuccessfully to suppress a giggling fit. I followed his gaze and saw Fran walking elegantly towards us. If I was the belle of the ball she was a supermodel and my jaw dropped as she matched John's smirk and gave him a lingering kiss on the cheek.

'Hi Beth,' she said with a genuine smile. 'I hear you call me "The Fearsome One".'

'I, I…' I stammered.

Fran laughed. 'I'm sure I gave you many good reasons. The important thing is that we are *all* on the same side now!'

We laughed, but despite this sudden feeling of peace on earth I was pleased when Joan took me to one side.

'Come on Beth, what's the punch line to this? When are we going to wake up and find out that it is all just a dream?'

'Sooner than I had hoped Joan. I spoke to my brother-in-law just before we came out. He called me to make sure that I was aware of the pitfall we are facing. He wanted me to come to the Ball knowing that what we have done is just the beginning and now the hard work will really have to start.'

Joan looked surprised. 'He obviously does not know the health service. Getting people to listen *is* the hard part. We, or rather you've, done the hard part. Now we have everyone talk-ing we can do anything.'

'But that's the problem Joan. The co-operation we have now is so precious, not to mention fleeting, that if we're not extra careful we'll damage it and get bumped back to square one or even worse.

'We're going to have to come up with even better ideas to keep the teams sweet. The walls will start building again the moment one of them suspects favouritism from management. More importantly we're six months away from budget negotia-tions, most people have holidays booked, the sun is shining and we have just overcome one little problem. Give it a few months and we could be dealing with a petulant medical staff who'll take even less notice of us than they did before because we have failed to keep the improvements coming.'

'But how can this be? We've just sorted out a major prob-lem.'

'I agree, but the problem we solved with the D&V outbreak will not be enough. Getting the senior medics involved was fantastic, it worked and will work again in similar circum-stances but do you remember the conversation we had about modelling, all those weeks ago?'

'When you asked me if other people had found solutions to problems?'

'That's the one. Harry reminded me of the reason for that conversation,' I paused to take a deep breath. 'Let me explain. The solution we came up with for the D&V outbreak was noth-ing new. In reality what we actually did was very similar to the Major Incident plan that kicks into play if we face a huge amount of casualties. The difference was the behaviour of the staff. They adapted to the situation because our plan made sense rather than being a standard procedure that lives on a managers' shelf.'

'Exactly!' Joan beamed. 'Now they will do what we tell them, we can start making real changes, real improvements.'

'Joan, don't you see, that this is where the danger is? Look, what we were able to do this week was to motivate people to improve the existing system because it made sense. They were clued up on the thinking because of the presentations. That was fabulous and it worked, but how soon will the memory of the presentations fade? How soon will their attention be taken by something else? These are really busy people and they have little time to ponder the workings of management. Does that make sense?'

'It does, but surely now that we've shown them what can be done they will go along with whatever we say...won't they?'

'Joan, you've just answered your own question. Why did you hesitate?'

'Oh hell... you're right, or rather Harry is. There is so much work to do.'

'Tell me what you're thinking.'

'OK... we agreed that the core problem is the lack of platform or mechanism for negatives to be addressed. Right?'

'Yes.'

'So, if this is right it means that last week's little demonstration was just a little taster of what can be done. Now we have to start work on the real strategy. One that will keep the medics engaged, that will interest the nurses and will tap into the experience of the support staff. Phew... we have got one big mountain to climb.'

'Absolutely! And I feel like I'm facing Everest in a pair of old running shoes!'

Joan laughed. 'Well, we're not dressed for mountaineering tonight, let's celebrate our achievements now and start on those foothills on Monday morning.'

A couple of cocktails certainly helped to relax us and we beamed at Max when he came to find us. However, our grins started to falter when he asked us to join a group near the bar.

As we tottered across the lawn the group came into view. Around a large table were Fran and John, the Chief Exec, Giles and his wife, followed by the Finance Director Nick and a woman whom logic told me was his wife or partner, then there were three empty chairs. Two of them had fresh, empty glasses placed in front of them. We were expected. Joan picked up on this as well and gripped my elbow.

'Uh oh, I don't think those cocktails were a good idea!'

I shared her sense of foreboding but could only giggle. I eventually managed to form the words, 'Joan, don't worry, we know what we have to do next, leave it to me.'

By the time we reached the table both of us were desperately trying to act nonchalant and unperturbed by the august gathering at the table. We even managed to feign surprise at the presence of some of the people at the table. A great show of pantomime, which fortunately for us was taken the way it was intended. There were a few empty champagne bottles on the table so it was a fair assumption that the assembled company was almost as *relaxed* as Joan and I.

After exchanging pleasantries, Joan and I became the centre of attention. Questions were being fired at us from everyone; What? How? Why? When? How many? How much? Who? Where from? How long? We did our best to answer them and soon Joan left the floor to me. After a while I realised that I had been talking for about 15 minutes without being interrupted. I don't even remember drawing breath. I stopped talking and looked around the table. All of them were staring at me waiting for me to continue.

It suddenly all became too much and I just stopped dead and took a big swig of Champagne.

'I'm sorry,' I stammered to Giles, the Chief Exec. 'I've just realised that I've spent fifteen minutes telling you how to do your job!'

Giles just looked around the table and laughed and began what almost seemed to me to be a prepared speech.

I found it difficult to concentrate on what he was saying as I was expecting him to be angry with me, but he wasn't. I was being used as an example 'of what our staff can achieve.' By the end of his delivery there was air of self-congratulation and at last I was able to drag Max onto the dance floor.

It was while we were clumsily swirling round the marquee that I discovered that while Joan and I had been acting like medical students at the cocktail bar, Max had been discussing the Trusts finances with Giles and Nick.

In turned out that rather than embarrassing myself by trying to tell Giles how to run the Trust I was, unknown to me, confirming many of Max's claims that it would be possible to improve the performance of the Trust without any new major investment—a pill that Giles and Nick found very hard to swallow. But the pill became sweeter and sweeter once Joan and I had performed our little double act of telling them how we managed to achieve the *impossible* without spending more money.

Joan and I had not realised that Max had worked out an Offer for the Board of the Trust that they would not be able to resist and that we were his unwitting stooges. It was a cunning plan as there was no way on earth that our performance could have been staged. It was from the heart, and the passion that Joan and I conveyed to our bosses was genuine and contagious.

I was beginning to see why Max was so successful at his job!

Chapter 38

If Max was first in the queue when the business politics skills were given out he must have been off sick when they doled out the ability to communicate with your own brother. The time of the Seager's visit arrived in a sudden rush along with plans of socialising and brainstorming. Max, however, kept himself out of the way and even managed to be in Germany on the day they arrived. I was furious and accused him of blame storming, but he shrugged and pointed out that he still needed to work for his company or we wouldn't have the funds for 4D.

It was fantastic to see Harry and Sarah at the airport. After all, they had been such a big part of our recent successes but it had been months since I'd actually seen them. The dogs also managed to make a huge fuss over them the moment they walked in the door. They say that an elephant never forgets, but neither do dogs, especially when these guests ignore all requests not to feed them treats from the table.

The scene was set, they had admired Max's English garden and we had lit the barbecue so we could start cooking soon after his arrival. However, Max phoned to say he had been delayed so we started without him and Harry donned the apron and did the caveman honours.

It must have been strange for Max to walk into that scene when he finally arrived. There was his successful life being lived by his kid brother, whom he had almost disowned. Harry looked uncomfortable as soon as Max appeared in the garden and immediately took off the apron as if relinquishing the family coat of arms to his elder sibling.

However, there were more urgent matters to attend to, as Winston and Maggie had to greet Max in their own spectacularly energetic style. Finally Max managed to free himself from their hairy embraces and the brothers walked towards each other. I couldn't help exchanging a knowing glance with Sarah—please let there be a truce!

'So,' Max said evenly, his face impassive.

'So,' Harry replied with an identical expression.

They squared up to each other and brought themselves up to their full, and practically identical height. Even the dogs sensed the tension and were now skulking behind my legs for protection. They could sense the challenge being thrown at their Alpha, their pack leader.

Harry slowly offered his hand to shake but Max ignored it.

Sarah and I looked at each other in horror. Finally Max broke the silence.

'You know you missed a few layers of resistance don't you?' He said in his best schoolteacher voice.

Harry frowned, but his eyebrows started twitching. Suddenly he burst out laughing.

'You stubborn old bastard!' He cried and threw his arms around Max who grinned as he returned his brother's embrace.

The dogs started barking excitedly and Sarah and I just looked at each other in confusion.

The brothers-in-arms finally broke apart. 'So…I guess we all fall down eh Harry?' Max laughed as the brothers remembered their days on the ice trying to out skate one an other and blaming other skaters for the groves in the ice that caused them to fall.

Harry grinned and threw him a playful punch that Max easily evaded. Max looked at the barbecue.

'What on earth have you done to those bangers?'

'Bangers?' Harry exclaimed. 'I know nothing about bangers, but those hot dogs are doing mighty fine.'

'Get real kid, we're in Blighty now so they're called bangers and you've cremated them!'

I looked over at Sarah in bemusement as I watched their good-natured bickering. 'What on earth was that?' I asked her.

Sarah laughed. 'I'm not sure but I think it has something to do with when they were kids. Harry told me how they used to skate on the local lake in the winter and after all the local kids had been on it the surface would be rough. From time to time one of them would fall and would claim that the ice threw them off balance rather than admit they had made a wrong move. It sounds as if our kids are willing to accept that there were things that pushed them apart that were no fault of their own.'

'Oh I see. No one is to blame, the system forced them apart, right?'

'Uh ha, sounds like the usual way Harry gets his way without apologising!'

'Yeah, Max too!' I laughed.

Chapter 39

The end and the beginning...
It was a year ago that I spat '*You* don't understand' to Fran. Just under a year actually. The journal I was keeping at the time ended not long after the Seager's visit. As we predicted, our lives became an express train ride and I was too busy holding on to find the time to write it all down.

The rest of Harry and Sarah's visit was a revelation to us both. They told us of their experiences with TOC and the training sessions and conferences they had attended. Sarah was using TOC in her primary school teaching and was able to give Max and I our first formal one-on-one lesson in TOC.

Luckily, Harry was able to introduce us to Ruth, the local TOC expert in our area. We were amazed to find out how wide-ranging her work was and how many areas of industry and commerce were already using her services. As a trainer she playfully admonished Harry for his long distance *teaching* methods but congratulated us on everything we had managed to achieve.

That was just the beginning. Our adventure with TOC was less than two months old. The more we spoke to people working with the tools, the more we realised we had to learn and everything seemed to accelerate from there. Our learning comprised of sending the 4D crew and hospital staff, including Joan, Fran and John on training courses and applying what we had learned to both the hospital and the developing bed management programme.

However, the most exciting time for me was when Ruth brought some TOC colleagues into the hospital to help with the implementation of one of the most powerful tools; Drum, Buffer, Rope[2], to the Emergency Department.

Until then I had been in the admissions trenches trying to keep the momentum going. The bed situation for the rest of the summer was much easier than it had been but we were all aware that we did not have time to relax. SARS was making the news and new strains of flu were popping up around the globe. As ever, we feared the inevitable. Winter was coming and we still could not free up enough beds for an epidemic. But the DBR solution installed in the autumn alleviated that worry and for the first time ever the Trust was able to report, with confidence, that the hospital was ready for the coming winter.

Despite the upbeat summer Harry kept dragging me down. 'What about the core problem? What are you doing to address it Beth?'

Each time he asked I had an excuse, but in truth I wasn't sure how to tackle it. I was lost. I knew that all we were doing was treating the constraints and by tackling just one at a time we were making more progress than we had ever done before. But in the back of my mind I felt that there had to be more, we needed to build a more robust organisation.

I started working with Ruth who helped me understand what was happening to me. My transition from an intuitive manager to one who made decisions based on provable logic was so complete that I was seeing the holes in the system everywhere I looked. What was the point in me doing all this work if it all fell down in the months and years to come? We would be back to the programmes Joan and I had discussed in the early

---

[2] **Drum, Buffer, Rope**. The name given to the TOC tool that **identifies** the slowest or weakest part of a process. Once known, the constraint, or bottleneck, is **exploited** as much as it can be after which the rest of the system slows or **subordinates** to the pace of the bottelenck to avoid building up a backlog. The constraint is then improved or **elevated** so that it is no longer the bottleneck after which the steps are **repeated** to find the next constraint which will take the system through the Identify, Exploit, Subordinate, Elevate and Repeat cycle so that the system contintues to improve.

days, ones that were a flash in the pan and then deemed to be no more than a failing passing fad.

Although I had attended some TOC courses by now, taking one-on-one instruction from someone other than Harry was strange but also very rewarding. There was no family baggage there and Ruth pushed me much harder than I thought I could go. The result was both astounding and simple. I needed to implement a solution to the core problem of *There is no platform or mechanism by which negatives can be raised and effectively addressed.* And the solution we came up with was simple.

First of all we needed a safe platform where staff could go and state their *negative*. To do this we invented a phantom person called Ivor Sicknote and published his password on the intranet. This meant that everyone could log onto the system as Ivor Sicknote and send an email to the UDE team that would be anonymous and non-traceable.

We soon had a pile of complaints that never seemed to follow the instructions we gave, but we figured that finally having a safe place to air one's grievances was too tempting and emotive to expect our long-suffering staff to take time to follow rules.

One person only picked up the incoming mail so we took great care in picking that person. They had to be honest, non-judgemental and fair. We could not pick a known gossip and we needed someone from the trenches to make sure that any seemingly trivial negatives were recognised as being important. Of course, we chose Sally. She was a natural for the job but took a little persuasion.

Now she spends a day a week working through the submissions. She separates the ones relating to bullying and harassment and hands them over to personnel and union reps to deal with.

She re-writes the others as generalised UDE's to ensure anonymity and posts them on the UDE web site so everyone can log in and vote on the UDE they most recognise. The UDE's with the most hits are worked up into a CRT. So far we have one more fully-fledged CRT from which we have been able to identify an operational issue around pathology reporting. Shortly this constraint will be no more and we are already seeking the next one.

The key to all of this has been addressing the *Mechanism* part of the core problem. Once we got to thinking about the *Platform* part of the solution the answer was simple. But we soon realised that we had to deliver sound solutions to problems or we would soon lose the support we had worked so hard to build. The *Mechanism* we adopted was TOC based naturally and by now we had the open support of the Board.

Each month, Joan and I would present a TOC update to the Board and ask for their decisions on the projects we were about to launch. In truth some of the projects were already underway, especially those that did not require extra funding, but we held back on the others until we got the go-ahead from the Board.

Soon the only question the Board members asked as we presented our projects was 'Will this bring us nearer our goal?' Of course we would not present an idea that did not, so securing funding for new projects became a simple exercise in common sense. If we can treat more patients, better, sooner, now and in the future and we can do it within our current overall funding budget the answer was always yes.

The flip side of this was the increase in the number of projects that were rejected by the Board because they did not meet the goal. We had predicted that this would happen and, as we had only been able to educate a handful of people in the trust we had to devise a way of checking project plans against the objectives of the Trust. We very soon realised that we needed to make a change to our goal statement. Now it reads: *Treat more PEOPLE, better, sooner, now and in the future.* Now it applies to our staff and students as well as our patients and the *Treat* part of it can be read two ways—treat as in interpersonal relationships or treat as in medically.

This change in the goal statement made us realise something. As a teaching hospital we actually aim to produce two

distinctly different products, to use manufacturing parlance.
Healthier patients and clinicians, not just doctors, but nurses,
technicians, paramedics, radiographers, physiotherapists, speech
therapists...the list is endless and without investing in producing these professionals we cannot hope to achieve our goal.

As soon as we recognised this in it's fullest sense, and remember we're talking about the rank and file staff discussing
these issues not the strategists or the Board members, there was
a huge surge of support for the students in the hospital. Now,
plans to upgrade their facilities with the aim of making this the
premier teaching Trust in the country are getting massive support from the staff.

A nice twist to the tale is that this has all been achieved
from Sally's work—she who is 'not paid to think.' She says she's
happy working in admissions and doing her UDE work one day
a week. In her own words she says that working in the department 'keeps it real' and that the 'trenches don't smell so bad
now.'

The trenches may be a healthier place to work now but my
days of synthetic uniforms are finally over. A few weeks ago I
accepted a promotion. I'd been fighting it for a while, but I finally gave in when the money on the table was too much to resist.

In the next few weeks I will start the final push to bed TOC
into the organisation. I will be working with personnel to develop the delivery of induction and Internet courses, which we
then plan to sell to other Trusts. We've put aside a year to
achieve this and after that who knows? I'm already collecting
UDE's from outside of the Trust and the field of Primary Care
looks very interesting. But that's another journal.

Guess who took my old job. Yup, Evil Eddy, or should I
say the 'now no longer Evil Eddy.' My job was advertised and
Eddy applied and was interviewed along with other applicants.
He shone. He had done his homework and presented his plans
for the department clearly and with a passion I would not have

thought possible. His *edges* have rounded off and he is relaxing more these days.

Sally mentioned to me that she suspected that Eddy had submitted at least 30 Negatives in the first month of the UDE search. She claimed to recognise his style of writing, but regardless of whether she was right about this, being able to see grievances that he agreed with being posted for all to see on the website seemed to calm him. He was no longer the lone voice and since then he was receptive to new ideas and willing to participate in projects providing they did not violate the triangle of 'What to change? What to change to? and finally How to change?' This is Eddy's new mantra! I'm not complaining, it's working and I'm confident that the best man got my old job. Not an inexperienced graduate but a foot soldier, he deserves it.

It was not all plain sailing outside the Admissions Department as we found sceptics wherever we tried to raise support, but we soon rooted them out and offered them the chance to attend training sessions. Joan and I kept a little black book of the Level of Resistance for the key players and soon the feedback from the training sessions was all we had hoped for. Layers of resistance were falling like autumn leaves. After so many Health Service *away day* training sessions that failed to deliver even an agreement to co-operate, the TOC sessions brought back fully tested and approved projects that were complete in their planning and which often cost next to nothing to implement.

Finally, no more 'You don't understand.' We all started to understand; we spoke about real solutions to real problems. We listened to our staff and in some cases the staff delivered project plans to us. At last the organisation was breathing again, it was alive and growing, but this time from the inside, not by bringing in more people. We were putting our own house in order and we were using fire resistant furniture!

Just after the Christmas holidays the hospital was hit with a severe outbreak of Norwalk, a nasty sickness and diarrhoea bug that threatened to close wards for indefinite periods of time.

This was the opportunity Max and 4D had been waiting for. By planning to move all infected patients to a single ward; bringing in specialist cleaning crews and reworking the nursing rota to keep potential *carrier nurses* with patients who were already infected, we managed to prove that the spread of the virus could be curtailed. Also, by planning to grant recovery time-off to the nurses who had worked on the infected ward the team was able to prove that closing beds would give more bed/days in the long run.

Implementing this plan was probably the most courageous move the hospital management had ever made but they did so with confidence and soon the outbreak was contained, just as had been predicted. The cost of the specialist cleaning crews was quickly offset against the lack of cancelled operations, the measurement that so many of the other hospitals were failing to reduce.

In fact the whole winter was relatively good for the service. As news of DBR spread from Emergency Department to Emergency Department, the number of reported 12 and 24-hour trolley waits fell across the country but where the hospital had only implemented DBR in the ED the number of cancelled operations increased.

It was obvious to those of us working the Electronic Bed Board programme that both ends of the process needed to be managed to truly get the improvements the service needed.

But more than this we needed the support and input from the staff on the ground and without them and their ideas none of the past year's successes would have been possible.

At the time of writing our hospital is now offering excess bed capacity to other Trusts. We are winning research grants because we have beds for patients who are pioneering new treatments and procedures.

So here I am relaxing in my garden as I bring my journal up to date. Except it's not the same garden as before. It's slightly bigger and even more *English* than the last one as it surrounds our beautiful thatched cottage. I won't go into details except that

Max has an irresistible urge to tell everyone he meets exactly how many hundreds of years old it is.

That's not the only news as we have just come back from a fabulous holiday to South Africa. Yes, a holiday! We're not worried that our subordinates are undermining us in our absence, or duplicating systems for the sake of it. We're not afraid that our bosses are going to ignore us, or anxious about every decision we make.

The highlight of the trip was watching John and Fran getting married in true African splendour. We also tried to emulate John's skill on a surfboard, but we both kept succumbing to the family adage—we all fall down.